ELIZABETH LOWELL

BARBARA McCAULEY

SUMMER Gold

D0311358

Silhouette Books

Published by Silhouette Books
America's Publisher of Contemporary Romance

SILHOUETTE BOOKS

SUMMER GOLD

Copyright © 2003 by Harlequin Books S.A.

ISBN 0-373-21813-3

The publisher acknowledges the copyright holders of the individual works as follows:

SWEET WIND, WILD WIND
Copyright © 1987 by Elizabeth Lowell

A WOLF RIVER SUMMER
Copyright © 2003 by Barbara McCauley

Visit Silhouette at www.eHarlequin.com

Printed in U.S.A.

ELIZABETH LOWELL
is a multi-*New York Times* bestselling author who,
individually and with her husband, has written over
fifty novels and has more than twenty-three million
copies of her books in print. Elizabeth Lowell has
won countless awards, including the Romance
Writers of America's Lifetime Achievement Award.
She also writes mainstream fiction as Ann Maxwell
and mysteries with her husband as A. E. Maxwell.
She presently resides with her husband in
Washington State.

BARBARA McCAULEY,
who has written more than twenty-five novels
for Silhouette Books, lives in Southern California
with her own handsome hero husband, Frank,
who makes it easy to believe in and write about
the magic of romance. Barbara's stories have won
and been nominated for numerous awards, including
the prestigious RITA® Award from the Romance
Writers of America, Best Desire of the Year from
Romantic Times and Best Short Contemporary
from the National Reader's Choice Awards.

CONTENTS

SWEET WIND, WILD WIND
Elizabeth Lowell

Chapter 1

*R*elax, Lara Chandler told herself silently. *Carson
has never set foot on the Chandler homestead—and
he never will. He hates even the thought of you.
You're safe here.*

As Lara heard her own thoughts, she smiled ruefully. She really didn't need to worry about running
into Carson Blackridge, on or off the small piece of
land that was surrounded by the Rocking B's lush
range. Carson had made it very plain the last time he
was with Lara that he had seen more than enough of
her. Even years afterward the memory of the moment
when she had offered herself and he had turned away
made her blush and then pale. She had tried to ex-
orcise the memory, but she had failed. Every time a
man had done more than hold her hand or kiss her
gently, the memory rose, freezing her.

Lara forced herself to take one deep breath, then another, trying to shake off the tension that had come over her ever since she had agreed to return to the Rocking B to write an informal history of a century of life on a Montana cattle ranch. With hands that trembled, she turned toward her suitcase, opened it and began to unpack with the efficient motions of someone accustomed to shuttling between two homes.

At least, normally Lara was efficient. Today her fingers seemed numb. The third time she dropped the mascara applicator that she rarely used on her thick black eyelashes, she made an exasperated sound. It had been four years since that humiliating incident with Carson. She should have gotten over it by now. But she hadn't. Four years wasn't long enough. She came from a long line of people for whom the past was very much a part of the present. Nor was there a safe place in the future for her to hide from the past. Whether she liked it or not, the past would always be there, all around her, inside her.

She had grown up listening to her grandfather's tales of the Rocking B as it had been a century before. As a child, the years separating her from the past had seemed insurmountable, a barrier as high as the glacier-carved mountains that surrounded and defined the ranch itself. As she grew up, the years shrank until they became as understandable, and almost as tangible, as the progression of the seasons.

Finally Lara had come to love the turning and re-turning of the years, grandparents seeing the faces of the past reborn in their grandchildren, the family stories told and retold until they became an informal history. She loved the larger human history as well, history written across the land itself, the extended family of mankind with its own rituals, its own unique patterns of disappointments and dreams passed from generation to generation.

History was a living part of Lara's personal life, and the Blackridges' Rocking B ranch was the center of it. She hadn't ''agreed'' to come back to do research so much as she had been compelled by her own needs.

Lara stood with her hands full of brightly colored underwear and looked around the room that her great-grandfather had built for the birth of his first child. To Jedediah Chandler, a free hundred-year lease must have seemed like a permanent grant. A homestead, not a leasehold. Yet in the end the land was only leased from the Blackridge family, not owned by the Chandlers, and the lease had expired two years ago. Larry Blackridge had extended the lease for the lifetime of Cheyenne Chandler, Lara's grandfather.

But Cheyenne was gone, and the homestead had passed into Blackridge hands. No more Chandlers would live in the expanded, often-repaired and much-loved family home that lay in the center of the Blackridges' Rocking B ranch. The name of the little valley would go on, however, passed from generation to generation as stories were told about the past. It had been called the Chandler homestead for the past century. It would be called that in a hundred years. The names of Blackridge and Chandler had become part of the Montana landscape itself.

Which meant that Carson Blackridge was very much a part of Lara Chandler, no matter how hard she tried to ignore him, especially there in the midst of the Rocking B. Every time she turned around, she would think of him, remember him, remember what he had done to her. He was part of her personal history—in many ways, the most important part.

"Fine," Laura muttered to herself. "So write a paper about Carson and file it under *M* for Mistake. Or Miserable. Misogynist, how about that?"

She sighed and gave up trying to characterize Carson in a single polite word. It would have been easier to forget him if he had made her unhappy while they were together. He hadn't. Having him close, seeing his rare smiles come more frequently while he was with her, talking with him, touching him, laughing with him… Miserable? Hardly. For a few short months she had lived in the center of rainbows, and sunlight had been a river of gold pouring into her outstretched hands.

"Sure," said Lara in a clipped tone. "Pigs flew then, too. Remember?"

Swiftly she emptied the suitcase, wondering with every movement if she had made a mistake coming back. There was nothing to tie her to the Rocking B but memories and a history that had no place for her. Her grandfather was dead. Her mother was dead. And the man who had never called her daughter was also dead.

Lara's hands hesitated as she remembered the call that had come to her aunt's house two months before. She had answered the phone. Carson's deep, gritty voice had told her that Larry Blackridge was dead. Hearing Carson's voice again after four years had been like being dropped into fire. She had barely heard the words he was saying for the sudden roar of blood in her ears. And then the words had penetrated. The man who had adopted Carson and never called him son, the man who had fathered Lara and never called her daughter, the man her mother had loved well but not wisely—Lawrence Blackridge was dead.

To this day Lara didn't remember what she had said to Carson, or if she had said anything at all. Her next memory was of standing in the thin March twilight staring at the phone in her hand. A wailing sound was coming from the receiver. For an instant she had wondered if the phone were mourning her dead father. Finally she realized that she had simply kept the phone off the hook too long.

Lara hadn't gone to the funeral. She had told herself that she had stayed away because it was too soon after her own grandfather's death to face the sadness of another loss. Yet even as she told herself that, she knew it wasn't true. Cheyenne Chandler had lived and died as he wanted to, in the center of the ranch he loved. After years of declining health, death had come to him as a friend, taking nothing from him that he hadn't wanted to give. She would miss Cheyenne for the rest of her life, but she wouldn't mourn him. He was still a part of her; his laughter and gentleness lived in her memories, and the love he had given to her was in every breath she took.

It was Carson she hadn't wanted to face, not sorrow. Lara still didn't want to face him.

"You don't have to," she reminded herself as she snapped the big suitcase shut and shoved it under the bed. "Your study covers 1860 to 1960. Carson's personal memories of the ranch are useless. He was too young."

The idea of Carson's being too young for anything made Lara pause. She had never thought of him as a child. To her, he had always been an adult and the nine years' difference in their ages an unbridgeable gulf. Even when they had dated, she had been more than a little in awe of Carson. That had faded gradually as her lifelong infatuation with him had deepened into love. She had thought that he returned her love.

M. For Mistake. File it.

Lara walked aimlessly around the room, grateful that Carson had left the homestead untouched after Cheyenne's death. As she quartered the room restlessly, her fingers brushed over odds and ends from her childhood. The ribbons she had won barrel racing in local rodeos were faded. The glittering sunburst of quartz crystals she had found years ago was dusty. The framed picture of her riding her first horse was also dusty. Absently she cleaned the glass with the long tail of her old red shirt. As she stared at the faded photo, she wondered if Carson had a similar picture of himself somewhere in the ranch house that lay in the big valley below, less than a mile and more than a world away from the Chandler homestead.

Though Lara tried, she couldn't form the picture of Carson as a young boy in her imagination. All her mind could see was Carson as he was now—taller than other men, stronger, tougher. The length of his bones made him look almost lean. It wasn't until she had stood close to him that she realized just how powerful he really was. His wrists were easily twice as thick as hers, his hands and shoulders half again as broad as hers, and his whole body was layered with the supple, cleanly moving muscles of a natural athlete. The closest he came to softness was in the long, thickly curling eyelashes framing eyes that shifted color without warning from green to amber. His mink-brown hair was also thick, with a tendency to curl at the ends when it was damp. The rest of his hair was thick, nearly black, warm and springy to the touch. She had loved to tangle her fingers softly in it.

Lara reined in her straying thoughts with the ease of too much practice. She buried her sensual response to the memories so automatically that she didn't even notice it. She had tried to date other men since Carson had rejected her so completely, but she had not been able to respond to them. Because she froze when they attempted to be intimate with their touches, she assumed that she was naturally cold. She hadn't been that way with Carson, but then, Carson had always been the exception to every rule. She had loved him before she had learned any defenses against love.

It was different now. She was very well defended. She had had the best teacher. Carson Blackridge.

Abruptly Lara decided that she couldn't yet face the cartons of family photos and mementos that awaited her in her grandfather's bedroom. Everything was just as it had been when the final heart attack had caught Cheyenne surrounded by the lifetime of memories he was sorting through and packing away. Eventually she would have to complete the job Cheyenne had begun, but she would do it as a scholar rather than as a granddaughter.

Eventually, but not right now. She wasn't ready to face her own personal history with a scholar's necessary detachment. There was no hurry. Carson had told her faculty advisor that the university's representative could live on the Chandler homestead for as long as necessary to complete the study; the Rocking B had no use for the old house. Whether Carson had regretted the open-ended offer when he learned that Lara Chandler was the university's representative— or whether he even knew that she was the historian who would do the study of the Rocking B—was never mentioned by her advisor.

In any case, Cheyenne's handwritten journals of his lifetime as the Rocking B's ramrod would just have to wait for Lara to sort through them. It was afternoon, the early summer wind was blowing silky and warm and she hadn't been riding in weeks. There were a few Chandler horses mixed in with Blackridge stock in the upper pasture. She would catch Shadow and ride over the long, rolling ridges and hidden side valleys that made up the Rocking B. She would say hello to the land she loved and would have to leave at the end of summer, when the oral histories had been collected and she had no further excuse to remain on the homestead.

Outside, Lara saw the small signs of disrepair that had come in the six months since Cheyenne had died. The barbwire was sagging in the boggy spot near the pasture seep. By spring calves would be able to wiggle out beneath the wire. The front gate, too, was sagging. By spring it would drag on the muddy ground, making life difficult for everyone coming to and going from the homestead. The lowest step on the porch was also sagging. By spring the step would be a menace waiting to trip the unwary.

But that wouldn't be a problem. By spring no one would be living on the homestead.

The mare that came at Lara's whistle was a graceful, spirited half Arab whose coat was the same blueblack as Lara's hair. Cheyenne had often teased Lara by saying that he had bought the leggy mare because he missed Lara after she went away to school. It might have been true; certainly Cheyenne had spoiled the mare in a way that he had none of his other horses.

"So you remember me, Shadow," murmured Lara, rubbing the mare's ears.

The horse bumped her nose softly against Lara's shirt and blew warm streams of air over her neck. Agile lips caught a long streamer of Lara's hair and began chewing.

"Hey," Lara laughed, retrieving her hair. "That's mine."

Serenely Shadow found another strand and began mouthing it.

"Must be that lemon shampoo," muttered Lara, grabbing her hair and backing away.

She fished around in her pockets until she found the rawhide strings she always carried when on the ranch. With flying fingers she bound her hair into a single long braid, tied it and flipped it over her shoulder. Immediately strands started to work loose and curl softly around her face, making her look younger than her twenty-two years. Her eyes were as clear and blue as a high-mountain lake—and as shadowed by hidden depths and currents. Her eyes hinted at mysteries and emotions that rarely ruffled her surface, just as the curving lines of her breasts and hips hinted at a womanly sensuality that only one man had ever touched.

Lara bridled the mare and led her back to the small barn. As she walked, she looked around several times, feeling as though someone were nearby. It wasn't an uneasy or frightening feeling. It was simply there, like sunshine. Yet every time she looked around, the countryside was empty of all but horses and cattle.

Inside the barn the feeling of another person being nearby diminished somewhat. With a shrug Lara began to curry the mare. As she worked, she realized that someone must have been caring for Shadow since her grandfather's death. The mare's coat had the sleekness that comes only from careful grooming, her long tail was free of tangles and her hooves had been trimmed and shod recently.

"Which one of Cheyenne's old friends have you wound around your delicate little hoof?" asked Lara. "Is it Jim-Bob or Willie? How about Dusty? Murchison?"

Shadow snorted and shifted her weight. Her long tail swished, sending flies buzzing off to find a less lively target.

"Not telling, huh? I don't blame you. If I had one of those tough old sons eating out of my hand, I'd keep it a secret, too."

Lara cinched the saddle tight, then automatically checked all the straps for wear as she did at the beginning of every summer when she returned to the ranch. The cinch buckle on the off side was new, as was the stirrup buckle. The webbing of the cinch itself had been replaced. With a muffled sound of surprise, Lara went over every bit of Shadow's tack. The homestead might be fraying at the edges, but Shadow's gear was not. It had been carefully reconditioned, all of it, from headstall to saddlebags. Nothing would fall apart or give way under sudden stress, throwing Lara.

"Well, Shadow. We owe somebody a double batch of chocolate chip cookies."

The mare nudged Lara firmly with a velvet muzzle, plainly wanting an end to preparations and a beginning to the ride. Shadow liked roaming over the land as well as Lara did.

"All right, all right," said Lara, shoving the mare's nose away from her stomach. "I hear you."

Lara led the mare out of the barn and mounted her swiftly, settling deep into the saddle. She expected a few wild minutes while Shadow worked off the months of not being ridden. Instead of a friendly round of bucking, Shadow immediately settled into a ground-eating lope. Somebody had been doing more than grooming and shoeing the mare. Someone had ridden her, as well. Someone who had demanded good manners and responsiveness but had done so in such a way that the mare's soft mouth and eagerness to be ridden remained intact.

"That lets out Murchison," Lara said, stroking the mare's black neck. "He's a good man, but he's got a heavy hand on the bit and spurs."

Shadow flicked one ear back toward her rider's voice. Then both the mare's ears shot forward. Lara looked up and saw the silhouette of a rider on the ridgeline to her right, which overlooked both the Chandler homestead's small valley and the Rocking B's ranch house in the larger, lower river valley. As the mare caught the scent of horse and rider, she nickered a welcome.

Lara didn't feel nearly so welcoming. She didn't need to see the distinctive patterns of the Appaloosa that was Carson's favorite mount to recognize the rider as Carson Blackridge. No man rode quite like him, sitting easily on the horse as though he had been born there rather than in a distant city. No other man had Carson's combination of strength, quickness and male grace.

Without hesitation Lara guided Shadow onto the left fork of the trail, away from Carson. Simultaneously her legs tightened around the mare's sleek barrel, urging a faster pace. Lara's reactions were completely unconscious. She had come to terms with her life as the illegitimate daughter of Lawrence Blackridge. She had accepted her mother's death ten years before in one of the summer thunderstorms that Becky Chandler had loved so much. Lara had accepted her grandfather's death and the loss of the home and the land she loved.

But she had not come to terms with offering herself to a man who hadn't wanted her in any way at all.

Lara could tell by Shadow's actions that Carson was pacing them along the ridgeline. He knew the land as well as she did. Soon the valley would narrow to a ravine that opened into the Rocking B's home pasture. Another path intersected that ravine, the path that Carson was on. Long before the safety of the pasture was reached, she would be trapped. She would have to see Carson up close, talk to him, acknowledge him in some way—and she had promised herself that she wouldn't have to do any of those things until she was ready.

She was not ready. Not now, when she was seeing her home for the first time since Cheyenne's death. Not now, when she was having to say hello and goodbye to so much. Maybe tomorrow. Or the day after. Next week. Next month. But not now. She was too vulnerable. She had always been too vulnerable with Carson.

Although Lara gave no signal that the distant rider would be able to see, Shadow suddenly veered left, sliding on her hocks down the steep, grassy hillside with the agility that made her a great rough-country horse. Bear Creek was conquered in a long leap, and then the mare settled in for some serious running. Lara bent low over Shadow's neck, feeling her braid come apart until her long hair unfurled in the wind like a black silk flag. Although she never looked back, she could tell the exact instant when the fleet little mare took her out of Carson's sight because the feeling of being watched went away. Slowly, gently, Lara brought Shadow back to a lope, secure in her freedom from Carson's presence.

Only later did Lara wonder what Carson had been doing on Chandler land. As far as she knew, he had never so much as ridden across the homestead. Perhaps that was the explanation—he was getting acquainted with a part of the Rocking B that was now his to manage. That would be like Carson. Whatever she might think of him personally, there was no doubt about his qualifications to manage a ranch. During the years since his father's stroke, Carson had proven his ability to make the land and the business thrive. He was a Blackridge in everything but blood.

Unfortunately, blood had been all that mattered to the man who had adopted Carson. Blood hadn't mattered enough for Larry Blackridge to divorce his wife and marry the woman who had given him a daughter, though. Lara had often wondered why. Like her illegitimate birth, Larry's obsession with a blood heir was well-known. Lara had never asked her grandfather to explain the actions of her mother's lover, or to explain her mother's continuing love for a man who would father a child and then never acknowledge it. That subject was the one topic that had been guaranteed to make sadness replace laughter on Cheyenne's weathered face.

In the end Lara had stopped wondering and simply accepted her parents' mysteriously interwoven lives as she accepted the summer lightning or the crystalline patterns of ice forming at the edges of autumn creeks. The reality of ice and lightning she understood. The mystery of them remained untouched, untouchable.

By the time Lara reached the broad river valley that was the heart of the Rocking B, she felt calmer, almost ashamed of having fled Carson. He had probably been as surprised to come across her as she had been to see him. And he had probably been relieved when she chose another trail, making it unnecessary for either of them to have a travesty of polite conversation. Surely he could be no more eager to confront her than she was to confront him. In fact, she was certain that it was a tribute to her faculty advisor's persuasive charms that she was on the ranch at all. She could just imagine what Carson had had to say on the subject of an informal "family" history of the Rocking B done by Larry Blackridge's bastard.

The sound of a long "Yoooooo!" called Lara out

of her thoughts. She turned and saw a man standing
in his stirrups, waving his hat in wide sweeps to catch
her attention. She recognized Willie and turned
Shadow quickly toward the cowhand. As the horses
came alongside, he bent over to give her a quick hug.

"You get prettier every time I see you, Lara. Got
your mother's eyes, and God knows He never made
nothing more blue. How's the city treating you?"

"I got a reprieve from concrete," Lara said, standing in the stirrups so she could reach Willie's dark
cheek with a kiss. "I'm on the ranch until Carson's
patience runs out or I pump the cowhands dry of
Rocking B stories—whichever comes first."

"Hell's fire, gal, we ain't never gonna run out of
tales, and that's a fact. Looks like you're here forever
and a day. We're all champing and prancing in place,
just waiting for you to unlimber your tape recorder
and make us famous."

"I don't want to interfere with your work," Lara
said quickly, voicing the same fear that she had to
her advisor. She didn't want to do anything that
would call down Carson's attention, much less his
wrath.

"Now don't you get to worrying about Carson,"
Willie said, patting Lara's hand with his gnarled,
work-scarred fingers. "He's already told the hands
that he's all for helping to educate the dumb bas—er,
city folks—that wouldn't know which end of a horse
bit and which kicked. He told us to be right helpful
to you. Not that we wouldn't have anyways. Chey-

enne's granddaughter is solid gold in these parts, and Carson knows it."

Lara gave Willie a dubious look. "Carson told you to help me? Are we speaking of the same Carson Harrington Blackridge?"

"The exact same fellow," Willie said, nodding firmly.

Lara made a sound that could have meant anything and nothing.

"Now I ain't saying that he don't have a few blind spots, same as anyone," continued Willie, patting Lara's shoulder in silent understanding. "He's a hard man but a good one, and the best damn ramrod this outfit has seen since it registered the brand—and that includes your granddaddy Cheyenne."

Lara gave Willie a startled look.

He nodded firmly. "And what's more, Cheyenne was the first to say so. Cheyenne didn't have no patience for computers telling a man what to do when it rains, or for cows throwing calves by bulls they never, er, met. Carson's not crazy about them computers, neither, but he knows what the ranch needs, and he sees that it gets it."

For a moment Lara didn't know what to say. Then she spoke in a soft, husky voice. "I'm glad Carson is good for the ranch. This land deserves someone who knows and loves it for what it is. The Rocking B is alive, just like we are, and it needs care. If you care for it, it will take care of you. Granddad knew that, and he taught it to me."

Willie's narrowed, dark eyes searched Lara's face,

seeing both truth and sadness in her expression. "If'n
you were to ask, I'm sure Carson would let you stay
on at the homestead as long as you want. Hell, he
said as much to me after the Queen Bi—er, after his
mother died."

Lara almost smiled at Willie's slip of the tongue.
Sharon Harrington Blackridge—known to the hands
as the Queen Bitch—had been a difficult woman to
get along with. But then, she had had reason. It
couldn't have been easy on her knowing that her husband's mistress and bastard were living on the ranch
less than a mile away from her home. Lara didn't
know why Mrs. Blackridge hadn't divorced her husband. Certainly there hadn't seemed to be much love
lost between them, even after Becky Chandler had
died. The Blackridges' enduring marriage was another mystery from Lara's childhood that she hadn't
pursued as she grew up, another part of her personal
history that was defined by silence rather than understanding.

"If'n you don't believe me," Willie continued ear-
nestly, "just ask Carson."

"No," Lara said quickly. She smiled to take the
edge off her refusal. "More than a hundred years ago,
Jedediah Chandler saved Edward Blackridge from being mauled by a grizzly. The Chandlers have lived
for a long time on that. The old debt has been more
than repaid."

Willie grunted and pulled his hat lower, a gesture
Lara knew well from her childhood. He disagreed, but
he wasn't going to argue the point directly. "Mebbe,"

he muttered under his breath. "But that don't say spit about new debts, do it?"

Lara pretended she hadn't heard because she knew that Willie hadn't meant her to hear. None of the hands had ever spoken to her about the circumstances of her birth or the man who was her father. Willie might compliment Lara on having her mother's blue eyes, but he would never mention the source of Lara's black hair, widow's peak and full mouth.

"What I thought I'd do," Lara said, her voice cheerful and determined, "is talk to the hands in the evenings after dinner. During the day I can go through Cheyenne's journals and take pictures of the ranch and read various documents that are part of the ranch history. And transcribe tapes," she added, sighing. That was one thing she wasn't looking forward to. Hours and hours and hours of typing when she would rather be out riding.

"Sure glad that steer ain't wearing my brand," Willie said, shaking his head. "These fingers never got the hang of a pencil. A rope, now," he nodded, smiling. "In my day, I was the champion roper of eight counties. Roped anything that moved." He settled more comfortably in the saddle, dug out a twist of chewing tobacco and bit off a hunk. "Did I ever tell you about the time the boys bet me I couldn't rope Larry's spotted bull? That old bull was the fastest, meanest—" Willie looked up suddenly as he caught movement at the corner of his eye. "Wonder what Carson wants."

Lara had seen the movement, too, and had recognized the big Appaloosa cantering toward them. "He's probably going to chew on me for keeping you from your work. See you later, Willie. I'd better get back and get to work myself."

A nudge of Lara's heels sent Shadow loping off across the huge pasture. There were three gates between her and the homestead on the roundabout route she had hurriedly chosen to avoid Carson. The last gate was in an isolated draw above the homestead. The draw was little more than a crease in the land where the wind gathered until it bent the grass in supple waves, like a hand stroking thick fur. The sound of the wind was like fur, too, cool and smooth and soft.

The beauty of the place was lost on Lara as she rounded the shoulder of a hill at a canter and dropped into the hidden crease. When she saw the rider dismounted by the gate, waiting for her, her first impulse was to spin Shadow on her hocks and gallop off in another direction. Any other direction. She would have done just that, too, but her body wouldn't respond to the frantic messages of her mind.

Carson Blackridge was less than ten feet away from her. She hadn't been that close to him in years. Nearly four years, to be exact. She had been naked then. She felt naked now.

"Hello, Lara. Welcome home."

Chapter 2

For long moments Lara simply stared at Carson. His eyes looked very green as he watched her, but she knew that at night, in lamplight, his eyes would be nearly gold. And in passion, nearly black. Or had it been contempt rather than passion that had darkened his eyes when he looked at her, touched her, undressed her?

"Carson."

The word was forced past stiff lips. Lara said nothing more, for the only words she had for him were from the hurtful past, like the images swirling up out of the locked-away places in her mind, memories she had spent years trying to forget.

He hadn't changed. He was still big, still powerful, still able to make her heart turn inside out with a look.

It had shocked her to see him standing there waiting for her. It was still shocking her, ripping away the careful layers of control built so painfully through the years, leaving nothing but naked vulnerability.

She had loved him. He had not loved her. She had told herself that she had gotten over that and him. She had been wrong. The scar tissue wasn't thick enough over the old wounds. He could still hurt her.

Carson's hand flashed out, grabbing Shadow's bridle in the instant before Lara would have spun the horse around and fled.

"Easy, baby, easy," he muttered.

At first Lara thought that Carson was speaking to her. Then she saw his big hand stroking Shadow's neck and realized that he was trying to soothe the mare, who had sensed the sudden race of fear in her rider. As Lara watched Carson, the years collapsed and she saw again that same hand so gentle on her own body, stroking away her fear as he had slowly unbuttoned her blouse and slid his hand inside. She had loved his hands then, so big, so warm, so unexpectedly tender.

With a shudder Lara looked away, fighting memories, fighting battles she thought she had already won—or at least had survived.

"Let go," she said, her voice little more than a harsh whisper.

"Look at me."

Lara's refusal was written in every tight line of her body.

Carson waited, then said quietly, "I made a mistake four years ago, Lara. I'm not going to let you make one now. Look at me.''

Her head turned sharply. Wisps of black hair blew across her face, but they didn't conceal her surprise. ''What?''

Carson's fingers closed over Lara's right hand. Gently he raised her palm to his mouth. His teeth pressed into the pad of flesh at the base of her thumb in a sweet, wild caress that sent a burst of sensation through her, igniting fires that had slept for years. When his tongue traced the tiny indentations in her skin left by his teeth, she forgot to breathe. Slowly his lips came to rest on her inner wrist, where her pulse beat frantically.

''That's what I'm talking about, little fox,'' Carson said deeply, looking at her.

Lara tried to pull her hand free.

''I want to start all over again,'' Carson said, holding on to her hand, his grip as gentle and implacable as his voice. ''I wanted to do it nice and slow, but you wouldn't let me. You've done everything but dive down a prairie-dog hole to avoid me.'' He released her fingers, frowning as she snatched back her hand. ''We're going to strike a bargain, Lara. If you stop running from me, I'll continue to give you the freedom of the Rocking B to work on your history. And that includes the documents and photos I have at the big house.''

For a few seconds Lara could only stare. She had desperately wanted those family archives for her history but had been afraid to ask for them. The first

Blackridge had been a photo buff at a time when photography was still an arcane art requiring a wagonload of equipment. Other Blackridges had been equally fascinated by photos. There were pictures up at the house that were literally priceless records of a time and a style of living that would never come again.

All of Lara's life she had wanted to be allowed to see those photos, but Larry Blackridge had kept the collection locked away from everyone, even his unacknowledged daughter, the last living Blackridge. The thought of being allowed access to that treasure trove was literally breathtaking to someone who loved history as much as Lara did.

Carson saw the look on Lara's face and smiled. "I thought that would do it. You really like the idea of getting your hands on those photos, don't you?"

She nodded slowly, knowing it was only the truth.

"Enough to stop running?"

Helplessly Lara nodded again.

"What happened four years ago won't happen again," Carson said, his voice deep, his eyes pinning her. "I never make the same mistake twice."

Lara didn't know which surprised her more—Carson's promise or the implication that she had just agreed to take up precisely where they had left off four years ago. She had not agreed to that at all. She would never permit herself to be that vulnerable again. The mere idea of it terrified her.

"Carson, I didn't agree to—to—" Lara made a helpless gesture with her hand as words failed her.

"Sleep with me?" Carson supplied smoothly, his

smile a slash of white across his tanned face. "I know. I just wanted you to be certain that there's no reason to run from me anymore. That's all in the past, dead and buried. I'm going to make damn sure it stays that way."

"Why?" asked Lara, not understanding. For nearly four years she hadn't had any contact with Carson. Nor had he appeared to want any. Now he was offering to... Exactly what was he offering to do?

For a moment Carson's face shifted into a hard expression that warned of both his famous temper and his equally famous determination. "Like I said, I made a mistake. That's all I'm going to say about it. It's history, Lara, and unlike you, I never look back."

Carson's words were clipped, final. Lara knew that the subject was closed and it would stay that way, no matter what her wishes might be. Confused, more than a little angry, she watched as he turned and opened the gate for her.

"I'll be around in the evenings if you want to go through the photos," he said. "Anytime after dinner is fine."

The thought of spending evenings with Carson shocked Lara's tongue into action.

"Thank you, but that's not necessary. If you'll just point out the boxes, I'll take it from there."

Carson's head snapped up. Beneath the dark brim of his hat, his eyes were like pale green crystal viewed through an amber lens. "Running already?" he asked softly. "Is that how you plan on keeping your end of the bargain?"

Lara opened her mouth, but no words came out. She swallowed and said tightly, "I have no desire to be alone with you, Carson. Surely that can't come as a surprise to you."

For an instant Carson's eyes closed, and an expression that could have been either pain or anger tightened his face into grim lines. When his eyes opened, they were bleak.

"For God's sake, I'm not going to attack you," he said flatly. "What happened a minute ago was more of a warning than a seduction. I'm a hunter. If you run, I chase—and I catch what I chase. If you stop running, I'll stop cornering you." Carson's mouth shifted into a hard smile. "So relax. I'm not exactly starved for female companionship, if that's what's worrying you. There are more than enough women around who don't run the other way when they see me coming."

It was foolish, insane, but Lara couldn't help flinching at the idea of Carson with other women. She had no hold on him, she never had, yet the thought of his big hands caressing someone else made Lara's whole body clench in silent rejection. He hadn't wanted her, but he wanted other women.

And he had taught her to want no other man.

Carson saw the tiny, betraying flicker of Lara's eyelids when he mentioned other women. Surprise showed very briefly on his face, to be replaced by speculation. He watched her stiff back as Shadow walked through the gate. Before he could say anything, Lara kicked Shadow into a canter, leaving Carson alone with the gate and the grass and the soft wind blowing around him.

Lara left the last of the dinner dishes to dry in the old plastic drainer that sat on the counter. Although it was seven o'clock, there was a lot of light and warmth left in the countryside. Montana was far enough north to have long summer days and equally long winter nights. Lara had always enjoyed both the light and the darkness, for each season had its special moments for her, its unique excitement.

As Lara dried her hands, she couldn't help thinking that the house seemed unnaturally quiet. She was accustomed to living alone but not to being alone in the old family home. She still expected to see her grandfather out of the corner of her eye, his legs stretched out on the old ottoman and smoke curling around his face from the pipe the doctor had forbidden and Cheyenne couldn't give up.

She didn't fight the tears that came suddenly to her eyes with the fresh realization that she would never see her grandfather again. She had known that coming back would be hard on her for a time. She also knew that occasional tears would help her to accept what could not be changed. There were so many good things to remember, so much of the past that deserved to be cherished and recorded. That was part of the reason she had come back to the ranch—to listen to the gentle ghosts of her childhood whispering to her, telling her about age and change and generations blending one into the other as naturally as summer blended into fall and winter into spring.

She might be alone, but she wasn't isolated, cut off from the rest of humanity. She was a part of history, both that of her family and that of the state she lived in, as well as of the nation and the larger international community of the world. Through that shared history, she was connected to life in countless ways that were both subtle and profound.

Lara's footsteps quickened as she went into the bedroom to change. The thought of being allowed to see the Blackridge archives had been bubbling through her all afternoon like a hidden spring. She didn't know what she would find. She did know that for a few hours she would live in another time, would see the land through the eyes of people long dead and would experience life in a new way. That was the endless fascination of studying history for her. History was her private time machine, letting her slide back through the years to share experiences and feelings and insights that would otherwise have been buried beneath the passing of generations.

It wasn't the conquerors or kings who moved Lara's mind and emotions. It was the ordinary people who worked and dreamed, cried and laughed and loved, bore children and finally died, leaving behind a legacy known only to the families who passed stories and more tangible mementos from hand to hand through the generations. It was those people Lara wanted to discover, those small histories she wanted to write, for they were the often unappreciated foundation upon which kings and conquerors and countries were built. For Lara, there was no excitement to equal the moment of discovery when a person long dead lived once again in her mind, teaching her the insights and dreams of another time.

"And if you stand around thinking about it any longer," Lara told herself crisply, "you're going to miss your chance to rummage through history tonight. This isn't the city. Folks around here go to bed early and get up the same way."

Her words drifted through the quiet house and dissipated in the larger silence of the land beyond.

"You're going to have to get yourself a cat or a dog to talk to."

Lara smiled wistfully to herself as she dressed. She loved animals, but the apartment where she lived didn't allow pets. She had tried goldfish. It just wasn't the same. There was life in a fish but no warmth, nothing to equal the gentle rasp of a hound's tongue or the purring contentment of a cat curled in her lap.

A critical look in the old, spotted mirror told Lara that everything was buttoned, zipped and clean. She had been tempted to wear something tonight other than her standard ranch uniform of jeans, boots and cotton shirt. All that had prevented her was the certainty that Carson would think she had dressed up for him—and he would have been right. She had been a girl rather than a woman when he had dated her. She wouldn't have minded wearing clothes that emphasized the difference four years had made in her body.

Unbidden came the thought that perhaps now he

wouldn't turn away from her. Perhaps now she was woman enough to hold his attention when he undressed her and looked at her.

Even as the thought came, Lara felt fear burst through her in a freezing wave. Never again would she be naked in front of a clothed man. Never again would she whimper with pleasure when a man's mouth touched her breast. There was no pleasure in that kind of vulnerability, only pain.

Lara turned away from the mirror, frightened by the unexpected, dangerous female vanity that had wanted Carson to admire what he had once rejected so cruelly.

What she didn't understand was just how womanly she looked despite her casual clothes. She had worn jeans for so many years that she didn't realize how they emphasized the length of her legs, the tempting curves of her hips and the contrasting slenderness of her waist. The cotton blouse was soft, fitted and clung to her breasts like an ice-blue shadow. The windbreaker she had tossed over her shoulders was a vivid scarlet that brought out the natural color in her cheeks and made her hair shine like polished obsidian. Her lips, too, were red, and their wide bow hinted at both humor and passion. Despite her lack of fancy clothes, she was more than enough to make a man's hands itch to follow her curves.

Lara had discovered long ago that a backpack was more practical for her than a briefcase and purse. The navy-blue pack was propped against the doorway in the living room, already stuffed with everything she

might need for her research that night. She shrugged
the straps into place and went through the door, closing but not locking it behind her. Because she had
never looked in the mirror while wearing the backpack, she didn't know that its straps snugged the
blouse tight across her firm breasts, subtly revealing
the sheer pink outlines of her bra and hinting at the
deeper pink of her nipples. The button between her
breasts strained at its fastening, allowing the puckered
cloth above and below to reveal flashes of smooth
flesh with each breath.

The slanting evening light turned the land to green
and gold and ruddy bronze as Lara walked along the
edge of the dirt road curving down into the big valley.
She could have driven to the ranch house or ridden
Shadow, but the mild evening fairly begged to be enjoyed on foot. One of her best memories of the time
when her mother had been alive was of walking over
the land with her in the evenings, when the earth itself
lay hushed beneath the condensing weight of night.

It was from her mother that Lara had learned the
savage beauty of mountain thunderstorms. Even after
her mother had died while hiking alone in an unexpected hailstorm, Lara had continued to walk the land
during times when the wild wind blew, seeing lightning even through her closed eyelids and feeling thunder in the very marrow of her bones.

As Lara approached the old ranch house, her steps
slowed. She had been in the big house eighteen times,
once for every Christmas before she went away to
school. It was not a unique tribute to her status as a

bastard Blackridge. Every other child whose parents worked or lived on the ranch had also been invited to the Rocking B's Christmas Day festivities. Santa— usually Cheyenne plus pillows, towels and the most unlikely white beard ever to grace lean cheeks—had handed out presents to squealing children in the shadow of a huge tree cut from a forest high in the mountains.

Lara didn't know when she had first looked at Lawrence Blackridge standing next to the tree and realized that he was her father. She did know that she had always instinctively avoided Sharon Blackridge, whose cold gray eyes were a fitting match for her tight-lipped smile.

That's over now. Mrs. Blackridge is dead. When I knock on that door, I won't have to pray that I'll be able to avoid her. So relax. I'm an adult now, a scholar invited here to do a history of the Rocking B, not just someone's bastard kid.

There was an assortment of ranch vehicles parked along the circular blacktop drive, including a flashy convertible that Lara didn't recognize. Somehow it didn't look like something Carson would have owned, which meant that the car probably belonged to one of the temporary hands the ranch hired every summer to help with branding, calving and rebuilding winter- ruined fences.

The ranch house was only a few decades old. Gos- sip said it had been built to amuse the Queen Bitch after she had discovered that she couldn't have chil- dren. The house was big, well insulated and finished in a combination of native stone and lumber, which blended beautifully with the spectacular setting. The door knocker was a polished brass horseshoe turned upside down to hold good luck within its deep curve.

The first time Lara used the knocker, she was so hesitant that the sound barely reached her own ears. The second time the clean metallic cry carried throughout the house. As the door began to open, Lara's heart wedged in her throat. She wanted to see history, not Carson Blackridge. When Yolanda's wrinkled face and wide smile appeared in the opening, Lara was almost dizzy with relief. The smile she gave the cook was so brilliant that the woman blinked.

"*Ai*, Lara, you are even more pretty than your mama. Come in. Let me look at you."

Lara walked inside and hugged the old woman who had been Cheyenne's favorite card partner as well as the ranch housekeeper and cook who had always had a treat on hand for any child brave enough to sneak through the backyard and tap on the kitchen window. Yolanda had been on the ranch for as long as Lara could remember.

"Hello, Yolanda. You haven't gotten a bit older. What's your secret?"

"You are too young to know," Yolanda said promptly, grinning and showing three gold teeth.

"Then I guess I'm just going to have to get old," Lara said, laughing.

Yolanda smiled. "You have eaten dinner?"

"Yes."

"Alone? At the homestead?"

She nodded.

Yolanda shook her head disapprovingly. "You must eat here from now on. It is not good to eat alone."

For a moment Lara couldn't believe what she had heard. More than any other single thing that had happened since she had come back, the invitation to dinner brought home to her the fact that Mrs. Blackridge was truly dead. Had she still been alive, Lara could have starved to death on the front porch before she would have received an invitation to eat inside with Sharon Blackridge.

Yolanda nodded as though she knew what Lara was thinking. "*Sí*," she said. "It has changed now that the Queen—Mrs. Blackridge is dead. It is a big house for just one man. Carson, he is lonely, I think."

Lara made a sound that could have meant anything or nothing. "Is he around now?"

"*Sí*. He told me if you come to bring you right to the library." Yolanda's face changed. "I think he will be glad to have some help with *la huera. Ai,* that one is as stubborn as a burro."

From the kitchen came the sound of a strident buzzer. Yolanda muttered a few Spanish words under her breath. "The cake," she explained. "It is ready."

"Go ahead. I'll wait."

Yolanda shook her gray head vigorously. "The library," she said, turning Lara and pointing her down the hall. "It is the room on the right. Go, go. He is waiting and so is my cake."

For a moment longer Lara hesitated, watching Yolanda's broad form vanish into the kitchen. Then she took a deep breath, squared her shoulders beneath the backpack and walked quickly through the living room. Everything looked strange to her, subtly out of place. She realized that it was the first time she had ever seen the room without a huge evergreen dominating the corner opposite the fireplace and holly wreaths burning greenly along the stone walls.

The library door was ajar. Lara knocked lightly on it, heard Carson's growled ''Come in'' and pushed the door fully open, taking a step into the room. That step was as far as she got before she froze.

Carson's shirt was open to his waist, revealing a thick mat of dark, curling hair. Light from the room washed over him like a caress, igniting small fires in his golden eyes and bringing the powerful muscles of his chest into high relief. His hand was rubbing the back of his neck as though to relieve muscles tightened by fatigue—or desire.

Too late Lara remembered that *la huera* meant ''the blonde.'' And that was just what the woman was, a tall, lushly built strawberry blonde who was reaching for Carson with manicured hands and pouting mouth. Her silk blouse was all but undone, showing the swell and sway of breasts unconfined by any bra. Carson was looking down at the smooth flesh being offered to him, and there was a sardonic curl to his hard mouth.

''What is it, Yolanda?'' asked Carson, closing his

eyes and rubbing his neck. "Does one of the hands need me?"

Lara couldn't force an answer past her lips. The sight of Carson's unbuttoned shirt had brought back an explosion of sensual memories she had kept buried for years, except in her uncontrollable, hotly twisting dreams—Carson stripping her clothes away with those big, warm hands and then bending down to her, his mouth caressing her breast until she thought she would die of the sweet fire bursting through her body.

But she hadn't died. Not in fire. She had frozen to death when he had turned away from her nakedness as though it repelled him.

Would he turn away from the blonde at the last instant as he did with me?

Lara looked at the woman's exposed breasts and open, shining lips. The blonde didn't look like a woman who expected rejection. She looked like a woman who knew very well how to please the man smiling down at her. The thought made Lara shudder as sweat broke in a clammy wave over her skin. A soft, choked sound came from her throat.

Carson's eyes opened as he spun swiftly and saw Lara standing in the doorway, her eyes blank, her hand raised as though to push something away.

"I'm—I'm sorry," Lara stammered. "Yolanda told me to—she said you—"

"No problem," Carson said dryly. "Susanna just stopped by to see if I needed company. I don't so she's on her way home." He rubbed his neck and moved his head to ease the tight, aching muscles.

"Coffee?" he asked Lara, ignoring Susanna and gesturing with his free hand toward a tray sitting on his desk.

"Let me, darling," Susanna said, standing on tiptoe to knead Carson's shoulders. "I know just where those old headaches tie you in itty-bitty knots."

Lara turned away before she saw Carson pull Susanna's hands from his body with a gesture that shouted of impatience.

"I'll—maybe tomorrow, or—" Lara gave up trying to talk coherently while her mind was reeling. She spun and all but ran toward the living room. She was halfway there when she heard Carson calling her name. She didn't even hesitate. Yolanda came rushing out of the kitchen as Lara reached the living room.

"You are leaving so soon?"

"Carson's—busy."

Lara's pale face told Yolanda that she should have been the one to open the library door. "*Ai*, that damned *huera*! She was after him again, no?"

"She was after him, yes. And she caught him."

Yolanda realized that, short of wrestling Lara for the door handle, she couldn't prevent her from leaving. "Go to the bunkhouse," Yolanda said quickly. "The hands, they are all hoping to talk with you. They tell me so just tonight. Go. You will see."

Lara bolted through the open door just as she heard Carson call her name again. She kept going without looking back.

"Damn!" snarled Carson as he stood in the hallway, frowning fiercely, his open shirt flapping in the breeze from the front door.

"*Ai*, no wonder the little one runs," Yolanda said, closing the door and throwing up her hands. "That is no way to win a wife, señor!"

Carson turned toward Yolanda. "What the hell—"

"I am old, señor, but not deaf or stupid. I hear the old man and his wife yelling at night. I know that he wanted what was only right and just for his blood child. I know that he wanted to see grandchildren from his own body inherit the Rocking B." Yolanda grunted. "And how can that happen but to have Lara Chandler become your wife, *verdad*? It is a thing much to be desired."

"Is that what you told Lara?" asked Carson, his voice low, deadly.

Yolanda lifted her hands to the ceiling and called upon God in torrents of Spanish.

"Answer me!" snarled Carson.

The old woman muttered and dropped her hands. "I am not a cow to be stupid about such things. I said nothing to the little one of what I know. The heart of a girl is not moved by what is necessary or right. It is moved only by love." Yolanda shrugged. "Or the appearance of love, *verdad*? *Ni modo*. It does not matter. Once *los niños* arrive, a girl loses her foolishness and takes her man for what he is—an animal made by God in one of his weaker moments." Yolanda glared at Carson. "But she is not yet big with your child, *hombre*. Walk soft, and whisper sweet things to her. And get rid of that *huera* cow!"

Carson's lips twitched, and then he threw back his head and laughed. Yolanda tried to continue glaring but couldn't. She laughed, too, shaking her head. She had raised Carson as much as his mother had. He could always get around Yolanda, and he knew it.

"All right, I'll whisper sweet nothings," Carson said, smiling. Then his smile faded, and his expression became as hard as the stone mountains. "But you be damn sure you don't say anything to Lara about Larry's last wishes, *comprendes*? I mean it, Yolanda. Stay the hell out of this."

The old woman looked at Carson and nodded slowly. She understood. If she interfered, nothing would save her from Carson's wrath. In that he was very much like the man who had adopted him.

"Carson?" called Susanna from the library door.

"Goodbye," Carson said carelessly, heading for the stairway that led to the second-floor bedrooms.

"I thought we were going to—"

"No." Carson's voice was firm. He didn't pause on the stairway. "I told you seven months ago that it was over. Go back to town and your banker boyfriend. Yolanda," he continued, raising his voice, "what kind of cake did you say Lara liked?"

"Chocolate," called the old woman to Carson's broad, retreating back.

"Bake one."

"Is your nose dead from *la huera*'s cheap perfume?" demanded the old woman. "Such a cake is right now cooling on the kitchen counter!"

"You're an angel from heaven," retorted Carson,

pausing long enough to wink over his shoulder at Yolanda.

Susanna watched the long, powerful legs vanish up the stairway just beyond her reach, heard the bedroom door slam shut and said a few very inelegant words as she stalked to the front door. Under Yolanda's baleful eye, *la huera* climbed behind the wheel of the convertible and roared up the driveway with far more speed than skill.

Carson didn't notice Susanna's angry departure. He was standing by the bedroom window, watching Lara hurry toward the bunkhouse. As he remembered the stunned expression on her face when she had seen his shirt open to his waist, he smiled like a chess player whose opening gambit has been an unqualified success. Whistling softly, he tested the stubble on his cheeks, decided it was too harsh for Lara's luminous skin and went to shave.

He would give her an hour. Maybe two. Then he would go after her. The thought of catching her brought a slow smile to his mouth and a flood of heat through his body. He never should have let her get away four years ago. He had wanted her ever since.

Now he would have her, and the Rocking B as well.

Chapter 3

Willie's narrow face split into a grin when he spotted Lara standing on the bunkhouse steps.

"Come in, gal, come in! We was just talking about you and wondering if'n you was going to drop by soon."

Lara's smile was a bit grim and her face was flushed, but no one seemed to notice. She was grateful. She had been as shocked by the sudden flood of anger she had felt while she walked to the bunkhouse as she had been by her response to the sight of Carson's bare chest.

Who did he think he was to ask me over to look at the Blackridge photos and then to dangle a cheap blonde under my nose?

Even as the words echoed in Lara's head, she realized that she had no right to ask the question. In the first place, she hadn't told Carson that she was coming over that night; she had left him standing at the gate without a word as to when—or if—she would come to the ranch house. In the second place, if he wanted to chase cheap blondes—or even expensive ones—through his library, it was none of her business. In the third place—in the third place—

Lara's thoughts fragmented on the memory of Carson standing and rubbing his neck wearily, his shirt open to the waist and light shifting over his powerful torso with each of his movements. It had been all she could do not to simply turn and run without saying a word. She had been very shy of men since Carson had rejected her. Even the thought of being naked and being touched by a man frightened her. She had once thought that making love would be beautiful, but Carson had taught her that it was hurtful and unspeakably tawdry. The shame of the moment when she had offered herself and he had refused still splintered through her at unexpected moments, freezing her.

"You remember Murchison, don't you?" asked Willie.

"Of course. Hello, Murchison." Lara repeated the greeting to Jim-Bob and Dusty. "Which one of you do I have to thank for repairing Shadow's tack and shoeing her?"

A chorus of disclaimers went up, capped by Willie's calm words. "Musta been Carson. When he heard you was coming, he had the old homestead cleaned. He caught Shadow and shook the kinks out of her, too. Guess he don't want you getting thrown. That's a right lively little mare, 'specially after running loose for durn near a year.''

Lara's mouth opened, but no words came out. She could hardly believe that Carson had gone out of his way to help her. Carson, who had barely spoken to her at Cheyenne's funeral. Of course, if she was honest, she hadn't given Carson much of a chance to say or do anything. She had looked right through him when he had tried to offer her comfort. The only crying she had done had been in Yolanda's understanding arms while Larry Blackridge had sat nearby in his new wheelchair, looking exhausted by the strokes that had ultimately killed him. Sharon Blackridge hadn't been at the funeral; she had died weeks before.

With an involuntary shake of her head, Lara put away the memory of Cheyenne's funeral and her unacknowledged father's illness. Both men had lived full, productive, active lives, surrounded by the country and the ranch they loved. There was nothing for her to pity or regret in that, no cause for her sorrow or grief. If she could die after a life that was half as interesting and constructive as theirs had been, she would know that she had lived well.

Willie finished the introductions without noticing that Lara's attention was divided between the past and the present. She smiled and murmured the correct words as she memorized the faces young and old that were in the bunkhouse. Twelve men, more than she ever remembered having lived on the Rocking B. The ranch had flourished under Carson's leadership in the past few years, as illness forced Larry Blackridge to give over the reins to his adopted, well-educated and very shrewd son.

The men who lived in the Rocking B's large bunkhouse were a mixture of youth and age and everything in between. That was common to big ranches, where men came and went with the seasons. Most of the hands had been born on a farm or a ranch somewhere in the West, but some of them had come from the East's overcrowded cities and had found a home in the uncrowded lands where cattle and sheep grazed. Some of the men, like Willie, were determined bachelors who were painfully shy with any woman they hadn't known as a little girl. Others, like Murchison, were divorced. Still others, like the handsome young man known only as Spur, had an appreciation of women that was uncluttered by any shyness or notions of the necessity of rings and vows.

Lara smiled around the circle of attentive faces once again. Behind the men she saw overstuffed chairs and well-used card tables with worn playing cards placed facedown where men had been sitting. Materials to write a letter were scattered across a scarred desk, and magazines were heaped at one end of a long coffee table. A television crackled in the corner as a laugh track tried to coax watchers into believing that the flickering sitcom was amusing rather than merely simpleminded.

"I'm interrupting you," Lara said. "Please, go

back to whatever you were doing. I just wanted to talk to Willie for a few minutes.''

Another chorus of disclaimers went up as Spur walked over and snapped off the TV. ''No way,'' he said, smiling as he turned to face Lara. ''Willie's been telling us all about you, but somehow he didn't get around to saying how pretty you are.''

Lara smiled slightly. Spur's charm was of the generic, automatic sort common to some men. It wasn't the specific kind of charm used by a man who was interested in a particular woman.

''I'll bet you have a lot of success with that line,'' Lara said dryly, smiling even as she let Spur know that she wasn't in the market for any lines, new or old.

Immediately the rest of the men relaxed and started ribbing Spur about his success with the ladies. Spur laughed, not at all put off by the teasing or by Lara's deft refusal of his invitation to join him in the oldest game of all.

''Is that what you're doing your research on— Western lines?'' he asked.

She shook her head, smiling. ''Nothing that spicy. I'm doing a history of the Rocking B from 1860 to 1960.''

''Before my time,'' said Spur. ''Before yours, too,'' he added, giving her an appreciative once-over with vivid blue eyes.

''That's what makes it interesting to me,'' Lara said, shrugging out of her backpack before Spur could offer to help. As she unzipped the biggest pocket, she glanced up. "You're sure I'm not interrupting?" she asked, looking particularly at the older hands.

"Hell, honey," said Jim-Bob, rubbing his grizzled head, "we been playing gin with each other so long we know the discards before we see them. No sport to it a'tall. We'd much rather talk to a sweet young thing."

"Well, if you find one, tell me and I'll let you go talk to her," Lara muttered as she rummaged in the backpack's huge pocket.

The men laughed and nudged each other appreciatively while Willie looked on like a proud papa. Knowing that Lara had not come to flirt with any of the hands allowed all of the men to relax and enjoy her company.

"The kind of history I'm doing," began Lara, laying out the tape recorder, "is informal. I don't care if you remember who was governor and who was president during the time your story takes place. What matters to me are the events and the people of the Rocking B ranch itself. I want the kind of stories your grandfathers told you, and the kind you would tell your friends or your children and grandchildren."

Lara looked up, glancing at each man's face, trying to make them understand why memories that might seem trivial to them were important to her.

"The Rocking B of the old days is gone," she said quietly. "It lives only in your memories, and in the stories you know about men and women who are now dead. Some of you have been here all of your lives, and when you were young, you worked with older hands who had also been here all of their lives. It was the same for those older men. They had been young once, and they had listened and learned from the Rocking B's old hands.''

The older men nodded slowly, remembering their youth a half century before, when they had listened to stories told by men who had been young before the century had turned.

"In a way," Lara continued, "the men who have lived in the Rocking B's bunkhouse are like a family passing stories down through the years. At least, it used to be that way," she said, grimacing toward the now-silent TV. "Telling stories used to be a major form of entertainment for ranch hands. That time is past. I want to gather all the old stories before they're forgotten. I want anyone who reads my history to be able to close his eyes and hear voices from the past whispering of horses and cattle and storms and sweethearts. I want people to know, really *know*, what it was like to live on the Rocking B a long time ago.''

Jim-Bob, who had once been quite a lady's man and who still cut a fancy figure among the local widows, rubbed his chin slowly. "You sure you want to know about the women, too? Not all of them were what you'd call respectable. Not that I'd know anything about it firsthand," he added hastily. "But I've heard some stories, sure enough.''

Lara hid her smile. "If my tape recorder blushes or faints, I promise I'll throw it away and get a sturdier model.''

Jim-Bob chuckled.

"The people who live on the Rocking B now aren't
saints," Lara said matter-of-factly, "and neither am
I. I'm sure it was the same in the past. I don't want
a sanitized kind of history. I want it just the way
you'd tell it if I weren't here listening. In fact, if my
being here bothers you, I'll show Willie how to
change the tape and bow out right now. Or, if you
like, you can write down any story you'd be embarrassed to tell out loud. But whatever you do, please,
please pass on the story. Don't let a wonderfully
funny or sad or simply human piece of history die
because you're embarrassed to share it with a
woman."

Jim-Bob looked dubious. "Some of the stories are
kinda raw, if you get my drift."

Lara smiled and said calmly, "If you're thinking
of the story about Hustlin' Annie and the bunkhouse
fire, or about Big Sally's Halloween surprise, or the
night Cheyenne's daddy ran naked all the way back
from town with a buttful of rock salt after getting
caught in somebody else's saddle—"

The laughter of the old hands drowned out Lara's
words. She smiled widely. "I grew up here, remember? And if it helps, the first informal history I ever
participated in researching was the life of a ninety-
year-old spinster living over on the Firehold River
who had worked in every whore-house in Montana.
After that charming old bawd, I'm shockproof."

"Sounds like Tickling Liz," muttered Willie.

"She said to say hello if I saw you," Lara murmured without missing a beat, "and to ask you if you

still were partial to dancing barefoot in the spring grass.''

Willie flushed to the roots of his thinning hair while the men around him howled with glee. Then Willie began to laugh, too, and there was a remembering kind of gleam in his eyes as he thought of the easy-smiling older woman who had long ago taught him why God had made girls one way and boys another.

After that the stories began to flow. Unobtrusively Lara finished setting up the tape recorder, checked the sound level and settled back to be an attentive audience. Tonight she would make no attempt to direct the stream of reminiscence and memories. The time for that would be later, after the men were accustomed to seeing her in their midst. Then she could ask for their oldest memories; they would answer in ways that would surprise even themselves, for the human mind works in amazing ways, dredging up incidents that the men would have sworn they had forgotten.

''...had this old spotted mare that just wouldn't hit the trail unless he had a cup of Java like the rest of the hands. Well,'' Murchison said, stopping long enough to light up a cigarette, ''the new man, Perkins, couldn't believe the mare liked coffee. He thought the hands were pulling his leg. So he ups and saddles the mare after breakfast, and she walks about ten feet and then she sits down in the middle of the trail,'' said Murchison. ''Swear to God. She sat right down like a big ol' hound dog and just dared Perkins to do something about it. Well, he kicked and he cussed, and that old mare just sat tight and rolled her eyeballs at him.''

''What'd he finally do?'' asked Spur, grinning.

''Well, by the time he gave up, the chuck wagon was long gone over the hill,'' Murchison continued, blowing out a stream of smoke. ''So Perkins spent half the morning chasing the wagon on foot and the other half hauling a bucket of coffee back to that wall-eyed ol' mare.''

''Did it work?''

''Nope.''

''Why not? Were they funning him all along?''

''Nope. Mare only liked coffee with cream. Last anyone saw of Perkins, that poor fool was running over the hills, trying to rope a mamma longhorn. To this day, I've heard that you can see him when the moon is just right and the calves are just getting up to weaning size.''

Lara's laughter blended with the deeper sounds of masculine amusement. She loved it when the men started talking about the horses they had known, for each man's life was intimately involved with the big, affectionate and sometimes epically willful animals.

''Did you ever hear about Wild Blue?'' asked Dusty.

Lara shook her head, although the name sounded vaguely familiar to her.

''He was a big stud that roamed around here way, way back, about the time the first Blackridge rode into the valley through South Pass. The Indians had tried to catch that mustang, but it was like trying to catch the wind. So they took their best mares and turned them loose to get bred by the wild blue roan. He threw some of the prettiest Appaloosa colts ever to eat Montana grass,'' Dusty said.

The cowhand's voice was slow, the words almost hesitant. He was more than seventy years old and had been born on the Rocking B. He had a lot of memories to search through for the threads of the story he was telling. Lara listened to both the words and the silences, letting the story grow in her mind, seeing again a time when horses ran free and were pursued by men just slightly less wild than the mustangs themselves.

The stories blended one into the other like streams joining a river running back through time itself. When it was necessary, Lara changed the tape unobtrusively, not interrupting the flow of words as she labeled each tape and entered it into her interview log.

Eventually the talk turned to the raucous celebrations that used to follow a roundup, when everyone would let off steam after the brutal work of catching, branding, dehorning and castrating spring calves. The square dances would go on until dawn and beyond, with couples sneaking away to be alone and then returning later, flushed with secrets.

Spur, who had been pretty well left out of the storytelling up to that point, brightened at the mention of dancing. With little urging Willie hauled out his fiddle, cranked the strings into tune and began to play all the old hoedown songs with surprisingly agile fingers. Spur turned out to be a superb square dancer whose family had a long tradition of calling dances all over the West. He began to chant the dances that he had learned and to demonstrate the rhythmic, exuberant steps that accompanied the words.

"This step is known as Over the Moon and Around the Mountain," Spur said.

Lara blinked. She was no authority on square dances, but she had the feeling that her leg was being very gently pulled. On the other hand, that kind of droll teasing was very much a part of ranch life both today and in the past. She had no objection to providing the men with a little entertainment at her own expense.

"Over the Moon and Around the Mountain," she repeated gravely. "That sounds, er, strenuous."

"Oh, it's not bad a'tall," drawled Spur. "Here, I'll show you."

He held out his arms. Lara hesitated for several seconds before lifting her own arms and stepping forward. As Spur pulled her into dancing position, she realized that Spur was every bit as tall as Carson and nearly as strong. The young cowboy's eyes were a very vivid blue, and his long, light mustache was worn in a drooping handlebar style that would have gone unremarked more than a century before.

"Ready?" he asked.

"I doubt it," Lara said, "but I'm game."

Spur winked. "That's my girl. Now start with your right foot."

Lara obediently put her right foot forward. Instantly she was swept off her feet, tossed into the air like a child, caught and swung around shoulder-high in a complete circle. She gave out a startled shriek and hung on to Spur as though he were a runaway horse. He laughed, set her on her feet carefully and grinned down at her.

"Over the Moon and Around the Mountain," he said. "Like it?"

"Er—"

"One more time."

"Spur—!"

Too late. Lara's feet left the floor before she could finish her sentence. This time Spur tossed her even higher, caught her even closer and swung her around twice. The men were all stamping and applauding and whooping their approval, and cutting a few fancy steps of their own while Willie made the old fiddle sing. Lara went Over the Moon and Around the Mountain so many times that she lost count. Before long she was laughing, breathless and too dizzy to do more than cling to Spur when he finally relented and set her on her feet to stay.

Suddenly the room fell silent. Lara pushed the hair back from her eyes and looked up. Carson was standing just inside the bunkhouse door. His expression was hard, and his eyes were the cold yellow of a winter sky after sunset. Although he was leaning casually against the door frame with his thumbs hooked into the waistband of his jeans, the angry tension of his body belied his relaxed stance.

"Any of you yahoos know what time it is?"

Carson asked, his voice the temperature of a February wind.

"'Bout eleven," Spur said. "Why?"

"Going to be a long day tomorrow," Carson said flatly. He pinned Lara with a glare from his narrowed eyes. "Have you lived in the city so long that you've forgotten how early dawn comes? These men have work to do, and they can't do it if they're staggering around half blind for lack of sleep."

"I'm sorry. I lost track of time," Lara said. Hurriedly she shut the tape recorder off and stuffed it into her backpack. "It won't happen again."

"You're damn right it won't," Carson retorted, straightening and walking slowly toward Lara with his hand out. "I'll carry that pack for you."

"Now wait a minute," Spur said, catching Lara's hand as she jammed the rest of her stuff into the backpack. "None of us are riding nighthawk so what we do after dinner and before dawn is our own lookout. If we want to help you with your research, we'll damn well do it!"

If the room had been quiet before, it became absolutely dead still as the older hands held their breath in anticipation of Carson's explosion. He had a well-deserved reputation for his rough temper. The men who knew him expected him to fire Spur on the spot. Instead, Carson simply looked at the young cowhand. Spur realized he was in trouble, but he wasn't going to back down from what he had said. He had a full measure of the proud independence that had been the hallmark of cowboys since the first man saddled a horse and tried to keep track of his cattle in the West's endless open range.

"It's all right, Spur," Lara said quickly. "Carson's right. I shouldn't have—"

A curt motion of Carson's arm cut off the flow of Lara's words. She bit her lip and wished she knew why Carson was so angry. It was late, yes, but not that late, and as far as she knew, only routine ranch work was scheduled for tomorrow. It wasn't as though she had kept everyone up late carousing on the night before branding or haying.

"This is the damnedest so-called 'research' I've ever heard of," Carson said icily to Lara. "Unless you're doing a thesis on how to pick up men. Is that it?" he demanded, glaring at her right hand.

Suddenly Lara realized that Spur still had his hand on her right wrist to prevent her from packing up and leaving. She eased herself from Spur's grip.

"Now that would make sense," continued Carson, warming to his topic with a vengeance. "You go around to all the bunkhouses and get handled by all the young cowboys and they take up a collection to thank you for being so soft and warm and willing. Hell, I'll bet a girl could make quite a nice living that way, if she didn't mind being known as an easy kind of female—or worse."

The anger that Lara had felt earlier that evening returned in a rush as Carson's sarcasm cut into her.

"An easy kind of female," repeated Lara tightly, yanking her backpack into place and pulling her hair out from beneath the straps with abrupt motions.

"Yeah, I guess you'd be an expert on loose women—
or worse—if that blond number who was undressing
you earlier tonight is any sample of your taste."
Lara's disdain vibrated in every word as she walked
toward Carson. "Well, Mr. Expert, if you wouldn't
hang around with easy females like that, you wouldn't
think that every woman was dying to go to bed with
the first man who would have her!"

Carson's hand shot out and clamped around Lara's
arm as she swept past. He leaned down and spoke so
softly that only she could hear.

"Maybe you're forgetting who was doing the offering and who was doing the refusing a few years
ago," Carson said in a low, deadly voice.

Lara looked up into his clear, cold eyes and felt
herself freezing inside, shame splintering through her
in shards of razor ice, cutting right through to her
soul. It was as though the years had never intervened.
She was vulnerable, naked, trusting, wanting—and he
was none of those things. He was armored, ruthless,
and all he desired was to see her shame.

A shame that she couldn't conceal. Naked.

Nothing had changed. She was as helpless now
against Carson as she had been years ago. The realization was devastating.

"Damn you," she breathed, shaking with humiliation. "*Damn you!*"

Lara slipped past Carson and ran out into the night
without stopping. She heard him call her name once
and then again, urgently, as though something other

than anger moved him. She didn't even hesitate in her flight.

Carson got to the doorway just in time to see the pale blur of Lara's blouse retreating along the road between the ranch house and the Chandler homestead. Behind him, in the explosive silence of the bunkhouse, he sensed movement. His hand shot out, and his long, work-hardened fingers clamped around Spur's arm in an unbreakable grip before the younger man could push past him and out into the night after Lara.

Unceremoniously Carson yanked Spur down the bunkhouse steps and around to the back, where no one could overhear.

"I'm going to tell you this once, cowboy, and only once. You listening?" snarled Carson.

Spur opened his mouth to say something, looked at the icy gleam of moonlight in Carson's narrowed eyes and decided that discretion was definitely the better part of valor.

"You're new to this valley," Carson continued, his words clipped. "You don't know about the Blackridges and the Chandlers, and I'm not going to waste my time educating you. All you have to know is this—Lara Chandler is mine. Got that?"

Spur hesitated, then nodded.

Carson looked at the younger man for a long moment, then nodded in turn, releasing him. "Good. Remember it."

"Or you'll fire me?" Spur asked, both curiosity and aggression in his voice.

Carson smiled thinly. "Hell, no, kid. I'll trash you. You want to work for me after you heal up, you're more than welcome. You're a good hand, Spur. One of the best I've got, despite the fact that you're barely old enough to drink hard liquor. But there are other good hands, and there's only one Lara Chandler."

Spur opened his mouth, shut it and smiled crookedly. "Well, you're living up to your reputation, Blackridge. Hard but fair. Know something? If Lara had given me the slightest come-on, I'd fight you and welcome to it. She'd be worth it. But she wasn't handing out any invitations to me or to anyone else that I could see." Spur shrugged. "So she's all yours and good luck to you. You're gonna need it. That filly is plumb skittish around men. She's real nice about it, but no is written all over her in letters a blind man could read."

Although Spur said nothing more, it was plain that he thought Lara's refusal extended to the tall, hard-looking boss of the Rocking B.

As Carson turned and went back to the ranch house, he was thinking the same thing. It had seemed so easy when Lara had flinched at the thought of him with another woman, and then she had found Susanna with him. Lara had taken one look at his open shirt and suddenly her eyes had blazed with memories. It was exactly the reaction he had hoped for.

What he hadn't expected was Lara's fleeing from him as though pursued by the hounds of hell. Before Susanna had dropped in, he had been set up in the library, hoping Lara would come over that night. He had expected to remind Lara of the sensual pleasures they had shared by the implied intimacy of the open shirt, then accept Lara's offer of a neck rub to ease his headache. She had the most marvelous hands. No one had ever been able to chase pain away as she could, with her sweet concern for his comfort and her knowing, gentle hands.

Carson cursed savagely under his breath. He hadn't meant to hurt Lara four years ago, and he certainly hadn't meant to hurt her tonight at the bunkhouse. Four years should have been plenty of time to get over being turned down by him. Until he had seen her flash of jealousy at the thought of him with another woman, he had been afraid that four years had been too damn much time to get over him, that she had forgotten entirely the months they had shared. He had assumed that during those years Lara had found more than one man willing to take what she had so sweetly offered Carson, a gift that he had been too caught up in the war between himself and his father to accept.

As always, the thought of some other man knowing Lara's warmth and lovely body made Carson's jaw tighten until it ached. He had been a pure, double-dyed fool to turn away from her, hurting her and complicating the hell out of his own life in the process; but nothing could be done about that now except to be sure not to repeat the mistake. He had missed his chance to be the first to teach Lara about the pleasures of sex. He would regret that the rest of his life. The thought of someone else sliding into that sweet young body had kept him awake more than once in the past few years. The memory of her bewilderment and pain and finally her overwhelming shame when he rejected her had kept him awake even more often than his enduring hunger for her.

Lara had looked the same tonight, surprised and hurt and then shamed all the way to her soul. The memory of her pale, absolutely bloodless face and haunted eyes turned in Carson like a knife, cutting him, making him grimace with the pain he had never meant to cause her. She was so fragile, so easily bruised, as sweet as a sun-warmed flower; he was a man not known for his gentle words and easy nature. The fact that Lara was still so vulnerable to him gave him both hope and fear—hope for his ultimate success in making her his wife, and fear that she had been too badly hurt ever to trust him again.

Damn you. Damn you!

Lara's words echoed in Carson's mind every step of the way to the dusty blue pickup. He got in, slammed the door and gunned the vehicle down the dirt road, wishing to hell that he had acted differently tonight. But he hadn't. He and his damn temper had taken one look at Lara all flushed and mussed from Spur's arms, and it had been all Carson could do not to take the young cowboy apart right there.

With an abrupt gesture Carson flicked the headlights on to high beam, hoping to pick out the pale color of Lara's blouse against the black of night. Nothing came back at him but the twin ghostly reflections of a cow's eyes as it grazed along the fence line.

Despite the urgency and impatience that was riding him, Carson kept his speed down well below the range of his headlights as he looked for Lara. He doubted that she had had time to get all the way back to the homestead, but there was no sign of her along the pale, moon-washed curves of the ranch road. Automatically he stopped, opened the homestead gate, drove through, then got out and closed the gate again. As he did, he heard the grating of wood over dirt and made a mental note to fix the gate. If it sagged any more, Lara wouldn't be able to handle the gate by the time the summer was over.

If she was still on the homestead.

The thought made Carson swear again beneath his breath. Lara had to stay. He simply would not accept any other possibility. It had seemed so easy after his mother had died. Even though Lara had refused to speak to him, he had been sure that if he could just lure her out to the Rocking B, time and proximity would take care of her coldness. For he knew that she wasn't a cold person at all. She was the exact opposite, at least as volatile and passionate as her own mother had been.

Carson frowned. He didn't like to think about Larry's mistress. He had grown up thinking of Becky Chandler and her bastard child as his enemies. Like his mother, Carson had blamed the Chandlers for the fact that Larry had never been much of a husband and even less of a father. Years later—far too late to prevent Carson from badly wounding Lara—he had realized that Larry's failings were his own and were not the responsibility of the passionate, blue-eyed woman Larry had loved when he could not love his own legal family.

It hadn't been an easy thing for Carson to admit to himself, but he had faced the reality of his adoptive father's lack of love and the reasons for it; then Carson had put it behind him and moved on to other things, things that were within his own ability to change or control.

It had always been that way with Carson. After he had learned whatever lesson was to be learned, he never looked back. For him, the past was a place of pain and mistakes, disillusionment and broken dreams. It held no fascination for him. He had never known his biological parents, and the people who had adopted him had done so for reasons that had nothing to do with wanting a child to love. He had no shared legacy of roots stretching back into time, securely placing him within a family history.

Carson had the future, though, and the future was his. He had earned it, and he was damned if he was going to let the mistakes people had made in the past take it away from him.

Chapter 4

Using the brilliant moonlight as her guide, Lara climbed quickly up the grassy ridge that rose between the ranch house and the homestead. The road snaked around the shoulder of the ridge, but instead of staying with the road, she had cut through the Rocking B's northeast pasture. It was a shortcut to the homestead, but she had no intention of going home just yet. She knew that would be the first place Carson would go looking for her, and somehow she had no doubt that he would pursue her. After all, she had run despite their agreement and his warning.

As Lara climbed, the memory of Carson's sarcasm on the subject of easy women flooded through her, goading her to greater speed. She couldn't blame him for thinking that she was easy. Once she had quite openly offered herself to him. He hadn't even had to ask. The aftershocks of that night and his refusal still shivered within her, shaking her, shaming her.

The top of the ridge was smooth, gently rounded and grassy. A breeze moved faintly, bringing with it sounds from the valley below. In the distance moonlight glittered along the length of the river that ran through the center of the Rocking B. The Big Green nourished the ranch's cattle and crops with water that had come down from the sawtooth mountain ranges that rimmed the broad valley. Much closer in, at the foot of the ridge, the ranch's lights glowed in shades of molten gold. The back door of the ranch house shut loudly, and a flashlight bobbed as someone walked across the yard. The air was so clear that it seemed as though the person were coming straight toward Lara.

She held her breath in the instant before she told herself that whoever was out walking couldn't be Carson. She had already heard his pickup go by on the ranch road and then turn up the fork that led to the homestead. When the flashlight vanished and the lights of a cottage came on, Lara let out her breath in a sigh, realizing that it had just been Yolanda going to her quarters for the night.

For a few minutes it was so quiet that Lara could hear her own heartbeat. Then two men came out of the bunkhouse and went toward the barn. She was too far away to distinguish words or identities, but the sound of easy male voices floated up to her in quiet counterpoint to the whispering of grass caressed by a summer breeze. A shiver coursed over Lara, a feeling that Cheyenne had once described as *the sensation of someone walking on my grave*.

Lara shrugged off the backpack and put on her windbreaker, even though the night wasn't chilly. She drew her knees up to her chin, stared down at the Rocking B and listened to voices drifting up into the beautiful, fathomless silence of the Montana night.

Once she had dreamed of being a recognized part of the family at the big house, of having Larry Blackridge acknowledge her as his daughter. She had believed that, if only those things would happen, she would be one of the people living forever amid the golden lights.

Lara's mouth turned down in a sad smile at her own expense. She had been very young then. Certainly too young to protect herself from her own dreams. Far too young to realize that she was Mrs. Blackridge's natural enemy, a living symbol of her husband's adultery, not a motherless child that Sharon might want to call daughter. Even so, the dream of belonging had died slowly, stubbornly, not breathing its last until Lara was a shy, awkward teenager whose greatest pleasure was watching Carson Blackridge from afar.

He had always fascinated her. From the very first time she had met him, he had been different from other men. As soon as she had stood in front of him, she had felt a shock of recognition that had shaken her, as though unseen, unknowable emotions already joined her and the tall, roughlooking adopted son of

Larry Blackridge. She had been thirteen years old when she had taken a Christmas present from Carson's hand. He had been twenty-two. It had been the first time that Carson had come to the Rocking B's celebration for the hands' children.

Even at thirteen, Lara had sensed the tension between Carson and his father. She had known without being told that Carson was giving out gifts under protest. Other people might not notice it, but to Lara, Carson's hostility was as tangible as the Christmas scent of evergreen that permeated the room. It had always been like that for Lara—she was as instinctively sensitive to Carson as a flower was to the sun.

Lara had neither sought nor discovered an explanation for her instant response to Carson Blackridge. It was simply a fact, like the color of the sky. Because she had no memory of a time when she hadn't been aware of Carson, she had never questioned that awareness. She had simply worshiped him with all of her young heart, and always at a distance. Her sensitivity to Carson's feelings had quickly told her that he wanted nothing to do with the thin, blue-eyed bastard whose mother had recently died in a storm. So she had watched him from afar, her eyes full of dreams and stirrings she was too young to name. He was aware of her, too; she was sure of it. It could not be an accident that he was never where she was on the Rocking B.

Years later, when Lara was eighteen and working at a restaurant in town during the summer before she began her classes at the university, Carson had allowed himself to admit that he noticed her. Not only did he acknowledge her, but he actually seemed to pursue her. He started coming several times a week to the café where she worked, and each time he was there, he flirted with her. When he had finally asked her for a date, it had seemed like a dream come true....

"Whoops!" said Carson, withdrawing his feet and catching the tray before anything could spill.

"Sorry," Lara said, feeling the heat of embarrassment climb up her cheeks.

"My fault," he said, smiling at her. "I'm a little big for these booths. I sort of spill out into the aisle."

She couldn't help looking from his stirrup-scarred cowboy boots to the muscular length of his legs straining against the faded fabric of his jeans. As always when he was within view, her heart beat too fast and simultaneously a strange weakness flooded through her, making her clumsy. She had nearly dumped a dinner in his lap out of sheer shock when she had recognized him sitting in her section of the café. He looked so relaxed, so utterly male, like a big mountain cat resting in a meadow, eyes half closed against the summer sun. Carson's eyes were like a cougar's, too, clear amber with a flash of dark green in their depths.

"You're perfect—it's the booth that's too small," Lara said without thinking. As she heard her words, she flushed again, feeling like a complete fool. She had overheard enough of the local girls talking about

Carson to know that he was much chased by women and rarely caught, and even then only for a short time. "Ketchup?" she asked quickly, setting a big hamburger and fries in front of Carson.

"Thanks, but I think the half bottle you brought earlier will hold me."

Lara looked away from Carson's thick, dark eyelashes long enough to realize that there was already a bottle of ketchup on the table, as well as steak sauce and mustard. She retreated without looking at him again.

It was the same the next three times he came in—her sudden heat and weakness, her clumsiness and unguarded tongue. She had dreamed of him for so long that his reality was overwhelming. She kept telling herself that she was being foolish, that he wasn't pursuing her, that he would never pursue her. His opinion of his father's former relationship with Becky Chandler was no secret. Besides, Carson had his pick of the sophisticated, experienced women who found their way to the Rocking B in hopes of catching and holding the interest of one of the most eligible bachelors in the state of Montana. What possible reason could Carson have to pursue a tongue-tied, blushing teenager?

The fifth time Lara glanced up and saw Carson watching her from what she had come to think of as "his" booth, she felt her heart turn over at the intensity of his look and the male heat in his slow, approving smile as she walked over to him.

"Hello, little fox," he said, gently brushing aside

the menu she offered and running his fingertips over her right hand. "How's the burn?"

The teasing endearment sent a helpless flush over Lara's cheeks, as did the gentle touch. The last time he had been in the café, he had told her that she looked like a fox at twilight—dark, shy, mysterious and very, very soft.

Lara looked down at her fingers, barely remembering that she had burned her hand a few weeks before. "Fine, thanks," she said, her voice husky. Her right hand felt as though it were on fire again, but this time it was from Carson's quick, gentle touch. "Do you want the usual?"

"Yes and no."

Lara smiled and prepared to make some revisions in the menu. Carson was one of the few customers who regularly got away with special orders. The café's owner was Yolanda's brother. Whatever Carson wanted was given to him without question, for the Blackridges had been very good to Yolanda's family through the years, sending their children to college and helping them get started in various small businesses.

"I'll have the steak and fries and blue-cheese dressing on the salad," Carson said.

That was the "yes" part of his order. Lara looked up from the pad, waiting for the "no" part.

"And for dessert I'll have you for a partner at the cattleman's dance this Saturday," Carson continued calmly.

Lara had actually started to write Carson's words

on the order pad when their meaning penetrated. Her head snapped up, and her blue eyes widened.

"What?" she asked, afraid to believe her own ears.

"I promise to hold your feet off the floor so you won't need to worry about getting trampled," he said, his eyes glinting with humor. The dances were notoriously crowded and sometimes rather rowdy.

Lara just barely prevented herself from blurting out that, if Carson was her partner, her feet would be so far off the floor anyway that they'd have to keep her on a leash like a carnival balloon.

"I—I'd love to—" Lara closed her eyes, hating the words that she had to say next.

"But?" he asked softly, watching her with eyes that missed nothing, seeing both her eagerness and her disappointment.

"I have to work," she said, her voice plainly unhappy.

"What time do you get off?"

"Ten o'clock."

"I'll pick you up at your apartment at 10:30."

Lara looked at Carson for a long moment before a smile transformed her face, making her glow like a delicate porcelain sculpture lighted from within. "Thank you, Carson. I'll look forward to it."

He hesitated, then smiled in return. "So will I."

Only later did she realize why his tone had struck her as strange. It was almost as if he had been surprised to find himself looking forward to their date. But that was absurd. If he hadn't wanted to take her out, there would have been no reason for him to ask her to the dance in the first place.

Lara left work early Saturday night and raced to her apartment, tearing the hated hairnet in her eagerness to be rid of it. She showered, washed and dried her hair and then brushed it until it shone like a raven's wing. The natural wave in the breast-length strands made her hair thick and luxuriant. Freed of the hairnet, her stylish, subtly layered haircut framed her face in soft, open curves that caressed her fine-grained skin like black flames. Against the darkness of her hair, her blue eyes had a jewel-like intensity and depth. She wore just enough makeup to emphasize rather than overwhelm her natural coloring, and a perfume that was as fragile as moonlight.

She hesitated in front of her closet, wishing that she had a dress as special as the occasion. Finally she settled for a white silk blouse that she had bought on sale a few weeks before and a swirling, floor-length skirt that was as black as her hair. A scarlet sash tied gaucho-style around her waist added a vivid splash of color that was repeated in her enamel earrings and matching bracelet.

With a frown Lara studied her reflection in the mirror, wishing she were older or had a spectacular figure or blond hair to her waist or a splashy designer dress or all four together. Then she wouldn't have to worry about Carson comparing her to the glittering, slinky women who always seemed to turn up at these affairs, making life miserable for their plainer or less wealthy sisters.

"Carson didn't ask one of those flashy types to the dance," Lara reminded herself out loud. "He asked me."

That continuing miracle still swept over her at odd moments, making her shiver with pleasure.

Another wave of pleasure went over Lara when she opened the door and saw Carson's surprise, quickly followed by his frank male admiration.

"Little fox," he murmured, looking at Lara from her gleaming hair to the black-nylon-clad toes peeking out of her high-heeled, patent-leather sandals. "You make me wish I weren't taking you out among the wolves tonight. I want to keep you all to myself."

Lara smiled and relaxed beneath Carson's genuine admiration. "Thank you," she said softly, no longer nervous about the coming date. Then, without stopping to think, she added, "Mountain lions don't need to worry about wolves."

Carson looked surprised again. His mouth curled into an odd smile. "Is that how you see me?" he asked. "A cougar?"

A quick sideways glance assured Lara that Carson was amused rather than put off by her frankness. "Yes," she said, picking up her little black purse. "Strong, rangy and graceful in a very masculine way. Not to mention your eyes." She smiled and looked away from him, saying, "But I suppose you're awfully tired of girls going on and on about your eyes."

Again Lara managed to surprise Carson, who had thought himself long past the age when a woman could show him anything new. He laughed suddenly and took Lara's hand, tugging her close to his side after she locked her apartment door.

"This may come as a shock," he said dryly, "but none of my dates have mentioned my eyes."

Lara looked startled. "Oh. Er, maybe it would be better if I went back to being tongue-tied."

"Only if my tongue gets to do the tying," Carson retorted, leaning past Lara to open his car door and glancing aside in time to watch the blush climbing up her face as the meaning of his words registered. He laughed again and ran the back of his fingers over her hot cheek. "Little fox, you're a real pleasure to tease. I didn't think girls still knew how to blush."

Lara groaned and tried to shield her face behind her hands. Gently Carson pried her fingers away.

"Don't hide," he said, kissing her flushed cheek and the corner of her mouth.

"You must think I'm a little fool," she whispered helplessly, shivering as she felt his mustache move over her sensitive lips like a silk brush.

"I think you're like a mountain creek on a hot summer day—clear, sparkling, sweet and tempting as all hell."

Lara would rather have been thought of as mysterious, sexy and complex, but she had just enough self-control not to say so out loud. She quit trying to hide her face and smiled at Carson rather uncertainly. He returned the smile with one of his own, a smile different from any she had seen from him before, as gently approving as a man watching a kitten chasing a teasing piece of yarn. When he bent and kissed her softly on the lips, she couldn't control her reaction or the small sound of her swiftly indrawn breath.

"Get in the car," Carson said, his voice deep, "before I decide to spend the night right here, kissing you."

Lara's red lips parted slightly as her breath came out in a rush. The thought of being kissed—really kissed—by Carson was both exciting and unnerving. His eyes narrowed as he read her instant response, but before he could move, she slid into the car. As he shut the door after her, he let out his breath in a soundless curse, surprised at the heat racing through his body.

The dance was held in the local Grange building. What the ballroom lacked in elegance it made up for in warmth and laughter. Everyone there knew everyone else, and the band knew all the favorite songs both old and new. By the time Carson and Lara arrived, most of the older couples had already gone home, leaving the floor to the violently energetic under-thirty set. The band had responded with the driving rhythms of rock music interspersed with slow, sexy ballads.

Carson found a small table, brought Lara a cola and himself a beer and pulled a chair around until he was sitting right next to her.

"To surprises," he said, smiling and clinking his glass lightly against hers.

She smiled almost shyly and took a sip. When she found that the drink hadn't been spiked, she let out a silent breath of relief. She hated the taste of alcohol, and she distrusted the dates who handed her a strong drink without asking her preference.

"Thank you," Lara said.

Carson's dark, thick eyebrows raised in silent question.

"For not giving me a drink that would bring down a bull," she explained.

Deep male laughter wrapped around Lara like a caress. After a moment she began to laugh, too.

"I outgrew that kind of maneuvering before I graduated from high school," Carson said, shaking his head.

"I wish more men had," said Lara.

"You have something against alcohol?" he asked innocently.

"Nope. It sure has something against me, though. First my forehead goes numb, then my head goes all twirly, and then I get sick as a hound dog that's been eating tall grass."

Lara's words stopped suddenly when she realized that she must sound about as sophisticated as a six-year-old. Carson shook his head and tried not to show his amusement, but in the end he gave up trying to control himself. He threw back his head and laughed with the kind of contagious humor that had other people turning and looking in his direction with a pleased smile. It got to Lara, as well. She forgot her embarrassment and laughed with Carson. She realized that she liked making him smile, hearing his deep laughter, watching the tight lines vanish from his face. It made her feel like a court magician bringing pleasure to a hard-working king.

Long, strong fingers closed over Lara's as Carson took her hand and squeezed gently. "You're not at all what I expected," he said.

The feel of Carson's warmth and strength radiated up Lara's arm in a wave of pleasure. When her breath came back, she asked, "What did you expect?"

As soon as the words were out of her mouth, Lara could have bitten her tongue. She knew precisely what Carson might have expected from an illegitimate child who was living alone in an apartment at a time when most girls of her age were still living with their families. Unfortunately, her grandfather couldn't afford a car for her to commute from the homestead to a job in town. Without a job there would have been no money for university tuition and books in the fall. Her apartment was very small; that and the fact that it was in a building partially owned by one of Cheyenne's old friends made the rental cost minimal. It was lonely living on her own but necessary if she wanted an education.

"Never mind," Lara said quickly, looking away from Carson. "I can imagine what you expected. Sorry about that, but I'm definitely not what the local gossips probably advertised. So don't feel like you have to stick it out here with me just to be polite. You can take me home anytime."

"How about tomorrow morning?"

The casual proposition shocked Lara. Her head snapped around toward Carson so quickly that her hair flew out and shimmered like black silk. She had called him a mountain lion—a predator—and that was exactly what he looked like then, his powerful body poised as though to pounce and his eyes almost yellow, narrowed in calculation.

A feeling of bitter disappointment washed through Lara, taking all the color from her, leaving behind only a pale shadow of her former animation. Carson hadn't wanted to be with her. Not really. He had just wanted to go to bed with her. She opened her mouth to tell him that she didn't sleep with men, even one that she had admired all her life. Her lips moved, but no words came out.

"You're totally innocent, aren't you?" asked Carson, watching Lara intently.

"Yes," she whispered finally, getting her voice back. She slipped her fingers from his and pushed back from the table. "I'm sorry. Thanks for being so honest about what you wanted from me. I should have guessed, but I'm not very…experienced." Lara's lips trembled, and her voice dried up. She swallowed, tried to speak and couldn't. "Goodbye, Carson," she managed, her voice so frayed it hardly carried beyond her lips.

Lara turned and quickly began to work her way through the fringes of the people crowding the dance floor. The band was playing a slow ballad that had a provocative, erotic rhythm. Couples clung to each other and swayed slowly from side to side, lost in a sensual world of warmth and closeness. Blindly Lara tried to slide through the dancers without causing a disturbance. She had just reached the edge of a small clearing in the crowd when Carson's hand closed around her wrist and tugged, using her own momentum to spin her around toward him.

"Carson, I won't—"

"Hush, little fox," he said softly, ending Lara's protest by pulling her into his arms.

"But I won't—"

"I know," Carson said, cutting across Lara's words and then kissing her lips gently. His hand slid beneath the black fall of her hair and stroked her spine soothingly. "Dance with me."

Lara hesitated, torn between her desire to be with Carson and her fear that he expected more from her than she wanted to give.

"Look at me," murmured Carson, taking both her hands and pulling them around his neck.

In the mirrored darkness of the dance floor, Lara's eyes were as enigmatic as twilight.

"I won't push you. I won't take anything you don't want to give me," Carson promised. "All right?"

"But you're used to—" Lara's voice broke as she tried to find a polite way to say that Carson was used to having women whenever the sexual urge struck him.

Carson's lips shifted into a smile that warmed Lara all the way to her toes. "That's my problem, not yours. You're different from my usual women. Let me enjoy that difference and don't worry about it. Okay?"

The breath sighed out from between Lara's unconsciously parted lips. "Okay," she said softly.

Carson's arms shifted subtly, moving Lara closer without making her feel trapped. His hand stroked the satin length of her hair, silently urging her to rest her head on his chest. As she did, her arms slid more tightly around his neck. With every breath she took, she smelled his unique male scent, a heady mixture of warmth and soap and a clean, faintly citrus aftershave. She matched his slow movements easily, unconsciously, fitting so perfectly into his arms that it was as though she had been born to be held by this one man.

Later, when Carson took Lara home, he did no more than brush his lips over her mouth and stroke her cheek with gentle fingertips. It was the same on the next date and the next. They talked and laughed and danced, and the weeks flew by. He never took her to the drive-in where couples groped and wrestled behind steamy windows. He never came into her apartment at the end of a date. Nor did he take her home to the Rocking B.

At first Lara was grateful that Carson was so careful not to push her sexually. It was a distinct difference from the way she had been treated before by boys her own age, most of whom seemed at the mercy of their newly rushing hormones. She had no doubt that Carson wanted her. She was inexperienced, but she wasn't ignorant. She knew exactly what caused the change that came over his body when he held her, kissed her gently, hugged her and kissed her and

kissed her again before he slowly released her at the
end of each date.

And at the end of each date, Lara wanted more.

It was almost three months before Carson slipped
the leash on his control. They had been chased inside
her apartment by a summer rainstorm that had washed
out their mountain picnic. Lara had set up the picnic
dinner all over again on the floor of her living room
and had sworn not to use any furniture or electricity.
They would sit on the floor, and when the sun set,
they would just light a camp lantern and pretend they
were back at Avalanche Creek's lush meadow.

As usual, Carson and Lara talked and laughed, and
with each word, each moment, she fell more and more
under his spell. She watched him with an intensity
that she didn't understand. Every breath he took,
every movement of his body, every small touch of his
fingers against her, sent shivers of awareness coursing
through her. And every instant brought her closer to
the moment when he would leave. Then he would kiss
her gently, hug her and let her go. She didn't want it
to end that way today. She wanted more. She needed
it in some mysterious, seething way that was so new
to her that she had no defenses against it. She didn't
even know that she needed any defenses.

Carson wanted more than chaste kisses, too. Lara
could see it in the hot gold of his eyes reflecting the
camp lantern and in the way his glance lingered on
her mouth, her hands, her breasts. When it came time
for him to go, he rose to his feet, pulling her after
him. As usual he kissed her, held her, kissed her

again; then he looked down at her parted lips silently begging for him. He made a husky sound that was almost a groan. His arms tightened around her like steel. In the flickering illumination of the camp lantern, his eyes were nearly pure gold, and like the light itself, they burned.

"Carson?"

"Little fox," he whispered, "would it shock you to feel my tongue touching yours?"

Lara hadn't liked it when other men had tried that particularly intimate kind of kiss on her, but the thought of being that close to Carson sent a shiver of excitement over her. She went up on tiptoe, circling Carson's neck with her arms, and then felt herself being lifted off her feet until her face was level with his. He fitted his mouth over hers with a single smooth motion. At the first hot touch of his tongue, she trembled and made a sound deep in her throat. Her arms tightened and her lips opened further as she tried to blend her mouth completely with his. When she moved her tongue over his, he tore his mouth away and let her slide down his hard body.

"Did I—did I do it wrong?" Lara asked. "Shouldn't I move my tongue, too?"

Half laughing, half groaning, Carson hugged Lara close and hard. "You did everything just right," he said hoarsely, fighting for control. "Oh, God, honey, you set me on fire all the way to the soles of my feet."

Her breath caught, and she looked up at him with blue eyes darkened by the beginnings of arousal.

"Is that good?" Lara whispered. "Do you like being—"

The words ended as Carson bent down and took Lara's mouth completely. Long fingers tangled in her hair, bending her head back and arching her body so that her breasts pressed against his hard chest. At the same instant his other hand slid down to her hips, lifting her into the cradle of his thighs, rocking her slowly over the hot, erect male flesh that strained against his slacks. His tongue moved in the same sensuous rhythms as his powerful body, the same rhythms that she instinctively gave back to him with her own tongue, her own body.

By the time Carson released Lara, she was dazed, trembling, half wild with feelings she had never known before. When his hands caressed the length of her body and then eased up over her breasts to seek and find the sensitive tips, her breath came in with a sound that was almost a moan. Her back arched again in a reflex as old as passion. He didn't have to ask if his hands on her breasts pleased her; her eyes were half closed, her lips were parted and her nipples had hardened into points that showed hungrily against the thin cotton of her blouse.

Gently, skillfully, Carson caressed the hard buds that had risen to his touch. Lara's whole body quivered in response. She didn't even know that he had unfastened her blouse and bra until she felt air bathing her flushed skin. The first touch of his fingers on her bare breasts was so exquisite that she moaned. When he plucked delicately at the eager nipples, she felt it all the way to her knees.

"Carson?"

The huskiness of Lara's voice was like an intimate caress. It fed the fires eating through Carson's control, burning him, consuming him. With one hand he flicked open the buttons of his shirt. Her eyes widened as she saw the dark thatch of hair curling across muscles and arrowing down to his belt buckle.

"I want to feel your breasts against me," he said quietly. "I want to watch those beautiful pink nipples nuzzle against my skin. Does that shock you?"

Slowly Lara shook her head, sending tendrils of hair whispering across her breasts. His hands tightened on her back, bringing her gently against his chest. He turned slightly from side to side, caressing her sensitized flesh with each small motion. She made a tiny sound and threaded her fingers through the male hair, kneading his muscular chest like a cat. Her eyes closed slowly, and her head tilted back as she gave herself to the subtle, ravishing sensations of her breasts caressing him and being caressed in turn. Pleasure expanded through her in wave after wave, shortening her breath until she was dizzy. She called Carson's name brokenly, barely able to stand.

"Yes?" he asked, his tone deep, gritty.

"I feel so strange." Lara's voice broke as Carson plucked at the tight pink crowns of her breasts, sending both fire and weakness radiating through her. As her knees sagged, she swayed against him. "Carson—"

He steadied her even as he eased her down to the floor. ''It's all right, little fox,'' he murmured, nuzzling her ear and then biting it delicately, making her shiver. ''Everything's all right,'' he said soothingly, smoothly removing her blouse and bra as he spoke, fully revealing the rose-tipped beauty of her breasts.

Lara heard the hiss of Carson's breath coming in swiftly, suddenly, and opened her eyes. He was looking at her bare breasts with a sensual approval that made her feel weak. If she hadn't already been lying down, her knees would have given way.

''Tell me if I shock you,'' he said huskily, bending down to her. ''I'll stop. I promise you.''

Before Lara could ask what Carson meant, his mouth had replaced his hand on her breast. The kiss was so sweet, so hot, that she cried out, arching helplessly as her nipple became even more erect beneath the moist, searching caresses of his tongue. Her breath came quickly, raggedly, reflecting the wild pleasure he was giving her. Without knowing it, she rubbed her fingers through his thick hair and held his head hard against her breast. He responded with a taut, urgent suckling that made her breath come out in a fragmented moan.

The wild race of fire through Lara's body left her defenseless, violently sensitized, seething with hungers she had never known. When Carson lifted his head to look down at the wet, erect nipple, she reached for him with a cry, aching for the feel of his mouth loving her again.

''Carson,'' she said throatily.

''More?'' he murmured.

But even as Carson spoke, he was lowering his mouth over Lara, pulling her deep inside, suckling hard on her until she made a ragged sound and her hips moved in the rhythms of his mouth tugging at her. His left hand kneaded her other breast, rolling the taut tip between his fingers, sending wave after wave of pleasure through her. Her eyes closed and her back became a bow that gave him her breasts with a sensual abandon that made him groan.

The hoarse sound was another kind of caress shivering through Lara, another flame licking over her hot skin. Pleasure swept away all her thoughts, all her inhibitions. She didn't even know the exact moment when he removed the rest of her clothes; she only knew that his hard, wonderful hand was stroking her bare stomach, her thighs, the midnight mound of hair at the apex of her legs. When he pressed lightly at her closed thighs, she shifted automatically, easing his way, too aroused to be hesitant or shy.

And then his fingers found the hot, aching nub hidden in her softness. She gave a broken sound as her hips rose against his caressing hand. When she felt fingers searching the rim of her softness and then sliding inside her, her eyes flew open in a wave of surprise and unexpected pleasure. She saw his face— taut, expressionless but for his mouth drawn with restraint. He was looking at her as he touched her, and his eyes blazed with hunger.

Suddenly his face changed as though pain were replacing passion. Slowly he began to ease his fingers from her body.

"Carson," Lara cried softly, lifting her hand to touch the hard line of his mouth. "It's all right. I'm not frightened. You don't have to stop. I love you. I've always loved you."

Carson closed his eyes and shuddered violently. He came to his feet in a single savage motion. For a moment he stood looking down at Lara, and then he said grimly, "You are your mother's daughter, all right, but I'm not my father's son. Using little girls just isn't my style. I'll find another way to get even with him."

Nausea rose in Lara's throat as her memories churned queasily. She had never remembered that night so vividly, her naked vulnerability and Carson's contempt like an impenetrable armor around him, her sickening eagerness for sex and his easy self-control, her trembling words of love and his cruel reminder of the circumstances of her birth.

She had borne much sly whispering for being the illegitimate, unacknowledged daughter of one of the biggest ranchers in the state, but it had been Carson's rejection that had nearly destroyed her. She had survived it but only at the cost of her ability to respond to men. Even the thought of being touched like that again literally made her go cold.

Only in her dreams was she a woman again, held once more in the arms of the man she loved.

Chapter 5

Lara sat on the dark ridgetop, her knees drawn up to her chest and her eyes staring blindly at the lights below while the past burned through her like black lightning. There were no tears in her eyes to reflect her memories of the night that Carson had rejected her so cruelly, so completely. She had called his name and had heard her answer in the door closing behind him. She had cried then, once, but never again. Humiliation had ultimately burned away her tears. After that there had been only shame. That had not burned away. She wondered if it ever would.

"I didn't mean to hurt you like that."

For a moment Lara thought that the voice was an echo from her former dreams, when she had longed to hear Carson explain what had happened, why it had happened, what had gone wrong that she had loved him and he had had no love at all for her.

But the voice wasn't a dream from the past. The voice was here, now, beside her; so was Carson Blackridge. With a muffled sound Lara looked away from him into the limitless Montana night.

"Don't turn away from me, little fox," Carson said softly. "Please. I'm sorry if I hurt you tonight. Seeing you with Spur made me jealous, and I lost my temper."

Lara's head snapped around so quickly that her hair flew out, brushing over Carson's hand as he reached for her. She had never heard Carson apologizing for anything. Not once.

"Jealous? I doubt it," she said finally. "A man who's interested in one woman doesn't spend the evening undressing another one. Or were you having some kind of complicated revenge on Susanna, too?"

There was more than enough moonlight for Lara to see the sudden narrowing of Carson's eyes and the flattening of his mouth.

"I didn't invite Susanna to the ranch, and I sent her on her way as soon as you ran out. She hadn't undone any buttons but her own. As for me—" Carson shrugged "—I'm used to being alone in the ranch house. Half the time I go around without a shirt. I didn't think that would shock you. Interest you, maybe," he added, smiling slightly, "but not shock you."

Lara looked at Carson's sensual, off-center smile and felt something in herself stirring as though awakening from a long, long sleep. The feeling frightened her.

"Interest me?" she asked, her voice tight as she forced herself not to remember the one time she had curled her fingers into the warm mat of hair that covered Carson's chest.

"It worked, too," he said bluntly. "If your eyes had been hands, I'd have been touched all over."

"No, thanks. I'll leave that to Susanna," Lara retorted.

"I doubt it," Carson said. "You don't like the idea of me with another woman, and it shows."

Carson's voice was calm rather than baiting. It was his very lack of inflection that was shocking, as though he had stated that Lara preferred her coffee black instead of with cream.

"I don't like the idea of sex, period," Lara said, but her tone wasn't as calm as Carson's had been. Emotions seethed through her words, through her hunger, confusion, fear and a sexual denial so deep, so ingrained, that she didn't even realize that it was underlying her other emotions, driving them, driving her. "I was—" Her voice shifted, splintered. She swallowed. "I was revolted by what I saw."

Carson's mouth flattened into an angry line. "I don't believe you."

She shrugged. "It's true. I don't like sex. Period."

"You liked it real well four years ago."

"People change."

"Not without reason," he retorted.

Lara shrugged again, but her body was so tight it

ached. She hated talking about sex, thinking about it, because every word, every thought, led straight back to the freezing humiliation of four years ago.

Carson looked at Lara and saw again the shame that had come over her in the bunkhouse when he had mentioned the past. He also remembered the look in her eyes tonight when he had stood before her with his shirt open. He remembered her reaction when he had mentioned that other women didn't run away from him. But most of all he remembered the shiver of response when he had gently bitten her palm. No matter how violently she protested, she was still vulnerable to him. He knew it. He could prove it.

And he was going to.

"When I touched you this morning, you trembled. That isn't the response of a woman repulsed by sex," Carson said flatly.

"I was afraid."

"Then it must have been because you were responding to me," he retorted.

Lara looked at her hand as though she could still see the marks of Carson's teasing, sensual caress. Her throat closed and her breath caught. She swallowed hard.

"You're known for your temper," she whispered. "You were angry with me this morning. You're much stronger than I am. You even admitted that what you were doing to me was punishment for running away from you. It...frightened me. If you had decided to punish me more, there wouldn't have been anything I could have done about it."

"Hell of an idea," Carson muttered.

With no more warning than that, his hard hands fastened onto Lara's arms. Carson's shoulders blocked out the moon as he bent over her. Before she could protest, she was lying on her back looking up into his face. Moonlight and night made a mystery of his expression. She saw his lips part, saw the white flash of his teeth and knew that he was going to kiss her with a lover's intimacy. The moment was like her dreams—and her nightmares. He would kiss her and she would respond, and when he had her helpless again, he would turn on her, tearing out her soul, leaving her empty of everything but pain. She couldn't go through that again. She simply *could not.*

Carson sensed the sudden stiffening of Lara's body as he brushed his mouth over hers. He felt the trembling warmth of her lips, tasted the freshness of her breath, and memories exploded through his body. He had never known anything half so sweet as the taste of her innocence when she had responded to his kisses long ago. He didn't believe that she was still innocent. Anyone as naturally sensual as she was would have experimented thoroughly before she gave up on sex, if she had really given up on it. Remembering her abandonment when he had made love to her four years ago, he doubted that she had given up anything that had obviously brought her so much pleasure.

God, he had been a fool to walk away from Lara, no matter how much he had hated his father at the time.

"Little fox," Carson whispered against her mouth, "I—"

Whatever he had meant to say was lost in Lara's choked cry as she tried to throw herself aside, twisting and turning, struggling to evade the kiss. Reflexively Carson held her still, controlling her with an ease that only increased her fear. She fought wildly, futilely, for he was far stronger.

After the first few instants Carson no longer tried to kiss Lara. He simply tried to protect both of them from her frantic struggles. Quickly the weight of his body pinned her against the ground as his legs and arms captured hers, stilling her, making it impossible for her to fight.

"Lara," Carson said urgently, "it's all right, honey. I'm not going to hurt you. Lara! Listen to me! You're safe!"

For a terrible moment Carson thought that she was too frightened to hear him. Then he felt her shudder and go absolutely limp beneath him. Instantly he rolled aside. He wanted to gather her against him, to rock her in his arms, to touch her reassuringly; but most of all he wanted to erase even the memory of the fear he had seen on her face when he had bent over her.

"Lara," he breathed, touching her pale cheek with aching tenderness. "Honey, I didn't mean to frighten you."

She looked up at him with wide eyes that were black in the moonlight, haunted. Then she turned her head aside. Carson took a deep breath and fought to keep his voice gentle when he would rather have screamed his raw rage at the man who had done this to her. After a few more breaths he felt calm enough to speak.

"Who was he?" Carson asked, his voice shaking with the effort of keeping it under control.

Lara drew a broken breath, too upset by her own wild, unexpected panic at Carson's touch to think coherently. She had had no warning, no chance to control her fear in the searing moment when she fought against herself and him without a thought to anything but getting away, fleeing, running and never stopping.

Suddenly Lara realized that that was what she had been doing for the past four years. Running from Carson. Running from herself. Running in a panic that knew no end. She thought she had gotten over him, but all she had done was flee from that awful moment when she had whispered her love and his expression had changed from passion to disgust.

"Who was he?" repeated Carson.

"What?" Lara asked, still dazed by her discovery that she hadn't solved her problem, she had merely run from it.

"Who was the man who raped you?"

Her head turned quickly toward Carson. "What are you talking about?"

"Don't be afraid to tell me," Carson said gently. "Who was he?"

Lara's mouth opened in disbelief, hardly able to accept that she had heard correctly. "No one," she said distinctly, "has ever raped me."

Carson's lips turned down in a sad smile. "It's all right, little fox. You can tell me."

"There's nothing to tell."

Slowly he shook his head. "It won't wash, honey," he said softly. "No woman as sensual as you were just turns off sex for no reason at all. What happened?"

Anger leaped suddenly in Lara, a bright, white-hot flame that burned through all her hesitations and fears. To hear Carson ask the same question that had pursued her through the years made her furious. He didn't know why she had run, why she was still running. He didn't even have the least idea of what he had done to her.

"How would you feel if you had been inexperienced and fascinated by a woman, but she wouldn't have anything to do with you for years, no matter how much you wanted her? Until one day she turned around and smiled at you and held out her arms and you ran into them."

Lara drew a shuddering breath and continued talking quickly, as though her life depended on crowding as many words as she could into as few seconds as possible. And in some ways it did. She couldn't run anymore. She was appalled that she had run so long and still had stayed in the same place—disarmed, vulnerable, frightened.

"And then she hugged you and kissed you and undressed you despite your hesitations," Lara continued almost wildly, "and when she had you naked and begging and crying for your love, she looked at you as though you were dirt and walked away saying you weren't good enough for her because you were a bastard. How the hell would you feel about that, Carson? Would you run right out and jump on the next woman who smiled at you, or would the mere thought of sex make your stomach turn over?''

Carson flinched as though Lara had struck him. "Lara," he said hoarsely, "little fox, listen to me. That isn't why I walked away from you that night. I never meant to—''

But Lara was still talking, four years of anger and betrayal pouring out in a headlong rush that nothing could silence.

"That's exactly what happened!" she countered, her voice raw. "Denying it won't change it, and it certainly won't change the way I respond to men because of it. I'll never be that vulnerable again. I'd die first!" She shuddered and turned her face away from Carson. "In a way, I suppose I should thank you for curing me of an affliction that seems to run the rest of the population ragged." She smiled bitterly. "But I'm sure you'll understand if I just tell you to go to hell instead.''

Carson studied Lara's profile, her long lashes throwing lacy shadows on her moon-washed cheeks, her lips trembling slightly. He let out a long, ragged breath and examined his clenched fists as though they might hold answers to questions he had never thought to ask until that moment.

"I've made it a rule never to look back," he said finally, bleakly. "The past is for people with roots, people who know where they came from. I don't. All I know is where I'm going.'' He looked at Lara. She was still turned away from him, still living in the moment when he had hurt her so badly and had never even realized it. ''I said I made a mistake four years ago and I meant it. Just like you're making a mistake now.''

Carson heard the whispering of Lara's hair as she turned back toward him. ''What do you mean?''

''You think I walked away from you because you're Larry's illegitimate daughter.''

Lara went very still. It was the first time anyone in the Blackridge family had openly acknowledged who her father was. ''Yes,'' she said, her voice as thin as moonlight.

''No,'' Carson said flatly. ''All my life I had two things shoved down my throat by my dear 'father.' The first was that I wasn't of his blood. The second was that you were. No matter how hard I tried, how much I accomplished, how good I was at what I did, it wasn't good enough. A *real* Blackridge would have done better. And you were the living proof. Dear old Larry never tired of telling me that you were the brightest, quickest, most beautiful, polite, respectful, graceful kid in Montana. You were better than any other kid at anything and everything you did. In short, you were a *real* Blackridge, although he never said it in so many words.''

Lara's mouth opened in silent shock. Never had Larry Blackridge said or done anything in her presence that made her think she had even been noticed by him in any special way. "But—" she began.

"No," Carson said, cutting across Lara's attempt to speak. "I'm going to tell you why I walked out four years ago, and I'm only going to tell you once. Then the past will be buried in the same grave our parents are, and I'll be damned if I'll go digging it up again. Ever!"

The hostility Carson felt toward the past crackled in every word he said. Lara could imagine what it had done to a man of Carson's pride to be belittled for something over which he had no control—the fact that he hadn't been born from Blackridge loins. Nothing he could say, nothing he could do, could ever change that simple fact.

It had been the same for Lara when she had been belittled by schoolchildren for being a bastard. Nothing she did, nothing she said, could change the fact of her illegitimate birth. She understood how that kind of unfair rejection could eat into a person's soul. She wanted to tell Carson that, but she didn't. She was afraid that if she interrupted again, he would simply stop talking. Then she would never know the answer to the question of why he had walked away from her love, if not because she was his father's bastard child.

"The older you got," continued Carson, "the more Larry shoved you down my throat. Partly he did it just to needle me because he was old and sick and I was young and strong and there wasn't a damn thing he could do about either one. But mostly he baited me as a way of getting even with me for not being

his real son.'' Carson swore tiredly and rubbed the
back of his neck, trying to ease muscles knotted by
tension. ''Anyway, I decided that I'd get even, too.
I'd go find this paragon of perfection, this *real* Blackridge, and I'd screw her and then I'd shove that fact
down Larry's throat until he gagged on it.''

Lara made an odd sound as she realized where
Carson's words were going, why he had sought her
out four years before, flirted with her, dated her, seduced her, rejected her. She put her fist against her
mouth and tried not to cry out in protest. He had never
wanted her, not ever, not even in the beginning.

''So I went to the café where you worked,'' Carson
said. ''I stood outside in the dark watching you for
about an hour before I went in. You reminded me of
a fox at twilight—graceful, wary, elusive. I expected
you to flirt with all the men. You didn't. You had the
same polite smile for everyone. You worked hard.''

Carson rolled his head and sighed. He hated talking
about the past. He hated even thinking about it. Talking and thinking only brought it all back, all the pain
and the rage and the hurt. And to what purpose? None
of it could be changed. Not one damned second of it.
But if it helped Lara to know why he had walked
away from her, he'd talk until his jaw locked. He
owed her at least that much.

And he needed her. Having her was the only possible way to defeat the past.

''So I went into the café and the first thing that
happened was that my big feet got in your way.''
Carson smiled wryly, remembering despite himself,

and not all of the memories were bad. Some of them were like rainbows shining in the midst of the stormy past. "You were so sweet about it. You acted as though my clumsiness were your fault. That surprised me. It wasn't what I'd expected. I'd thought that any girl with looks as stunning as yours would have been spoiled to death by the men around her."

Lara's eyes widened as she stared at Carson. She had never thought of herself as unusually attractive. The realization that he had thought of her that way warmed her subtly.

"After the first few times I ate at the café, I found myself looking forward to going back. I enjoyed watching you, and you enjoyed watching me. I could tell by the blush when I turned and caught you at it." Carson's voice softened. "When you said you'd go to the dance with me, I could hardly wait for the weekend. I had heard all the gossip. I thought that your sweet innocence was just an intriguing kind of act, a way of making the moment even hotter when you finally gave in. Then you opened the door and stood there in that sheer silk blouse and sexy, floaty skirt, and your hair was all soft and loose and begging for a man's fingers, and I was sure that I'd have you before the night was over."

A tiny shiver coursed through Lara as she listened to Carson's deep, gritty voice painting a picture of the past that was unlike any she had in her own mind. *Is that how he saw me? A sexy little tease who pretended innocence only to make the chase more interesting?*

The realization that Carson's image of Lara had

been so different from her own image of herself expanded through Lara's mind like a shock wave, rearranging every memory it touched. It was as though reality were a book in which each chapter contained a different version of the same story, and everyone who looked at it saw a different chapter, a different slice of history, a different view of life; now she was reading the chapter Carson had read, with the result that her own view of the reality of the past was changing with every word, every new insight. It was disorienting, dizzying, and at the same time it was exciting, almost miraculous, another page from the past revealed.

Lara had felt a similar excitement before, when her research had turned up a fact that changed everything, rearranging the past before her very eyes. That had been the fascination of history for her. History wasn't dead—it was alive, immensely vital, capable of infinite change. The realization that her own personal history was also fluid, vital, changing, gave Lara hope for the first time in years. Nothing was fixed. Nothing was final. Everything was possible.

Carson's words sank into Lara, sliding past old barriers and fears, touching the vulnerable core that had never died.

"And then you looked so shocked when I called your bluff," Carson said. "I couldn't believe you were that innocent, until I saw your face. You had gone pale. No actress is that good. When you apologized for being a virgin and told me you understood that I wouldn't want to waste any more of my time on you, I felt as though I'd been sandbagged. By the time I realized that you were every bit as sweet and innocent as you seemed, you were lost in all the dancers.''

Lara bit her lip, remembering again how she had fled across the dance floor. It had been like a nightmare. No matter how she had twisted and turned, there had been no clear exit, no way out of the room. Trapped. Even the thought of it made her heart beat faster.

''I sat there and told myself there was no point in chasing you, I wasn't going to get my revenge by screwing you. And then I remembered how you had smiled when you saw me walk into the café. You didn't smile at other men like that. Whether you knew it or not, you wanted me.'' Carson hesitated, then added, ''I wanted you, too. You could make me hot with a look. And you kept surprising me. I enjoyed that. It had been a long time since I'd found anyone half so intriguing.'' He smiled a swift, off-center smile and ran the back of his index finger along Lara's cheek. ''Hell, little fox, I still haven't found anyone like you.''

Startled, she flinched at the touch. Carson's mouth flattened into a grim line. He wished that he had never started talking, wished that all of it had never happened, wished that he had a clean slate with the woman lying so close to him, wrapped in the black shroud of the past, a past that was strangling the only future he had ever wanted. He had to find a way to unwrap the clinging shroud or there would be no fu-

ture, nothing but the past repeated, hopes and dreams
dying.

"Then you curled up so trustingly in my arms on
the dance floor," he said, the words clipped. "You
fit perfectly against me and you smelled like a sweet,
wild spring wind. I wanted you until it felt like I was
being pulled apart."

Again Carson had surprised Lara, making the huge
pages of history turn again, shifting reality, revealing
yet another new truth. He had wanted her. No matter
the ultimate outcome, he had truly wanted her once.
She heard it in his deep voice, saw it in his hands
clenched against the memories of hunger.

"I kept on wanting you," Carson said. "I told myself it was revenge I really wanted. That was why I
kept on seeing you, talking with you, laughing, enjoying myself. Revenge. Every day brought me closer
to the time you'd give in and I'd go back to Larry
and tell him 'like mother, like daughter.'" Carson's
breath hissed out in a savage curse. "Most of the time
I even believed that it was revenge I was after. I had
to believe it. There couldn't be any other reason for
seeing you. Larry couldn't be right—you could *not*
be the perfect woman for me. You were my mother's
enemy and my enemy. You always had been. You
always would be."

Lara lay very still, trying not to even breathe. The
complex emotions in Carson's voice flicked over her
like burning threads, scoring her.

"I didn't ask myself why I avoided any chance of
actually getting my revenge by seducing you," con-

tinued Carson. His tone was oddly distorted, as though he had flattened all emotion from it. "I could have teased and nudged you into bed a lot sooner, but I avoided even being alone with you. Damned funny way for me to go after my revenge, wouldn't you say?"

Carson resumed rubbing his neck, speaking matter-of-factly, not expecting an answer from Lara. "Then the storm came that day and chased us inside. We were alone, and you were watching me with eyes that made me ache. So beautiful. So curious. So hungry. I tried to leave before I touched you. I swear to God I tried not to—"

Carson made an abrupt sound, a harsh word that was bitten off before it could offend Lara.

"Then I told myself one kiss, just one," he said, turning toward Lara, looking at her. "I should have been able to stop, but I couldn't. I'd wanted you so long, and you trembled when I kissed you. Passion, not fear. You were burning and so was I. When I kissed your breasts and you moaned, I nearly went crazy. You were more beautiful than I had imagined, and I'd spent more than one night undressing and loving you in my mind."

A visible shiver went through Lara. Once Carson would have assumed that it was desire. Now he was afraid it was revulsion. He continued speaking quickly, not wanting her to get up and flee his words as he described things she no longer could bear even to think about.

"And then you were naked," he said. "All that

softness, all that fire. Mine. When I touched you, really touched you, I felt the proof of your innocence. So did you. You looked at me and said that it was all right, that you weren't frightened, that you loved me."

Carson's voice changed as emotion seethed beyond his control once again. "At that instant I knew I couldn't do it. I couldn't take your virginity for revenge. Suddenly I despised my father and your mother for their years of adultery, for all the pain they had caused other people in the name of the lie called love." Carson grimaced, his face expressing exactly what he thought of love. "I knew all about love. At best, love is a trick you play on yourself. At worst, it's a trick you play on the unwary, the innocent— like you that night. Innocent. Trusting."

Carson's fingers dug into the muscles knotted at the base of his neck, physical symbol of the tension knotting his mind. He hated digging through the pain and failures of the past.

"I wanted to yell at you to wake up, to look at reality, to understand that I was your enemy," Carson said harshly, his voice resonant with anger. "Your innocence enraged me. But most of all I was furious and completely disgusted with myself for being so caught up in the past that I would use another person as I had almost used you. I had hated Larry for years for not being able to control his sexuality even to the point of preventing his mistress's pregnancy. Yet there I was, about to do the same thing with you. I had no way of protecting you that night, and you were too naive to have protected yourself.''

Carson shuddered suddenly. ''And you know what?'' he asked roughly. ''That thought was the most exciting of all. Something of me growing in you. Something new. Something untouched by the past. A child. Our child.''

The sound Carson made then was too harsh to be called a laugh. It was more like a hoarse echo of pain. It cut deeply into Lara, telling her how little she had known about Carson four years ago—and how much she still cared that he had been hurt by the past, too. He was still hurting. Like her. Hurting and not knowing how to make it stop.

Without realizing it, Lara's hand went out to Carson in an instinctive gesture of comfort that stopped short of actually touching him.

''Nothing escapes the poison of the past,'' Carson said flatly. ''I spent most of my life fighting that particular truth. I lost. But I finally learned that you can limit the damage by not looking back. So I don't look back. I go after what I want for the future and *to hell with the past.*'' He turned and searched Lara's face, trying to read her emotions beneath the mysterious veils of moonlight and darkness. ''Do you understand now?'' he asked softly. ''It wasn't you I walked away from that night. It was the past.''

Lara didn't realize that she was crying until she felt the heat of her tears against her cool skin. Carson brushed away the tears with a gentle fingertip, then brought his hand to his lips, tasting her tears.

"Don't cry, little fox," he said hoarsely. "The past isn't worth the salt in your tears. The past is dead. Buried. Don't let it hurt you anymore. Don't let it hurt us. Don't let it ruin our future."

Lara closed her eyes, releasing the last of her tears. "Carson," she whispered shakily, "what do you want from me?"

He started to speak, then remembered her raw fear when he had tried to kiss her a few moments ago. The sexual implications of marriage would send her fleeing down the hillside like the wind.

"Another chance," he said, which was as much of the truth as he felt Lara could handle, as much of the past as he would allow to intrude into the present.

"Why?"

"I enjoyed being with you four years ago," he said simply. "I want that again. We had something that I've never found with any other woman. I've wanted you for years, but I let the past get in the way."

Slowly Lara shook her head. "I don't have anything to give you anymore," she said, her voice breaking.

"That's not true."

She looked at Carson's narrowed, intent eyes and didn't know whether to laugh or cry. "Haven't you listened to me?" she asked hoarsely. "Even when I was a child, I had already learned to fear the passion that drew my mother and your father together, causing so much pain for her. Then you—we—" For a moment there was only silence while Lara fought to control herself. "I didn't know how very powerful desire could be, until you touched me. I didn't know how much I could love, until I loved you. And I didn't know how much I could be hurt, until you walked away from me.'' She let out a shaky breath. ''I can't be that vulnerable again, Carson. I simply can't. If you walked away again it would destroy me.''

''I'll never walk away,'' he said flatly. ''I can't.''

Lara bit her lip and shook her head slowly.

''So to avoid the possibility of being hurt in the future, you're killing yourself by inches now,'' he said. ''Is that it?''

''I was fine until I came back here.''

''Were you?'' asked Carson softly. ''Or were you just so badly poisoned by the past that you were afraid to let yourself feel? Like me.'' He ran his fingertip down the silver trail of a tear until he reached the corner of Lara's mouth. ''When you trembled today, it wasn't all fear, was it?''

''Carson, I—''

''Was it?''

Lara shivered as the ball of Carson's thumb stroked her lower lip very lightly, tracing the full curve.

''Give us a chance,'' he said, his voice low, coaxing. ''Stop running long enough to get to know me again. I won't drag you into bed. I promise.'' He smiled crookedly. ''As Cheyenne would say, my intentions toward you are strictly honorable, more than you know.'' Carson hesitated, then made a movement with his hand that was impatient, almost angry. He wanted to talk of marriage but knew it was too soon.

"I won't do to you what my father did to your mother," Carson said finally. "I won't dishonor you."

"But if you don't believe in love—" Lara's voice stretched and broke into silence as she remembered his words. *Love is a lie, a trick played on the unwary.*

"Do you?" Carson asked, his tone curious, his expression surprised.

"Despite all the pain, my mother loved your father," whispered Lara. "My grandfather loved the grandmother I never knew. He talked about her until the day he died. And he and my mother loved me. I loved them. Yes, I believe in love."

Carson's smile was bittersweet, almost yearning. "Then you're stronger than I am, little fox, or much more naive." He lifted Lara's hand to his mouth and kissed her palm with such exquisite restraint that she barely felt the warmth of his lips before he lifted his head and looked straight into her eyes.

"If you eventually decide that you want me, remember this: I would never turn you into a kept woman for others to sneer at and condemn. I would never get you pregnant and then not marry you. I would never allow a child of mine to be sold like I was or to be raised as a bastard like you were. If you trust yourself to me, I will take care of you and our children. Always. The future, Lara. Not the past."

Lara closed her eyes and felt her palm tingling where Carson's lips had brushed over her. He was sometimes a hard man, even a fierce one, yet even his worst enemy had to admit that Carson's promises were as solid and unchanging as the mountains themselves. As she listened to his words again in her mind, she felt them sinking into her like an intangible balm, healing places she hadn't even known were raw. Carson would not seduce her and then abandon her to a lonely pregnancy and an even more lonely life as a single parent. Nor would he condemn his own child to a life of illegitimacy in a time and a place where such things still mattered. He might not believe in love, but he did believe in personal responsibility.

That was why he had walked away from her four years ago. It hadn't been disgust with her. It was simply that he had been too decent to use her for revenge like that.

Slowly Lara's eyes opened. She looked at the long, powerful body of the man stretched out on the grass so close to her. Moonlight and shadows outlined his strength, heightening every line of his body; his need was a long ridge of moonlight and darkness rising against his jeans. Oddly, the blunt evidence of Carson's desire reassured her. Despite his obvious physical hunger, once he had understood her fear, he had made no move to touch her in any way but gently.

She drew a slow breath.

"All right," Lara whispered. "Another chance."

"No more looking back?" Carson asked, his voice urgent, as though he needed reassurance as much as she did.

"Carson," Lara said very softly, her voice breaking. "Oh, Carson, the past isn't dead. The more you learn about it, the more it changes. That's not something to fear or avoid. It's a miracle. It allows you to grow past pain, to heal.''

"You're wrong," Carson said flatly, his voice as bleak as his eyes. "For us, the past is dead. It has to be, or the future is dead, too. Believe me, Lara. Please. The past can't heal us, but it can destroy us. Let it be. Let the dead bury the dead.''

Lara opened her mouth. No words came out. There was an emotion close to desperation in Carson's flat words. He believed what he was saying and wanted her to believe, too. He wanted the past dead, buried, gone, untouchable, unspeakable.

Carson came to his feet in a swift, lithe movement and held out his hand to Lara. After an instant's hesitation she took it, allowing herself to be pulled toward him. She walked with him back down through the moonlight and darkness over Blackridge land, going toward the Chandler homestead—going toward the past, feeling the future tugging at her hand, letting the warmth of Carson's skin drive away her doubts.

Chapter 6

Lara turned off her tape recorder and stretched, flexing fingers that were numbed from working the old manual typewriter that was all she could afford. Despite her aching back and sore fingers, she smiled at the neatly stacked sheets of paper. Willie had finally broken down and told her a carefully edited version of the day he had danced barefoot in the spring grass with the woman who later became known as Tickling Liz. Willie's halting, hesitant words had sketched in the lines of a society and a time when *lust* was the only word used to describe all sexual feelings outside marriage. Yet it had been more than lust for Willie, and perhaps even for Liz. Surely no woman who was merely a whore would have taken so much gentle care in seducing a terribly shy boy.

Slowly Lara leafed through the papers again, but she didn't need to see the words. She could still hear Willie's thin voice and see the memories glowing in his eyes.

...and I took off my boots so I wouldn't hurt her if I missed a step. She smiled up at me and laughed soft and low, and for a time life was warm and sweet as summer honey.

Lara knew she would never again look at Willie and see simply a gnarled old cowhand. She would also see the boy he had once been, dark-haired and strong for his years, holding a woman in his arms while she taught him all the different ways there were to dance.

That was the kind of knowledge that Lara wanted in her history of the Rocking B. It was a ranch and a state and a country built by men and women like Willie and Liz—neither saints nor devils, simply people who had been born into and had grown up in a world they hadn't made, a world inherited from their parents. And, like their parents, like themselves, the world was imperfect. Often it seemed that there was more hate than love, more hurting than healing, more death than life. Yet even in the very worst of times, some people still loved, still healed, still created life in the midst of death. It was those people who left the world a better place than they had found it, not the conquerors and kings who marched hard-shouldered through history.

Smiling, Lara let the pages of Willie's memories drift from her fingers back onto the scarred oak table.

She knew her gentle views of history would never be as popular as the fierce cycles of ambition and bigotry, war and betrayal that most people thought of when they heard the word *history*. Those things existed, of course, and they had changed the outward appearance of countries and the distribution of various peoples since the beginning of time. But beneath those outward changes lay the unchanging reality of human emotions, human needs. That, too, was history, and it was a history far more enduring than any royal dynasty or national boundary.

"Lara?"

The sound of Carson's voice whisked Lara out of her history project and into the present. Her breath caught for an instant and her heartbeat speeded up. It had been two weeks since she and Carson had made their truce on the ridge between the ranch house and the homestead. She had seen him every day and most evenings, but it hadn't been to research the Rocking B by going through the boxes of old papers and cabinets of photographs. Instead, they had simply talked after dinner about what Carson had done that day on the ranch or what interviews Lara had done for her history project. After they had discovered a mutual passion for cribbage, they spent many hours pegging up and down the ivory cribbage board that Larry Blackridge's great-uncle had carved from the horns of a massive elk he had shot for winter meat nearly a century before.

"Door's open," Lara called, frowning and wishing that time hadn't gotten away from her. Now it was too late to shower and change clothes before she went riding.

Even as Lara realized that she wanted to look pretty for Carson, uneasiness prickled through her. She shouldn't care whether he found her attractive. But she did. It was there in the quickened beat of her heart and in the breath wedging in her throat as he walked into the small living room. He filled the doorway. Even with his hat off, he had to duck beneath the lintel. In his cowboy boots he was six feet six inches tall.

Carson saw Lara's sudden, intent stare and stopped moving toward her. "What's wrong, honey? Did I startle you?"

"No. It's just—you're so much bigger than the men who built this house."

Carson's green-flecked, golden-brown eyes traveled down the curving length of Lara's body with a posses-siveness that he didn't bother to conceal. "Don't let it bother you. You're bigger than the women were then, too. We'll fit together perfectly, just like we did when we danced."

For a moment Lara was speechless, totally sur-prised by the sensual implications of Carson's words. He hadn't touched her even in the most casual way since the night he had led her down off the ridge and squeezed her hand in farewell at the homestead's door. Yet the look in his eyes right now was enough to light fires in a snowbank. Even as Lara's own eyes widened, she felt a soft bloom of heat deep within her body.

"Carson, you promised," she said, her voice sounding husky, almost breathless.

"I'm not touching you," he pointed out, smiling slowly as he looked at the escaped tendrils of her hair curling around her face, teasing her red lips.

Carson may not have been touching Lara physically, but his smile sent another pulse of heat expanding through her. She realized that at some level she wanted to be touched by him, just as she wanted to be pretty for him. For a moment fear and excitement warred within her.

Carson saw the fear. Even as he told himself not to worry, it had only been two weeks, his smile faded. Two weeks, and nothing had changed. She was still afraid. Would it be the same after two months? Six? Sixteen? Would he lose the only future he wanted because of the mistakes of the past?

He closed his eyes, fighting the rush of fear that came when he thought that Lara might not change in time, might not turn to him with trust instead of fear in her eyes before it was too late. He could not let that happen. He could not let the past win again, taking everything he wanted, everything he needed.

Suddenly Carson felt each separate ache in his body, legacy of the tiredness that had come to him because he had cut short his sleep in order to spend more time with Lara and still get all the ranch work done. Unconsciously he rubbed his neck, trying to loosen muscles knotted by too much work, too much tension, too little peace of mind.

"Carson?" asked Lara softly, hating to see the light and laughter go out of his eyes.

He looked at her, forcing a smile. "Ready to look at those old boundary markers?"

"I—I packed a picnic lunch if you…that is, I know how busy you are and—" Lara stopped speaking and made an uncertain gesture with her hands.

Carson's mouth softened into a true smile. "Clever little fox. How did you know that I needed to get away from accounts and breeding books for a while?"

"Because it's so beautiful outside," she said promptly, smiling because she had chased the darkness from his eyes. "Everyone knows it's bad for your health to be inside on a day like this."

"You have a swimsuit?" he asked.

She nodded.

"Bring it. We'll go up to Long Pool."

"Is it warm enough?" she asked, thinking of the clear green water of the Rocking B's favorite swimming and fishing hole.

"We'll swim fast," he suggested wryly. "Or if you're too chicken—"

"Never," she interrupted quickly, rising to the bait. "I joined the Polar Bear Club as soon as I was old enough to swim. I was so little they had to put me on a fishing line and dunk me like a worm."

Carson laughed, and the lines of strain bracketing his mouth dissolved, making him look much less intimidating. For an instant his hand stroked Lara's shining black hair in a gesture of appreciation for her company. Even though he withdrew his hand almost as quickly as he had extended it, she felt the brief touch all the way to the soles of her feet.

"I've got to get a few things," Lara said huskily. "Why don't you sit down?"

"I'm afraid I'd fall asleep," he admitted, muffling a yawn.

"There's coffee on the back of the stove."

Carson's eyes flew open, revealing flecks of green as well as the familiar golden brown. "You have no idea of the things I'd do for a cup of coffee right now."

"Then I'd better get you one before I find out," she said quickly, a smile tugging at her lips.

"Chicken," he said as she retreated.

"I'm a fox, remember?" she shot back, refusing to rise to the bait again. "They aren't chickens—they eat 'em."

Carson's low chuckle warmed Lara. She loved being with him like this, teasing and laughing and enjoying each other. And if his eyes flared with desire from time to time, that, too, was warming.

By the time Lara had combed her hair and added a swimsuit and towel to her picnic collection, Carson was finishing his second cup of coffee. He looked more alert, but Lara couldn't tell whether that was the result of the coffee or the sight of her teal-blue two-piece bathing suit dangling from one end of the rolled towel. Although he said nothing, his dark brown eyebrows rose in a silent show of anticipation.

They decided to swim and eat lunch before tackling

the photographing of the Rocking B's various boundary markers. The ride to Long Pool was only a few miles, but there were six gates. Lara got in and out of the pickup each time like the well-brought-up ranch child she was, grumbling for the last three fences that the only reason Carson had brought her along to the swimming hole was so that he wouldn't have to open all the gates himself. He agreed with a solemn voice and a wicked smile that lighted up warning signals and nerve endings all through Lara's body.

The first rush of the spring melt had already passed, restoring the Big Green to its normal summer size and clarity. Despite the river's name, it wasn't very large. In most places the Big Green wasn't a lot more than a hundred feet wide. Nor was the river particularly deep, except in the pools, which were often twenty-five feet deep or more, having been gouged out during spring floods. At the pools the water poured in swiftly on the upstream end, churned in shades of white and green and blue, and then flowed sedately toward the shallow, downstream end of the pool where eddies swirled slowly and smaller trout fed.

Thickets of willow and an occasional granite boulder taller than Carson studded the riverbanks. He spread their picnic quilt in a nest of grass shielded from the wind by one of the huge boulders. In addition to being a windbreak, the pale granite made a very good heat reflector, adding several degrees to the already warm picnic site.

With a sigh of pleasure, Carson sat down on the

quilt, pulled off his boots and socks, tossed his hat aside, unbuttoned his shirt halfway to his belt and rolled up his sleeves. Lara watched the quick, efficient motions of his hands with something close to fascination. It had always been like that for her—watching Carson's combination of size, strength and coordination had never failed to please her.

When Carson had finished making himself comfortable, he closed his eyes and turned his face up to the sun with an appreciation that made Lara's heartbeat quicken. More than anyone she had ever met, Carson was alive to his senses and to the physical world around him.

"You can change here or in the thicket," Carson said without opening his eyes. "I won't peek."

Lara's cheeks flushed suddenly with a warmth that had nothing to do with the sun. The thought of being naked in front of Carson frankly terrified her. It was too close to her memories, to her nightmares. Even the idea of wearing a swimming suit around him made her very uneasy.

"I don't—it's not hot enough to swim," she said quickly, looking away from him.

Carson's eyes opened. He looked at Lara for a long moment, seeing her fear, sensing the darkness of the past reaching forward into the sunny day. He could have pointed out that it was at least eighty degrees in the sheltered spot, more than warm enough to be comfortable in a swimsuit, but he knew that it wasn't the temperature that was preventing Lara from swimming. She had been naked when he had walked away from her four years before. He had been fully dressed. She remembered that as well as he did, probably better, and she had no desire to duplicate the humiliating moment.

With a silent curse Carson yanked off his shirt. He had hoped that swimming together would help diminish Lara's nervousness about being less than fully dressed around him. He had even hoped to see a flash of sensual interest in her eyes when he eventually stripped to his swim trunks. Instead, he was afraid that he had done nothing but increase her fear, reinforcing the past's dark grip on his future.

Wide-eyed, Lara watched Carson's lithe, muscular body emerge from the concealment of his clothes. She was so caught up in the moment that she wasn't even aware of staring at him. She hadn't fully realized just how powerful he was until she saw the bunch and flow of his strength unblurred by concealing cloth.

Carson's legs were long, muscular, and gleaming with hair that was so intense a brown it was almost black. Vaguely Lara noticed that he had worn swim trunks beneath his jeans and that he must have spent a lot of time at Long Pool through the years because his legs had the same tan that his chest did. His shoulders were half again as wide as her own, and his chest tapered to a lean waist and hips that were the result of both a lifetime of hard physical work and a genetic heritage that was unknown but must have been excellent.

"What are you thinking?" asked Carson, his voice low.

The words were as soft and unthreatening as the breeze sliding through the grass. Lara answered automatically while she admired sunlight pouring like honey over Carson's body, making everything it touched gleam with golden light.

"Your parents must have been physically perfect," Lara said simply.

For an instant Carson didn't understand that Lara wasn't referring to Sharon and Larry Blackridge but to the unknown man and woman who had conceived him. When Carson did understand, he looked down at his own body as though he hadn't ever seen it before. It was the first time he had looked at himself through a woman's eyes, seeing the raw strength of his own flesh compared to Lara's smaller, softer body. It occurred to him that it was a miracle she trusted him enough even to be alone with him. The difference in their physical strength was so great that it had to be frightening.

And then Carson realized that not only did Lara trust him, but also she approved of the very differences between their bodies.

"You're amazing," he said, shaking his head.

Lara looked up into his eyes, surprised. "What?"

"I'm twice your strength, half again your size and must look about as hairy and generally cuddly as a hungry grizzly. Logically, you should be running away from me and screaming. Yet you stand there and tell me that my parents must have been physically perfect. You're amazing." He laughed and held out his hand to her. "Come on, my brave, crazy fox. Walk with your tame grizzly down to the river."

Smiling almost shyly, Lara took Carson's hand, enjoying the warmth and strength of his touch. He interlaced their fingers until their palms met and rubbed with a sweet friction that sent tiny quivers of awareness through her. She giggled when Carson winced as his unprotected feet found the stones lying in ambush along the way to the river.

"Tenderfoot," she teased.

"Literally," he agreed, smiling crookedly as he boosted Lara onto the top of a huge, water-smoothed rock ledge that overlooked the deepest part of the pool. "Even though I go barefoot around the house a lot, I still have to toughen up my feet every summer." He braced his hands on the chest-high granite outcropping that made up the ledge and levered himself up next to Lara in a single, easy motion. "It's worth a few stone bruises, though," Carson continued, sitting next to her, close but not crowding. "The men have learned not to bother me when I head for Long Pool. They know I come here when I need some time to myself."

Glancing sideways at Carson, Lara saw both the lines of strain on his face and the subtle signs that he was relaxing in the presence of the rushing water and radiant sun. She could understand the soothing lure of the pool. The patterns the water made were almost hypnotic, as was the sound of the river itself, and the sun was a continuous caress over her whole body. Deep inside herself, she sensed knots loosening, releasing her from a tension that had been part of her for so many years that she had come to accept it as normal. But it wasn't. She was learning it with every breath she took, relaxation overtaking her like a benediction.

Lara wished she were in her swimsuit so that her body would be free to absorb the warmth and peace unhindered by clothes. Being naked would be even better, feeling the sun over every inch of her skin, all knots loosening until her body softened and turned to honey.

The thought would have startled Lara if she hadn't already been so undone by the sun and the murmuring green water. She hadn't enjoyed being naked for years, not since she had curled around herself after the door had closed behind Carson and she had felt cold to her soul.

That was the past. This is now. Go away, memories. Let me dream in the sun. It feels so good, both the sun and the dreaming.

Closing her eyes, Lara leaned back to brace her weight on her hands and turned her face to the sun. Carson watched hungrily, wishing that it had been his touch that had brought the sensual softening to her mouth. He wished that he could settle her gently between his legs, letting her rest her weight on his chest while he kissed the sensitive center of her palm and the tempting line of her neck. Then she would use his bare thighs as an armrest, stroking him with her soft fingers while he unfastened her blouse and her bra and held her breasts in his hands.

The direction of Carson's thoughts had an immediate and unmistakable effect on his body. Abruptly he decided that it was time to go swimming in the river's bracing green water. If Lara saw him before he had his unruly sex under control, he doubted that she would feel quite so relaxed around him. In fact, she would probably run like hell.

The small sounds that Carson made as he stood up were lost in the soothing rush of the water. He went into the pool in a shallow dive. Lara blinked, looked around and saw Carson swimming cleanly downstream. When the water became too shallow for swimming, he turned and swam upstream, his body slicing through the water with the speed and grace of an otter. She remembered hearing that he had been on the swimming team at the university during one of the best seasons the team had ever had. As she watched, she had no doubt that Carson's presence had contributed to the team's success.

It was also clear that he was at home in the water in a way few Montana ranchers were. He swam easily, swiftly, powerfully, as though the pool were only fifty feet long instead of more than fifty yards. She wondered if Carson's father had been a swimmer, too, and if his sheer physical beauty had caused some girl to succumb to an ill-advised passion.

But that was something Lara suspected she would never know. If Carson had any curiosity about his biological parents, he had never expressed it aloud. As he had told her two weeks before, he never looked back. In all their hours of talking, if the past had been discussed, it was because Lara brought it up. That included any of the past, not merely what had happened between them four years before. Carson would talk freely enough about the ranch's history and the old stories the cowhands told around the bunkhouse at night, but when it came to talking about the Blackridges and the Chandlers, Carson usually found a way to change the subject; and the closer the questions came to the past four years, the more quickly the subject was changed.

The soothing, sibilant, rushing sounds of the river beckoned to Lara, unraveling her thoughts. It was warm on the big rock where she sat, almost hot, and the breeze had died to nothing. A sheen of sweat slicked her skin, making her itch to go swimming. Carson was heading upstream on either his fifteenth or sixteen complete circuit of Long Pool. She had lost count, and he showed no signs of slowing.

Lara slid off the ledge, went back to the picnic blanket and shook out her swimsuit. She undressed almost slowly, savoring the feeling of freedom that came as her confining clothes dropped onto the quilt. She hurried only when she replaced her bra with the swimsuit top, and her panties with the bottom. The suit was the most modest one she had been able to find short of buying from the granny racks in the local department store.

The one-piece suits that were cut up to the hipbone and down to the navel weren't to Lara's taste. Nor did she like the handfuls of strings and tiny patches that were called bikinis. The blue two-piece she had finally selected was more than most women wore and less than Lara had hoped to find. Yet she had to admit that the sun felt like silk on her exposed skin. It made her want to close her eyes and stretch completely, holding out her arms to the pouring warmth.

The river, however, was a good deal less warm. Lara stood undecided on the edge of the rock ledge that rimmed the deep pool, letting water drip from the foot that she had dangled briefly in the pool. A long, dark shape glided closer to the ledge. The shape evolved into Carson shooting up out of the depths, shaking hair and water from his eyes. He hung suspended in the clear water, making lazy motions with his hands to stay in place against the current.

"Come on in," he offered, watching Lara through half-closed eyes. He was grateful for the hard swimming and the cold water because she looked delicious standing there, her body poised between advance and retreat. He wanted to pull her into the water and feast on every lovely inch of her.

"Aren't you going to tell me the water's fine?" Lara asked hopefully.

"Actually, it's pretty warm for early summer."

"Damned by faint praise, as Shakespeare would say," she muttered.

Carson laughed. "It's not that bad, honey."

Lara gave him a look that clearly said she didn't believe him. Then she dove in and came up gasping.

"You beast!" she said, trying to get her breath. "Why haven't you turned blue!"

"You just got all hot lazing around on that rock,"

Carson said, grinning. "Come on. We'll swim you warm again."

After Lara had done a few quick circuits of the river pool, she was warmer. After six more she was getting a little breathless. When Carson turned and began the thirteenth full circuit, she groaned and rolled over on her back, letting the current take her downstream the easy way. Carson noticed that she was missing, turned, swam back and drifted alongside her.

"I've found—the secret of—your great body," Lara panted, fighting for breath.

"Swimming?" asked Carson lazily, smiling at her, pleased by her words.

"Sort of. Your father was—a deep-sea diver. Your mother—was a mermaid."

"That explains everything but the fins," Carson said gravely.

"Fins?" Lara asked, looking at the clean, powerful lines of his body as he drifted next to her. "You aren't wearing any swim fins."

"Right. No fins a'tall," he drawled. "Just fur."

"That explains it," she said, smiling slightly.

"What?"

"Why I'm cold. No fur," she said succinctly.

Carson remembered the sight of Lara standing in the sun, her smooth skin gleaming with warmth between the blue bands of her suit. She was right. There hadn't been a bit of fur showing on her. With an effort he dragged his thoughts away from the memory that there was one place where she was softly, beautifully furred.

"Ready to get out?" he asked.

"What was your first clue?"

"Shriveled blue lips."

Lara buried Carson in a wave of water plowed up in front of her cupped hand before she turned and raced for the ledge. She thought she had made it when she felt his hands clamp over her thigh. Then his fingers slid slowly down her leg and off her foot, freeing her. She felt suddenly weak, but she pulled herself out onto the ledge in time to watch Carson come out of the water in a smooth rush. He shook his head, spraying water every which way. She would have done the same if she hadn't been afraid of beating herself half to death with her heavy single braid.

The first thing Lara did on the way back to the quilt was step on one of the rocks lying in ambush. Her breath caught at the unexpected pain, and she stumbled. With no warning Carson scooped her up into his arms and calmly continued walking toward the quilt.

"And you call me a tenderfoot," he said teasingly.

Carson looked down at Lara for only an instant before he concentrated on the vague trail to the quilt. The ground didn't need that much of his attention; he was simply afraid that she would see the desire in his eyes. Her breasts swelled temptingly from the top of her suit, water beaded like diamonds in the shadow cleavage between and her cold-hardened nipples were clearly defined by the blue cloth. He remembered all too well a time when it had been the heat and moisture of his mouth rather than a cool river that had made her nipples hard. He wanted that time to come again with a force that shook him.

"There you go," Carson said lightly, depositing Lara on her feet on the soft quilt. With swift motions he shook out her towel and wrapped it around her shoulders. "Warm enough?"

Lara nodded. "Thanks," she said, knowing that she sounded a bit breathless but unable to control it. "You're so strong." Instantly she winced, wishing that she had said anything else or at least hadn't sounded quite so awed. "I'm not used to being carried," she added quickly, as though that explained her words. "In fact, no one but you has called me little since sixth grade."

"Strength comes in handy with a mean steer," Carson said matter-of-factly as he dried his face on his towel.

He concentrated on briskly rubbing his hair dry and biting his tongue so that he wouldn't say how soft Lara had felt in his arms and how sweet it had been to know that she trusted him at least that much. She had allowed him to carry her. That simple fact went through him like lightning, warming him more than the sun.

Lara sat down and buried her face in her own towel, grateful that Carson had accepted her words as though people told him every day that he was surprisingly strong. Perhaps they did. Especially women. After all, it was only the truth. With unnecessary force

Lara jerked out the rubber band that was holding her braid and yanked her fingers through her dripping hair, wincing and wishing that she had never thought of Carson's powerful arms wrapped around other women.

"Hey, easy there," Carson said, kneeling and gently pulling Lara's hands away from her hair. "Let me do it."

Without waiting for her agreement, he began carefully separating her braid until black strands fell slick and gleaming halfway down her back. He took his towel and wrapped her hair in it, squeezing gently until the excess water was absorbed. Then he shifted to a dry part of the towel and rubbed her head slowly.

A small sound of pleasure escaped Lara as Carson massaged her scalp. The flash of uneasiness she had felt when he had picked her up was completely gone. He had made no attempt to increase the intimacy of the moment, although she knew he wanted her. It was as clear as the blunt ridge of flesh rising against his swim trunks.

The fact that Carson was aroused didn't frighten Lara. She knew that he couldn't prevent his desire from showing—but he could prevent himself from pushing her, demanding something that she wasn't prepared to give.

"Where's your comb?" Carson asked, rubbing Lara's scalp slowly, feeling its warmth seep up through the towel to his fingertips. His hands paused. "Unless you mind?"

Lara opened her eyes slowly, mesmerized by the

gentle massage. "Mind?" She blinked against the bright sunlight and closed her eyes again. The twin black arcs of her eyelashes cast delicate shadows over her cheeks. "Mind what?" she murmured, sighing with pleasure.

Carson smiled as he bent and kissed Lara's hair so lightly that she felt nothing. He glanced around the quilt until he spotted a bright red comb peeking out from beneath Lara's discarded jeans. Carefully he combed out her long hair until it lay over her back like a polished ebony fan. Then he picked up the brush that had also been underneath Lara's clothes. With slow, firm movements he brushed her hair until it was dry and silky and clung to his fingers like a lover with each stroke of his hand.

After the first few minutes Lara stopped trying to stifle her appreciative murmurs. Having her hair brushed was a luxury as unexpected as relaxing beneath the sun's heat had been. Carson absorbed her small sounds of pleasure hungrily, for each one was a separate caress, a separate sign of hope. The brush dropped unnoticed to the quilt as he substituted his palm smoothing over the glistening black strands, stroking her slowly, taking an intense pleasure in the softness of her hair against his skin.

Long, strong fingers eased into Lara's hair, searching beneath the silk, finding the warmth of her. Carson massaged her scalp with slow, sure motions until she came unraveled in his hands and leaned against him, letting him support her relaxed body.

"You're very good at this," Lara said. Her words

were as languid as the motions of her head rubbing against Carson's hands in return, increasing the pressure of his fingers. She was too relaxed to guard her thoughts and questions. She sighed and asked, "Who taught you?" And then she bit her lip at the question. It was none of her business who Carson had been with, who he had caressed, who he had seduced. "Never mind, I—"

"You taught me," Carson interrupted, leaning down to inhale the sweet fragrance of Lara's hair. "I've never forgotten how good it felt at the end of a long day to have your hands rubbing through my hair, unraveling all the knots of tension and disappointment, leaving me at peace."

Carson's words were another kind of caress touching Lara, sliding past her defenses, making her eyes brim with unexpected tears.

"Was it really like that for you?" she whispered, turning to look at him over her shoulder.

"Such beautiful eyes," Carson said. "They've haunted me." He bent and brushed his lips over Lara's. "Yes," he whispered. "It was really like that. And that, too, has haunted me."

For a long moment Carson looked at the memories and shadows darkening Lara's eyes. He knew she was remembering how it had ended between them—pain rather than peace. Silently he cursed himself for bringing up the past when the present had been so unexpectedly sweet.

"If you must remember the pain," Carson asked in a low voice, "why can't you at least remember the pleasure, too? I remember, and I wake up hot and shaking. Pleasure, Lara, not pain. I want a chance to make more of those memories so that when we look back years from now, the past won't be a cold chain wrapped tight around our lives, strangling our future.''

Lara closed her eyes and shivered, and even she didn't know whether it was from fear or the sudden memory of Carson's face taut with need and pleasure as his tongue laved the sensitive pink peak of her breast. As though he were caressing her like that again, her nipple tightened, sending currents of pleasure radiating down through the pit of her stomach, making her want to moan. She wanted to see his mouth on her again, to feel his heat and need—and she was afraid to give herself to him again, to share his heat and need.

"What is it that frightens you so?" asked Carson. His voice ached with the effort of being gentle when he wanted to tear the answers from Lara, ending her pain and his own, putting the past behind them once and for all. "Did I ever hurt you physically?"

Silently Lara shook her bowed head, sending a soft black cloud of hair sliding over her shoulders, concealing her breasts.

"Are you afraid that I will?"

Again she shook her head. Despite Carson's physical strength, she didn't fear him in that way. Even when he had wanted to use her only for revenge, he had been unfailingly gentle with her.

"Did you like being touched by me?" he asked, his voice both soft and persistent.

This time Lara nodded her head, but she still didn't look up at him. She didn't want to meet his eyes, for she knew that too much of her hopes and fears could be read on her face.

"Then what is it, little fox?" Carson asked, tilting Lara's head up with his hand beneath her chin.

Lara didn't fight his touch, but she refused to open her eyes. She tried to speak, swallowed and forced out the words. "I'm just afraid to give myself to you again."

There was a long, taut pause while Carson looked at Lara's beautiful, troubled face. He smiled suddenly, crookedly, and his thumb touched her lips like a kiss. "Then I'll just have to give myself to you instead."

Lara's eyes flew open. "What?"

"Yeah, I know. It's a terrible sacrifice," Carson said gravely, his eyes brilliant with laughter and other emotions that were far stronger, far more complex. He held out his hands to her. "Take me, honey. I'm all yours. You can comb my hair and rub my scalp until I turn to butter and melt in your hands. You can talk to me, ride with me, stand quietly and watch the sun go down with me, dress or undress me, touch me, explore me, do as much or as little as you like. Anything. Everything." The laughter faded from Carson's eyes but not the emotions that turned his eyes to molten gold. "Except run from me," he said. "No more of that, Lara. That belongs to the past, and the past is dead."

Carson's eyes were intent, golden, and the hands he held out to Lara didn't waver. Slowly she put her hands in his. She expected her fingers to be enveloped in his warmth and strength, but he made no move to hold her more tightly. She realized that he was silently reinforcing his words. He had given himself to her.

What she did with that gift was for her to decide.

Chapter 7

The faded daguerreotype showed a ragged pile of rocks on a windswept ridge. Below the ridge was a wide, fertile valley with a river winding through it. There were no fences, no man-made landmarks, nothing but grass, the river and thickets of willow and alder. Tiny dots scattered across the grass in the picture could have been deer or perhaps even elk.

Lara knew that the dots weren't cattle, for the first of the Blackridge herd was being driven up from Texas when the photo had been taken more than a century ago. She had found the daguerreotype tucked in among her grandfather's mementos. It had been Cheyenne's old-fashioned, formal hand that had written the note glued to the back: *The first marker on the Rocking B. Photo probably taken by Carson*

Blackridge after Civil War and before first herd arrived in 1867.

The curved lens of Lara's magnifying glass glittered in the sunlight as she slowly moved the lens over the length of the photograph. After a moment she looked up, studying the valley below her, searching for landmarks that hadn't changed in the past century. Over the past few weeks she had learned to ignore the modern reality of fences and missing trees, the houses that had been built and the bend in the Big Green that had moved subtly south.

Shadow shifted her weight, stamped to discourage a fly and went back to her three-legged doze. The horse's motions didn't distract Lara. She had become accustomed to Shadow's habits in the four weeks that she had been living on the old homestead. A lot of Lara's time during those weeks had been spent on horseback, talking to the older hands as they rode the land and remembered other rides, other times. Between interviews she had searched for and ultimately found all but one of the Rocking B's original boundary markers.

Even Carson had been drawn into the search for the missing marker after the picnic at Long Pool. Together Lara and Carson had gone through the old deeds and surveys that he had brought out of safety-deposit boxes in town. With his help Lara had compiled a list of boundary markers and their probable locations. She had spent days tracking down the markers and photographing all of them. Except one.

The one whose daguerreotype was in her hands right now.

"Dammit," she muttered. "This has to be the ridge and the right place on that ridge. And it was about this time of year, too. The flowers in the foreground are blooming, and the snow has melted back to the higher peaks. It was about this time of day, as well. The shadows match, and the angle of the sun on the Big Green and even the wind bending the grass so that—"

Abruptly Lara straightened in the saddle. "Of course! The grass!"

She slid off Shadow and began quartering the ridgetop for several hundred feet in all directions. It was hard work. This part of the Rocking B had been withdrawn from grazing for the past three years, allowing the land and the plants to rest. As a result the grass was waist-high in places. Lara waded through it as though it were a living green river. Several times she spotted the pale gleam of stones jutting up through the grass, but each time she was disappointed. The stones were naturally scattered rather than gathered by man and piled to mark the first eastern boundary of the Rocking B.

After a few minutes sweat began to shine on Lara's cheeks. Though it was barely a week into June, the land was hot and sweet with summer's bounty. At the moment Lara wished the sun were a wee bit less generous with its presence. A cooler day would have made plowing through the grass more pleasant.

"Lose your watch?"

Lara's head snapped up at the sound of Carson's voice. She had been so intent upon her search for the markers that she hadn't even heard him ride up.

"Carson! Where did you come from?" she asked, her eyes lighting up with pleasure at seeing him so unexpectedly.

The look on her face went through Carson in a shock wave of warmth. Lara had smiled at him like that in the past, when he had appeared without warning in the café where she had worked. He hadn't seen that particular smile in years. He hadn't known just how much he had missed seeing it.

"One of the cows was down along Hat Creek," Carson said, gesturing over his shoulder with his thumb. "I saw you pacing back and forth up here and came to see what was going on."

"Looking for that darn boundary marker. How's the cow?"

"Dead," he grunted, rubbing his neck. "Third one this week. Probably just a coincidence—they were all old cows—but I called the vet, anyway." Carson sighed, and his hand dropped to the saddle horn. "So you're still looking for that pile of rocks. Why? Do you need it that bad for your paper?"

Lara paused, wondering how she could make Carson understand. It wasn't that she needed the marker for her personal history, it was just that the marker was a lost piece of the past waiting to be discovered. "I guess I just love finding missing pieces," she said.

"Never give up grubbing around in the past, do you?"

"Nope," Lara said cheerfully. "It's too much fun."

She wiped her forehead on her sleeve and pulled her hat back into place, missing the sudden tightening of Carson's face as he realized that the longer a piece of the past's puzzle eluded Lara, the harder she would look to find it.

And there was one piece of the past that simply had to be left unfound.

All Carson could do was thank God that what had to remain hidden wasn't part of the time covered by Lara's history. That part of the past would be exempt from her too-intelligent, too-careful scrutiny.

Lara looked up and saw Carson's changed expression. "I know, I know," she said, smiling uncertainly, "you'd just as soon never have to look at any part of the past. Well, I'm a historian, and I love grubbing around in the past."

After a moment Carson smiled almost unwillingly. Despite his fear he enjoyed seeing the light in Lara's eyes when she was in close pursuit of something she enjoyed.

"Hell, I don't suppose much harm could come from finding an old pile of rocks." Carson dismounted and walked over to Lara. "Let's grub together until suppertime."

"You're sure?" she asked hesitantly. "I know you're not interested in the Rocking B's history."

That was putting it tactfully. Lara knew that Carson

had a hostility toward the Rocking B's past that was both deep and, to her, inexplicable. Sometimes she wondered if the hostility might have come from the fact that he had been raised knowing that he didn't "belong" to the ranch's history. Would that be enough to make Carson hate the past?

Although Lara very much wanted an answer to that question, she knew that she wouldn't bring up the subject directly. She hated to see Carson's face tighten into harsh lines, and it always did when they talked about the recent past and the Rocking B ranch.

"I'm sure I don't mind," Carson said, rubbing his neck again. "Beats hell out of looking at dead cows."

"No argument there," Lara said, making a face.

"So how do we go about this low-budget historical survey?" Carson asked dryly, kneading his neck one more time before giving up. The headache had started the day he had held Larry Blackridge's will in his hands; there were nights when Carson wondered if the pain would ever end.

"First you hold my hand," Lara said.

"Yeah?" Carson's face softened into a smile as he peeled off his work gloves and stuffed them into his back pocket before offering his hand to her. "Holding hands, huh? Maybe I've been wrong about this history stuff all along."

Lara looked at Carson's gentle smile and tired eyes. Impulsively she took his hand between both of hers and brought it to her lips. She kissed his palm softly, brushing her lips over the sensitive skin before pressing it to her cheek. She felt his fingers tightening slightly, returning the caress. The restraint of the gesture made her want to cry. He had been so careful to keep his word, not to press her in any way. He had given her so much companionship and laughter—and she had given him nothing in return.

"You're working too hard, Carson," Lara whispered. "You look so tired. I don't want you to wear yourself out over an outdated boundary marker that means nothing to you."

Carson closed his eyes for an instant, feeling the softness of Lara's cheek pressed into his hand, savoring it with an intensity that was just short of pain. Since the picnic by Long Pool, Lara had touched him more frequently, been more at ease with him physically, but not nearly as much as he had hoped; and at no time had she suggested that the touching go beyond her hand in his as they walked out across the ranch and watched sunset transform the land into a place of fire. Yet he looked forward to those times with an intensity that made him ache.

And now she was looking at him with concern in her beautiful eyes.

"I don't mind, little fox," Carson said, his voice deep. "The best part of my day is the time I spend with you."

Lara didn't know whether she stepped into Carson's arms or he stepped into hers. She only knew that she felt as though she had truly come home.

At first they held each other tightly, as though they were afraid that something would happen to separate them. Gradually their arms loosened while Carson rocked Lara slowly against his chest, stroking her hair and back with his big hands, wordlessly telling her how much it pleased him to hold her. It was the same for Lara. Her arms were around his lean waist and her head was resting against his chest as her hands kneaded gently down the muscles of his back, trying to relax the tension that was rooted so deeply in Carson that he had forgotten a time when it hadn't been there.

When Lara finally tilted back her head to look at Carson's face, his eyes were closed and an expression of peace had replaced the lines of strain on his face. The knowledge that she could bring him such ease with something as simple as a hug made her ache with emotion. She should have done this weeks ago. She had wanted to. Every time she saw him at the end of the day, his face weary, his right hand automatically rubbing his neck, she had wanted to hold him and soothe him until he relaxed and smiled down at her as he had done years ago.

"I have a better idea than tramping around up here until it's too dark to see," Lara said softly.

Carson rumbled deep in his throat, a sound that was more a bass purr than a word. Lara smiled. Without thinking, she brushed her lips lightly over his shirt. He felt it. She could tell by the subtle tightening of his arms around her. Yet his hand never hesitated in its slow, gentle stroking of her hair.

"It's Yolanda's night off, isn't it?" continued Lara.

Carson rumbled again, somehow managing to make the sound both contented and questioning at once. She laughed softly and hugged him close for just an instant.

"Why don't I cook dinner for you at the homestead?" Then, quickly, Lara added, "Bring the ranch accounts with you, if you like. I know you're behind in them. After dinner you can work on them while I go through some of Cheyenne's mementos. Then I'll feed you dessert and give you a back rub because you hate doing the accounts so much that it always ties you in knots. How does that sound?"

Carson's smile radiated through Lara. "Like heaven. We'll do it right after you show me a little more of your hand-holding history research. I figure you should get something out of this deal, too."

"You don't have to plow through all the grass with me."

"But I want to," Carson murmured, shifting his weight, subtly easing Lara closer to his warmth. "I like holding hands with you. And I like this so much that—" A tremor went through him. "Oh, God, Lara, I love holding you."

The whispered, barely audible words sent an answering tremor through Lara. Her arms tightened, and she held Carson very hard for a few moments. Then she looked up at him. The intensity of his amber eyes made her breath shorten. She wanted him to kiss her but knew that he wouldn't, even though it was obvious he wanted to very much. He had been careful to keep the promise he had given to her a few weeks before. He had done nothing to make her afraid. Nor would he do anything now. If she wanted to be kissed, it was up to her to take the initiative.

"Can I...kiss you?" Lara asked. Her voice was hesitant, and her eyes mirrored her own inner conflict. She wanted the kiss, yet even as she leaned toward him, her memories warned her of danger.

"I'd like that," Carson said, looking at her mouth, his voice gritty.

Again Lara felt the small shiver of response take Carson's strong body. And again he did no more than tighten his hold on her for an instant. That reassured her. As much as she wanted to be in his arms, to know again the pleasure of his touch, the memory of what had happened four years before still had the power to make her want to turn and flee.

Carson could sense Lara's uncertainty. Despite the hunger that sent tiny, uncontrollable tremors through him, he didn't bend down and take the lips that trembled very slightly as Lara looked up into his eyes. She knew that he wanted her. Standing as close as they were, she could feel the proof of his desire. So he waited for her to come to him, knowing that she would feel more secure that way, knowing that she had to want him enough to overcome her fear.

Lara stood on tiptoe and kissed the corner of Carson's cleanly shaped mouth, then pressed her lips against his. She had meant to feel only briefly the firmness and warmth of his lips and then to retreat as gently as she had advanced. But the silky texture of his mustache and the smoothness of his mouth sent sweet memories rippling through her. Some small corner of her mind recognized that Carson was right; she should try to remember the good as well as the bad.

And it had been very good to open her lips beneath his, to taste and feel his mouth consuming her softly.

Hesitantly Lara's hands crept up the front of Carson's shirt. Her lips brushed over his once, twice, and then her arms came around his neck, allowing her to lean against him. Instantly his arms shifted, supporting her as he gathered her even closer to his body. She opened her mouth slightly and kissed him again, expecting him to take her mouth with a single hot stroke of his tongue.

When that didn't happen, Lara pulled back and looked up at Carson. His eyes were closed. The taut, intense look of concentration on his face left no doubt that he was enjoying the soft kisses. Reassured, Lara kissed him again, nuzzling against his firm lips, hoping that they would open in response to her caress. But they didn't.

Puzzled, frustrated, Lara wondered how to get Carson to open his mouth for her. She had had no experience in being the leader in this kind of sensual play. It had taken her a long time even to accept a date after Carson had rejected her, and the men she had dated had been more than willing to be the aggressors. In the end that was what had made Lara retreat; the men were demanding the very thing that she had once offered Carson. She simply hadn't wanted any of the men enough to take the emotional and physical risk of offering herself again. As a result she was no more experienced in lovemaking now than she had been four years ago. She wanted to increase the intimacy of the kiss she was sharing with Carson, but she didn't know quite how to go about it.

Lara kissed Carson again, pressing harder against his mouth. That was more satisfying because she could almost taste him, but it was still much less than she wanted. Again she pulled back, looking at his mouth as though it were a puzzle she was trying to solve. When she finally glanced up, he was studying her own mouth with equal intensity.

"Carson?"

A questioning kind of purr was her answer.

"Why won't you—" Abruptly Lara's courage deserted her. Putting what she wanted into words suddenly seemed more intimate than any kiss she could imagine. She was about to abandon the whole idea when she shifted her weight and felt the blunt, hard ridge of Carson's sex pressing against her torso. The certainty that he wanted her gave her the nerve to try again. After all, he had already taken the risk for her; he had made her the gift of himself two weeks ago when they had been at Long Pool. Now it was up to her to find out how to unwrap that gift. "Why won't you open your mouth for me?" she asked in a rush.

"Do you want me to?" Carson asked, smiling a slow kind of smile.

"Yes," she said huskily, "but I don't know how to make you." She heard the last words and winced. "I don't mean 'make you,' exactly," she muttered. "That sounds awful. I mean I want you to want to—"

She stopped again, realizing that she already had hard physical proof of his wanting her. "I mean, I don't know how to tell you I want you to open your mouth without just coming right out and saying it," she admitted in a rush, flushing. She buried her hot face against his shirt. "Oh, Carson, I don't know what to do," she said miserably. "All I really know about kissing is what I learned from you four years ago."

Carson's expression changed, surprise replacing passion for an instant. Somehow he had assumed that, even if Lara hadn't given herself completely to a man during the past four years, she had at least gone in for the kind of heavy petting that made the question of virginity a technicality rather than a real issue of inexperience.

The realization that he had hurt Lara so badly that he had all but crushed the expression of her sensual nature shocked him. She had meant what she said when she had cried *I love you*. He hadn't believed in love then. He still didn't—not in the same way she did. But he was learning just how deep Lara's feelings ran, and just how badly she could be wounded. It made him want to give her a pleasure as deep as her capacity to feel emotion.

Carson gathered Lara closer, kissing the top of her head. "There's nothing wrong with telling me what you want," he said, the words soft and gentle. "In fact," he murmured, moving just a little against Lara, teasing and easing his hungry body with the same motion of his hips, "it's sexy as hell to hear you say that you want my mouth. But if talking makes you feel shy, just run your tongue over my lips.'' He laughed softly, deep in his chest. ''I can guarantee that I'll get the message. I'll even make you a deal. Whatever way you touch me, that particular kind of touching will belong to both of us. But until you do it first, I won't do it at all. Okay?''

Lara looked up, saw gentle amusement, anticipation and hunger in Carson's eyes. She smiled. ''Okay.''

She went up on tiptoe again, nuzzling against his lips, enjoying the firm feel of his mouth. Slowly her lips parted and her tongue hesitantly brushed the full curve of his lower lip before circling to trace the deeply indented peaks of his upper lip. She felt the shiver of Carson's response and heard the thick, stifled sound of his groan. His mouth opened, and his tongue repeated her caress exactly, leaving an exciting trail of warmth and moisture around her lips.

Breath rushed out of Lara's mouth in a sigh that sounded like Carson's name. The tips of their tongues met, retreated and touched again. It wasn't enough. She wanted her lips to be pressed hard against his and her mouth to be fully joined with him while his tongue stroked hers. It had been that way once. She remembered it vividly. He would kiss her like that again if she could just show him what she wanted.

Lara's fingers slid up into Carson's thick hair, sending his hat tumbling to the ground not far from where hers already lay. The pressure of her fingers brought his head down to hers. She tilted her head a little, then a little more, trying to find the angle that would allow the greatest contact with his lips. Even after their mouths were fully joined, she continued moving her head slowly, rocking back and forth, remembering that he had once kissed her that way and she had felt a wave of sensation clear to the soles of her feet.

Carson made a thick, inarticulate sound of pleasure as he felt Lara's warm breath sigh into his mouth. In an agony of suspense, he waited until Lara's tongue rubbed over his, silently telling him what she wanted him to do to her. His arms flexed as he straightened, lifting her off the ground until her face was level with his. He teased her tongue slowly, luring her deeper and deeper into his mouth until the sensual trap was sprung and he could fill her mouth in return.

The shiver of Lara's response set fire to Carson. It was all he could do not to carry her down into the tall grass and join their bodies even more deeply than their mouths. He wanted it with a violence that shocked him. In that instant he learned that, although he had taken other women since he had turned away from Lara, he hadn't really wanted them. Not like this, with his blood rushing and gathering heavily between his thighs until his head spun and his knees wanted to give way, tumbling him into the soft grass with Lara still in his arms.

With an almost harsh sound Carson slowly lowered Lara until her feet were touching the ground again. He didn't know how or where he found the control not to keep on going, to pull her down with him and cover her sweet, forgiving softness with his own hungry need.

When Carson's arms loosened, Lara swayed slightly as her legs gave way. She realized that if he let go of her completely, she would slide down his body and end up in a boneless heap at his feet. The certain knowledge that she would fall unless he supported her was all that gave her the strength to pull her mouth away from his, ending the deep kiss.

"Hold me," Lara said, her voice so husky that it didn't sound like her own. "My legs—" She tried to take a breath, only to have it break into pieces with a ragged sound. She laughed helplessly. "What have you done to me, Carson? I don't have any more bones than a spoonful of honey."

"Funny you should mention that," he said, his voice deep, almost rough. "I was going to say the same thing." Automatically he bent down to capture her mouth again, then realized what he was doing, the pursuer rather than the pursued. He straightened and took a deep breath. "You go to my head worse than Willie's 180-proof white lightning."

Lara blinked and then smiled, pleased that she wasn't the only one who felt a little weak in the knees. "Do I?" Her breath caught with a husky, intriguing vibration. "I like that idea," she admitted.

Carson made a sound that was a cross between a growl and a purr. Lara felt as much as heard it. Her eyes went again to his mouth. It was reddened from the force of their kiss and from the blood beating heavily through his body. Slowly Lara went up on tiptoe, supporting herself by leaning against Carson's chest, feeling his heat and strength radiate through her blouse until her heart beat as rapidly as his. She closed her eyes and strained upward until her lips barely touched his. The tip of her tongue went out and whispered over his lips as lightly as her breath.

"Are you doing it deliberately?" he asked, his voice both sensuous and rough.

"What?"

"Torturing me."

The tip of her tongue nuzzled the corner of his smile. "Am I torturing you?"

"Yes," he said, but there was no anger in the word, simply an underlying masculine purr of pleasure and laughter and hunger.

Suddenly Lara remembered one of the ways Carson had "tortured" her years ago. She caught his lower lip between her teeth and tugged delicately, running the tip of her tongue along his resilient, captive flesh. Carson's laughter was replaced by a deep sound of desire. His tongue slid beneath her upper lip, making her gasp. As her teeth parted, he tilted his head and fitted their mouths together smoothly, hotly, no longer worried about who was pursuer and who was pursued. She was asking for his mouth, aching for it, and they both knew it.

Lara felt the kiss throughout her whole body, lighting up nerves that had slept too long. The sweet friction of his tongue on hers, the taste of him, the heat and pleasure of his mouth, every aspect of the kiss swept through her. She didn't know that she whimpered deep in her throat as her knees gave way. Nor did she know that her breasts were pressed against his chest and her mouth was straining against his every bit as fiercely as his was straining against hers, as though they both wanted a single kiss to bridge the dark chasm of misunderstanding and years that lay between them.

It cost Carson all his strength to slowly, slowly end the kiss, although even then he held Lara as though she were his last hope of peace after a lifetime of conflict. They both were breathing quickly, unsteadily, soft bursts of sound and heat. He had never wanted a woman so much, not even the night he had turned and walked out on Lara.

"I never knew how hot a kiss could be," Carson said huskily, watching Lara with eyes that were dilated by passion until there was only a narrow ring of green-flecked gold around the pupils. "You'll have to let me take time out, or I'm going to forget all my fine promises and drag you down into the grass."

The thought both intrigued and made Lara wary. Carson could sense passion in the rosy softness of her mouth and uneasiness in the sudden stiffening of her body against him. He nodded slowly.

"I know," Carson said heavily. "It's too soon for you, isn't it?"

Lara closed her eyes. "I'm sorry," she whispered.

His thumb stroked lightly over her sensitive lips, silencing her. "Hush, little fox. There's nothing to be sorry for. You gave me more with that kiss than I deserve."

"But you...that is, you're—"

Helplessly Lara's glance went down to the thrusting evidence of Carson's desire. His own eyes followed hers, and he smiled crookedly.

"Yeah, I sure am. Sorry if it bothers you, but there's not a hell of a lot I can do about it when I'm around you."

"Bothers *me*? What about you?"

Carson laughed softly as he brushed his lips over Lara's forehead. "Honey, after a kiss like that, I'd be a lot more bothered if all I had in my jeans was a pocketknife."

Biting her lip, Lara tried not to laugh as she looked up at Carson from beneath a black fringe of eyelashes. Then she gave up and let laughter bubble out.

"Just for that," Lara said finally, fighting for breath as she held out her hand to Carson, "I'm going to lead you down the primrose path of history."

"Is that where the primrose path leads?" Carson asked dubiously, lacing his fingers through hers. "I always thought it went to something more, um, exciting."

"Depends on how you define excitement."

"Guess," he said succinctly.

Lara flushed, but the color had more to do with pleasure than embarrassment. "Did you really like it?" she whispered, hardly able to believe that the kiss had been real.

"Oh, yes," Carson said, slanting her a sideways grin. "I really liked it. But I know scholars are trained to go to the original source for their information. So feel free to do some truly original research. Rummage around in my pockets and see what comes to hand."

Carson's expression was such an outrageous combination of sober encouragement and frank sensuality that Lara forgot to be embarrassed. With a small shock she realized that the thought of sliding her hands into his pockets right now made nerves quiver deep inside her body.

She was quite certain that she would find more than a pocketknife.

"I think, for now, I'll settle for researching the Rocking B's first boundary marker," Lara said, unable to meet Carson's eyes or to entirely suppress the small, very female smile that tugged at her mouth.

When Carson saw the smile, a raw stroke of desire ripped through him. His hand flexed slowly, making his palm rub over hers as hotly and completely as his tongue had. "Where do we start?"

It took a moment for Carson's question to register in Lara's mind. The sensuous promise of his skin moving over hers had scattered any thoughts of history and the Rocking B's original boundary markers. At the moment the present was far too sweet for her to care about the past.

"Where do we start to…?" she asked, her voice trailing off as she met Carson's eyes.

Lara looked at Carson. The angle of the sunlight had caught his eyes and turned them into brilliant topaz jewels. Light tangled in the thick hair she had so recently run her fingers through. The slanting radiance brought out high-lights of deep chocolate and darkest bronze. The play of colors and sliding light shifted with each of his breaths, changing before her eyes, fascinating her.

"Lara?"

She blinked, but he didn't vanish. He still stood before her, radiant with the late afternoon light, as strong and as perfect as though he had condensed from the land itself.

"Lara?" asked Carson softly, wondering why she had gone so still.

"You are so...perfect," she said helplessly.

The emotion that closed Carson's throat for a moment had nothing to do with desire. She was coming to him so trustingly, so...perfectly. And he knew that he could not match her perfection.

"Oh, God," he said raggedly, closing his eyes against the light's burning clarity. "I wish I were, Lara. For you. Just for you. But I'm not perfect. Remember that when I fail you," he whispered. "Remember, and try to forgive me."

Lara felt herself being lifted even as she reached for Carson. She held him tightly, trying not to cry, wanting desperately to ease the wild pain she had seen in his eyes before they closed.

"It's all right, Carson," she said huskily, holding him. "Whatever it is, it's all right."

He held her until he ached, knowing that it wasn't all right, knowing and praying that she would be able to forgive him when she discovered what he had done.

Chapter 8

"You're sure you'll be all right?" asked Lara anxiously.

"The doctor, he told me there was nothing wrong that a few weeks off this ankle will not cure," Yolanda said, gesturing to her left ankle, which was thoroughly swathed in elastic bandages. Sighing comfortably, she propped her foot on a hassock and settled back in the worn, overstuffed chair that dominated her cabin's small living room. "Now do not worry about me. The bunkhouse cook, he said he would bring me my meals until my sister's daughter gets here tomorrow. And the hands—they have spent more time walking through my house than watching cows."

Lara smiled, knowing that it was true. Ever since

Yolanda had sprained her ankle slipping on a throw rug, two things had happened: all throw rugs on the Rocking B had vanished or had been fixed in place, and the men had taken turns watching over Yolanda until her niece arrived from Billings.

"There is one thing you could do," Yolanda said slowly, "if you would not mind."

"I don't mind," Lara said, without waiting to hear what Yolanda needed. "What is it?"

"Carson he hates old Mose's cooking. If you could fix dinner for him, I would not feel so bad."

"Of course."

Yolanda smiled like a cat curled around a bowl of cream. "Thank you, *niña*. That is very good. You better hurry. Carson, he is a very big man, very hungry, and the hour, it is getting late."

Lara glanced at her watch. "Do I need to run to town for supplies?"

"No. Everything that a woman needs is already there." Yolanda closed her eyes and smiled to herself, nodding slowly. "*Sí*, everything."

Shutting the door softly behind her, Lara crossed the ranch road and hurried toward the big house. It was no trouble for her to cook for Carson. Lately he had eaten more meals at the homestead than he had at the ranch house. In fact, Lara hoped that this evening would provide the perfect opening to ask if she could finally see the documents, photos and other memorabilia that composed the Blackridge archives.

She had hinted around the subject several times before. Each time Carson's expression had subtly changed, telling her that he would just as soon not confront the question of the past and the Rocking B, the Blackridges and the Chandlers. Sometimes Lara thought that it was almost as though having found a way to bring her close without using the Blackridge collection as a lure, Carson regretted having promised her access to it at all.

After Lara did a quick survey of the kitchen garden and refrigerator, she decided that Yolanda had enough food to feed the Rocking B and the neighboring ranches as well. It was too late to cook a roast, but there were some thick steaks that would be more than enough for dinner. A few minutes in the garden yielded tiny new potatoes, baby carrots and baby peas. Lara remembered that Carson loved raw spinach but wouldn't touch it cooked so she gathered two handfuls of greens for a salad. Humming quietly, she carried her vegetable loot into the kitchen.

By the time Lara heard Carson walk into the laundry room just off the kitchen, the whole house was filled with the smells of dinner. She heard the water run as he sluiced off the worst of the sweat and dust, but she didn't hear him come into the kitchen behind her. As always, he had left his boots in the laundry room. He came in barefoot. There were moccasins set out for him to wear, but he ignored them unless the house was really cold.

''And here I thought all those good smells meant that I was going to have to apologize to Mose for slandering his cooking all these years,'' Carson said, coming up to stand behind Lara as she washed spinach leaves in the sink. His arms slid around her waist as he bent to nuzzle the line of her neck. "You look good enough to eat." His tongue flicked out over her warm skin. "You taste good enough, too. You're in trouble, woman. I'm a very hungry man."

A spinach leaf appeared beneath Carson's nose. Growling rather fiercely, he ate the green leaf all the way down to Lara's fingertips and then began nibbling on them, too. She laughed and turned in Carson's arms to give him a welcoming kiss. Since they had searched hand in hand for the boundary marker nearly a week before, she had become much less wary of him physically. Despite the hunger that Carson couldn't conceal, he had kept his word; he kissed Lara often, and passionately, but he didn't push for any greater intimacy than she had already offered in her previous caresses.

At the times when Lara felt herself aching for more than kisses, she knew that she would have to be the one to take the lead. Without a word being said, Carson's actions had assured her that there was no way she would ever be undressed and then rejected again; it was for her to do the undressing and, if she wanted, the rejecting. That reassured her, just as Carson's passion and restraint reassured her. He was doing everything he could to make their growing relationship risk free for her. The realization that he was perceptive as well as passionate made her feel cherished. These days when Carson touched her, she responded without fear.

Slowly Carson pulled Lara close, fitting her along

the length of his body with a sensuous precision that sent fire racing through both of them. There was no question of giving or taking, pursued or pursuer. The kiss claimed both of them equally, making a shivering heat blossom deep within Lara. She loved the feeling of being pressed along Carson's powerful body, and she trembled with pleasure to feel the hard rise of his desire and know that she was causing it.

Only after the long kiss was over and Lara looked up into Carson's face did she see the lines of fatigue and the darkness beneath his eyes.

"Carson," she whispered, kissing him very gently, "you look so tired. Aren't you sleeping well? Is something worrying you?"

His whole body tightened at the question. "I sleep," he said, nuzzling the corner of Lara's mouth.

What he didn't say was that he lay awake for a long time each night, trying to decide whether it was better to tell Lara the whole truth now and almost certainly lose everything he had ever wanted, or to wait and pray that he would never have to tell her at all. There was no guarantee that she would ever find out. And even if she did, it might be years and years in the future. By then she might understand. By then she might care enough about the life they had built together to be able to forgive him.

"Is something wrong with the ranch?" Lara asked hesitantly. "Are the inheritance taxes—"

"No," Carson interrupted, his voice almost harsh. "Larry planned for everything. Too damned well!"

Carson's arms tightened as he bent down, asking

for and taking Lara's mouth in the same motion. She wondered what Carson had meant by his comment, but as always the heat of his kiss scattered her thoughts. Even as part of her realized that this always happened when the subject of the Rocking B or Carson's father came up, the rest of Lara responded to the need that lay beneath Carson's searching kiss, a need that transcended the hard insistence of his sex pressing against her softness. She didn't know where that greater need came from; she only knew that she ached to answer it, to ease Carson's mind as well as his body.

Slowly Carson and Lara separated, sharing many tiny, swift kisses that spoke eloquently of their reluctance to be parted.

"I'll shower," Carson said, his voice husky. "I must smell like a polecat."

Lara smiled. "You smell like a man who has worked hard and ridden hard. You smell hot and—wonderful."

With a thick sound Carson stepped back quickly. "You keep that up and I'm going to find myself suggesting that you take a shower with me," he said, smiling and very serious at the same time.

Carson turned away before he could see the widening of Lara's pupils or the sudden intake of her breath as she thought of sharing a shower with him. She waited for fear to come at the thought of being naked with him. All she felt was a flash of uneasiness that was quickly overwhelmed by a rush of desire.

"How long before dinner is ready?" he asked, not looking back.

"How long do you want?"

"Give me fifteen minutes."

"Fifteen minutes," she agreed.

It seemed like a very long quarter hour to Lara before Carson returned, filling the kitchen with his male presence and deep voice.

"I'd kiss you again," he said, "but I don't trust myself to stop before dinner is as cold as well water."

Lara looked at Carson's damp, freshly combed hair, dark mustache and smiling lips and decided she didn't trust herself, either. She served the dinner with easy, efficient motions, then sat at his right hand and began to eat. Between bites she asked questions about the water and the grass, the calves and the cows, the price of beef and feed. The ebb and flow of the Rocking B's seasonal work had always fascinated Lara, for it gave her a deep sense of being involved in processes and cycles that went far back in time and would continue far into the future.

"…vet said that it was nothing but coincidence that I lost those three cows so close together," finished Carson.

Lara let out an audible breath of relief. "I was worried that the cattle you bought at the beginning of summer might have been carrying some disease."

"That thought occurred to me about once an hour after the third cow died," Carson agreed wryly. "Just old age, though. It was a hard winter, and raising a calf takes it out of old cows. They dropped strong calves, though. They're going to make it.''

"Doesn't surprise me," Lara said tartly. "They darned near pulled my arms out of the sockets tugging on the bottle.''

Carson's eyes kindled with laughter and pleasure as he remembered the picture she had made with her legs braced and a healthy bull calf nursing hard on the oversize bottle she was holding. Carson had finally moved to stand behind her, wrapped his arms around her waist and anchored her so that the calf didn't pull her right off her feet. As they struggled to keep the bottle from being yanked free by the eager calf, they had begun laughing so hard that they had ended up falling down in the hay while the calf trailed milk all over both of them.

And then they had forgotten the calf and the barn and the men working nearby in the other stalls. Carson had pulled Lara into his arms for a kiss that had left him hard, aching, shaking with hunger at the feel of her body so soft and unafraid beneath his.

"You can hand raise my babies anytime," Carson said, leaning back in his chair, his voice gritty and his eyes tawny beneath the dining room's warm lights.

Something in his clear, intent eyes made Lara breathless, as did the thought of feeding his babies— and not the four-legged variety, either. She realized then how much she would like to feel Carson's child growing inside her, forever joining their destinies beyond any human ability to sever. The thought ex-

ploded softly through her, making her melt in waves
of emotion that left her trembling.

"I'd like that," Lara whispered, her voice as soft
as the sensations shivering through her.

Carson heard her words, and he knew that Lara
wasn't talking about raising calves.

"Lara—" he began, looking at the woman sitting
next to him at the table.

Then his words stopped as he saw Lara's tongue
flick out to pick up a stray crumb from her lip. With
a throttled groan he bent and caught her mouth beneath his, turning his head until her lips opened. He
kissed her with slow, aching rhythms of his tongue.
When he finally lifted his head, he was breathing too
fast, and so was she.

"White lightning," Carson said hoarsely.

Once Lara would have blushed or felt uneasy at
seeing the raw desire on Carson's face. Now, seeing
his need simply made it more difficult for her to drag
air down into her lungs.

"You make the coffee," he said, standing abruptly.
"I'll take care of the dishes."

"I'll help."

"Honey," Carson said, his voice almost rough, "if
I brush up against you in the kitchen right now, I'll
trip you and beat you to the floor." He saw the sudden parting of Lara's love-bruised lips, heard the swift
intake of her breath and wanted nothing more than to
feel her naked and willing and hot beneath him.
"Don't look at me like that," he warned, but his
voice was caressing rather than harsh.

"Like what?"

"Like you want to eat me for dessert."

Carson's eyes narrowed into hot gold slits as he realized that Lara had never thought of touching him that way before—and thinking of it now had made the pulse in her throat beat faster. When a shiver of response coursed over her skin, it was all he could do not to grab her.

With a small sound Lara tore her eyes away from Carson's hard, hungry body. "Coffee," she said faintly.

Carson didn't trust himself to say anything at all. He grabbed two handfuls of dishes and went into the kitchen. After a few minutes he heard Lara walk into the kitchen and turn on the fire underneath the old-fashioned drip coffeepot he always used.

"Carson?" Lara's voice was hesitant, as though she were unwilling to disturb the increasingly fragile control that both of them had over their emotions.

"Hmmm?"

Carson's vague rumble of encouragement was all Lara needed. "Would it be possible for me to look at some of the Blackridge historical papers and photos tonight?" she asked in a rush, as though afraid Carson would somehow manage to change the subject in midquestion as he had so many times in the past.

It was the request that Carson had been heading off successfully since the day he had held out the family archives as a lure to draw a shy scholarly fox closer to him. He wanted to change the subject, to deflect her, to do anything but agree to let her rummage through the Blackridge papers, raking up a past that belonged to her in a way that it would never belong to him—a past whose cold shadow could extend even into the present and future, destroying the delicate growth of friendship and desire that was bringing Lara closer and closer to him with every breath.

Yet Carson knew that if he kept refusing to allow Lara into the Blackridge archives she would begin to suspect that his reluctance went much deeper than a simple dislike of the past. She would begin to ask questions. Once that happened, she wouldn't rest until she found the answers. There would be no hope of deflecting her. He had seen that already, her joy and persistence in uncovering historical facts that was as much a part of Lara as her stunning blue eyes. Once she had found out about the old boundary markers, she had pursued them like a prospector after the mother lode, even though the markers had no immediate relevance to her informal history of the Rocking B. They were simply there, a tangible part of history, and she wanted them.

It was the same for the Blackridge archives.

Although Carson had carefully removed any documents dating later than 1960 from the boxes, he still hated turning those records over to Lara. They contained too many hints of what had finally driven Larry Blackridge to draw up his morally crazy but legally unimpeachable will.

Carson didn't want Lara's curious, intelligent mind anywhere near the Rocking B's recent history. Yet he knew that he had stalled as long as he could without raising Lara's curiosity. As of tonight, giving the records to her had just become the lesser of two evils.

And Carson hated that, too—being forced by the past to choose among evils. But it was not the first time. Nor would it be the last.

"Take the coffee into the library," Carson said quietly, "but don't touch any of the stuff lying around until I get there. Bring some cognac, too. I could use it."

Surprised by Carson's tone and by the implication that she somehow wasn't to be trusted alone with whatever was in the library, Lara said nothing. She poured coffee into an insulated carafe, found two big mugs, put them on a tray and carried it over to the liquor cabinet. When she opened the polished walnut doors, she spotted an array of glasses as well as liquor. She pulled out a snifter for Carson. After a moment's hesitation she added another snifter to the tray, deciding that she wouldn't mind a taste of cognac herself. As always, the subject of Blackridge history had created tension between Carson and her. She wished that he would talk about the problem instead of ignoring it, but so far he had resisted every effort she had made to follow that particular line of conversation.

"It's the decanter to the left," Carson said without looking up from the dishes he was stacking casually in the dishwasher. "The square one."

Lara looked at the row of cut crystal decanters that had been Sharon Blackridge's pride. They were all filled with liquids of varying colors and potency. Only one of the decanters was perfectly square. It was filled with a liquor the exact shade of Carson's eyes when he stood at sunset looking over the land he loved.

The door to the library was ajar. Lara nudged it with her shoulder until she could carry the wide tray through. Cartons were stacked everywhere, floor and coffee table and couch alike, as though every closet in the ranch house had been cleaned out and the contents packed for storage elsewhere. The only place free of boxes was Carson's desk, which was covered with various papers, breeding books and ranch ledgers. Fortunately, there was enough room for the tray, as well. Lara would not have moved a single box even one inch after what Carson had said to her in the kitchen.

She set the tray down on the desk and poured coffee and cognac. Scrupulously not looking into the few cartons that were open, she eased down onto the couch in a narrow space between boxes. Cautiously, she drank her coffee and occasionally sipped the cognac, inhaling the fragrant, potent fumes. She moved as little as possible so as not to disturb the precariously balanced boxes.

From what Lara could see, nearly all the cartons were new. Each had been labeled in a general way. The words she could see—daguerreotypes, ranch accounts, personal mementos, old photographs—were all written in the same strong, blunt hand. Carson's, she assumed. From what she had heard, Larry Blackridge had been too ill before he died to do anything as strenuous as sorting through generations of accumulated family records.

Lara didn't notice Carson standing in the doorway watching her while she looked at all the cartons. He could read the intense curiosity and eagerness on her face as easily as he could read his own handwriting on the boxes. For a moment he wished futilely that Lara had been interested in knights and dragons or shoguns and warring city-states—anything except the history of ranching in general and the Rocking B in particular.

But that had always been her passion, just as becoming a "real" Blackridge had always been his.

Without a word Carson walked into the room, shifted boxes off the couch, grabbed his coffee and cognac and sat next to Lara. He sensed her watching him with a curiosity that grew greater with every second he didn't speak. From her reaction he knew that his expression must have accurately reflected how he felt inside—cold, closed, hard. Trapped. He put his foot against a box of papers and abruptly shoved it onto the floor, making room on the coffee table for something other than the dusty residue of Blackridge history.

Lara set her empty coffee mug and nearly untouched cognac beside his in the cleared space on the coffee table. Biting her lip unhappily, she turned toward Carson.

"I just realized how unfair this is to you," Lara said quietly. "There are six cartons of Cheyenne's journals and mementos back at the homestead, and I haven't had the courage to open even one of them. Even the thought of going through all the pictures and personal treasures was just too painful.'' Lara closed her eyes against the sudden sting of tears. ''So instead of coping with my feelings and reading Cheyenne's journals, I come here and ask you to rummage through your own family mementos, your own pain. I'm sorry, Carson. That was terribly selfish of me.''

Strong arms closed around Lara as Carson lifted her onto his lap. He tucked her head against his shoulder and kissed her gently, repeatedly.

''Sweet little fox,'' Carson said huskily, kissing Lara's eyelids, ''you wouldn't know how to be selfish if someone gave you step-by-step instructions.''

Lara's lips trembled as she tried to smile. ''Oh, Carson,'' she whispered suddenly, burying her face again his neck, ''sometimes I miss Cheyenne so much that—'' Her voice broke.

Carson's arms tightened around Lara as he rocked her slowly against his chest. ''Go ahead and cry,'' he murmured, stroking her gleaming black hair and kissing her forehead.

''It isn't the kind of pain that crying makes better. This makes it better, though,'' she said, closing her eyes, letting Carson's presence seep into her, filling her with warmth. ''Having you hold me is…healing.''

''Yes,'' whispered Carson. ''For me, too.''

For a long time there was no sound but that of Carson's hand gently stroking the raven silk of Lara's hair. Finally he began talking quietly, his voice so deep that she could feel the words resonating through the hard bone and muscle beneath her cheek.

"Larry was like you," Carson said, "obsessed with the Blackridge family history, the Blackridge blood-lines. He had genealogical charts drawn up that began with the Battle of Hastings and stopped with Larry Blackridge." Carson made a sound that was partly amusement, partly disgust. "I doubt if there's any truth in the damn charts beyond Great-Grandfather Blackridge—or was it great-great?" Carson shrugged, dismissing the distinction because it no longer mattered to him. "Whichever. The Blackridge who piled up those boundary stones you can't find on Windy Ridge. Beyond him, I think those fancy charts are a load of raw crap."

Carson leaned forward, holding Lara in place with one arm while he reached past her with the other and snagged a snifter of cognac between his fingers. He offered her some, watching hungrily while she took a delicate sip and licked her lips. He wanted very much to lick her lips for her, to bend his head and taste the sweet warmth of her mouth. But he knew that he had to talk first, to try to make her understand why he was so hostile to the recent past. He had to tell her enough to dull her curiosity about him per-sonally...and not so much that her curiosity found a new, much more dangerous direction.

Frowning, Carson took a sip of the brandy, sighed and wondered how to begin talking about his least favorite subject. He leaned back against the couch once more, taking Lara and the snifter with him. The subtle movements of her body as she found a new balance in his lap were an exquisite torture. He hadn't known a man could want a woman so much, in so many ways. Not for the first time he cursed his parents for the power struggle whose ramifications were still shuddering through his own life, threatening to tear it apart. He should have married Lara four years ago, when she had wanted him.

But it had been impossible then.

"For a while," Carson said almost roughly, "I was just as wild about the Blackridge family tree and history as you or Larry. I was still young then. I still believed that one day my dear adoptive 'father' would look at me and see his son instead of a changeling who had been foisted off on him."

Lara's eyes widened and darkened. She wanted to ask what Carson meant. Hadn't Larry wanted to adopt a child? And if he hadn't, why had he gone through with it? But the sight of old pain and anger drawing Carson's face into dark, tight lines made Lara ache. She didn't want to hurt him by asking unnecessary questions, questions he might answer if she were just patient and listened quietly.

Carson swirled the rich amber cognac around and around in the crystal glass for the space of several breaths before speaking again.

"But no matter how much I tried, how hard I worked, how much I wanted it, Larry never looked at me as his son," Carson said finally. "It never seemed to occur to him that a baby might grow up feeling that the man and woman who raised him were

actually his parents in the only sense of the word that
mattered, and that the child might want to love and
be loved by those parents.''

Carson shrugged impatiently, as though throwing
off the grasp of the unhappy past. ''The only part of
being a parent that mattered to Larry had to do with
extending his bloodline. The rest was sentiment, and
God knows Larry never had much use for that.''
Carson swirled the liquid again and added softly,
''Except with your mother. I have a feeling that was
as close as Larry ever came to loving. And you, probably. For your blood. His blood.''

*And may he spend eternity regretting his obsession
with blood*, Carson added silently, bitterly. *He sure
as hell made everyone else regret it while he was
alive.*

Lara's fingers moved to cover the strong hand that
had tightened on her hip. She didn't know what to
say. She did know that Carson's thoughts must have
been even more painful than his words.

''None of it is your fault,'' she whispered, lifting
Carson's hand and rubbing her cheek slowly over it.
''You were everything a reasonable man could want
in a son.''

Carson's curt laugh made Lara wince. ''Too bad
Larry wasn't a reasonable man,'' Carson said savagely. ''But it's over now, over and done and buried
with him. He fouled up enough lives in the past. I'll
be damned if I'll let him foul up any more in the
future.''

As Carson's words echoed in the silent room he

knew that he had the answer to the question that had been keeping him awake nights: No. He would tell Lara nothing. The bitter result of the power struggle between Sharon and Larry Blackridge would be buried with them, never to see the light of day again.

"To the future," Carson said, lifting the brandy snifter, "and to hell with the past."

He drank swiftly, draining the potent liquid. He leaned forward, traded the empty glass for the other one and settled back again without loosening his hold on Lara.

"Where were we?" he asked. "Oh, yes. The precious Blackridge family archives."

Lara winced again and said nothing. She had a better understanding of Carson's bitterness now. Everything in the room was a reminder of a family that he had tried desperately to belong to. In the end Larry Blackridge had never allowed Carson to be more than a stranger who happened to share the same living quarters.

The thought of growing up like that made Lara ache in silent sympathy. Being a bastard had been difficult for her at times, but she had always known that she was loved. She hoped that Sharon Blackridge had somehow made up for Larry's inability to love his adopted son. Yet even as the thought came, Lara doubted that it had worked out that way. Sharon Blackridge had been a proud woman rather than a loving one.

"There they are," Carson continued, waving the snifter of brandy in a wide arc that included the chaos of cartons and boxes. "At one time I spent a lot of time pouring over this junk, looking for the key to Larry's respect. I guess I figured that if I knew as much as he did about the Blackridges, I'd somehow magically become one."

Carson's laugh was harsh, but the arm holding Lara was not. With a sigh he bent and brushed his lips over her silky black hair.

"I spent damn near as much time learning the family history as I spent on getting a bachelor's degree," he said. "It didn't make me a Blackridge, though. Nothing did. Nothing would. Larry told me that so often that I finally believed him. I'm not a Blackridge and I never will be. So after he died, I was tempted to burn all this junk to ash and throw it to the wind."

Lara's breath came in with an audible rush at the idea of so much history being destroyed. Eyes wide and dark, she studied Carson's face. Once she would have thought that the smile curling the corner of his mouth was cold, unfeeling, almost cruel. She knew better now. She could see the hurt beneath the hard exterior, the lingering remnants of the child who had never belonged, no matter how hard he had tried.

Sadly she realized that in some ways it must have been a relief for Carson when Larry died. The Rocking B was Carson's home now. He finally had a place where he belonged, a place where he would no longer have to feel like a stranger every time the man who refused to be his father looked at the son he had adopted but never accepted into his heart.

Very gently Lara brushed her lips against the warm,

slightly rough skin along Carson's clenched jaw. He turned to look at her, and for an instant his eyes burned into hers like those of a cougar brought to bay. Then he bent and gave her a kiss that tasted like cognac and fire. When the kiss ended, he looked at her again, his tawny cat eyes clear and hot.

"Then I decided that what the hell, maybe some good could come of all this Blackridge stuff in the right hands. So it's all yours, Lara. May you get more joy out of it than we did."

Chapter 9

Carson watched Lara's dark head as she bent over the coffee table, sorting through yet another box. The floor was checkered with documents, photos and mementos divided into decades. When the pile of material Lara was building threatened to slither off onto the floor, Carson gathered everything up in his big hands.

"Are these for the 1910 pile?" he asked, stifling a yawn.

Lara made a noise that he thought sounded positive, but he wasn't sure.

"Lara?"

She looked up from the photograph in her hand. Tears magnified the blue depths of her eyes. Carson's hands opened. A cascade of photos and papers poured unnoticed to the floor.

"What is it, honey?" he asked, reaching out to her.

Wordlessly Lara held out a handful of faded color snapshots. "These were buried in with all the early 1900s photos. I don't know why."

Carson looked at the picture on top. He recognized Long Pool, the water-smoothed granite ledge and the swirling, tumbling wealth of the Big Green. There was a young woman stretched out on the pale granite, sunning herself as unself-consciously as a butterfly. She was slender, elegantly shaped, and her hair was the color of the sun. Although her face was turned away from the camera, Carson had a visceral certainty that the woman's eyes were the brilliant blue of a high-country lake.

"Your mother," he said, no question in his tone.

Lara nodded.

For a moment Carson's hand tightened on the snapshots as though he would fling them across the room. He stared down without seeing anything, wishing that he had looked for more than incriminating documents when he had gone through the archives. He could have spared Lara the pain of meeting her mother's ghost so unexpectedly. Slowly, almost against his will, he slipped the first photo from the group and put it underneath the others.

The sound of the camera must have alerted Becky. She had propped herself up on her elbows, turned and smiled. Carson's breath hissed out of him as though he had taken a blow. He had seen that smile before, when he came upon Lara unexpectedly and she turned toward him, her face glowing with pleasure. If he had

had any doubt about who was taking the pictures, he no longer did. Only one man would have been able to light up Becky Chandler like that, the man whose mistress she had been for thirteen years, the man whose bastard child she had given birth to.

The next snapshot was a stunning close-up of Becky looking into the camera, approving of the man she saw. The angle of the light told Carson that this picture had been taken later in the day. Becky's lips were slightly swollen, her cheeks were flushed and her hair was a wild radiance around her face. She had the languid, sensual look of a woman who had been loved recently and well.

Carson's body tightened as he wondered if Lara would look at him half so approvingly after they finally made love.

The last snapshot made Carson go as still as Lara had. It was a close-up of Larry Blackridge, but it was a Larry whom Carson had never before seen. His father was smiling with affectionate indulgence while Becky took his picture. Despite the gentle curve of Larry's lips, his pale blue eyes blazed with emotion as he looked at the woman who held the camera.

And there was no doubt that it was Becky Chandler who had taken that picture. Larry had never smiled gently at anyone else. In fact if it weren't for the picture in Carson's hand, he would have sworn that Larry had been incapable of that much tenderness, that much intensity, that much passion.

Or was it love that Larry had felt, as well as passion? Had he loved Becky, but not enough? Had he loved the Rocking B more, and chosen it over Becky?

Because Larry couldn't have had both of them legally, the woman and the land. He had had to choose. Sharon had seen to that. Then Larry had tried to have the last word in the long, bitter struggle over love and the land; in doing so, he had inadvertently ensured that Carson would have neither love nor land if Lara found out what Larry had done.

"I—I didn't realize mother was so beautiful," Lara said, her voice aching. "The photos I have of her are either as a child or after I was born."

Carson looked down at the haunting, bittersweet pieces of the past held in his hand. He had hated Larry because he was cold, stubborn and occasionally cruel in his determination to have his way. Yet Larry had also been a man caught between two overwhelming loves. He had kept both the land and the woman, for a time. When a storm had taken the woman and left him with only the land, Larry's cruelty had become more than occasional.

Carson hadn't thought about any of that, even though he had been old enough to see Larry as more than the man who refused to be a father. Carson had been twenty-one when Becky Chandler died, yet he had not seen his father's grief. Carson had seen only his mother's hurt and humiliation, and his own. He had not asked if Larry might have found something in his mistress that his wife could not provide, or if a cruel necessity had doomed him to marry the wrong woman. Carson had simply hated Larry without trying to understand him at all.

And then Carson had gone out and poured that hatred like acid over a girl whose only crime had been to laugh with him, to ease his fatigue at the end of a long day, to bring him passion, to trust him and to make him feel alive in a way that he had been trying to recapture for the past four years.

"I've heard that women in the first flush of love often are beautiful," Carson said quietly, looking up at Lara. "I know that I've never seen a woman half so perfect as you were the night we ate a picnic in your apartment."

Carson saw memories darken Lara's clear eyes and draw her face into lines of pain. His mouth turned down in a bitter curve.

"That's all you remember of that night," he said. "Pain. Humiliation. I gave you no pleasure at all, nothing to repay your warmth, your trust, your— love." His fingers opened and the colored fragments of the past fluttered down like autumn leaves. "Oh, God, little fox," he whispered, his voice shaking. "There are times when I wish I could crawl out of my skin and die."

Carson came to his feet in a wild surge, but before he could turn away, Lara had thrown her arms tightly around his hips, holding him close.

"It wasn't like that!" Lara said fiercely, scratching her temple against his silver belt buckle and not even noticing. "You made me feel like the most beautiful woman ever born. And when you kissed me, touched me—'' Her voice broke. She moved her cheek caressingly against Carson, feeling the hard warmth of his body beneath the faded jeans. ''You turned me into fire and I—I burned. For you. With you. Nothing was ever that beautiful for me. Nothing. That's why it hurt so much when you—when you—''

Carson's fingers tangled in Lara's thick, silky hair as he held her tightly. ''I'm sorry,'' he said hoarsely. ''If I had known I was going to hurt you so much, I never would have walked into that café.''

He felt the shudder that went through Lara as though it were his own.

''Then I'm glad you hurt me,'' she said, her breath ragged. ''If that was the only way we could be here, now, together, then I wouldn't take back a second of the past. Do you hear me?'' she asked urgently, tilting her head back from his waist and looking up at him. ''Not one second. It was worth it, all of it, for this.''

Carson looked at the deep, brilliant clarity of Lara's eyes and felt his throat close around emotions he had never felt before. ''You are so beautiful to me,'' he whispered hoarsely, stroking her cheek with fingers that trembled. ''I'd give everything I have to take back what I did to you.''

''You can't take back the past,'' Lara said, turning to kiss the hand that was touching her cheek. ''You can only understand it, forgive it and go on to build a different future.'' Her head pressed tightly against Carson as her arms held his hips in a hard hug. ''But until you understand and forgive,'' she said, caressing his body with her cheek, her hands, her mouth, as though touches could make him understand what words could not, "until then you're like a fly in amber, imprisoned forever in the past. Don't do that to yourself, Carson. Please."

After a few moments he let out a long, ragged breath. He eased his fingers back into the silky warmth of Lara's unbound hair and rocked her head slowly, gently, against his body.

"How did you get to be so wise in so few years?" he asked softly.

"I learned from you."

Carson laughed sadly. "Pain, yes," he said. "But not understanding or forgiveness."

Silently Lara shook her head, disagreeing. "I didn't understand what happened four years ago. It…froze me. Now I understand. I can grow again."

And forgive?

Carson thought the question had existed only in his mind. He didn't know that he had whispered the words aloud until Lara answered him.

"Yes," she said, her arms tightening around his hips. "Oh, yes."

"No," Carson said quickly, hating himself because he could not tell her about the rest of the past, the part of it that could be understood but not forgiven and overcome. "I have no right to ask you for anything, least of all forgiveness."

"And I have no choice but to forgive," Lara said, turning her face into Carson's warm body, kissing nim blindly. "I love you." As she felt his hands clench almost painfully in her hair, she smiled sadly against the worn fabric of his jeans. "It's all right, Carson," she said softly. "I'm not asking you to love me in return. I know you don't believe in love. But I do, and I love you."

Carson was still for so long that Lara finally loosened her arms enough to look up at him. His eyes were tightly closed, his expression almost agonized. A tear glittered against the thick darkness of his lashes.

"Carson?" she said, her voice breaking.

He opened his eyes and looked down at her. "You're right. I don't believe in love. Not the way you do. And I don't deserve your love," he said hoarsely, "because I can't return it. But I want it. Oh, God, how I want it!"

"It's yours," she said simply. "It always has been."

Carson pulled Lara to her feet and into his arms, kissing her eyes and her cheeks and the cool smoothness of her hair. His caresses were like warm rain falling over her, bathing away the bitter residue of the past. She gave back the kisses as tenderly as she had received them, holding his face between her hands, trembling as she tasted the single tear that had escaped his control.

The world shifted around Lara as Carson sank back down onto the couch and lifted her into his lap, holding her in his arms as he whispered her name over and over again. She closed her eyes and held him in return, drinking the soft sounds of her name repeated by the man she loved. Gradually she became aware of the hard warmth of Carson's body, the power of his arms and the trembling sweetness of his lips brushing over her hair, her eyelashes, her mouth. She shivered and knew that she wanted more than those tender, fleeting caresses. But did he?

Lara turned her head and caught Carson's mouth with a sensual skill that he had taught her. When her tongue touched the corner of his lips, she felt the instant shudder of his response. He opened his lips and waited for her to accept the invitation. Though he ached to, he was afraid to take control of the kiss. He needed her too much. If he slipped the leash on his control just one fraction, he didn't trust himself to stop until he was finally sheathed inside her softness, drinking her passionate cries while he poured himself into her as he should have done long ago.

When Lara's tongue teased his, Carson groaned and returned the caress with slow, deep, primitive rhythms of his tongue that were unlike any kiss he had ever allowed himself with her before. As she trembled, he realized what he was doing, seducing Lara rather than following her lead, breaking the spirit if not the letter of his promise to her. With an effort he forced himself to stop pleading for her body with every movement of his tongue.

"Again, please," whispered Lara, pressing against Carson as she slid her hands deeply into his hair. "Oh, yes, again. I like that kind of kiss."

"Do you?" he asked, opening his eyes, looking at the velvet warmth of Lara's mouth, wanting it.

"I felt it all the way down inside me," Lara whispered.

"Oh, God," groaned Carson, consumed by a wild lightning stroke of desire that was like nothing he had ever felt before. His fingers speared into Lara's rich, thick hair, holding her still for the claiming of his mouth. "I know where you felt it," he said huskily as he slowly lowered his lips to hers. "In a place that's soft and hot and made for me. Someday you'll let me touch you there, taste you, be part of you. But until then kiss me the way I just kissed you, kiss me and imagine what it would be like if our bodies were as deeply joined as our mouths."

The words sank into Lara and exploded softly, sending heat coursing through her, heat and a heavy sweetness that made her breath wedge in her throat. Carson's mouth fitted hers with hot perfection, and his tongue thrust slowly, completely, into her. As he resumed the primal mating rhythm of tongue against tongue, Lara made a sound deep in her throat and clung to him, giving her mouth wholly to him, imagining....

When the kiss finally ended, they were both trembling and breathing too fast, too hard. Lara's hand moved restlessly from Carson's hair to his shoulders and then to his neck. She loved feeling the masculine textures of his skin and touching the dark hair that curled up in the opening of his shirt. She dipped her fingers beneath his collar, seeking more of his heat, more of his textures. The feel of his skin against the palm of her hand made air hiss sharply into her lungs.

She leaned forward, wanting to kiss him, to taste him, to rub her cheek against the thick, springy hair that lay like a shadow beneath his shirt; but everywhere she turned, every way she touched, cloth was between her and her desire.

"Carson, could I—"

"Yes," he said instantly, interrupting her.

Lara smiled and traced his lips with her fingertip. "You don't even know what I was going to ask."

"I don't care," Carson said simply, looking at Lara with eyes that were molten gold. "There's nothing you could ask me that I would refuse."

Lara looked at Carson's lips and felt weakness course through her. She wanted his mouth but not merely for another kiss. She wanted to feel his mustache brushing against her naked breast, his tongue stroking her nipple, the moist heat of his mouth caressing her. That was how it had been years ago. Surely it could be that way again. She wanted it until she ached, but she was too shy to put her need into words.

"Can I have the shirt off your back?" she asked wistfully.

Humor and passion flared in Carson's eyes, making the centers widen and darken even more. "Yes."

She waited expectantly, but he made no move to undress himself. "Carson?"

"It's yours, little fox," he said, smiling slowly. "All you have to do is take it."

Hesitantly Lara lifted her hand. Carson's shirt had snaps rather than buttons, and the snaps were stubborn. Sitting as she was with one of her arms around him, her body half leaning against his chest and wrapped in his arms, she could use only one hand to open his shirt. She tugged again at the first snap. The cloth pulled toward her, and the snap stayed shut.

Smiling despite the sensual anticipation that had made his whole body tighten until he ached, Carson lifted Lara, shifting her position until she was sitting astride his lap. The thought of sitting the same way without having clothes between them made him shudder. The hard length of his sex ached in response to the blood pouring through his body and pooling hotly between his legs. He pulled Lara's head down, drank deeply from her mouth and slowly released her.

"Now," Carson said huskily, "try again."

Lara's hands were trembling. She pulled on the snap and heard it give way, revealing the darkly sensuous gleam of his hair. She stroked him lightly, then more firmly until her fingertips were combing through the warm, springy hair. The second snap gave way more easily than the first, and the third more easily still. Her hands slid inside the shirt and then slowly pushed it open until she could rub her face across Carson's chest, turning from side to side, stroking him with her cheek as well as her hands.

Lara's curious, exploring fingertips brushed over and then returned to the small, erect nub at the center of Carson's nipple. She rubbed gently, savoring the unexpected, different texture. His groan caught her by surprise. She glanced up, startled.

"Shouldn't I—" she began.

"God, yes," Carson gritted, cutting across her hesitation. "Touch me any way you want, every way you can think of, whatever you dreamed. Do it all, honey, every bit of it." He stretched his arms out along the back of the couch. "I won't give you back the pleasure. Not yet. Not until I know without a doubt that you want me." He smiled with sensual promise. "Go ahead, my shy, curious little fox. No matter how you touch me, you won't shock me. I promise you."

Hesitantly, then with growing confidence, Lara found and caressed the tiny, erect points of his nipples, watching Carson as she did. She saw his eyes become heavy lidded and his mouth become frankly sensual. Seeing his pleasure so clearly was like being licked by a loving fire. She leaned forward until her hips were just brushing his, and then she stroked him with her tongue in the same rhythm as her fingers teasing his nipples. She felt him strain toward her, pulling against the boundaries of his self-imposed limits.

Knowing that Carson would keep his word was as exciting for Lara as the feel of his warm, naked skin. Slowly her mouth quit teasing his lips. She kissed his cheek, the line of his jaw, his neck, and then sighed as her tongue probed a darkly curling thatch of hair on his chest until she found the erect, eager nipple beneath. The thready groan that answered her caress made her shiver as though she were the one being touched. She had never guessed how exciting it would be to arouse Carson. She bent down and caressed him as she ached to be caressed, with teeth and tongue and mouth. His breath went in raggedly even as she felt his thighs tighten between her knees. That, too, was exciting.

Lara turned to find and tease Carson's other nipple, only to discover that his shirt kept on getting in the way of her exploring hands and mouth. With an exasperated sound she tried to open the rest of the snaps, only to be defeated because the shirt was tucked in at Carson's lean waist. This time she didn't wait to ask for permission. He had already told her she could do anything she wanted, and she was impatient to take him at his word.

Smiling, Carson watched as Lara tugged out the long shirttails. He leaned forward obligingly, making it easier for her to slide the shirt off his shoulders. When she got sidetracked tracing the lines of muscle on his left arm with her tongue and then her teeth, Carson moved slowly with each caress, increasing the pressure, silently telling her that he approved of her sensual exploration.

Lara straightened to look at the powerful shoulders she had just revealed beneath the dark cloth of his shirt. Carson was even more magnificent than she had remembered. She breathed his name and returned for another taste of his hot skin, hungry for him in a way that she could neither name nor satisfy.

"If I'm going to get this shirt off you, you'll have to take your arms off the back of the couch," Lara pointed out.

The husky sound of Lara's voice made desire twist through Carson. The low, intimate timbre told him that she was enjoying the sensual play every bit as much as he was. Slowly he lowered his arms. Rising slightly up on her knees, she pushed the dark fabric down his back. She had peeled the shirt all the way down to his wrists when she realized that the cuffs were still fastened. Not only that, but the shirt was now so tangled that she couldn't even find the snaps.

Suddenly Lara felt foolish. She had no practice at seducing a man, and everything she did proved it. Yet when she looked up into Carson's face, all she saw was approval and desire.

"You're very patient," Lara said quietly as she went back to work on Carson's cuffs. "I'm no good at this."

"You're sexy as hell," Carson said deeply, watching the fine trembling of Lara's fingers. "Knowing that you've never undressed another man, watching your face as you discover just a few of the things you can do to me, seeing you shiver every time your tongue touches my nipple—God, little fox, it's so sweet and hot it's a miracle I haven't lost control." Carson saw her startled look and smiled. "No, I didn't mean lose control as in pouncing on you. I meant lose control as in coming right here. Does that shock you?"

Lara started to say yes, then realized that it wasn't quite the truth. Surprise her—yes. He was so open with her, as though he wanted her to know at all times that he was vulnerable to her. And then she realized that that was exactly what Carson was saying. He had given himself to her. That meant being naked in more ways than simply not wearing clothes.

"No," Lara said softly, smiling as she bent over his cuff once more, "I'm not shocked. I'm…pleased."

Her smile almost undid every one of Carson's good intentions, as did the innocent pressure of her thighs on either side of his. So close, so very close, and so very far away from the blazing act of intimacy he wanted.

The last snaps gave way. Lara pulled off one sleeve and then the other, dragging the shirt across Carson's lap in her eagerness to get rid of it. She felt his hips jerk softly when her hand brushed across his jeans. As she looked down, she saw that he was fully aroused and that she had inadvertently touched him.

"I'm sorry," she said quickly. "I didn't mean—"

"Oh, God, little fox," he interrupted raggedly. "Just do it again and I'll forgive you."

Lara looked at Carson's face, wondering if he was joking. He stretched his arms across the back of the couch again, underlining his vulnerability.

"Whatever you want," he said, his voice a gentle rasp.

Lara stared into Carson's amber eyes for a long moment. The only sound in the room was his quickened breathing as he watched her in return. Almost imperceptibly her hand moved forward, hovering above his jeans. He held her eyes and smiled a slow, inviting smile that made her heart turn over. She let her hand settle over him. She felt the barely controlled surge of his hips, heard the sudden, fierce hiss of his breath and almost lost her courage. Then the heavy-lidded pleasure revealed by his golden eyes made heat and weakness shiver through her. Gently she increased the pressure of her hand on his hot, hard flesh.

"I can feel your heartbeat," Lara said, her eyes wide, her tone husky with surprise.

Carson felt an odd combination of tenderness and violent desire. Tenderness won. He let out a long breath and forced himself to relax against the couch, opening himself to whatever caress she might want to give him. As softly as a breath her fingertips traced his length. Against the sun-faded roughness of his jeans, her hand was slender, graceful and so utterly feminine that he had to look away or risk losing control.

"What should I do?" she asked softly.

"Pet me, honey."

His voice was too gritty, too thick, but he couldn't control that any more than he could prevent the blood from beating heavily in the erect flesh beneath Lara's caressing fingers.

"Oh, God," he said, moving subtly against her hand. "I wish I could make you feel as good as you're making me feel. I wish—"

The word ended in a hiss as Carson thrust almost helplessly against Lara's hand, increasing the pressure of her palm against his hungry body. Suddenly she wanted to be able to hold him, to run her hands over him without the barrier of clothes, to know him with an intimacy that she had never shared with any man. She wanted it so badly that her hands were shaking.

"Carson?" asked Lara raggedly.

The sound of his name was another caress, almost as hot and every bit as sweet as her hand stroking him, and her eyes watching him were like blue fire. Without a word Carson shifted his hands from the back of the couch to the waistband of his jeans. The steel buttons gave way in a fast, soft ripple of sound. Wordlessly Lara moved aside. He peeled off his clothes and kicked them under the coffee table. Watching her, he leaned against the cushions and forced himself to put his arms along the back of the couch again, leaving himself utterly open to her eyes and her touch.

It was the hardest thing Carson had ever done, to be naked when Lara was clothed, vulnerable when she was not, aching for her until he thought it would be easier to die than to go on without having her; and suddenly he wondered what it would be like if she told him that he didn't measure up and then walked out without a backward look. The realization of what it must have been like for her made ice twist through his guts.

"Lara—" he said hoarsely.

But Carson could say no more for Lara's hands were smoothing over his chest, his waist, the long, taut muscles of his abdomen and the rigid muscles of his thighs. She traced the shadow of dark, curling hair as it tapered to his navel and then flared out again into a thick thatch. There her hands hesitated until

Carson felt as though he were being stretched on a rack.

"I can see your heartbeat now," Lara whispered. "It's so fast, so hard. Oh, Carson, do you really want me so much?"

Before Carson could answer, Lara cradled him between her palms. To feel her warm hands holding him was like being connected to a soft current of electricity. To see her delicate fingers caressing him was like sliding into fire. Carson felt control slipping away beneath the sweet, wild friction of her skin over his naked desire.

"Oh, baby, stop," Carson groaned.

Stricken, Lara looked up into his eyes. "Am I hurting you?" she asked. Her voice, like her hands, trembled.

Carson's answer was a thick sound that could have been a laugh. Deliberately he moved his hips, sending his hot flesh sliding between her hands again and again, slowly, deeply.

"Harder," he rasped and then shuddered uncontrollably when she responded by giving him what he had asked for and more, her hair tumbling freely down his naked torso and her mouth learning the hot, changing textures of hair and skin. "No, that doesn't hurt," he said, groaning again. "It just feels too damn good to bear. A little more and I'm going to shock you."

"You won't shock me," Lara said. The words were as soft and hot as her breath trembling against his aroused skin.

Carson laughed roughly. "The hell I won't. I've wanted you for years, dreamed of you until I woke up sweating and tied in knots. But I never dreamed anything this hot, this wild. God, you're killing me so sweetly that I—" He groaned and moved even as Lara's hands did. "No more," he said, wrapping his fingers over her wrists, forcing her to be still.

"But I want to know," she whispered, smoothing her cheek and her hair over the hard muscles of his abdomen. "I want to know how it is for you when I please you."

The thought that Lara wanted to know his body that intimately almost cost Carson what control he had left. With a thick sound he covered her hands with his own. He moved once, very slowly, and then forced himself to stop.

Lara looked at Carson completely, from the thickly curling hair of his head to the powerful lines of his torso and down to the different, ultimately masculine flesh that responded so hotly to her touch.

"Oh, Carson, don't you know how perfect you are?" she whispered, caressing him with her hands, her cheek, her lips. "Nothing you do could shock me."

Lara felt the current of response going through him, felt the instant when his whole body tightened, felt the pulsing groan that came all the way from his soul, felt the sweet heat of him filling her hands to overflowing. Watching him with her eyes half closed, smiling, she pleasured him slowly, loving him.

"Come here," Carson whispered finally, pulling

Lara up his body with hands that shook. "I have to kiss you, feel you against me, all of you, or I'll go crazy. I want to touch you the way you touched me, tease you until you shiver and cry and melt all over me like honey. Then you'll know what you've done to me. You'll know how it feels to want it until you could scream and then to have it, all of it, given to you with a loving smile. You'll know—"

The words ended in a husky sound as Carson's mouth fitted over Lara's and his tongue seduced her in the primal rhythms she had just learned. His big hands smoothed over her, shifting her until she fitted against him in a long caress. She felt him move beneath her, stroking her with his body and his hands as his tongue thrust into her soft, hungry mouth. By the time the kiss ended, she was twisting slowly against him, trying to ease the tension that had tightened her body until she shuddered repeatedly. She wanted his hands to soothe her and to set her on fire, she needed his touch, yet no matter how she twisted, his hands slid away from intimacy.

"Please," Lara whispered.

"Anything," Carson said, clenching his hands into fists to avoid breaking his word, taking her before she asked for him. "Just tell me."

"I want—" Her voice broke as she looked into the hot gold of his eyes. "Everything. I want things I don't know how to ask for. Undress me," she whispered, trembling. "Touch me. Help me, Carson. I— hurt."

His hands swept up her body until her breasts were

cupped in his palms. The sweet pressure felt so good that Lara couldn't control a whimper. When he brushed her nipples with his thumbs, she had to bite her lip against a wild cry of pleasure. He teased her gently, hotly, tugging at her breasts until her nipples were hard and radiating bursts of fire that consumed her. When his hands moved away, she twisted helplessly, seeking his touch again, needing it with an intensity that made her groan.

"Easy, love, easy," Carson said thickly, gently laying Lara on the couch as he slid off and knelt beside her. "Let me undress you. It will feel even better without any clothes."

He wanted to unbutton her blouse slowly, kissing each new bit of skin until he found the dark pink buds that were hidden beneath cloth and lace. But her wild little whimpers and the thought of all her hot, sweet secrets waiting for him made it impossible to draw out the moment.

"Next time," Carson promised Lara hoarsely as he stripped away her clothes, tossing them onto the coffee table heaped with photos, scattering bits of the past on the floor. "Next time I'll go so slow you'll think you're dying, but now—ah, God, you're beautiful!" he groaned as the last bit of cloth fell away, revealing all of her.

Lara felt a flash of unease when the room's cool air touched her and she realized she was naked. Then she saw Carson's approval in the blazing gold of his eyes, heard it in his deep voice, felt it in the big hands smoothing reverently down her body. When his tongue touched the tight peak of her breast, she arched in helpless reflex, thrusting her aching nipple more deeply into his mouth. Carson's long fingers spread beneath her back, pulling her even closer, holding her for the loving, tugging pressure of his mouth.

Pleasure shimmered through Lara's body. She cried out, and her hips moved in languid, sinuous rhythms. Carson's teeth raked tenderly, and she cried out again. This time when she moved her hips, there was an answering warmth and pressure as his hand eased between her thighs, tenderly cupping her softness. Unerringly his thumb found the tiny bud that ached to be caressed. He stroked her slowly, gently, drinking in her small cries, and she opened to his touch, withholding none of herself. His deep voice told her of her beauty and of the pleasure she brought to him when she gave herself so sweetly to his caresses. He cherished the soft, feminine secrets that she had given to him, stroking her with his fingertips and tasting her between each husky, loving word.

Inside Lara an expanding wave of pleasure burst, showering her with tingling warmth. She felt another wave gathering and then another and another, each one more intense, each one both releasing and paradoxically increasing the tension that grew deep within her. She trembled suddenly, almost frightened by the unfamiliar sensations claiming her.

Her eyes opened and she saw Carson watching her as he loved her with his hands and his words. She felt the velvet brush of his tongue in her navel and then the unexpected, exciting touch of his teeth on her soft inner thigh. As she saw the vivid darkness of his hair against her pale skin, she knew that she should feel shy or fearful, but the passion that had flushed her body had burned away everything except her need for the hot, intimate caresses he was giving her.

When his hand moved between her legs again, testing her softness, the tension that had been gathering in her tightened with sudden violence. She moaned brokenly, balanced on the brink of a pleasure so great it was nearly pain.

''Carson!''

''Let it happen,'' he said huskily. ''Give yourself to it, to me. It's all right. I'll keep you safe.''

Carson's head bent down and he caressed Lara so tenderly, so intimately, that her fear splintered and fell away, leaving nothing to inhibit her pleasure. She abandoned herself to him as wave after wave of sensation swept through her, shaking her, melting her, setting her afire. Sensual triumph glittered darkly in Carson's voice as he encouraged her, in his eyes as he watched her and in the hot, knowing movements of his hands and his mouth over her softness. He felt the wildness gathering deep inside her, a wildness that he had called from her innocence, a wildness that he had focused within her and would finally release.

With a smooth, powerful movement Carson settled between Lara's legs, teasing her with his own violently aroused body. Her eyes opened, heavy lidded and black with desire.

"Carson?" Like her eyes, Lara's voice was dark, heavy.

"Yes, little fox," he said deeply. "You're finally going to be mine. Is that what you want?"

Lara's answer was a broken sound of pleasure coupled with a motion of her hips that brought Carson closer. She felt him gently pushing against her, easing into her, becoming a part of her. She had expected pain or discomfort or shyness, anything but the exquisite pleasure that radiated through her with each slow, rocking motion of his hips. Her skin was hot, slick with passion, and so was his, making every movement of his body over hers a shivering, sliding caress.

"Does it hurt?" Carson asked, the words rough with the effort of controlling himself.

Lara tried to answer, but the sight of him rising over her, shaking with passion and restraint, swept away her ability to speak. She breathed in suddenly—and that simple movement tightened her around him, sending the first currents of ecstasy racing through her. Her back arched, and she drew up her legs in an instinctive effort to hold him more deeply, to make the ecstatic instant last and last.

If there was any pain when Carson took Lara completely, it was lost in the pleasure bursting within her, melting her around him. When he felt her hot and sweet, tightly sheathing him, he pressed even deeper, rocking slowly against the bud hidden within her softness. He heard his name become a broken cry on her lips as she abandoned herself utterly to him, moving with him until they both were overtaken by the unleashed ecstasy they had called from one another.

And then they clung to each other, shaking with the wild pleasure that was sleeting through them, so deeply joined that neither knew whose skin was caressed, whose name was called, whose body had shattered and been reborn in the endless moment when they had been not two but one.

Chapter 10

The first lambent radiance of dawn slid silently from windowsill to floor, then crept softly across the pillows, waking Carson. Slowly he eased from the warm, scented tangle of limbs and sheets, kissing Lara gently again and again. Then he stretched fully, smiling to himself. He could barely believe the changes that the past six weeks had brought. Before it had been as though he was stranded in the past, caught as Lara had been caught, an insect paralyzed within the unforgiving amber of time, helpless to go either forward or back. Then Lara had allowed him to make love to her, healing both of them and filling him with a radiance that even the sun could not equal.

The gold band on Lara's left hand gleamed in the same warm color as Carson's eyes. He bent and took her hand reverently, kissing the wedding ring before he turned over her hand and smoothed another kiss into her soft palm. She was so beautiful lying there asleep, smiling just a little as though she were feeling his loving caresses even within her dreams.

"Good morning, Mrs. Carson Blackridge, my beautiful little fox," he murmured, rubbing his cheek against her palm. His eyes closed and his fingers tightened almost imperceptibly, as though something were trying to take her away. Emotions burst through him powerfully, more emotions than he could name or understand. It was all he could do to breathe. He lay quietly, watching her, sorting out the explosion of feelings, separating the familiar from the unfamiliar.

One familiar feeling was desire. There was no doubt of it. Making love with Lara was an incandescent pleasure that grew hotter and better with each sweet repetition. It was the same for her. She came to him without inhibitions, eagerly, making him feel so much a man and then celebrating his manhood with him in the most elemental way. With her he drank the wild, consuming wine of sensuality and found ecstasy glittering in the bottom of the shared cup.

There was also the familiar, cold presence of fear. Carson had no doubt of that, either. He would never feel secure in his shared life with Lara nor even in her love, for it could be torn away from him at any instant by a past that might refuse to stay buried. Knowing he could lose her was an agony that sometimes brought him upright in bed in the middle of the night, his body clammy with the residue of a dream too black to remember.

That, too, was familiar to Carson. He had spent a lifetime knowing what it was to want and to want and never to have. He had learned that wishing and wanting and hard work didn't necessarily make dreams come true.

What was unfamiliar to Carson as he lay and watched Lara was the aching tenderness he felt toward her; he wanted to give her the sun and the moon, the earth beneath her feet and the very air she breathed. He wanted to infuse her with the sweet warmth she gave to him simply by being alive. He wanted to make her smile, to drink her laughter, to see her eyes light when he called her name. He wanted things for which he had no words, simply unfamiliar yearnings sweeping through him until he could only murmur her name as he bent down to her, breathing air that was still warm from her body.

Lara stirred sleepily beneath the covers, reaching for Carson before she was even half-awake. The gesture sent a lightning stroke of tenderness and desire through the man who watched her with eyes that were as gentle as the dawn itself. Lara's sensuality was a continuous revelation to Carson, but it was her generosity of spirit that was unspeakably beautiful to him. She never measured or withheld her caresses, waiting for him to say or do something that might pleasure or repay her. She simply smiled and touched him, pleasing him, because his pleasure was also hers. It was the same for him. Seeing her face light up when he appeared, hearing her breath catch when his kiss changed from welcoming to consuming, feeling the boneless melting of her body against him—those things transformed his lonely inner silences as surely as sunlight transformed night.

Although Carson knew that Lara ached to hear *I love you* from his lips, she never pleaded or pouted until he gave in. She didn't even apply the unsubtle pressure of saying *I love you* and then waiting for him to speak in return. She rarely said the words herself except when the ecstasy he brought to her consumed all barriers and the words poured out, setting fire to him in turn. Her breathless, broken declarations of love satisfied him in a way that he could neither explain nor understand; he only knew that he lived for the words and the shared smiles as well as for the blazing, shattering pleasure he found deep within her body.

Carson lowered his head and nuzzled Lara's lips gently. He felt them shift into a smile as her arms snaked around his neck and a warm, impudent tongue teased the corners of his mouth. Desire arced through him. He pulled her into his arms and gave her a long, deep kiss. Before it ended, she was clinging to him hungrily.

"Last chance," he said, ending the kiss with a reluctance that told of the blood beating heavily through his veins.

"For what?" Lara asked. Her fingers slid down the long, powerful muscles of his back to his hips, caressing the resilient flesh, savoring his hard strength.

"Don't ask me, honey," Carson said, laughter curling beneath the words. "You're the one who told me to get you up at dawn."

"I did?" Lara blinked and frowned sleepily. "Oh, yes. Now I remember. I wanted to make the final selection on those pictures so I could take them into town to be duplicated before Mr. Donovan goes to court."

"*Donovan?*" Carson felt all the warmth of dawn change to icy midnight. He pushed up on his elbow and looked down at Lara. "What do you need him for?" Carson demanded. "Why do you keep wanting to see him? Is something wrong that you're not telling me about?"

Lara yawned and shook her head at the same time. "I've been trying to set up an interview with Donovan for weeks, but either you needed me for something on the ranch or he had to be in court, or—" Lara yawned again and turned to rub her cheek against Carson's warm, furry chest. "Anyway, I figured since half of the Donovan family has owned the neighboring ranch for the last century and the other half of the family has been the Rocking B's lawyers for the last hundred and twenty years, Donovan would have some good stories for my history. I hear he has an incredible memory. He's got to be almost eighty, and he's still practicing law."

Even as Carson opened his mouth to tell Lara that she couldn't see Donovan, he realized that he would have no reason to give her when she inevitably asked why. There were other ways, better ways, to put off the potentially dangerous interview. Much more pleasant ways. His hand slipped beneath the sheets. Slowly he smoothed up the taut flesh of Lara's thigh, traced the crease where leg joined torso, dipped into the dimple of her navel and continued upward to the soft weight of her breasts.

"I've got an incredible memory, too," Carson said, his tone deepening. "Want to reward me with an interview?" His fingertips teased Lara's nipple into a taut peak of desire. "I remember how hard and yet velvety you get," he said, rubbing a tight pink crown with his thumb. "Then I remember how sweet you taste and how warm your mouth is."

His tongue slid between Lara's teeth with a lover's ease, drinking the small catch of her breath as she turned toward him. He kissed her until their heartbeats were hard, rapid, and she was clinging to him.

"Then I remember how incredibly soft you are," he whispered, easing his hand down to the apex of her thighs. Delicately he sought and found her most tender flesh. He groaned as he felt her changing even while he touched her, becoming softer, hotter, preparing herself to accept the gift of his body. "God, Lara, you don't know what it does when I feel your willingness to take me. You're so damned sexy it's a wonder I ever get out of bed."

Lara laughed softly and tangled her fingers in the thick, rumpled thatch of hair curling down Carson's body. "It's you, not me," she whispered as she nuzzled his neck. "You touch me so perfectly." She shivered suddenly, and her hips began to move against his caressing hand. "Just thinking about how it's going to be makes me want to—"

Carson savored the moan that took away Lara's words, felt the hot melting of her at his touch. Then her warm, appreciative hands slid down his body, and he forgot to breathe.

"Come inside me, love," she whispered, caressing his hard length, pleasuring him, promising him even greater pleasures with her smile.

Carson swept aside the covers with one motion of his arm. For the space of several ragged breaths, he simply looked at the woman who could turn his body to fire with a look, a touch, a smile. Lara's skin was gilded by dawn and flushed by passion. She lay nude before him without fear or shyness, her body open, inviting him to become part of her once more. When he looked at her breasts, the nipples tightened as though he had touched them with his tongue. It was the same for her navel, a visible ripple of sensation chasing across her taut skin. When his gaze lingered over the glossy black mound below, her knees flexed and her body moved in helpless need.

"Carson," Lara said huskily, reaching for him, "you're killing me."

He smiled slowly down at her, memorizing every bit of her sensuality and beauty. "But I'm not even touching you," he said reasonably.

"I've noticed," she retorted. "That's what's killing me."

Lara traced the length of Carson's powerful body with her fingers until she found the rigid evidence of his hunger. She nipped very lightly at his aroused flesh with her fingernails. Blood beat visibly, heavily, in him, telling her the cost of his restraint.

"I have a cure for too-rapid heartbeat," she whispered, tugging softly at him with her fingertips.

"Do you?" Carson asked, smiling crookedly even as his hips moved in sensual response to her touch. "Maybe I should go get your tape recorder or take notes. Medical science needs to know how to slow down—"

Carson's teasing tone changed to a groan as Lara shifted position suddenly, gracefully, and he felt the wild, intimate heat of her mouth loving him. A shudder racked his body.

"Oh, God, baby," he gritted, torn between residual laughter and a desire so hot he could scarcely breathe. "I hate to tell you, but that's not going to slow my heartbeat down one damn bit!"

Lara laughed softly, and that, too, was a wild kind of caress against his erect, very sensitive flesh. With a thick sound Carson reached for her, only to have her slide like sunlight through his fingers. The cool black silk of her hair fanned across his thighs. He reached for her again, wrapping his fingers securely in the ends of her long hair, but instead of pulling her back up his body and into his arms, he found himself utterly captive to the piercing pleasure she was giving him.

With a groan of hunger and passion, Carson released Lara's hair in order to slide his fingers down the curve of her waist and hip, seeking the silky skin of her thighs until he finally caressed the melting softness that waited for him. He felt her hunger, her shivering heat, her welcoming body, and suddenly he knew that he had to be sheathed within her or he would be pulled apart by the violence of his own need.

"Lara," Carson said hoarsely, "I've got to have you."

She heard the urgency in his voice, felt it in the sudden trembling of his body as he lifted her over him. All teasing gone, she came willingly to him, opening her legs to ride his narrow hips as she settled into place on his body. Carson's face was dark and harsh with need, his eyes almost black, his body drawn as taut as a massive bow. His visible need sent a burst of passionate heat through Lara, melting her even as he slid deeply into her softness with a smooth thrust of his hips.

Lara couldn't understand the words Carson said, for they were blurred by the thick, hard driving of his need, but she saw the transformation of his face when release came, the pleasure so intense that it tore him apart in great, shuddering bursts that made him cry out. Then her own transformation came, her own release, and cries of pleasure and love rippled out of her in the endless moments before she collapsed across his broad chest, breathing as hard as he was.

It was a long time before their frantic heartbeats slowed and their breath came at normal intervals. Even then Lara and Carson remained joined, loving each other with gentle kisses and warm hands smoothing over skin still flushed with pleasure. Smiling to herself, Lara put her cheek against Carson's chest and began silently counting his heartbeats.

"See?" she said triumphantly, nuzzling his nipple. "It worked."

A rumbling, purring sound of contentment replaced the rhythm of Carson's heartbeat in Lara's ear. "Sure did," he said deeply. "Better every time. Better and better and better again. I can't wait for the—"

"That's not what I meant," she said, interrupting, laughing gently. "I was talking about your heartbeat. It's way down. Barely sixty-six a minute. See? It worked. I cured you."

Carson laughed aloud and hugged Lara close, wondering how he had ever gotten through the days before she had come back to the Rocking B and to him as warily as a fox tiptoeing through twilight.

"One time doesn't prove anything," he pointed out, nipping sensually at Lara's ear.

"Oh, yeah?"

"Oh, yeah," he said huskily, tracing the curved shadow at the base of her spine until his fingertips found her feminine heat and softness once again. "Didn't you learn anything about the scientific method in school?"

Lara's thoughts scattered with each slow, gliding caress of Carson's fingers between her legs. "Science?" she asked. "You mean like friction generating heat and—" She shivered and gasped as he found and stroked the exquisitely sensitive focus of her desire.

"I mean like repeatability," Carson said, rolling

over, taking her with him. "Didn't you know?" he asked, smiling down at Lara with a combination of possession and humor and passion. "That's the basis of the modern scientific method. If you can't repeat an experiment, then you can't draw useful conclusions from the data."

"I never was very good at science," admitted Lara.

"I'll teach you."

"That's kind of you," she said gravely. "Not many men would have the patience to teach—Oh!" Her words fragmented into a soft cry of pleasure.

Carson's hand moved slowly as Lara tried again to speak. More soft cries of pleasure came from her lips. She saw the heavy running of Carson's blood in the pulse beating in his neck, felt it as he grew inside her with every heartbeat and knew that soon he would fill her to overflowing. The thought was unbearably exciting, as was the slow movement of his hips rocking against her.

"Yeah. *Oh*," Carson said thickly.

He lowered his head and took her mouth as completely as he had taken her body. She took him in the same way, wanting him deeply, heat bursting through her in anticipation of the shimmering ecstasy to come.

This time when their heartbeats finally slowed, they fell asleep in a sweet, hot tangle, not knowing whose skin was being caressed, whose tongue was tasting the slick residue of passion, whose laughter was trembling within the joined peace of their bodies.

Even hours afterward the memory sent exquisite frissons shivering through Lara, distracting her from her task of sorting the Rocking B's photo archives into piles according to her first, second and third choices to illustrate her history. The more she and Carson made love, the more ways she found to please him. Tender or wild, gentle or fierce, he brought her an ecstasy so great that she sometimes wondered if she would survive the sweet violence of her release. She had discovered that she brought Carson an equal ecstasy; that, too, was a shattering sweetness pouring through her veins each time she realized it anew.

Sighing, Lara decided it was just as well that she had missed her chance to catch Donovan in town; her mind was just too scattered to interview a lawyer right now. For the eighth time she looked from the photo in her right hand to the photo in her left. They both showed weathered men riding gaunt horses. Behind them Texas cattle with horns as long as ax handles poured through a narrow gap into a Montana valley that had never before known anything except deer and buffalo. It was the end of one era and the beginning of another, and it had been captured by a man who knew that he had driven his cattle into a place in the history of his country as well as into a lush, ungrazed land.

Lara put the paired photos aside, unable to choose between them. Instead, she thought about tonight, when Carson would be through with his work. After dinner she would give him a back rub and listen as he talked about the small crises and unexpected pleasures that had come to him during the day. When the knots were gone from his neck and shoulders, he would pull her into his lap, lean back against the couch and ask about the progress of her history.

She had discovered that Carson had very acute perceptions on the subject of human needs and the land itself, about the kinds of things that didn't change whether the time span being considered was months or millennia. And, for a man with a pronounced hostility toward the past, Carson had an excellent eye for the photo that told the most about the land, the men and the moment they had been frozen in time by a camera. She had come to value his insights as much as she valued his laughter and the muscular power of his body. Every day she loved him more.

Lara worked steadily, rapidly, sorting through photos. Most went into a reject pile. The next biggest pile consisted of photos that might be suitable for illustrating her history. Off to one side there was a pile she reserved for sharing with Carson. The pictures in that pile showed everything from a tough old bald-faced cow with three calves peeking out from beneath her belly to the Rocking B's old ranch house adrift in a sea of snow and moonlight.

There was a series of wedding pictures, too, each ceremony more elaborate than the last. The same lace scarf had been worn by three generations of Blackridge wives—four, now. The fragile, delicately wrought scarf presently lay in Lara's dresser drawer, her most prized possession after the wedding ring that fitted so smoothly on her hand.

She smiled softly, remembering the morning after they had first made love. Carson had awakened her by putting his hand over her womb and saying that they would be married as soon as possible because he had been too crazy with desire even to think of protecting her last night. Nor would he protect her in the future, unless she wanted it, because the thought of his child growing in her womb was unbearably sweet. But only if she wanted it, too…

Lara sighed and put her hand just below her waist. Oh, yes, she had wanted it. She had wept when her period had finally come nearly three weeks late. Carson had held her so gently, kissing away her tears, telling her that it was just as well—if he were any happier, he would burst like the Roman candles they had seen at the Fourth of July celebration in town. Besides, he had added, kissing her more deeply, he had discovered that he was selfish. He didn't mind keeping her all to himself for a while longer. That way he had it all, the anticipation of a child in the future and the reality of a generous, abandoned lover right now.

A tiny smile tugged at the corner of Lara's mouth as a shivery feeling invaded the pit of her stomach. She loved being Carson's woman, his wife, his lover, the future mother of his children. Someday she hoped that he would realize that she was also his beloved. Sometimes after they had made love, or when she rubbed away the tension that tied his shoulders in knots, or when she woke up and found Carson watching her with eyes that were almost gold—sometimes then she had the feeling that he wanted to tell her something, something that was very difficult for him to say.

Was it *I love you*?

Were those the words Carson seemed to be searching for and unable to find? If so, then she wanted to tell him that it didn't matter whether he talked of love or not. If the words were so difficult, so painful for him to speak, she didn't have to hear them in order for her life to be complete. Hearing his laughter come more often now that they were married, seeing a smile erase the harsh lines from his face when he looked at her, feeling the brush of his fingers over her cheek when he walked by her chair, those things spoke eloquently of his feelings for her. It wasn't necessary to hear the words, too, especially if saying them brought pain rather than pleasure to the man she loved.

"Such a beautiful smile. What are you thinking about, little fox?"

"Carson!" Lara came to her feet in a rush, her face radiant with the unexpected pleasure of seeing Carson in the middle of the afternoon. "I thought you weren't going to be back until dinner. Did you get all the cows moved to the new pasture?"

Carson's arms came around Lara and he lifted her feet off the floor, holding her in a hard, warm hug. "We're just about done. Murchison and Spur are combing out the strays right now. I'm playing hooky," he added, nuzzling Lara's ear and the curve of her neck.

"I'm glad," she said softly, kissing his cheek, combing her fingers through his hair, loving him.

For a moment they rocked slowly in place, absorbing the sweetness of holding and being held. Lara felt her eyes burn suddenly and blinked back tears. He had come like this to her so many times in the past weeks, surprising her with a fragrant wildflower or a colorful, water-polished stone he had plucked from a creek bed.

Once he had come in unexpectedly and taken her up on the low ridge above the ranch. There he had told her to close her eyes and listen. There was a strong west wind that day, blowing through the narrow ravines that twisted down from the high, rugged mountains beyond the ranch. The wind was sweet, warm, wild and had a sound that was both beautiful and so lonely that it had torn at her heart. When she had told Carson how she felt, he had said, *Yes. That's why I brought you here. Together we can share the beauty and hold the loneliness at bay*. And then he had drawn her so close that she couldn't tell whose heartbeat she felt in her blood.

"Do you have a few minutes?" Carson asked. "I've got something I want to show you."

"Of course," said Lara, ruffling the slightly shaggy hair at Carson's neckline with her fingers, enjoying his warmth and the changing textures of skin and hair.

"Good. Let's go before they go back into hiding."

"They?"

"You'll see," Carson said, putting Lara back down

on her feet and taking her hand, tugging her toward the door.

On the way out Lara deliberately ignored the litter of pictures and documents scattered across every available surface in the library. She was a little behind schedule on her history, although her faculty advisor had told her to take as much extra time as she needed—as Carson's wife, Lara wasn't likely to be kicked off the ranch for asking questions, looking for boundary markers and being generally underfoot in her quest for the Rocking B's history. Besides, it was much too beautiful to be inside, even with something as fascinating as old photos to sort through. The day was alive, she was alive and Carson's hand felt so warm in hers.

Carson helped Lara into the pickup truck and drove along a winding, rutted ranch road. He drove to a distant corner of the Rocking B, where the pasture had been cycled back into grazing land at the beginning of summer. A few sleek cows stood belly deep in wildflowers and grasses, searching among the abundant greenery for favorite forage.

Carson parked the truck, lifted Lara out and took her hand in a warm grip. Smiling, he ignored her questions and curious glances. He led her along the path that cattle had made to the tiny lake where springwater welled up in clear, sweet ripples. The pond was ringed by a thick growth of reeds and cattails.

Motioning for silence, Carson led Lara up the back side of a small hill that overlooked the pond. The grass had been recently walked on but was already springing back into upright position. At the top of the hill, Carson pulled Lara down into a nest of fragrant grass laced with flowers. Once seated, Lara was all but hidden by the tall greenery. Carson sat behind her, pulled her between his legs so that she could rest against his chest and got out the binoculars he had taken from the truck.

"We're upwind here," he murmured, the words a bare thread of sound, "so we'll have to be quiet. Sound carries real well over water, and she's skittish as hell. I don't blame her, either," he continued, quartering the pond with binoculars. "If I had that many—there she is! Poor baby. She doesn't know whether to strut or hide under a rock."

Lara felt as much as heard the low chuckle vibrating in Carson's chest.

"Here," he murmured, giving Lara the binoculars. "Look just to the left of that small willow. See her?"

The warmth of Carson's breath on Lara's neck distracted her. "See what?" she whispered, adjusting the glasses. "What am I supposed to—Carson!" Lara murmured suddenly, her tone soft yet urgent with excitement. "There's a mother duck out there with so many ducklings around her that she looks like a city under siege!"

Carson rumbled softly, a cross between a chuckle and a purr. "Isn't she something?" he whispered. "When I spotted her, I couldn't wait to bring you here. I've never seen a duck with that many babies."

"And you're right," Lara whispered, laughter curling through her words. "The poor thing doesn't know whether to strut with pride or hide under a rock and have a moment of peace." For a time Lara counted silently, finding and losing ducklings as they wove around their harried mother. As the number rose, Lara spoke softly aloud, hardly able to believe what she was seeing. "...twelve, thirteen, fourteen," she counted slowly, trying to keep track of the darting, bobbing bodies. "Fifteen!" she breathed. "My God. Fifteen of the fluffy little darlings. Maybe some of her luck will rub off on me this month," Lara added softly, smiling to herself.

Carson's expression changed, intensity replacing humor on his face. He closed his eyes and brushed his lips over Lara's hair so delicately that she didn't even feel the caress.

"Are you sure, little fox?" he whispered, kissing Lara's neck with the same aching mixture of emotions as when he had kissed her wedding ring while she slept. "I want you to be happy."

Lara lowered the glasses and leaned back against Carson's warm, broad chest. "I want your baby," she said softly.

She felt the shudder that went through him at her words. She heard his breath catch and felt a small, hot trail of moisture as he pressed his cheek against hers.

"Carson," Lara said softly, her voice shivering with emotion that she had moved him so.

"Before you, no one ever wanted me, really. Not the woman who had me, not the man and woman who adopted me, not the women who lined up hoping to marry a big ranch,'' Carson said, his voice husky, his arms tight around Lara. ''Then you came back and you wanted me despite the way I hurt you four years ago. The thought that you really want my baby, too—''

With a husky sound he gave up trying to speak and simply held her while the soft summer wind whispered through the tall grass around them. Finally his arms loosened, and he kissed her as though she were more precious than life itself.

''I'd better get you back,'' Carson said reluctantly. ''I'm taking up too much of your work time. I know you wanted to have the pictures in to be duplicated last week. And we were late getting up this morning.''

He smiled at the memory even as he realized that the longer Lara took with her historical research, the greater the danger that she would put too many pieces together. And the longer he was with her, the more he understood just how much was at stake. Since he had been fifteen, he had understood that, if he wanted to have a home and be part of a real family, he would have to do it himself. Yet the more women he had had, the less possible the dream of a home had seemed, until he had all but forgotten it.

Then Lara had come back, turning life inside out, revealing to him how empty he had been and how richly she filled him. He was still discovering that richness, still growing to meet the promise of her generous spirit. At times he could almost feel old, scarred layers of himself splitting and falling away, allowing room for new thoughts, new hopes, new laughter, new emotions—even the ability to cry.

Lara turned slightly against Carson's chest and smiled up into his eyes. Against the backdrop of lush grass, the green in his eyes eclipsed the amber, reminding her of Long Pool in late afternoon, clear emerald water sparkling with points of deep golden light.

"You have the most incredible eyes," she whispered. "Always changing, always beautiful."

Smiling, Carson bent and smoothed his mustache over Lara's cheek. "If I start telling you about your incredible, beautiful body and the lovely way it changes when I touch you," he said, nuzzling along her jawline, "we'd be lucky to get back to the ranch before the first snow, much less in time for dinner."

"Is that a threat or a promise?" Lara asked softly, turning and catching his lower lip between her teeth for an instant.

"Let's find out," he invited.

Carson saw how tempted Lara was in the seconds before she sighed and stroked his mustache with her fingertips. "I should get those pictures so I can catch Donovan before he goes on his vacation."

Carson was too close to Lara to prevent her feeling the sudden stiffening of his body at the mention of Donovan's name. She saw the instant deepening of the brackets on either side of Carson's mouth as his lips flattened. At that moment she realized that, whenever the lawyer's name came up, Carson changed the subject in one way or another. It was the same when she tried to make or keep various appointments with

Donovan—somehow, inevitably, something always came up to prevent her from seeing the lawyer.

"You don't want me to see Donovan, do you?" Lara said quietly.

"No." The word was clipped, cold, as bleak as the flat line of Carson's mouth.

"Why? Surely you can't still be angry about that note he sent after he found out we were married. I'm certain he didn't mean to imply that the reason for our hurried marriage was that I was pregnant," Lara said, smiling crookedly. "He's too much a gentleman of the old school to be so crude."

Carson closed his eyes and fought to hold on to his temper as he thought of the note the old lawyer had sent: *Fast work, boy. Larry knew you real well, didn't he? I presume the heir is soon to follow, ensuring that Larry's progeny will be part of the land forever, world without end, amen.*

Indignation and outrage had crackled in every slashing line of Thackery Donovan's handwriting. Carson had seen it, even if Lara hadn't. He had wanted to kill the old man for even hinting at what it was his moral duty as a lawyer to keep confidential. But Larry's will had been like a burr under old Thack's saddle since the day Larry had walked in and demanded that his will be redrawn. No matter how Thack had fought and shouted about "immoral" or "crazy" or "stupid," Larry hadn't been swayed. It was legal, and that was all that mattered. Larry had known what he wanted. If he couldn't have it, no one else could have what he wanted, either.

World without end, amen.

"Carson?" asked Lara softly.

Abruptly he focused on Lara rather than on the cruel, destructive and indestructible past.

"Thackery Donovan is like Larry," Carson said finally. "If you let him, he'll take all the joy out of life. Thack is part of the past. You and I don't live there anymore." Carson bent and kissed Lara's lips, breathing his warmth into her, breathing her warmth in return. "You're happy now, little fox," he whispered. "We both are. Keep away from Thack, and we'll stay that way." He smiled slowly, teasingly. "Besides, you have enough stuff scattered around the library for six university degrees. What do you need with more junk?"

"There are gaps in the Rocking B's legal record," Lara said, her voice quiet, her eyes intent as she tried to make Carson understand. "The firm of Donovan, Donovan and Donovan can fill those gaps from their files." Then, urgently, she added, "Carson, the past can't hurt us anymore. Some things that happened were sad and bitter, but some things were beautiful, too. It all balances out in the end."

"Don't you believe it," he said flatly. "The past will tear us apart."

Carson's voice was so hard, so certain, that Lara was frightened. She had hoped, as he became happier in his own life, he would have less hostility toward the pageant of history that brought her so much joy. But it hadn't happened that way. If anything, his hostility to their personal past before their marriage had grown greater with every day they were together.

"See?" Carson said, his tone heavy as his thumb traced the downward curve of Lara's mouth. "We were so happy a few moments ago, but now—" He swore softly, savagely. "Tell me what you need. I'll get the damned papers for you. Just stay the hell away from Thackery Donovan!"

Chapter 11

Lara pushed back from Carson's desk and stood up very carefully. She had discovered just a few moments ago that the room had an alarming tendency to revolve around her if she stood up too fast. She was afraid that she had finally caught the respiratory flu that had been making the rounds of the Rocking B. The older hands had been hit hardest, with Murchison and Willie spending two weeks in bed and two more recovering. Murchison had gone back to work too soon; the flu had rebounded and put him back in bed. Spur had been down for three days, then back to work and then down again. Carson had run a slight fever for one day, slept a few more hours than usual that night and been back in the saddle no worse for wear the next day.

All the men had joked that the flu was a blessing in disguise: it made them lose their appetite, which was just as well, because Mose's cooking was worse than usual. As for Yolanda, her niece had taken her back to Billings for a long-overdue vacation. Now that Lara was caring for Carson, there was no reason for Yolanda not to spend time with her nieces and grandchildren.

Lara had sailed through the flu weeks blithely, cooking for the men who were hungry, setting out aspirin and antibiotics that had been prescribed for the hands who needed them, making sure that there was a steady supply of cool, tempting fruit juices on hand to drink. As man after man fell ill, got well and relapsed into flu again, she had assured the cowboys that her health was a clear-cut case of the superiority of clean living over the kind they obviously favored. They had been too tired to give her more than a half-hearted raspberry in rebuttal.

Seeing them all so listless and pale had squeezed Lara's heart. Instead of working on her history project, she had spent most of her time going from ranch house to bunkhouse, checking on the men, calling the doctor when the fevers went higher than one hundred and three degrees and then driving to town for another round of antibiotics for the latest flu casualty. Dr. Scott had taken to calling her Lara Nightingale.

Only to herself did Lara admit that she was more tired than usual lately and much less interested in food. She had very much hoped that those symptoms signaled the early stages of pregnancy. It had been seven weeks and four days since her last period. She hadn't said anything to Carson yet because the last time her period had been late, it had come after seven weeks and five days. She didn't want to raise his hopes, only to disappoint him again.

But as the room swayed gently around Lara and her skin roughed up with a sudden chill, she bitterly conceded defeat. Flu, not pregnancy, was sapping her normal vitality. Flu, not pregnancy, had taken away her appetite.

"Damn, damn, *damn*," Lara said as hot, unexpected tears spilled down her face.

She wiped them away with a hand that shook. Lately her moods had been unpredictable, which had raised her hopes of pregnancy, but this sudden drop into despair was ridiculous. She had gone to the doctor after her previous period had been so late. Dr. Scott had assured her that her body was fully functioning and that sudden changes in a woman's life—like marriage—could throw off her menstrual cycle. It was nothing to worry about. If she wasn't pregnant after six or eight months of trying, she and Carson should come in for a thorough workup. Until then, he advised, they both should just relax and enjoy the process of conception.

Lara's lips trembled between smiling and crying as she thought that never had a doctor's advice been so enthusiastically followed. The currents of passion flowing between herself and Carson increased in depth and intensity each time they made love. When Carson gave her a certain look or a certain smile, fire shimmered through her. It was the same for him. A look, a touch, and she could see his blood begin to beat heavily, filling him with sensual heat.

Lara shivered suddenly and rubbed her arms. She could use some of Carson's heat right now. It was cold for September. Yet when she went to check the thermometer on the library wall, the mercury was nudging eighty. It wasn't cold for the season. It was hot.

And so was she. Too hot.

As Lara turned away from the thermometer, the library seemed to darken for a moment. She braced herself against the wall until the dizziness passed. Ruefully she conceded that the older hands hadn't been joking when they had called this bug the worst one since the Second World War. The only silver lining to this particular flu cloud was that it didn't have you hanging your head in the toilet until you prayed you would die. This bug just laid you out for a few days or weeks while the world passed by in a fever haze, followed by the kind of exhaustion that made you sweat if you walked across the room.

The bug hit fast and hard. Spur had barely been able to ride in from the range. Lara had suspected that he was making more of his sickness than there was. Now she knew better. Waves of weakness washed over her. She was grateful that all she had to do was get to the library couch. Walking to the bedroom would have been beyond her. As she groped for the couch, she told herself that she would have to apologize to Spur for teasing him about being too sick to ride.

With a sigh Lara tumbled onto the couch and lay there for a moment, trying to get up the strength to pull the afghan off the back of the couch and cover herself. Then she realized that she had already pulled the blanket off and fallen on top of it. To cover herself she would have to roll to her side in order to free the afghan. That would take a lot of energy. She fell asleep before she decided whether moving aside was worth the trouble in order to get warm.

"Take care of Socks for me, would you, Willie?" asked Carson, handing over the reins. "I want to check on Lara. She looked kind of pale this morning."

"She hasn't been to the bunkhouse since last night," offered Willie, taking the big horse's reins. "'Course, only one of the hands is still down, and Jim-Bob ain't all that sick now."

Carson took the front steps two at a time, smiling in anticipation of seeing Lara's face light up with pleasure when he walked in. For the first few weeks after they had argued over Thackery Donovan, Carson had been worried that Lara would piece together too much of the past from the legal documents he had reluctantly gotten for her, but as far as he knew, she hadn't done more than leaf quickly through the papers, checking dates against a column that contained the cryptic entries referring to the reams of oral history she had typed up.

He had helped her as much as possible, wanting the damn project over and done with so that he could draw a breath without waiting for his newly discovered, unexpectedly beautiful life to blow up in his face. The fear of losing everything was always there, a cold shadow of the past lying beneath the brilliant warmth of the present.

Pausing in the living room, Carson listened intently. No quiet sound of movement came from the kitchen where Lara had taken over Yolanda's duties. No muted click of keys came from the computer he had taught Lara how to use, saving her hours of time as she worked on her paper. In fact, there were no sounds at all. Frowning, Carson stood without moving, wondering if Lara had gone to the Chandler homestead to work on Cheyenne's notebooks.

At the thought of the homestead, Carson smiled to himself, remembering Lara's look of stunned delight when he had given her the deed to the homestead as a wedding present. He had wanted her to have it. He had wanted her to know beyond doubt that she was as deeply rooted on the Blackridge ranch as anyone who had ever lived there. He had wanted to give her the security of having her own place, her own piece of the earth no matter what happened. And if the worst happened, he prayed that the homestead would keep her from turning her back and simply walking away from the past, the Rocking B and him.

With a silent, savage curse Carson shoved the bleak thought back down in his mind. It wouldn't come to that. Somehow, someway, he would prevent that.

A small sound came from the library, as though a stack of papers had slithered across the floor. In three long strides Carson was across the living room. His boots scuffed softly on the narrow rug in the hall leading to the library. The door was ajar. He pushed it open a bit more and slipped in, waiting to hear the swift intake of Lara's breath when she spotted him standing there.

The only thing Carson heard was the same odd, slithering sound. He walked further into the room. What he saw made his heart turn over. Lara was struggling to sit up on the couch, but even as he watched, she slumped backward. The sound of her clothes rubbing over the leather couch was what he had heard.

"Lara!"

She turned toward his voice. "Carson? I—" Her teeth chattered. "Cold," she said raggedly. "So cold."

"It's all right, little fox," he said, scooping her up off the couch, holding her close to his own warmth. "I'm here. I'll take care of you."

The instant Carson touched Lara, he knew that she was a lot sicker than any of the men had been. She literally burned beneath his touch, yet he could feel the chills shaking her. He wondered how long she had lain on the couch, too weak even to pull the afghan over herself. The thought twisted through him, hurting him as nothing before ever had.

She had been helpless, and he hadn't even known.

Carson carried Lara upstairs and put her under the covers. Pausing only long enough to kick off his boots, he slid in next to her, pulling her close once more. He held her while chills racked her slender body. He stroked her slowly and spoke softly, telling her again and again that she would be all right, he would take care of her, he would warm her and she would sleep and then she would be well again. He doubted that she heard him, but he kept talking, anyway. It helped to keep his own freezing fear at bay.

He had been afraid of losing her, but never like this, having her life slide through his fingers like twilight bleeding into night.

Even as the thought came, Carson told himself he was being foolish. Lara was young, healthy, rippling with laughter and vitality. She simply had the flu. In a few days or weeks she would be well again. She would look up at him and smile, and then she would nuzzle against his mustache, teasing him until he made love to her and she came apart in his arms, crying his name and her love.

She would be all right. She had to be. Anything else was unthinkable.

When the last of the chills finally faded, Lara sighed brokenly and lay without moving in Carson's arms. He waited until he was sure that she was asleep before he eased carefully out of bed, tucking the covers around her to keep her warm. She whimpered softly, restlessly, searching blindly for him even in her fever-ridden sleep.

"I'm here," Carson said quietly, stroking Lara's hair. "Rest, little fox. I'll be right here the whole time."

With his free hand Carson picked up the receiver of the bedside phone, punched in the doctor's number and waited impatiently for Dr. Scott to take the call.

"Another hand down with the flu?" asked the doctor.

"It's Lara. I found her on the couch, too weak to sit up."

"Fever?"

"Like hell itself."

"How high?"

"You tell me. Her teeth are chattering too hard to put in a thermometer. Her skin feels like an oven."

"Nausea?"

"All she said was, 'Cold. So cold.' As soon as the chills stopped, she fell asleep."

The doctor grunted. "How does her breathing sound? Too many of these flu cases are going straight into pneumonia."

Carson's expression became even more bleak. He bent over and listened to Lara for a minute before turning back to the phone.

"Her breathing sounds okay," said Carson. "A little fast, maybe, but she's not having any trouble that I can hear.''

"I'll be out in two hours. Keep her warm and quiet. Get her to drink something if you can. If her breathing changes, prop her up in bed and call me right away.''

Carson hung up, looked at the clock and then back at Lara lying bundled up in the middle of the bed, her black hair streaming out over the covers. She looked too small, too pale, her fingers fragile against the forest-green bedspread. Gently he picked up her hand, kissed it and tucked it beneath the covers once more. She murmured something and turned toward his touch. He stroked her hair until she sighed and curled up against his thigh, calm again.

He picked up the phone, dialed the barn and told Willie that he was in charge of the Rocking B until Lara was well.

The hours until the doctor came passed in slow motion for Carson. He lay next to Lara, holding her, stroking her hair, listening to each breath as though his life depended on it. She seemed to slip in and out of sleep, never waking enough to focus on her surroundings, never sleeping deeply enough that a sound or a movement wouldn't disturb her. Yet she always seemed to know that he was there. No matter how restless she became, she moved toward rather than away from him. The realization made Carson's hands tremble as he stroked her hair. He kissed Lara gently, repeatedly, feeling emotions seething inside him, pressing against old scars, old boundaries, until they cracked and gave way, letting him breathe again, letting him grow.

Motionless but for his hand stroking Lara, Carson lay beside her. Finally he heard Dr. Scott at the front door. With a last caress Carson got up and went to let the doctor in.

"How's she doing?" asked Dr. Scott.

"Sleeping, kind of. Restless. Hot. A few more chills, but not as bad."

Dr. Scott grunted. "Drink anything?"

Carson shook his head. "Wasn't interested."

The doctor grunted again. He followed Carson through the bedroom door, took one look at Lara's pale cheeks with their scarlet fever banners riding high and bright, and pulled a thermometer out of his bag.

"Wake up, Mrs. Blackridge," he said, shaking Lara's shoulder firmly.

Lara mumbled and stirred. When her eyelids finally opened, her eyes were glazed.

"Put this under your tongue and keep it there."

Lara's eyes closed again, but she kept the thermometer in place while the doctor took her pulse and blood pressure, and listened very carefully to her breathing. He managed to do it all without uncovering more than a fraction of her body at a time. Even so, her skin roughened up with chills. She didn't complain. She seemed more asleep than awake, disoriented by the fever. Dr. Scott removed the thermometer, looked at it and then at Carson.

"You folks using contraceptives?" asked the doctor.

Carson looked startled. "No."

"Thought so. Well, that makes things a wee bit trickier."

"What the hell does that mean?" demanded Carson, fear leaping in his blood.

"Take it easy," Dr. Scott said, lifting his shaggy gray eyebrows at the intensity of Carson's response. "All it means is I have to find out if Lara's pregnant before I treat her. If she is, then we'll have to be real careful about what we give her in the way of medicine. There's always a chance—minor, but still a chance—that the pregnancy might be adversely affected, even terminated, by some medications."

"Listen," Carson said bluntly, "there's a major chance that *you* will be 'adversely affected' if you don't do everything possible for Lara. That's my bottom line, Doctor. My wife. I want her well again. I want to come into a room and see her smile. I want to walk with her at sunset when loons sing on the pond. I want to show her every wildflower and every—"

Abruptly Carson looked away, unable to speak. The sight of Lara lying so pale and still beneath the doctor's ministrations had gone into Carson's heart like a knife. Normally Lara was alert, vibrant, quick to respond to a word or a touch. Yet as he looked at her now, he doubted that she heard or understood much of what was going on around her.

"I hear you, Carson," the doctor said gently. "How long has it been since her last period?"

Carson tried to think, but the image of Lara's pale, still face kept interfering. "Five weeks. No. Seven."

"Probably too soon to tell without tests, but—" Dr. Scott shrugged and set aside the thermometer.

Disturbing the covers as little as possible, he slid his hand beneath the sheet and began to probe gently at Lara's abdomen. He hesitated, probed some more and then pulled the covers aside and started unfastening her jeans. Lara stirred and muttered, shivering. Carson pulled the spread up so that it covered as much of her as possible without interfering with the doctor's examination.

"Carson?" she asked.

Her voice was so thin that it frightened him. "I'm here, little fox," he said, taking her hand. "Dr. Scott wants to examine you before he gives you any medicine."

Carson couldn't tell from Lara's dazed, too-dark eyes whether she understood. All he could be sure of was that she pulled his hand down to her cheek and sighed, taking comfort from his presence.

"I'll be damned," the doctor said finally, pulling the covers back into place. "Feels like she's at least three months along. I'll have to run some tests to be sure, but if I were a betting man, I'd put good money on you being a papa come spring."

"But she had a period," Carson objected. "She can't be—"

Dr. Scott interrupted. "It happens that way with some women. Mrs. Blackridge? Lara? You following this?"

Carson turned and saw tears running down Lara's face and pooling in the upturned curves of her smile. The doctor smiled in return.

"Guess you're tracking well enough," he said. "Was your last period heavy, light, normal?"

"Light." The word was a raspy sigh. "Very…light."

"Any more bleeding since then?"

Slowly Lara shook her head.

"Cramps?"

"No," she whispered.

"Nausea?"

Again she shook her head.

Dr. Scott grunted. "You might be one of the lucky ones." He smiled up at Carson, who was looking stunned. "Cat got your tongue, Carson?"

Slowly Carson bent and kissed Lara's eyelids and her cheeks and the fingers that were intertwined with his. The hand that lifted to stroke his cheek was too hot, trembling with weakness, but no touch had ever moved him more.

"I'm going to give you a shot," Dr. Scott said, pulling a syringe from his traditional black bag. "I'll be leaving some antibiotics in pill form, too. Take them until they're gone. Drink eight ounces of fluid an hour, or I swear I'll give it to you IV. Hear me?"

Lara nodded.

Dr. Scott drew a blood sample, gave Lara a shot and packed up his bag. Carson followed him out into the hall just beyond the bedroom.

"Will she be all right?" Carson asked bluntly.

"She'll be fine. Flu and the third month of pregnancy is a double whammy, but she's strong. As for the baby, it'll be fine, too. Mother Nature has a way of taking care of the fetus first and the woman second."

"That doesn't comfort me," Carson said in a clipped tone.

Dr. Scott laughed. "Yeah, well, get used to it because that's the way it is. As far as Mother Nature is concerned, people are just an egg's way of making more eggs. Reproduction is first. Everything else is second. But don't fret about it. Women have been doing it long enough that they've got it down pretty well by now."

"That's why they go to hospitals to have their babies, right?" retorted Carson. "Don't try to con me, Doctor. I've seen enough cows give birth to know that things go wrong."

"Statistically, it's—"

"Screw statistics!" Carson grated. "Lara isn't a number!"

The doctor sighed. "Been a rough few weeks for you, hasn't it?" he asked mildly. "All the hands sick and then most of them relapsing, work piling up, new marriage to adjust to. Less than that has been known to put an edge on a man's temper."

After a visible effort Carson reined in his emotions. He ran his hand through his hair, took a deep breath and tried to explain. "I want her well again," he said simply. "I...need her."

"Don't you want the baby, too?"

"Hell, yes, I want it. I want it a lot," Carson said, his voice vibrating with intensity. "*But I want Lara more.*"

"No reason you can't have both. I'm being straight with you about that, Carson. Your woman is going to be fine. Now go back in there and let her know you're near and solid even if the rest of the world is all distant and fuzzy."

Carson watched the doctor walk away and told himself that everything was going to be fine. Lara would get well. There was no reason to feel as though the past were poised like an icy winter avalanche, ready to rush forward, burying everything, crushing warmth and life from the present, leaving only memory and loss and a lifetime of regret.

The first three days of fever passed very quickly for Lara and with glacial slowness for Carson. By the fourth day her temperature had returned to normal. By the sixth day she was more than strong enough to be bored lying in bed, but the doctor had wanted her to stay in bed for two more days. She had demanded, wheedled and finally bribed Carson with kisses to bring her research material to work with; even so, he only brought her enough for an hour's work at a time.

Two at the most. The rest of the books he gave her were mysteries.

Sighing restlessly, Lara looked out the window. There was a side yard enclosed by tall fences covered with climbing roses, giving total privacy both to the yard and the bedroom itself. The roses were a soft profusion of colors and fragrance, and the grass was a green invitation to come out and lie quietly in the sun. Lara wanted to be out there where thousands of petals trembled in the warm breeze. She wanted to feel sunlight all over her, drawing out the last residue of sickness, leaving her vibrant and burnished with heat. The only thing that kept her in bed was her promise to Carson.

"You look good enough to eat," Carson said, standing in the doorway with a batch of new magazines in his hand.

"Carson!" she said, turning toward him, smiling with surprise and delight. "You're back early."

He smiled and looked at Lara with open appreciation. The rose lace gown he had given her the day before made her skin glow. "Has anyone ever told you what a beautiful smile you have? It lights up a whole room."

Lara watched Carson walking toward her with his powerful body and easy, loose stride and wondered how she had been so lucky to win him when every woman in the state of Montana had been setting traps and laying snares for him since he had turned sixteen.

"Here," Carson said, fanning the magazines across the bedspread. "One of everything."

Lara held out her arms to Carson, ignoring the colorful cascade of magazines. She felt the warmth of his arms sliding around her, the tantalizing brush of his mustache across her lips and the intimate flavor of his kiss.

"Mmmm. Raspberries and cream," he said, slowly releasing her. "My favorite."

"You taste like the wind," she said, smoothing her cheek over his. "Sweet and wild."

Carson's hands tightened on Lara in the instant before he controlled the desire that prowled so hotly within him. He had gone without women before in his life, but it had never affected him with the intensity that going without Lara for the past week had.

"Carson?"

He nuzzled her hair and made a sound that managed to be both a deep purr and a question.

"I want to go to the side yard and lie in the sun. Just those few steps won't hurt me," Lara said quickly, anticipating Carson's objections. "It's hardly much farther than the bathroom and I've been managing that quite easily for the last three—"

The tumble of words stopped as Lara felt herself being lifted into Carson's arms. His long fingers snagged the comforter that lay across the foot of the bed. Within moments Lara found herself lying in the sun, feeling the heat of the ground seep up through the comforter Carson had spread over the grass for her.

"Anything else?" he asked, smiling.

"A hug?"

Carson stretched out beside Lara and gathered her into his arms. For long moments they simply held each other, absorbing the sunlight and the warmth and the husky murmur of bees sliding between soft petals to touch the nectar hidden inside. Slowly Lara's hands crept into the open collar of Carson's shirt, then her fingers softly undid the snaps on his shirt. With a sigh of pleasure, she worked her fingers through the thick, warm hair covering his chest. When she touched the smooth disk of his nipple, it immediately hardened into an erect nub. Desire poured through Lara in a hot, sweet wave.

"Carson," she whispered, seeking his mouth, finding it.

For a few moments Carson allowed himself to enjoy the deep, sensual kiss. Then finally, reluctantly, he captured Lara's caressing hands, kissed them and tucked them back around his neck.

"Carson?"

"Not yet, honey," he said huskily. "You're still weak as a kitten."

"Only compared to you," Lara retorted, kneading the thick muscles of his shoulders. "Dr. Scott said it would be all right."

She felt the sudden stillness of Carson's body.

"When did he say that?"

"I called him this morning," Lara said. "He told me I can 'resume marital relations' anytime I want. I want, Carson."

A tangible shudder of desire went through him. His heartbeat surged, filling him with heat. He fought to control the total response of his body to Lara's invitation. It was no use. A word, a kiss, and he was hard, ready, aching to be sheathed within her loving warmth.

"Are you sure?" Carson whispered. "You were so sick when I found you in the library. It...frightened me a little," he said. "Oh, hell, Lara, it terrified me," he gritted, burying his face in the black silk cloud of her hair. "I don't want to do anything that would hurt you."

"Then you'd better make love to me," she said, threading her fingers deeply into his thick, cool hair, seeking and finding the warmth of his scalp beneath. "I want you so much that it's a kind of hurting."

"Lara," Carson said hoarsely, his arms closing around her with an intensity that he could barely restrain. "My sweet, warm, beautiful woman." Reluctantly he released her and stood up to pull off his clothes. "I'll make it good for you, honey."

"You always make it good for me."

Anticipation shivered through Lara as she watched Carson's powerful body emerge from his clothes. Her breath caught as she saw how aroused he was. When he knelt beside her, she ran her fingertips down his torso to the hard, erect flesh where his blood beat visibly, hotly. When she stroked him, his whole body tightened as though he had brushed against an electrical current. For a few moments he allowed himself to enjoy the sweet torment of her caress before his hands swept down, catching her trembling fingers, removing them from his hungry body.

"It's too soon, baby," he said, his voice thick with passion and regret as he brought himself under control. "You're so weak you're shaking."

Lara made a sound that was caught between a laugh and a sob. She looked up at Carson with eyes that were nearly black with passion.

"I'm shaking because I know what kind of pleasure is waiting for me," she said huskily. "Take me there, Carson. Go there with me."

It was Carson's fingers that trembled this time. He whispered Lara's name as he traced the soft curve of her lower lip. Then he bent over her and tasted the warmth behind her lips so gently that the kiss was like a sigh. She had expected a passionate claiming as sudden and hard as his obvious need for her. The delicate, exquisitely erotic tasting of her mouth made her shiver wildly, for it was a violent contrast to the pulsing heat of him against her thigh.

"Carson," she whispered, feeling the restraint in every ridge of muscle on his back. "You don't have to hold back. I'm—"

Lara's words became a cry of passionate surprise and pleasure as his fingertips slid beneath the silky peignoir and stroked the soft skin behind her knee.

GET 2 BOOKS FREE!

To get your 2 free books, affix this peel-off sticker to the reply card and mail it today!

MIRA® Books, The Brightest Stars in Fiction, presents

The Best of the Best™

Superb collector's editions of the very best books by some of today's best-known authors!

★ **FREE BOOKS!**   To introduce you to "The Best of the Best" we'll send you 2 books ABSOLUTELY FREE!

★ **FREE GIFT!**   Get an exciting surprise gift FREE!

★ **BEST BOOKS!**   "The Best of the Best" brings you the best books by some of today's most popular authors!

GET 2

HOW TO GET YOUR
2 FREE BOOKS AND FREE GIFT!

1. Peel off the MIRA® sticker on the front cover. Place it in the space provided at right. This automatically entitles you to receive two free books and an exciting surprise gift.

2. Send back this card and you'll get 2 "The Best of the Best™" books. These books have a combined cover price of $11.98 or more in the U.S. and $13.98 or more in Canada, but they are yours to keep absolutely FREE!

3. There's <u>no</u> catch. You're under <u>no</u> obligation to buy anything. We charge nothing — ZERO — for your first shipment. And you don't have to make any minimum number of purchases — not even one!

4. We call this line "The Best of the Best" because each month you'll receive the best books by some of today's most popular authors. These authors show up time and time again on all the major bestseller lists and their books sell out as soon as they hit the stores. You'll like the convenience of getting them delivered to your home at our special discount prices . . . and you'll love your *Heart to Heart* subscriber newsletter featuring author news, horoscopes, recipes, book reviews and much more!

5. We hope that after receiving your free books you'll want to remain a subscriber. But the choice is yours — to continue or cancel, anytime at all! So why not take us up on our invitation, with no risk of any kind. You'll be glad you did!

6. And remember...we'll send you a surprise gift ABSOLUTELY FREE just for giving THE BEST OF THE BEST a try.

SPECIAL FREE GIFT!
We'll send you a fabulous surprise gift, absolutely FREE, simply for accepting our no-risk offer!

Visit us online at
www.mirabooks.com

® and TM are registered trademarks of Harlequin Enterprises Limited.

BOOKS FREE!

Her leg flexed in sensual response, opening her body to his touch. His hands stroked lightly, tracing her thighs, brushing over the midnight hair that concealed so many honeyed secrets.

The silky caress of the peignoir retreating up her body, the whispering touch of Carson's mouth and the tangible warmth of the sunlight pouring over her bare legs made Lara moan. When she felt the brush of Carson's fingers behind her other knee, she drew up that leg as well, giving herself to Carson and the sun. Though he knelt between her legs so closely that she could feel the brushing of his rigid flesh against her softness with each hard beating of his heart, still he did not take what she wanted so much to give.

Lara called Carson's name as flames of need licked over her. The word was a throaty plea, then a gasp as the peignoir slid up over her breasts to reveal the pale, satin skin and the velvety hardness of her nipples.

"Raspberries and cream," Carson said huskily. "I could eat you, little fox. You give yourself to me so sweetly that I—" His voice thickened. "There aren't any words. There's only this."

Carson's tongue touched each nipple and delicately traced the aureole, savored Lara's visible trembling at each touch. He took off the frothy lace peignoir and let it slide from his fingers, wanting nothing between his body and the woman who came to him so perfectly. Slowly, as gently as sunlight itself, he kissed her lips and the hollow of her neck, the creamy swell of her breasts and their deep pink crowns, the shadow pool of her navel and the smooth curves of her thighs. His hands moved over her legs in tantalizing caresses, shifting her subtly with each touch until her legs were drawn up against her body in a gesture of trust and sensual abandon.

At the first touch of his fingertips tracing her layered softness, waves of pleasure radiated through Lara. She opened her eyes and tried to say Carson's name, but all that came out was a broken sound of pleasure as he looked into her eyes and caressed her again. He smiled as he felt her melting at his touch, wanting him. The slow, sweet friction of his palm made her moan. Lara tried to tell Carson that she needed him, but all that came out was a husky sound. A languid fire spread up from his caress, ravishing her as sweetly as his touch. She tried to speak again but forgot the words as she felt him slowly begin to take her. The sensation was so exquisite that she closed her eyes and her body arched helplessly, silently pleading for more of him. He answered her with a small rocking motion that sent showers of pleasure through her. His name came from her lips in a ragged sigh when he finally filled her, only to retreat slowly, leaving her empty once more.

"Carson," she whispered, looking up into male eyes that were dark pools of need and a pleasure so intense that it was nearly pain.

Slowly he came to her again, filling her completely, rocking against her gently, perfectly, teaching her with every sweet movement that passion could be expressed in many ways; and that pleasure could build so subtly, almost secretly, that there was no warning of the ecstasy poised to consume her. Seeing his face taut and his powerful body misted with sweat, feeling him move with such restraint inside her, suddenly made her body unravel in tiny, endless ripples that were so exquisite she wept without knowing it.

Carson held himself tightly within Lara, both sharing and increasing her climax with small, powerful movements of his body. Then he was overtaken even as she had been, and he poured himself into her until he cried out unknowingly, consumed by an ecstasy both fierce and endlessly sweet.

When the last aftershocks of pleasure finally stopped sweeping through their joined bodies, Carson kissed away the tears caught in Lara's black lashes. He rolled onto his side, taking her with him, holding her close. The breeze lifted a corner of the comforter. He caught it and pulled it over Lara, kissing her with tender care. She smiled and curled more closely against him, loving him so much that she was afraid to put it into words because she didn't want him to think that she was asking him to say the words in return.

Finally, with aching tenderness, Lara brushed her lips against Carson's warm, salty skin and relaxed completely in his arms. He returned the kiss as gently as it had been given to him, holding Lara close while she drifted into sleep, holding her and wishing with all his strength that he could absorb her into his very soul, shaking with the force of that wish.

"Little fox," he whispered, "what am I going to do if you leave me?"

There was no answer but the wind lifting Lara's hair across Carson's cheek in a silky caress.

Chapter 12

"Mmmm," Lara murmured as Carson slowly released her mouth from his kiss, "I thought I was bribing you into bringing my research papers. Now I wonder who's bribing whom?"

A smile that was both beautiful and oddly haunted transformed Carson's face. Even though Lara had been up and around for a week, fear still clutched at Carson's heart every time he remembered how helpless she had been in the library when he had found her.

"I'm bribing you," he admitted huskily, looking down at Lara as she sat cross-legged on the bed, fully dressed. "I want you to take it easy, even though Dr. Scott said you could go out and brand calves if that's what you wanted to do. Stay here. Be here when I come back."

The urgency beneath Carson's words caught at Lara. "Don't worry about me," she said, taking his hand and bringing it to her lips. "I'm fine, Carson. Good as new. Better," she added, grinning and putting a hand on her slightly rounded stomach. "I'm twice as good. Go on and take care of the ranch. I hate to think of how much work you've put off to take care of me the last two weeks."

"After the fever broke, I enjoyed every bit of it." Carson hesitated, then looked at Lara with eyes that were intent, luminous…oddly haunted. "You've given me so much, Lara," he said simply. "More than I can tell you. If I've been able to give even a small part of it back to you, I'm glad."

The door closed gently behind Carson, leaving Lara alone but not lonely. The echo of Carson's deep voice and the memory of the golden warmth of his eyes as he looked at her made loneliness impossible. Smiling, she reached for the stack of documents that dealt with the legal aspects of the Rocking B's history from 1940 to 1960.

Feeling more vital and alive than she had in years, Lara tackled the last two decades of the Rocking B's history that she needed for her thesis. There were many papers dealing with small loans for seed and fertilizer, loans that were repaid within nine months. Some of the notes amounted to little more than IOUs written by hand on notebook paper. Others were more formal.

One document in particular intrigued Lara. It was

dated March 17, 1949, and signed by Larry Black-ridge, but it hadn't been drawn up by any of the Don-ovan lawyers. If the first page was anything to go by, the document seemed to detail the circumstances un-der which Larry Blackridge would borrow at no in-terest a large sum of money from Monroe White.

"White," muttered Lara. "White. Have I heard that name before in connection with the Rocking B? A shirttail relative of some kind? Must be. Who else would loan money with no collateral and no inter-est?"

Lara pulled over a notebook and began to read, pen poised to take notes. The more she read, the less sense the document made. Wryly she reminded herself that impenetrable prose was a common problem in legal documents. With a sigh she began the first page all over.

Gradually Lara realized that she was reading a pre-nuptial agreement between Sharon Harrington and Lawrence Blackridge. Monroe White was Sharon's maternal grandfather, a man of enormous wealth. Once the legal language was boiled down, the details emerged in all their emotionless austerity. Sharon, a woman of thirty-four years, was to be wife "in every sense of the word" to Larry, a man of twenty-four years. In return for said marriage, she would bring a dowry of fifteen thousand dollars, which would im-mediately be given to her husband. In addition, the White family would agree to guarantee loans at no interest for the future development of the Rocking B as long as the marriage remained intact.

The document went on for page after page of all but unreadable fine print, yet the basic meaning was inescapable. Monroe White had purchased a nearly bankrupt rancher for his beloved, regrettably unattractive spinster granddaughter. Larry had married Sharon not out of love but out of desperation; he had been on the verge of losing the ranch that meant more to him than anything else in the world. White had been a shrewd negotiator. Nowhere did the document allow for Larry to divorce Sharon without immediate forfeiture of the Rocking B. If Sharon wanted the divorce, she in turn forfeited all right to the Rocking B, to repayment of past loans and to custody of any children of their union.

Unconsciously Lara sighed as she set aside the sad circumstances underlying Larry's marriage. The document answered one question left over from Lara's own childhood. She now knew why Larry hadn't married the mother of his illegitimate child. He had loved Becky, but he had loved the Rocking B more. As for Sharon… If the rumors Lara had heard all her life were true, in the beginning Sharon had loved Larry Blackridge with a spinster's hopeless passion for a man too young and too handsome to come to her without the lure of money.

And in the end Sharon had hated Larry with all the fury of a woman scorned.

Frowning, Lara returned to the documents. Nothing

unexpected turned up until nearly six years later. There was a terse note signed by a doctor at the Mayo Clinic, who bluntly stated that Sharon Harrington Blackridge was sterile beyond the ability of medical science to cure. Three weeks later another legal document appeared. This, too, had not originated in the offices of Donovan, Donovan and Donovan. In exchange for unspecified ''expense money,'' an unnamed minor agreed to turn over her baby for adoption by the Blackridges. Two months later baby John Doe legally became Carson Harrington Blackridge, son and heir of Lawrence and Sharon Blackridge. The day the adoption was registered, the sum of one hundred thousand dollars was transferred to the Rocking B's ranch accounts from the estate of Monroe White.

Tears blurred Lara's eyes for a moment. Behind the stark fiscal transactions were lives that cried out with pain. She knew from her research that the three years preceding Carson's adoption had been devastating for the Rocking B. Falling beef prices, brutal blizzards, disease—all the bad luck that ranchers are subject to had descended simultaneously on the Rocking B. Larry had gone deeper and deeper into debt. In the end he had been forced to choose between his dream of conceiving a blood heir and ownership of the Rocking B itself.

Nowhere in all the massive legalese was there any clause indicating Larry's willingness to love the child he had bought and then adopted; but then, nowhere in the Blackridge history had Lara found any indi-

cation that love had been important to Larry. The land
was, though. That and blood relationships. In the end,
the land had been the stronger obsession.

Without realizing it, Lara rested her hand just below her waist as though to reassure the unborn child
that it was wanted, loved and would be cared for with
all the understanding she and Carson could command.
The baby would never become a pawn in a power
struggle between mother and father as Carson had
been between Sharon and Larry. The baby would
never have to look in a mirror as Carson had done
and know that he hadn't been wanted, not really, not
as a child to be loved. Sharon had wanted a family.
She had bought both the child and Larry's compliance
in an adoption that it was obvious he had never
wanted. Larry's price had been one hundred thousand
dollars.

Sadly Lara put aside the thought of how it must
have been for Carson as a child, growing up unwanted
by the only father he had ever known. Tears blurred
her vision. She forced herself to control them. If she
thought about Carson now she would lose all the
emotional distance from her subject that a researcher
must have. Later she would think about the personal
sadness, the irreversible pain. Later she would cry for
the lonely boy who had become the man she loved.

Grimly Lara returned to the papers. She almost
missed the document that indirectly had shaped her
own childhood. It was another loan paper, another
transfer of White money to the Rocking B's empty

coffers. It was the loan that had made possible the doubling of the Rocking B's boundaries, creating an empire in fact as well as in Larry's dreams. What caught Lara's eye was the document's date—six months to the day before she was born.

The paper contained a clause which stated that Larry would never, in any covert or overt way, acknowledge any but legitimate offspring. If he died before Sharon, the ranch would go in its totality to her and Carson. If she died first, her half would be held in trust for Carson, with Larry acting as administrator. If Larry tried at any time to will, sell, assign, give away or use as collateral for a loan any part of the ranch to anyone except Sharon or Carson Blackridge, all debts owed to the White estate would become immediately due and payable in full.

In effect, if Larry acknowledged Lara as his illegitimate daughter, he would lose the Rocking B. There was no way he could have repaid the huge "loans" the White estate had made to the ranch through the years unless he sold the land itself.

"My God," Lara said softly to herself, setting aside the document with a shaking hand. "How Sharon must have hated Larry, hated my mother, hated me. Sharon held the Rocking B like a sword over Larry's head for almost forty years. He must have hated her in return—and the 'son' she had forced him to accept as an heir when all Larry had ever wanted was a child of his own blood to inherit the ranch that had been Blackridge land since the Civil War.''

It eased an old, old hurt to know that Larry hadn't refused to acknowledge Lara because he was in some way ashamed of her. The man who had smiled so indulgently into Becky's camera hadn't scorned the child of that illicit affair. He had been a man caught in a cruel vise. The fact that it had been largely a vise of his own creation didn't make the situation less painful or the outcome any less tortured.

And then a thought came like black lightning, dragging darkness and cold behind. Carson must have hated Becky, hated Lara. They had the one thing he did not have—Larry's approval.

''Oh, Carson,'' Lara said softly, looking blindly down at the documents scattered across the bed. ''How terrible it must have been for you. And how ironic that from such hatred came such beauty for us. If you hadn't wanted to get even with Larry four years ago, you never would have come close enough to me to know me as myself rather than as a living symbol of so much of your unhappiness.''

Tears burned in Lara's eyes as she remembered that night four years ago. But they were tears of a different sort, understanding rather than humiliation, shared pain rather than shame.

''The miracle, my love,'' she whispered, ''is that you didn't utterly destroy me four years ago when you had the chance. How hard it must have been for you to walk away from the revenge you had wanted all your life.''

Lara closed her eyes and tried not to cry as she realized how close she had come to never knowing Carson as a friend and lover, husband and father of her child. All those sad, tangled lives, a past that had been so cruel that Carson simply refused to discuss it even now, just as he refused to believe in love. She didn't blame him for that. If she had been raised as he had been, watching what ''love'' had done to Sharon and Becky and Larry, she doubted that she would be strong enough to risk what would certainly seem like the agony of love.

''Someday you'll understand, Carson,'' she whispered, running her fingers slowly over the thick, smooth surface of the paper in her lap. ''The past is behind us, not in front of us. Their sadness isn't ours, nor are their hatreds. We're beyond that. We've found our own battles. And we've won.''

Yet even as Lara whispered the words, tears slid silently down her cheeks. The documents she had just read had made the huge book of history turn over a new leaf, bringing her a new understanding of the past and the present. The new knowledge was poignant, even painful. She had a deeper understanding of why Carson sometimes watched her with haunted eyes. He had never been loved. Even now he found it all but impossible to believe in her love, and so he expected it to be taken away without warning.

Let the dead bury the dead, and the living get on

with living. The past can't do anything for the present except ruin it.

How many times had Carson said those words to her in one variation or another?

And how many times had she tried to make him understand her love for all the small acts and large emotions of history that had shaped the present?

Carson's hostility to the past was as deeply rooted as Lara's fascination with it. No, that was wrong. His hostility was greater. He feared and hated the past because it had almost destroyed him. He was still fighting it, still trying to climb out from under the cold dead weight of the past and live securely in the warm possibilities of the present.

Lara knew that it wasn't an easy process for Carson. Last night she had awakened to find him sitting up in bed, rigid. His skin had been clammy to her touch. She had been afraid that he was having a relapse of the flu that had made everyone on the Rocking B so miserable, but when she had asked him if he felt all right, he had said only *I dreamed you were gone.* Then he had made love to her with aching intensity, as though he were trying to take her into himself all the way to his soul. Even when they finally slept again, he had held her tightly, as though he still feared waking and finding her gone.

And what had he said this morning as he left her surrounded by the heaped documents of the past? *Stay here. Be here when I come back.*

Lara brushed futilely at the tears that welled more

quickly than her hand could carry them away. The understanding of the depth of Carson's past wounding was as painful to her as if she herself had been the one raised without love. She wanted to go to Carson, to tell him that she loved him and would never leave him, to hold him and be held by him in turn. Yet even as the impulse came, she knew that it was more for her own comfort than for Carson's. The hurt was new to her. It wasn't to him. It was as much a part of his life as the Rocking B itself.

"Use your head, not your heart," she told herself, wiping away the last of her tears. "You can't change in a day the lessons that took Carson a lifetime to learn, and it's both stupid and cruel of you to try. You know it's all right to believe in love because you've always been loved. Carson has only allowed himself to be loved by you for a few months. Give him enough time to let love become part of his past as well as his present. Then he'll be able to look at the future without fear. That's how you can heal him. Hold him when he wakes up in the middle of the night. Be there in the morning. Love him."

Gradually Lara's tears dried as she forced herself to stop thinking about Carson and get to work sorting and sticking two decades of Rocking B legal documents into neat piles. When she finished, she labeled and set aside the piles with a feeling of relief. Research had never been an unpleasant chore for her, but these last two decades of the Rocking B's history had simply been too painful for her to enjoy researching them. The worst was over, though. No more basic research had to be done. She could begin to organize her paper.

As a reward for a hard job conscientiously completed, Lara turned to the box of Cheyenne's journals that Carson had brought over from the homestead for her to read. She loved the spare wit and deeply felt descriptions of the land that were the hallmarks of her grandfather's observations on the ranch, people and life. She had read through all Cheyenne's journals except the one dealing with the years of her own life because she hadn't needed those years for her research. Nor had she felt strong enough to deal with her own past before this moment. But after seeing the circumstances that had shaped Carson's life, she turned to her own history as to a healing balm.

Lara lifted the heavy leather-bound book onto her lap and leaned against the bedstead for support. One of the enduring threads of her childhood had been the image of Cheyenne pulling a big leather book from a locked cupboard and going to the kitchen. On the nights when Cheyenne had spent hours writing by lamplight, or when he had carefully fastened photos, letters and other small mementos to the pages, Lara had watched, fascinated.

When she had asked to look at the whole book, her grandfather had always gently refused, saying that he was writing a personal history that shouldn't be read until he had told the last word. After all, there wasn't much point in reading a book without an ending, was there?

Lara had never been able to refute that logic, and, in time, Cheyenne had written the last word.

As soon as Lara opened the book, she confronted her own history staring back at her. There was a picture of her mother at fourteen, standing between two big men. One of them was Cheyenne. One was Larry. She had an arm around each man and her head tilted in laughter. She was giving Larry a sidelong glance that was a compound of mischief and elemental female awareness of an attractive male. Larry was looking at her with an odd expression on his face, as though a stranger stood in the place of the girl he had expected to find. The picture was dated two years before Lara's birth. Beneath the picture was a single line of Cheyenne's elegant writing. The writing was dated the day of Lara's birth.

Sometimes I think it all began that day.

For a moment Lara had to fight an impulse to close the book. She felt like an eavesdropper. The thought brought a bittersweet smile to her mouth. Wasn't eavesdropper just another name for historian? If she could stir through the embers and ashes of strangers' lives, surely she had the courage to stir through her own.

I'm worried about Becky.

There followed a long page of a father's concern over a daughter who was too pretty for his own peace of mind. Nowhere was Larry Blackridge mentioned.

After that there was no entry for several months
except those referring to cattle and the land, the small
crises and triumphs of ranching that had remained un-
changed through history. Finally Lara came to a line
that had been written and then underlined later, with
a note added in the margin giving the date of the
underlining.

*Larry's wife must be giving him hell. He's been
over here more often than he's been home. Becky's
getting a boot out of cooking for 'her men.' Larry's
getting a boot out of it, too. Never known him to laugh
so much.*

In the margin the date was a year to the day before
Lara had been born.

There was more about the ranch on the following
pages and then a segment where pages had been torn
out. On the frayed remainder of one page was the
terse statement: *Some things are better left unsaid.*

Instinctively Lara knew that the missing pages
dealt with Cheyenne's feelings on learning that his
young daughter was pregnant with Larry Blackridge's
child. Lara closed her eyes for a moment, wishing that
her own birth hadn't caused so much pain for the
people she loved.

She turned the page and saw a cardboard-mounted
picture of a newborn baby, wrinkled and tiny, staring
unblinkingly into the camera. The cardboard had been
glued over a page of Cheyenne's observations on the
nature of raising cattle in a cold country. Obviously
the picture had been added later. Across the bottom

of the cardboard were a few lines written in an unfamiliar hand. As she read, Lara realized that it was her own mother's handwriting.

You were born today, daughter. You were born to me and only to me. You are mine in a way no one else will ever be. I will call you Lara, which means 'shining,' because you are the light cast by my love for Larry. Hello, Lara Chandler, with your rosy cheeks and tiny little fingers. I love you.

Tears welled again behind Lara's eyes. She ran her fingertips over the lines as though through them she could touch the woman who had died before her daughter ever truly knew her. Staring blindly at the page, Lara wished suddenly that she could tell her mother so many things, not the least of which was that Lara had loved her, too.

There were other lines on the cardboard, lines written by Cheyenne.

Found this after Becky's funeral. Figured it was a more fitting way to welcome a child into the world than the poison that spilled out of me when I first found out Becky was pregnant.

Lara smoothed her fingertips lightly over the words. How like Cheyenne to overcome his own bitter disappointment and grow into a larger love. Never once had he made Lara feel like anything but a beloved, welcome addition to his family. Never once had he even hinted that the birth of his granddaughter wasn't every bit as joyous an event as the birth of his own daughter had been.

"You were a rare man, grandfather," whispered Lara. "You gave so much to me. I'm glad that you lived long enough for me to love you in return."

The pages turned beneath Lara's fingers, pages revealing Becky's love for Larry, pages detailing Cheyenne's stoic acceptance of what he could not change. Only rarely did Cheyenne's anger surface, and then only at what he perceived as an injustice toward the one truly innocent party in the whole tangle—Lara.

The Queen Bitch got on her high horse again. Told me I couldn't bring 'that bastard' to the Christmas party. I told her I'd see her in hell before I'd hurt my own granddaughter and that, if she didn't want us at the party, she'd better be standing in the doorway with a shotgun and a round in the chamber.

And then a few days later:

Larry apologized for the QB. Said Lara was of course welcome to the Christmas party. I told Larry that if he didn't muzzle that bitch on the subject of Lara, he could find himself another ramrod. I don't blame his wife for hating Becky, but I'm damned if I can see any reason to take it out on Lara. A sweeter child God never made.

The pages turned faster and faster beneath Lara's hands, memories swirling around her, history changing with each new insight, each new understanding, each new point of view. Her mother died in a mountain storm, leaving behind a child who didn't understand why she was alone. Larry's mistress died in a mountain storm, leaving behind a man who became more cruel with the passing of each loveless day. Cheyenne's daughter died in a mountain storm, leaving behind a father who knew only that Becky had loved well but not wisely. An adulteress had died in a mountain storm, leaving behind her lover's wife, a woman whose emotions had twisted and shrunk until nothing was left of her but a single-minded desire for revenge on the man who had never loved her.

And through all the seething years, an adopted boy grew up always beyond the reach of love, always wanting it, never having it, until finally he believed that vengeance, not love, was the only human emotion that endured.

In a strange way Becky's death brought together the two men who had shared her life. When life had troubled either Larry or Cheyenne, they sought each other out, sometimes to talk, often simply to share a silence that demanded nothing, because each man knew that there was too much between them ever to be either described or eased with something as intangible as speech. Each crisis in their lives was bluntly stated in Cheyenne's increasingly frail hand. By the time Lara turned fourteen, Sharon Blackridge had had her first bout of cancer and surgery. When the cancer recurred, Larry came to Cheyenne in the middle of a spring blizzard.

Larry wants me to make sure that Lara doesn't marry anyone until Sharon is dead. I told him that seeing as how Lara is only fourteen, he didn't need to get all in a lather about her love life just yet. He

*didn't say a word, just looked at me. I knew then that
he'd had Becky before she was fifteen.*

*Came real close to killing him right then. Hadn't
felt that way in years. Hope I never do again.*

It was a long time before Larry's name was mentioned in the journal. Lara read about the ranch, her
grandfather's pride in her grades and his regret that
he wasn't rich enough to send her to college. The
pages turned and the years with them, and she was
working at the café in town.

I'm worried about Lara.

The words went through Lara like a cold wind,
echo of Cheyenne's worries years before, when
Becky was young.

*Heard that Carson was courting her. A good man
and a fine cattleman, but lacking tenderness. And
she's such a gentle little thing. Considered warning
her, but didn't. Everybody's got to measure his own
dreams. She's eighteen, and she's had a crush on him
since she was thirteen.*

*Hell, I should go down on my knees and thank God
that Carson didn't notice her sooner, like Larry did
Becky—or if Carson did notice, he was too damned
decent to seduce a child.*

*Good thing the Queen Bitch is too sick to care
about gossip. She'd make life hell for Carson and
Lara both.*

The entries became more and more sparse, with
greater lengths of time separating them, as Cheyenne's health began to decline. Larry's first stroke

was noted, as was Cheyenne's own heart attack. Sharon Blackridge's long, slow descent into death was recorded, ending with the day of her funeral.

Lara turned the page, began to read and felt reality dropping away from beneath her feet in an icy, terrifying rush. She read the lines, then read them again, unable to believe, refusing to believe. Yet even as she fought the truth, she felt a page turning over, history shifting inexorably, revealing a new part of the past, a new clue to a truth that tore mercilessly at her soul. She wanted to hurl the book from her, to scream denials, to tear the page out and burn it to ash as bitter as the end of her dreams; but all she did was numbly read the lines again and again, hoping against hope that she was wrong.

First day back from the hospital. Good to be here again, but I came home to die and I know it. It's time and then some. All that holds me here is little Lara. She's such a gentle thing. I pray to God that she'll find a man worthy of her, but I doubt that I'll live to see it. She hasn't so much as looked at a man since she stopped seeing Carson a few years ago. I wonder if—

There was a break in the sentence and in the journal, as though something had interrupted Cheyenne. His next words told Lara what that interruption had been.

Larry came. Told me that he'd finally outfoxed the Queen Bitch. She thought she'd fixed it so that he would never have a child of his own blood inherit the ranch. But as soon as she died, Larry drew up a new will. When Larry dies, Carson has one year to marry Lara. No marriage, no inheritance. And it has to be a real marriage. Carson has two years to get a child or to prove that Lara is sterile.

After a long time Lara forced herself to stop reading and rereading the lines as though she could somehow make the words change by sheer effort of will. She turned the page with a hand so cold that she couldn't feel the heavy texture of the paper. There were no more entries in Cheyenne's journal.

Lara turned back to Cheyenne's last entry, irrationally hoping the words had changed. They hadn't. She closed her eyes, unable to bear the rich sunlight flowing through the windows over the bed. She tried to think constructively, to apply her intelligence to this discovery as she would have to any other new historical fact, but all her thoughts revolved relentlessly around Carson's cruel deception, returning to it again and again, unable to think past it.

An act. All of it. He never wanted me. Not four years ago. Not now. An act. All of it. He never wanted me. Never wanted. Never. Me.

Lara wished that she could cry to ease the ache and burning of her eyes, but no tears come. She felt as though all her strength had vanished in a single terrible instant, leaving her worn and old, unable to cry out in anger or agony or even despair, a stranger in her own body, a stranger in her own life.

She had been so sure of herself and love, so sure

that her understanding of reality was valid and Carson's was not.

She had been wrong.

There was a reason Carson had never said he loved her. He didn't. He never would. Four years ago he had sought her out for the sake of revenge on Larry Blackridge, but Carson hadn't been cruel enough to follow through. Four months ago he had sought her out because she was the key to ownership of the Rocking B. That was the "mistake" Carson had referred to when she had asked why he wanted her back. He had let her get away four years ago when he had her roped, thrown and ready for branding. But he hadn't known at the time that Sharon would die and Larry would attach unthinkable terms to the inheritance of the Rocking B.

There was also a reason Carson hadn't tried to protect her from pregnancy. It wasn't because he had been too caught up in the passions of the moment to remember to guard against conception. It wasn't even because deep down inside himself he had wanted to have a child to raise and love. It was because the sooner she was pregnant, the sooner he was secure in his claim on the Rocking B.

Like Larry, Carson had wanted only the land. Like Larry, Carson had married a woman he didn't love in order to keep the Rocking B.

Lara heard the front door slam and wished suddenly that she had had the sense to flee while she could. Yet even as the thought came, she knew it was too late. The pages of history had already turned, taking her with them, imprisoning her in a world she had understood too late. She was married. She was pregnant.

And she was in love with a man who loved only the land.

Was that how her mother had felt? Caught in a trap of her own making? Pregnant. In love with the wrong man. No place to flee because everywhere she went she would drag the heavy golden chains of her love behind, chains anchoring her to a man who loved the land more than he loved the mother of his child.

History repeating itself generation to generation, a loveless legacy of ambition and power passed from father to son, world without end, amen. Bitterly Lara thought that maybe the traditional historians were right. Maybe men had always loved the land and the glory more than they had loved the women who made their damned dynasties possible.

World without end, amen.

Chapter 13

"Lara, that Canadian storm is sweeping a few loons down our way," called Carson from the stairway, coming closer with each word. "If the storm holds off, let's go out to the pond and listen to them sing to the rising moon. It's the most beautiful—" Carson's words stopped abruptly when he saw her. "Lara? What's wrong, honey? Are you sick again? Should I call Dr. Scott?"

Eyes closed, Lara made a weary gesture with her right hand. "It's all right, Carson. You don't have to pretend anymore."

Confusion replaced concern on his face. "Pretend? Pretend what?"

"That you care."

"About what? The loons? Honey, you're not making any sense."

"About me." Lara's hand went over her womb. "About us," she whispered.

Carson went very still. "What the hell are you talking about?"

"About the sins of the fathers," Lara said bitterly, feeling a hot, almost violent rush of anger through her blood. She looked at Carson for the first time, and her eyes were black with pain and unwanted knowledge. Her words were tight, formal, as though she had chosen them for a treatise. "About history and land and the inheritance thereof. About men who love the land more than they love anything else, even the women who love them. About Larry and Sharon and Becky. About you and me. About the Rocking B and marriage."

Lara watched Carson's expression become as bleak as her voice. Without a word he came to stand over her. He saw the open journal, spun it around and read the last page. He began to swear tonelessly, the words all the more terrible for their lack of emotion. He turned toward her, reaching out to hold her.

"Lara—" he said hoarsely.

She knew then beyond any doubt that it was true, every word of it, every cruel betrayal. She flinched from Carson's hands. "*Don't.* The act is over. You had your dream. I had mine. Too bad they both couldn't come true."

Carson's hands flashed out and closed on Lara's face, pinning her beneath his glance. "It's not what you think! I wanted you before Larry ever wrote his goddamned will!'' Carson forced himself to slow down, to take a deep breath, to cope with the disaster he had foreseen and yet had prayed would never come. ''What we have is too good to throw away. When you get past your first anger, you'll see that,'' he said urgently. ''You have to. I won't let you go, little fox.''

''Why? You've got all you ever wanted—revenge and the Rocking B. Or was there something in the fine print of Larry's will that Cheyenne missed? Some kind of bizarre minimum time limit for marital relations?'' asked Lara, and the bitterness of her words drew her mouth into a thin downward curve.

Carson's eyelids flickered, the only pain he allowed himself to reveal. He had known this might happen, but he had hoped so desperately that whatever they had built together would withstand the blow. Now the cold certainty was growing that he had been wrong. The blow had come too soon. She looked too pale, too remote, as icy and untouchable as a winter moon.

Chills chased over Carson's skin.

''Do you really want to know the fine print?'' he asked, his expression bleak.

''I'd be a fool if I didn't. I'm tired of being a fool.''

Slowly Carson released Lara from his grasp. ''You want revenge, is that it?'' he asked, curiosity and something else in his tone, something very like the agony that was clawing at Lara. ''I guess I can't blame you for that.''

"I want to know the dimensions of the fool's paradise I've been living in," she corrected.

"'Fool's paradise.' Is that how you think of our time together?"

"Spare me the fake sentiment," Lara said, clenching her hands together. "I can take the rest but not that. Not that!"

"Lara," Carson said achingly, reaching toward her again.

When she flinched away, his hands dropped to his side. He closed his eyes. He had anticipated losing her, but he hadn't known how much it would hurt. He hadn't allowed himself to know. He had told himself that she loved him. Surely she would understand that he had wanted her as well as the land. But she didn't. And when he thought about it, he couldn't blame her for that, either. He had gambled on her love being great enough to hold them together, no matter what. He had lost.

Carson's eyes opened slowly. There was nothing to show what he was feeling except the deep brackets on either side of his mouth.

"Cheyenne hit the high points well enough. The rest is simple," Carson said, his voice so controlled that it was toneless. "In the event of a divorce, the Rocking B's title is transferred to our children, with me retained as ranch manager until the day I die, unless I'm the one who sues for divorce. In that case the ranch simply goes to Larry's grandchildren and I drop out of sight as though I'd never been born, never lived on the Rocking B, never—'' The words ended in an abrupt silence.

"And if there are no grandchildren?'' Lara asked quietly.

Carson went absolutely pale. He tried to speak but could not.

Lara saw his agonized fear that she would end the pregnancy, and beneath her anger pain turned and cried out. *Why couldn't he have loved me just a little? Why do I have to feel his pain even now? Will it ever end? Will that child I'm carrying even now grow up only to break its heart on the cruel realities of the past?*

"Don't worry, Carson,'' she said tiredly. "You won't lose the Rocking B at this stage in the game. I won't get an abortion just to get even with you. There's been enough cruelty and vindictiveness in the history of the Rocking B. I won't be part of it any longer.''

Slowly Lara closed Cheyenne's journal and set it aside. As she did, other answers came to her, other pages of history turning and bringing new understanding of her recent past with Carson Blackridge.

"No wonder you didn't want me going over all the old Blackridge documents,'' Lara said. "You were afraid I'd find out about the will. When were you going to tell me? After the child was born?'' She stared at Carson for a moment and understood. "You weren't going to tell me at all, were you?''

"You were happy," he said simply. "What possible good would have come from making you sad?"

Lara had no answer for that but her own pain radiating through her in waves, threatening to overwhelm her. She couldn't allow that. She had to think. She had to act. She had to decide how she was going to spend the rest of her life.

But no matter how fiercely she tried, nothing came to her mind except pain. She closed her eyes and wished again that she could cry. She felt Carson's hard, warm hands gently circling her face, tilting her up to meet his eyes.

"Has it been so bad being married to me, little fox?"

The tears that Lara couldn't cry raked her throat, all but choking her. "When I thought that you wanted me…that someday you might come to love me." She swallowed, but it didn't help. Her mouth was as dry as her eyes. "Living with you was very beautiful. But now that I know you never wanted me—" A shudder racked her. "Oh, God," she said hoarsely, "why didn't you tell me why you wanted me to come back to the ranch?"

"I've wanted you for years. You were afraid of me. If I'd told you, you would have run again, the way you had been running for years. And by the time you were no longer afraid of me." Carson looked hungrily at Lara's dark, haunted eyes and the pale, beautiful bow of her mouth. "I liked seeing you happy, little fox. I liked what we had together in bed. I liked having you run toward me, smiling.''

"Yes," Lara whispered bleakly. "I can believe that. It meant that you had the Rocking B locked up tight.''

"That's not—" began Carson.

"Stop it!" she cried suddenly. "The truth is written all over the Rocking B and the Blackridge history!'' With an effort Lara controlled herself. "I understand why you did what you did. In time I'll even be able to forgive it. But what I can't forgive is the way you let me fall in love with you all over again. Or was that your final revenge on me for being Larry's bastard?''

There was a long silence. At the end of it, Carson looked drawn, older, alone. "Can you look at these last few months and believe that?" he asked.

"Can I look at that damned will and believe anything else?''

There was another long, taut silence. When Carson finally spoke, it was in a tone that Lara hadn't heard for months, clipped and hard; his eyes were the deep, icy amber of a February dawn. Yet there was a yearning beneath his words that twisted Lara's heart.

"That's why I didn't tell you. You said you loved me, but I knew there wasn't enough love in the world for you to believe that I wanted you with or without Larry's will. So I said nothing. I wanted to heal you and myself and the past. I wanted—" Carson's mouth became a hard, bitter, downward curve. "You weren't the fool, little fox. I was. I knew more about love than you did, and yet I still hoped. I should have known better. Sharon loved Larry, and she made his life pure hell. Larry loved Becky, and he put her through a different kind of hell. You loved me and I—'' Carson made a sudden, chopping motion with his hand. "Hell of a thing, love."

Suddenly he turned and walked away. A few moments later Lara heard the sound of the front door closing.

She lay without moving for a long time, trying to think, unable to do anything except hurt. Finally she knew that she couldn't bear being inside the bedroom any longer. She pulled on a light jacket and walked quickly to the only haven left to her, the Chandler homestead.

Yet that, too, had somehow changed. Lara looked around the familiar, worn interior of the homestead and wondered why she should feel a stranger in her own home. She knew every seam, every pit, every gouge in the walls and floor. She knew the faded colors of the throw rugs and the threadbare patterns of the chairs by heart. Each crack and chip in the heavy pottery plates was an old friend, as was the mismatched silverware stacked in wooden drawers whose corners were rounded by use. Every room, every window, every fall of light and shadow in the old house called silently to her, *Remember me?* And the answer was always, *Yes, I remember you.*

Then why did she feel adrift, lost?

Lara's blue-black eyes searched each room as she paced the small house yet again. She had come to the homestead to think because thinking had been impossible at the Blackridge ranch. The things she remembered there were too new, too raw with pain for her to do anything but flinch.

She didn't want to remember the way Carson had looked before he had turned and walked out of the house. He had the ranch. Wasn't that what he had wanted? Land, not love? Then why had he looked so sad and angry? Had she missed some vital page in the history of the past? Had she interpreted the facts of her own personal history mistakenly or too narrowly, with the result that her conclusions outraged truth in the very act of supposedly discovering it?

She had had that kind of distorted focus on reality once before. She had been so sure that Carson had walked out on her four years ago because she was Larry's bastard. So sure...and so wrong. Carson had walked out because he was too decent to seduce a virgin for revenge. That fact hadn't changed with the revelation of Larry's will. That fact remained.

Carson was a decent man.

In school Lara had read scholarly works whose only purpose had been to distort historical facts in the service of the author's own prejudices. She had always felt that those works represented the most distasteful sort of trickery, intellectual lies masquerading as enduring truth. But was she doing that very same thing now? Had she remembered only the most damning incidents from the past four months, and had she interpreted them in only the most damning ways?

Why did the light go out of Carson's eyes when he knew that I had discovered the truth? He had what he wanted. Didn't he?

Didn't he?

There was no answer but the wild cry of a Canadian wind flowing around the mountains, wrapping them in clouds.

Suddenly Lara's own skin seemed too small for her. It was the same for the room, the house itself. She had to be outside. She had to be beneath nothing more than the untamed sky, had to see nothing smaller than the massive thrust of mountains, had to hear nothing but the long cry of the wild wind.

At that instant Lara realized why her mother had always walked out alone during the most violent thunderstorms. In the immense, shattering thunder, no one would hear her scream.

A gust of wind tore the front door of the homestead from Lara's hand. The door banged against the wall, fully open. The door banged again, as though to remind Lara that she had forgotten to close it. She didn't notice. As she hurried out into the yard, she pulled on the mountain parka that she had automatically grabbed from its hook beside the door. Behind her the door banged again, then slammed shut.

Lara scrambled to the top of one of the rolling, grass-covered ridges in back of the homestead and stood for a moment. All around her huge clouds raced and boiled, churned by a muscular wind. Some of the clouds were the color of freshwater pearls. Others were as dark as the mountains whose peaks they concealed. After a glance she hurried on. She knew exactly where she was going. Her mother had taken her there on gentler days, when sunlight rather than thunder poured over the land.

But her mother had also gone there to drink the wild storm winds, and she had gone alone.

Before the first vague forerunners of thunder trembled through the air, Lara reached her destination. A long, rocky spine rose from a grassy ridge. In some places the layered rock had been worn to little more than a jumbled mass of boulders. In other places, a cap of harder rock jutted out over the ridge where softer rock had already been worn away. The result was a low, shallow cave overlooking the valley of the Big Green.

Lara ducked beneath the overhang, sat with her knees pulled up against her chest and waited for the storm to break. And as she waited, thoughts shivered and twisted like clouds called by the raging wind, thoughts escaping her control, reminding her of the very things that she had fled from the Blackridge house in order to forget. She fought the seething memories, throwing back cold truths to take the warmth from a remembered time when she had believed in love. Like the wild wind, the arguments raged in her mind.

Sometimes Carson's hands had trembled when he touched her.

Lust, nothing more. Simply lust. A biological reflex having nothing to do with tenderness and caring and love. He didn't love her.

He had let her fear fade before he touched her. He hadn't pushed her sexually in any way at all. He had kept his promise even when passion had made his whole body hard with need.

If he had pushed, she would have run away and he would have lost the Rocking B.

He had let her undress him. Let her touch him. Had made himself naked and utterly vulnerable to her. Had given himself to her. He had taken all the risks. He hadn't been forced to do that by her fear because her fear had faded with each of his smiles, his deep laughter, his amber eyes approving of her. He could have seduced her much more quickly if he hadn't tied his own hands. After the first weeks she wouldn't have been afraid to make love with him. He must have known that. Yet he had held back. He had kept his word. He had let her come to him.

Lara sat very still, waiting, but there was no cold refutation to take away the warmth of that memory. If seduction had been Carson's only goal, he had acted foolishly by being so restrained. Carson wasn't a foolish man. Therefore, seduction hadn't been his only goal.

With that realization came another memory. It shook Lara like the wind, just as it had shaken her that night in the library when Carson had looked at her with such agony and regret in his eyes for having hurt her years ago: *Oh, God, little fox. There are times when I wish I could crawl out of my skin and die.*

Lara shuddered violently and made a broken sound that was swallowed up by the long howl of the wind. She remembered something else that he had said: *Love is a lie, a trick played on the unwary.* She had been easy prey. She had walked into his arms as trustingly as though he had never betrayed her in the past. But he hadn't betrayed her years ago. Not really. He had stopped short of the cruel, unforgivable act of seduction and revenge.

And then came the cold, undeniable refutation of warmth and companionship. In the end he *had* tricked her. He hadn't told her about Larry's will.

Wind howled and moaned through the valley, bringing an icy foretaste of the storm to come. Thunder rolled in the distance, a vibration more sensed than heard. Below her, scattered at the edge of the wide green valley, was the Blackridge ranch and the Chandler homestead. Her home.

Even as the sight of home reassured Lara at some deep level of her mind, she realized that Carson had never had that kind of reassurance. But he had wanted it. He had needed it. A home. A place that was his own after a lifetime of being told that he didn't belong on the Rocking B because he wasn't a child of Larry's body. How would Lara have felt if she hadn't had the certain knowledge that the Chandler homestead waited for her when the storms of life threatened to tear her apart? How had Carson survived without the silent, enduring presence of home and love to give him strength?

No wonder he had hungered deeply for the Rocking B. It represented the security he had wanted and never gotten from life. With Larry's death the ranch should have become Carson's. He had earned it. It should finally have become the home where he belonged beyond argument or the ability of man to alter. And the ranch had belonged to him—until Larry's will was opened, and Carson was told that, if he wanted the ranch, he had to seduce Lara into marriage and motherhood.

Silently Lara asked herself if she really expected Carson at that point to risk everything he had ever wanted on the goodwill and sympathetic understanding of a girl whom he had hurt so badly that even four years later she ran from the slightest chance of meeting him face-to-face.

And then she remembered that Carson had been trying to see her or lure her to the ranch for more than a year. He had called her faculty advisor and suggested the topic of the Rocking B history while Sharon and Larry Blackridge were still alive. Carson couldn't have known about Larry's will at the time. The will hadn't been drawn up until Sharon died.

I've wanted you for years, dreamed of you until I woke up sweating and tied in knots.

That was why he had tried to get her to the ranch. Lust. Just lust.

Yet even as the cold thought came, Lara found herself unable to believe it. Lust was too simple to explain the complex emotions Carson had shown her. Did a man in the grip of wild lust take such tender care to arouse and then wholly satisfy an inexperienced partner? Did a man who knew only lust sit by a woman's bedside for days while she lay in the grip of a fever that had nothing to do with sex? Did lust drive a man to break his workday and take a woman up to a remote pond—not for a quickie in the grass but to count baby ducks? Did lust make a man cry at the thought of a woman wanting his child?

No.

Then a cold thought came, threatening the warm memories. A man who was worried about getting a woman pregnant and keeping her content might do those things. Marriage was only the first step in securing the Rocking B. The ranch wouldn't be within Carson's control until a child was born.

Lara shivered suddenly, though the wind rarely reached beneath the sheltering overhang. She couldn't believe that Carson was so cold, so calculating, that he would plan and carry out an intricate campaign of gentleness and sharing simply to assure himself of his hold on Lara and the ranch. She just didn't believe it. She didn't know why, but—

She frowned suddenly, reaching back to the blurred time of fever for a memory that was eluding her. She stared out across the land as though the answer were there rather than in her own memory. As sudden lightning stitched across the darkening sky, words came to her, Dr. Scott's and Carson's voices echoing in what Lara had thought was a fever dream but realized now was reality.

I want Lara well. I...need her.

Don't you want the baby, too?

Hell, yes, I want it. But I want Lara more.

Carson couldn't have known that she would hear and remember those words. They couldn't have been the result of calculation rather than emotion. He wanted her more than he wanted the baby that would give him control of the Rocking B.

Yet she had believed that he wanted the land more than anything else.

What if Carson wanted what the ranch represented rather than the land itself? A home. A place to live that was his own. A place where he would be welcomed when he was worn and hungry and cold. A place where he could go to sleep at night and know that someone would smile on seeing him in the morning. A place where he was accepted no matter who his parents were or were not, a place where he was loved whether or not he was perfect in every way.

I'm not perfect. Remember that, and try to forgive me when I fail you.

Had he failed her?

"He doesn't love me!"

Lara didn't know that she had cried out until she

heard her own words echoing back from the overhang. "Love me. Love me. Me. Me." She put her head in her hands and trembled, but her thoughts drove on relentlessly, searching out another page of reality, a different understanding.

Did the fact that Carson didn't love her prove that he had failed her? How would her life have been different or more complete if Carson had loved her? Would he have been a more thoughtful, passionate lover? Would he have taken better care of her when she was sick? Would he have given her small caresses as he passed her chair at night? Would he have surprised her with wildflowers and shiny river stones and a mother duck with a raft of fluffy babies? Would he have fought tears at the realization of how badly he had hurt her four years ago? Would the light have drained out of his eyes when her bitterness poured over him, slicing through his hopes of home and happiness until he—

"Stop!" Lara cried out, as though it were something other than her own words battering her. "Oh, stop—"

But it didn't stop. Ruthlessly Lara's memories and intelligence worked together, pages turning, reality slowly shifting, presenting a new view of its complex truths. Understanding raked through her, forcing her to look at Carson and herself, forcing her to realize that truth came from looking at what a person did rather than what he said or did not say. Carson hadn't said he loved her, *but he had treated her as though she were the most precious thing on earth to him.*

If that wasn't love, what was?

And she, who had cried out her love for Carson, had stripped him of his dreams in a single, bitter torrent of words.

Was that an act of love?

And where was he now, the man she loved? Was he out walking in the storm because he couldn't bear to go back to the pain and emptiness of a house that was no longer a home?

With a choked cry Lara scrambled out from beneath the shelter of the overhang. Instantly the wind swirled around her, flicking tiny whips of ice-tipped rain across her cheeks. She didn't feel it any more than she heard the sudden massive thunder rolling off the peaks. All she heard was the echo of her own questions and the shattering reverberations of her answers.

At first Lara thought that the shout came only from her own need, her own dream. Then it came again, tumbled by the wind, Carson's voice calling her name. She turned and saw a wall of blue-black storm racing toward her from the northwest. Lightning arced in an incandescent dance between cloud and earth. An avalanche of thunder came, shaking the land. Carson rode swiftly toward her in front of the storm, spurring his horse across the land at a speed that made her heart stop with fear. She called his name, knowing that he couldn't hear her, unable to help herself from crying out.

Within minutes Carson brought the horse to a plunging halt in front of Lara. He paused only long enough to swing her up into the saddle in front of him before he put his spurs to the big horse again. It responded with the eagerness of an animal that knew it was finally heading for the shelter of the barn with a storm in violent pursuit.

As the horse raced up to the Rocking B's ranch yard, Willie hurried out of the barn and grabbed the bridle. Cold rain pelted down, mixed with stinging hail. Thunder cracked over the land, burying everything in an endlessly breaking wave of sound. Willie said something, but the words were utterly lost. Carson understood anyway. He kicked out of the stirrups, grabbed Lara and raced for the house as Willie ran with the horse toward the barn.

Lightning came again, strike after strike of white light that bleached color from the land. The bang of the ranch house door was lost beneath hammer blows of thunder so immense that the ear registered only an eerie silence. Cloud and earth slammed together in a massive avalanche of hail.

Lara clung to Carson, trembling as the storm battered the house with stunning violence. All she could think of was that Carson could have been caught out there without shelter, looking for her, and she would have been safe beneath the rock overhang and he wouldn't have known. The pieces of ice that were

even now scouring the land could have scoured his
unprotected body. He could have been thrown, the
horse could have fallen, he could have been hurt and
then he would have lain helpless in the ice and wind
until he died.

That was what had happened to her mother—an icy
trail, a fall, a cold too great for human warmth to
overcome.

Lara looked up into Carson's eyes, wanting to ask
him to forgive her for not understanding him better,
wanting to tell him that she loved him, wanting to say
everything at once. The drumming of hail buried her
words. It was the same for him. She saw his lips moving, saw the burning intensity of his eyes and heard
nothing at all.

She came up on tiptoe, straining toward him, even
as her fingers searched through his thick dark hair,
pulling him toward her. His lips were cold from the
wind and so were hers. She knew that the heat of him
burned beneath, and she knew that she had to reach
it, had to touch the hot rush of his life. She felt herself
being lifted suddenly as his arms came around her
with crushing force. She was holding him the same
way, as though she could become part of him if she
just held him tightly enough. His kiss was a promise
both wild and sweet, a sharing that needed no words.

Around them the storm raced by, taking with it
both thunder and ice, leaving silence behind.

"I'm sorry—"

"—forgive me."

"I should have trusted—"

"—my love. I love you. I love—"

The sudden words glittered in the silence, fragments of overlapping thought and need, and neither he nor she knew who spoke which words, who apologized and who forgave. Their words, like their love, belonged to both of them equally.

Epilogue

"Carson? Is that you? Are you finished already?"
Lara asked.

She looked away from the computer screen, smiling with anticipation and love at Carson as he came into the library, wondering if he had brought something special to share with her. Last week it had been a river stone that looked as though tiny, creamy flowers bloomed within a gray-green matrix. Two weeks ago it had been an evergreen bough perfectly spangled with rain.

And once, in autumn, he had taken her to lie within his arms and listen to a loon's tremulous call while night condensed around them.

"Just something I want you to see," Carson said, bending down and kissing the nape of Lara's neck. "Do you have time?"

She turned and put her hand on his cheek. "For you? Always."

Carson turned and caught Lara's palm against his mouth, silently cherishing her. Then he pulled her to her feet, smiling as she trusted herself to his strength without hesitation.

"How's it coming?" he asked, looking at the computer.

"Much better. You did a wonderful job of matching the men's memories with the Blackridge daguerreotypes," she said, putting her arms around Carson's neck. "Have I thanked you for that?"

"Every day you're with me, every time you smile, but don't let that stop you," Carson murmured, bending down to her lips. "I love the way you thank me. I love thanking you in return."

Gently Carson pulled Lara against him, savoring the soft heat of her mouth, the generosity of her response and the firm, pregnant curve of her body pressed against him. Finally, reluctantly, he released her.

"If we don't get going, the next storm will move in and there won't be anything to show you until spring," he said.

Refusing to answer questions, Carson bundled Lara into a parka and tucked her into the pickup. He drove until he was at the base of a long, low fold of land. The shape of the ridge tickled Lara's memory. Together they climbed the gentle rise. Summer's lush grass had been cured by frost and woven into a dense, tawny mat by autumn rain and wind. Soon the storms of winter would come, pulling a thick white blanket over the land, protecting it while it slept and dreamed, resting in preparation for the sweet violence of spring.

"Close your eyes."

Obediently Lara closed her eyes. She felt the world tilt as Carson lifted her into his arms. Smiling, she hid her face against his warm sheepskin collar, telling him without words that she wouldn't peek. After a time the world shifted again as Carson carefully set her back on her feet.

"Now?" she asked.

Without answering, Carson stepped behind Lara, put his arms around her and pulled her into the sheltering warmth of his body as wind stirred over the open land.

"Now," he said.

Lara looked. Before her the Rocking B's pastures lay on either side of the Big Green's shimmering curves. A scattering of cattle grazed, and a rider wove through them. Except for the fences, little had changed since the first Blackridge had ridden into the valley, gathered a handful of stones and begun to build a new life.

And that was what Carson had brought Lara to see. In front of her, no more than an arm's length away, was the tumbled mound of native stone that had marked the first boundary of the westering dream that had shaped a family, a state and a nation.

"You found it!" Excitement rippled in Lara's

words. "This is where it all began, the Blackridge dream and the Chandlers', all those long years ago. I can touch the very same stones, see the same valley, stand on the same ridgetop—and it's all here, everything!"

Lara turned in Carson's arms, giving him a radiant smile. His hand slid inside her parka, and he spread his fingers wide over her rounded body. Beneath his palm he felt their child stir as though impatient to be born and to walk upon the land as his ancestors had before him and as his own children would in their own time. Carson never tired of feeling that mysterious, eager life beneath his hand, of knowing that his child was growing within Lara.

"Yes," Carson said huskily, brushing his lips across hers. "It's all here, everything, right in my arms, and its name is love. I love you, Lara."

He felt the tremor that went through her as he lifted her into his arms. The kiss they shared was like the wind sweeping over the land, sweet and wild, touching everything, joining the past and the present into a future that would be as beautiful and enduring as history and the land itself.

* * * * *

A WOLF RIVER SUMMER
Barbara McCauley

* * *

To Mary-Theresa Hussey—
an editor whose boundless energy and unwavering
dedication to her work inspires everyone around
her. This one's for you!

Dear Reader,

What a thrill it's been to tell Clay and Paige's story! Clay had been grumbling at me for some time to find him a woman—not just *any* woman, mind you. A dependable, intelligent woman who won't expect love. A woman to willingly share his bed, but not his heart. Ah, but men are such silly creatures, aren't they?

So come along for the ride. It's a wild one, with more than one sharp turn and bump along the way. And the final stop—well, you'll see...

Sincerely,

Barbara McCauley

Chapter 1

When Clay Bodine came to town, folks took notice.

It was a rare sight to see the Wolf River County rancher drive into town in his dusty, black pickup. So rare the residents called his appearances a "Bodine Sighting." Before that black pickup even turned onto Main Street, phones lines were already sizzling, ears were already burning. Curiosity had more than one store owner sweeping a sidewalk they'd swept only an hour before, and window shopping—in spite of the one hundred plus degree heat—tripled in popularity.

For the most part, the good people of Wolf River minded their own business. But small towns were small towns, after all, and the fact that Clay had made himself so scarce for the past fifteen years had created an aura of mystery around him that simply couldn't be ignored. Not that folks didn't understand *why* Bodine had kept his distance. They understood completely. But still, what happened to Clay and his family when he was fifteen was water under the bridge. Though they might not have forgotten, everyone in Wolf River had long since moved past that difficult time.

Everyone except Clay.

Today, Clay's pickup had barely passed the Papa Pete's Diner before noses were pressed to glass, everyone hoping to catch a glimpse of the elusive Texas cattleman. Inside the barbershop, bets were placed where Bodine was headed. George Simon, the barber, laid a buck down it would be Peterson's Feed and Grain. Hugh Foderman doubled the odds it would be the bank. Ronald Weeder put his money on the department store. Clay hadn't been shopping since last Christmas, Weeder said, and the man had needed new boots then.

When the dusty pickup passed the feed and grain store, then the bank, as well, Weeder grinned and stuck his hand out to be paid, only to watch as Clay drove right past the department store, too.

"I'll be damned," Weeder muttered, and all three men stared at Clay's tailgate.

"Where's he going?" Hugh craned his neck.

"Beats me," George said, scratching his ear. "'Cept the hotel, the drugstore and that little antique store, ain't much down at that end of town."

"There's the library," Weeder added.

George and Hugh both hooted at the idea of Clay

Bodine going to the library, then George said, "A buck on the hotel."

"Two bucks on the drugstore," Hugh determined.

Only because he was stubborn as a mule, Weeder folded his arms and lifted one of his two chins. "I'm going with the library."

Stepping out onto the sidewalk to get a better view, the men watched Clay's pickup pass the intersection of Main and Bristle, then pull into a parking spot.

"I'll...be...damned." Weeder shook his head in amazement, then grinned at his dumbfounded buddies. "Pay up, boys."

Paige Andrews made prudent use of her lunch break from Wolf River Library by shopping at the drugstore. She'd made a list just that morning—cotton balls, hair pins, reading glasses, in-sole cushions for her work shoes, a catnip mouse for Eudora and the most recent copy of *Quilter's Monthly*. She lingered over the magazines for a moment, even picked up a copy of *Celebrity Circle* and browsed through it, but since she didn't own a television set, most of the pretty faces inside the glossy pages were unknown to her.

Paige had been thinking about buying a TV. She knew she was probably the only person in Wolf River who didn't own one. For that matter, she was probably the only person in Texas who didn't own one. But her grandmother had not approved of whiling away one's time with "that sort of horsefeathers," so for the past twelve years, the only television Paige had watched had been at her best friend Rebecca's house, or her ongoing Friday evening date at Bernie Pratt's apartment.

Not that anyone would exactly call take-out pizza and watching *Jeopardy* with Bernie and his mother a *date,* but at twenty-six, that was about as exciting as Paige's personal life had been since she'd finished college five years ago.

Still, Grandma Millie had not approved of her only grandchild visiting a man's house unchaperoned. Though Paige had reassured her grandmother that Bernie was well behaved, Grandma Millie had harrumphed. "There better not be any hanky-panky going on, Paige Eloise Andrews," Grandma had said.

If only there were, Paige had always thought. Not that she considered Bernie her dream man. But he was always a gentleman, even when he kissed her goodnight. He never groped or pushed himself on her, though she had always secretly wondered what it would be like if maybe he had been a little more... forceful.

As if I were the type to instill that kind of ardor in a man, Paige thought with a silent sigh.

No, Bernie was exactly the right type of man for her. He had a stable job at the bank. He was comfortable to be around. He was dependable. All important, admirable traits in a man. Since Grandma Millie had passed away six months ago, Bernie had commented on more than one occasion that he didn't think it was a good idea for a young woman to be living alone, which led Paige to wonder if he was working up the courage to pop the question.

But the real question, Paige thought, was what would she say if he did?

Her shopping list completed, Paige paused at the candy display and picked up a package of red licorice whips to add to her basket. She had a group of five-to-seven-year-olds coming into the library for story-telling this afternoon, and she always enjoyed giving the children a treat as much as they enjoyed receiving one.

Paige had barely reached the end of the aisle when she heard the excited murmuring of Sheila Gordon, the drugstore clerk, and Daphne Pringle, a waitress from Big Bob's BBQ, coming from the front of the store. When Paige stepped around the corner, she saw both women standing at the front glass window.

"I'm telling you," Sheila said. "I saw him go in there."

"Were you wearing your glasses?" Daphne asked. "You know you're blind as a bat without them. It could have been one of his ranch hands."

"Of course I was wearing my glasses." Sheila gave an indignant toss of her short, red curls, then straightened her thick, tortoiseshell glasses. "It was him, all right. I saw him plain as the mole on Marilyn Monroe's face."

"It's just hard to believe." Daphne shook her pretty blond head. "What in the world would Clay Bodine be doing at the *library,* of all places?"

Paige froze. Clay Bodine had gone into the library?

Her library? Sheila must have made a mistake, Paige thought. Clay Bodine had never come into the library before. At least, not in the five years Paige had worked there.

Wouldn't that just figure, Paige thought, stepping closer to Sheila and Daphne. The most interesting man in town comes to the library where she worked, and it's one of the few times she wasn't there.

The story of my life.

"There he is! It's him! It's really him!" Daphne grabbed Sheila's arm as Clay stepped out of the library and stood on the sidewalk. The black Stetson he wore shadowed his face, but there was no mistaking the six-foot-four-inch rancher.

"Ohmigod." Sheila uttered a low groan. "I think I might faint just looking at him. That man is *fine.*"

Paige felt her own pulse quicken as she looked at the man herself. Clay had the solid, muscular build that came from the hard labor and long hours of working a ranch seven days a week. His legs were long, his shoulders strong and wide. Today he wore a denim jacket and jeans, a weathered, soft blue that matched his eyes, Paige knew, and remembered the day five months ago when she'd opened her front door and he'd turned those incredible eyes on her....

"Ms. Andrews," he'd said, touching the brim of his black Stetson.

She'd been so stunned, she'd simply stood there and hadn't uttered a word. They'd only met once before, the summer she had turned eighteen and worked at the doctor's office before going off to college. Clay had brought his grandfather in for an eye infection and an exam, but Paige was certain that Clay wouldn't have remembered her, even though she certainly remembered him.

"I heard your '57 Chevy is for sale," he'd said in a voice as thick and dark as molasses. "That right?"

Paige had blinked, then nodded. Her grandmother had bought the car new, but had barely put ten thousand miles on the engine driving it to the grocery store and back. It had been parked in the garage and covered for the past twenty years, and was in perfect condition. Paige had considered keeping the vintage car, but she had her own little blue sedan, and the reality was, she needed the money to help pay funeral and medical expenses. Paige had put the For Sale notice on the bulletin board at Peterson's Feed and Grain just that morning.

"What's your price?" he'd asked.

Price? She hadn't even thought about a price. And staring into Clay's rugged, handsome face had seemed to rob her of the ability to speak, let alone think. "I—I don't know. Whatever you think it's worth, I suppose."

He'd stared at her for a long moment, which had only flustered her all the more, then pulled a check out of the pocket of his blue chambray shirt and handed it to her. "That's a fair price," he'd said. "You can hold on to it if you want to think about it for a while or ask around to make sure I'm not taking advantage of you."

"I'm sure you wouldn't do that," Paige had said

quickly, then felt herself blush when his gaze narrowed and met hers. "But wouldn't you like to drive it first?"

"Not necessary. I know I want it. I'll come back later and pick it up."

He touched the brim of his hat again, then turned and strode away. He'd already gotten into his truck and started his engine before Paige even looked at the check. Eleven thousand dollars! She gasped at the unbelievable figure. That would not only pay for the funeral, but the rest of her grandmother's medical expenses, as well.

The car couldn't possibly be worth that much. She'd tried to wave him back to tell him he'd made a mistake, but he'd already driven away. Who would pay that kind of money for an old car? Paige had thought in amazement.

But she found out later, after she'd gone on the Internet, that a lot of people would have paid around that price, though Clay had given her top dollar without so much as driving, or even looking at the car.

"Do you think the rumors about his ex-wife are true?"

Sheila's question to Daphne brought Paige back to the present. Clay still stood in front of the library, his hands on his hips as he glanced impatiently about. Cars slowed to stare at him. He glared back.

"What woman would leave a man who looks like that?" Daphne stared longingly at Clay. "Plus the man has more money than he knows what to do with.

A woman would have to be crazy to leave a man like Clay Bodine. Besides," Daphne added, "no one knows for certain if he really was married or not. She never came to town once in the three months they were supposedly married, then suddenly she was gone."

"Judith Parcher insists that Clay did her in," Sheila whispered. "She says he buried her on his property somewhere and told everyone she'd run off."

"Judith Parcher's a lunatic and an old biddy," Daphne said defensively. "She also swears she saw Elvis bull riding at the rodeo last week."

Both Daphne and Sheila laughed at that, and even Paige found herself smiling at the absurdity. She'd lived in a small town long enough to know that most rumors were based on very little fact. *The Life of Clay Bodine,* as told by the people of Wolf River, would sit nicely on a library shelf next to all the other great works of fiction.

And if *she* wrote the book, Paige thought as she watched Clay glance at his wristwatch, it would sit on the erotica shelf. Since he'd bought her grandmother's car, Paige had had more than one fantasy about the sexy rancher, though she'd never tell that to a living soul—not even her best friend, Rebecca. Paige especially liked the one where he made love to her in a barn stall on fresh hay, and then there was the one in the meadow, beside a creek where Clay—

"He's coming this way!"

Sheila shrieked, then made a mad dash toward the cash register, then stood casually behind the counter.

Daphne shot for the magazine rack and snatched up a magazine, pretending to be engrossed in the pages.

Not wanting to be caught standing at the window, Paige quickly stepped away, but stumbled over a display of bagged dog food. Her basket tumbled from her arm, and the contents scattered across the floor.

He hadn't time to stand around on street corners all day and be gawked at, Clay thought as he strode across the street. He had a mare that had already bagged up in preparation to foal, ten missing cows in the far east section of his ranch and a pile of paperwork that was quickly spilling over the sides of his desk.

He'd rather face a cornered, angry bull than that mountain of paperwork, but from the time he'd taken over the ranch after his grandfather had died, Clay had vowed never to trust anyone with his ledgers but himself. He'd kept that vow, but the cost had been burning the midnight oil on more nights than not—which had left him little time for other midnight activities of a much more pleasurable nature.

A situation he intended to remedy very soon, he thought, and walked into the drugstore. A bell tinkled over the door and Sheila Gordon, a woman he'd dated once in high school, looked up from behind the cash register, then placed a dramatic hand over her well-endowed chest.

"Why Clay Bodine—" Sheila's eyes were big and round behind her thick glasses "—what a surprise."

"Sheila." Clay knew that Sheila, along with

Daphne Pringle, had been watching him from the window. He glanced over at Daphne—who was supposedly reading an issue of *Ranch and Farm Science*—and watched her lift her gaze with feigned surprise. Clay had never dated Daphne, but had known her from high school, too.

"Hi, Clay," Daphne purred. "Haven't seen you in ages around here. You're looking good."

"Thanks." He spared the blonde a nod. "You, too."

A sound from behind the magazine rack caught Clay's attention. He looked down and saw the soles of a pair of black leather loafers.

"Is there something I can help you with, Clay?" Sheila asked hopefully.

"No, thanks."

Daphne's smile widened as he moved closer, then faded when he moved past her. He stepped behind the magazine rack and saw Paige on her knees, reaching for a small, cloth mouse the same pale shade of gray as the long-sleeved, calf-length dress she wore. She'd obviously dropped her shopping basket and was occupied with picking up its spilled contents. Several long strands of wispy, sandy-brown hair had escaped from the tight knot at the base of her neck. "Ms. Andrews."

When he knelt beside her, she stiffened then looked up slowly. "Mr. Bodine."

Even her eyes were gray, he noted, with a tint of green around the iris, fringed by thick, dark brown lashes. He hadn't noticed her eyes when he'd come to her house a few months ago. Nor had he noticed her skin was pale as a baby's and appeared to be just as smooth and soft, too.

But he'd had no reason to look then, either.

He reached for a package of foot pads lying on the floor and handed it to her. Her cheeks colored bright pink as she snatched the package from him and threw it into her basket. "Thank you."

They both reached for the bag of red licorice at the same time and when their fingers brushed, she yanked her hand away as if she'd been burned.

Good Lord, but the woman was jumpy, Clay thought.

He tossed the bag of licorice into the basket, then— much to her distress—took hold of her elbow and helped her to her feet.

"Could I speak with you for a few moments?" He held on to her arm, had the distinct feeling she would have run if he hadn't.

She stilled at his question, then blinked slowly. "You want to speak…with me?"

Clay could practically feel Daphne and Sheila's eyes burning into his back. "Somewhere private?"

"I—" Page clutched her basket tightly to her "—is this about the car?"

With Daphne and Sheila hanging on every word, he could hardly tell Paige why he needed to speak with her. "Yes," he said loud enough so the other women wouldn't need to strain to hear. "I wanted to talk to you about the car."

"Is something wrong with it?" The distress in her

gray-green eyes turned to worry. "If there's a me-
chanical problem, maybe I can have Wayne at the
repair shop take a look at it and I'd be more than
happy to—"

"It's more of a paperwork issue," he said. "If
you'd just give me a few minutes, I'm sure we can
clear it up."

"You can use the back office," Sheila offered eagerly. Both women had stopped trying to pretend they
weren't listening. "Larry won't mind. He's out for
the rest of the afternoon, anyway."

"Thanks." Clay moved toward the back of the
drugstore toward the pharmacist's office, tugging
Paige along with him. She held onto her basket as if
it were a life preserver and she was drowning.

Inside the small, cluttered office, Clay closed the
door behind them, then let go of Paige's arm. She
stepped quickly away.

"I hope you haven't changed your mind, Mr. Bodine," she said nervously. "The car—"

"Just call me Clay," he said evenly. "And this
isn't about the car."

"It's not?"

He shook his head. "I lied about the car so no one
would know the real reason I wanted to speak with
you."

She furrowed her brow. "The real reason?"

"Look, Paige, in about fifteen minutes, it's going
to be all over this town that you came into the back
office of the drugstore with me. Now that doesn't

bother me in the slightest, but I suspect it might bother you.''

As if to confirm his statement, she shifted awkwardly.

God, but this was going to be harder than he'd thought. He'd spent the past two days going over this moment in his mind. What he would say. How he would say it. But now that he was actually standing here, he couldn't remember one word. Something about this woman disarmed him. Maybe the expression of innocence shimmering in her eyes, or maybe the sound of absolute amazement in her voice.

Dammit, anyhow. He tugged his hat off and dragged a hand through his hair. ''Paige—is it all right if I call you Paige?''

''All right.''

''Why don't you put your basket down and sit?'' He gestured toward the chair behind the pharmacist's desk.

''Thank you, but I'd rather stand.''

''Please.'' He wasn't used to saying the word and it left a bitter taste in his mouth. ''I promise this won't take long.''

She hesitated, then sat, but still kept a death grip on the basket.

Clay walked to the office door and opened it. Daphne and Sheila jumped back, then quickly scurried off. Shaking his head, Clay closed the door again and faced Paige.

''How much do you know about me?'' he asked.

His question obviously confused, as well as surprised her. "What do you mean?"

"I assume you've heard about me, about my family and all the other rumors that have circulated over the years."

"I—" She glanced away, then said quietly, "I've heard."

"So you know that my father embezzled a large sum of money from the bank fifteen years ago, and that he went to prison?"

She brought her gaze back to his. "Yes."

"And you know that I paid the money back?" he asked. "Every penny, and interest, too?"

"Mr. Bodine—"

"Clay."

"Clay," she said his name hesitantly. "Why are you telling me all this?"

"You also probably heard that my mother left Wolf River right after my father was arrested," he went on without answering her question. "She couldn't face the humiliation. I was fifteen at the time."

Clay watched Page's face soften, saw the familiar expression of pity in her eyes. The knot in his gut tightened. He didn't want her pity, dammit. He didn't want anyone's pity.

He expected the typical "I'm sorry" from her, but when she set her basket down, then folded her hands over her knees and kept her gaze on his, quietly waiting, the knot in his gut loosened.

"I went to live with my grandfather on his ranch," he continued. "The Rocking B. When he died four years later, I inherited twenty thousand acres and a small herd of cattle. In the past eleven years I've increased the herd tenfold and established myself as a reputable horse breeder.''

''Dutton's Disciple won the blue ribbon at the county fair last August,'' she said almost wistfully.

He lifted a brow at her comment, thought it odd that she would have known his top stud horse had won a prize almost a year ago. He wondered what other surprises the Wolf River librarian might have for him, then forced his attention back to the reason he was here.

''Almost six years ago,'' he went on, ''I married the daughter of a wealthy businessman in California, but she—Nancy—left me after three months of living on the Rocking B and filed for divorce. In spite of the various rumors that have circulated, my ex-wife is not locked in my basement.''

''I hadn't heard that one,'' Paige said, her eyes wide. ''I heard—''

When she stopped herself, then bit her bottom lip and glanced away, Clay almost laughed. ''She isn't buried on my property, either, if that's the one you heard.''

Paige stared at him for a long moment, then shook her head. ''I still don't understand why you're telling me all this.''

''Just give me a minute and you will.'' He let out a long breath, then continued, ''Nancy was killed in a boating accident in the Caribbean last month. Her parents contacted me to give me the news.''

"I'm sorry," Paige said quietly.

While he'd certainly never wished Nancy any harm, it still surprised him that he felt nothing for his ex-wife. No grief. No sadness. Just…nothing. "I'm not here for sympathy."

"Then why are you here?" she asked. "What is it that I can possibly do for you?"

Clay leveled his gaze with Paige's. "You can marry me."

Chapter 2

Paige blinked.

You can marry me?

She blinked again.

Obviously, she hadn't heard him correctly, even though she was sitting no more than three feet away and he'd spoken quite clearly. She'd been a twisted bundle of nerves from the moment he'd asked to speak with her. She'd barely been able to breathe, let alone think clearly. In her anxious state, she must have had some kind of strange, momentary brain dysfunction.

What woman *wouldn't* be absolutely flustered by the man, Paige thought. His presence filled the small office. His blatant masculinity, his dark intensity, his rugged good looks. Heavens, he should carry smelling salts for all the swooning women he left in his wake.

"Excuse me?" she finally managed, though the words sounded like a tiny little squeak. She watched as he prowled to the door of the small office, then turned abruptly and faced her.

He dragged a hand through his thick, dark hair. "I didn't mean to blurt that out."

Of course he hadn't. Paige released the breath she'd been holding. *Thank God.*

"I'd intended to ask you to marry me *after* I'd explained everything," Clay said. "I just got a little ahead of myself."

A little ahead of himself? Paige felt her heart stop. That was the understatement of the century. Good Lord, he *had* really asked her to marry him. Too stunned to reply, or even react, she sat still as a stone.

"It wasn't just Nancy's death that the Barringtons called to tell me about." A muscle jumped in Clay's jaw. "It turns out that when Nancy left me, she was pregnant."

Paige managed to find her voice, but it was no more than a whisper. "You have a child?"

"She'll be five in August. Her name is Julia."

Clay's eyes softened as he spoke his child's name. For a moment, Paige saw the wonder there, and the longing. "She never told you?"

"No." The hard glint of anger returned. "I never saw, or even spoke to Nancy after she left. There was really no reason to. Our lawyers handled everything."

"But I don't understand." Paige shook her head. "Why would she keep your own child a secret from you?"

"It probably would have delayed the quick divorce she wanted. That we both wanted," he added. "Plus she knew me well enough to know that if I'd been aware of her having my child, I would have insisted on visitations and joint custody. She wouldn't have wanted that kind of inconvenience in her life."

What kind of a woman, what kind of a *mother,* could deprive her own child of a father because it might inconvenience her? Paige wondered. It was beyond her imagination. "What about Nancy's parents? Did they go along with their daughter keeping Julia from you?"

"They told me they didn't approve, but Nancy was insistent they keep quiet. Shortly after she had the baby, Nancy picked up with a musician in Los Angeles and started touring with his band. The Barringtons have practically raised Julia. They feel that she should stay with them."

"Why did they contact you at all, then?" Paige asked.

"Because my name is on the birth certificate," he said flatly. "Either Nancy wasn't thinking clearly when she filled out the paperwork, or she knew she'd always have an ace in the hole if she ever had a need for me or my money. In any event, with Nancy gone, the Barringtons needed my permission to gain legal guardianship. They contacted me two weeks ago and offered visitations."

Paige lifted her brows in disbelief. "Just visitations?"

He started to pace again. "I told them I'd settle for

nothing less than full custody. We had one court hearing in California and the judge set up a visitation schedule to allow my daughter to get to know me. I managed to have the case transferred here to Wolf River and there's a hearing scheduled in a few weeks to determine custody.''

"You're her father." Paige frowned. "Of course the court will award you custody.''

"The Barringtons will bring in the best lawyer to fight me." His mouth set into a hard line. "My lawyer has already prepared me that they'll use the fact I'm a single father against me.''

"Nonsense," Paige said firmly and straightened her shoulders. "Single fathers win custody disputes all the time.''

"Since they've raised her from infancy, the Barringtons will contest that they are better suited to meet Julia's needs.''

"But you have rights," Paige insisted. "Surely the judge will take the entire situation into consideration.''

"My lawyer feels confident, but I can't assume anything." Clay looked directly at Paige. "I need to do everything I can to stack the odds in my favor, and that means having a wife.''

The intensity of Clay's blue gaze made Paige swallow hard, but she did not look away. "You're serious," she whispered hoarsely. "You really do want me to marry you.''

"I'm dead serious.''

A mixture of alarm and excitement rippled through her. It was ridiculous. Preposterous. Unthinkable.

And yet thrilling at the same time.

"There are dozens of women in Wolf River you could ask," Paige said, shaking her head. "Women more attractive and more interesting than me. Women you'd have much more in common with. Why in the world would you ask *me?* You don't even know me."

"I know what I need to know." He moved closer to her. "I know you're twenty-six, that you graduated from Texas University and you've worked at the Wolf River Library for five years. I also know that your parents were killed in a car accident when you were twelve, that you lived with your grandmother until she passed away six months ago, that you aren't engaged, though you do spend Friday evenings with Bernie Pratt."

Stunned, she simply stared at him. Other than the fact he'd bought the car from her, Paige wouldn't have thought that Clay Bodine had known she existed. "How—how do you know any of those things about me?"

"This is Wolf River, Paige. You don't even have to ask to know most folks' business," he said evenly. "But it's not as if I picked your name out of a hat, either. I carefully considered several women, but you were—are—my first choice. I'm not looking for a trophy wife. I need a mother for my daughter, someone who's dependable and stable."

"You'd actually marry someone you don't even know?" Eyes wide, she stared at him. "You really think that a marriage without love would be the best environment for your daughter?''

''Mutual respect and consideration between two people is more important than love,'' he said dryly.

They were *all* important to a marriage, Paige thought, but clearly, based on the tight set of Clay's jaw, he wasn't looking for, or interested in, love.

''And since I would like more children,'' he went on, ''ours would be a real marriage in every other way.''

A *real* marriage? He meant *sex*, she realized. Her heart stopped, then began to race.

''Unless—'' he lowered his voice when she did not respond ''—you find the idea of sleeping with me repulsive.''

''Of course you aren't repulsive,'' she blurted out, then felt her cheeks burn at her outburst. She quickly glanced down at her folded hands and wished the floor would open up and swallow her whole. ''But...I don't even *know* you, we don't know each other. Like that, I mean.''

He stepped closer to her, so close that denim brushed her knees. Even that tiny contact sent shivers coursing through her. ''Do you want children?''

''Of course I do,'' she replied softly.

''Then marry me,'' he said firmly. ''We'll have as many as you want.''

She'd always dreamed of a large family, especially because she'd been an only child. But her dream had included a husband who loved her, and she loved back. Not an arranged marriage with a man she barely knew.

This entire conversation was absurd. Shaking her head, she stood, careful to avoid touching Clay. She reached for her basket, then stepped away and turned to face him squarely. "I wish you luck in finding the right woman, Mr. Bodine, but I'm sorry I can't help you."

His mouth thinned, then he nodded stiffly. "Thank you for your time, Ms. Andrews."

"Goodbye."

She turned and opened the office door, prayed that he wouldn't see how her hand was trembling or her legs were shaking.

She felt his eyes burn through her back as she walked away. At the front register, she somehow managed to face Sheila and Daphne and smile, then casually mentioned that Clay had needed additional paperwork for the car she'd sold him. Still, Paige knew it wouldn't be long before the entire town heard about the drugstore encounter between Clay and herself.

It didn't matter, she told herself. By the time the town heard, they'd have a bigger, better story to tell—that Clay Bodine had found himself a wife.

Page couldn't wait to hear who the lucky woman would be.

The twelve-by-fifteen foot glass-and-steel greenhouse behind the Rocking B barn had a twenty-four hour controlled temperature between seventy-eight and eighty-four degrees with a humidity level of eighty percent. Misters turned on every hour for five minutes. Overhead lights, ordered from a specialty nursery in Florida, glowed for exactly ten hours and twenty minutes per day. If any system were to fail, an alarm would sound inside Joe's apartment over the bunk house.

Growing exotic orchids in Texas was not what you would call easy.

Gravel crunched under Clay's boots as he stepped into the greenhouse. The air smelled of damp earth, and except for the soft sound of Beethoven's Moonlight Sonata drifting from an overhead speaker, it was like stepping into a wild jungle.

"You raised in a barn?" Joe grumbled from the other side of the greenhouse. "Close the damn door."

Joe Morgan had been foreman at the Rocking B for twenty-five years, and the older man's moods, like the tropical flowers he so loved to grow, were unpredictable.

"I *was* raised in a barn." Clay shut the door. "You ought to know."

Joe glanced up from the yellow cymbidium he was carefully pruning with a pair of clippers. His sun-weathered, sixty-two-year-old face softened around the eyes. "If you weren't mucking out a stall, you were sleeping in one. Can't remember how many times Rita Mae had to drag you back to town."

Even as a child, Clay had felt more at home here at the Rocking B than in his parents' big house at the edge of town. Every time he disappeared, which was often, his mother would send their housekeeper to the ranch to bring him back.

"Rita Mae didn't mind." Clay stopped to examine an odd spike of red and gold stripes sprouting from a pot. "You being a widower with two young boys, she had hopes of being the next Mrs. Joseph Morgan. You shoulda married her while you still had a couple of good years left in you."

"One wife was enough." Joe snipped off a dying spike of yellow flowers from the plant. "I had a ranch to help your grandpa run and a family to raise. A woman takes time and patience. Two things I didn't have."

The truth, Clay knew, was that Joe had simply never stopped loving his first wife. It was the reason he'd taken over the care of her orchids, so he could keep not only her plants, but her spirit alive, as well. He groused constantly about the amount of attention the plants required, but it was a labor of love.

"So what brings you out here at this hour of the night, boy? Wait, let me guess." Joe reached for a spray bottle and gave the plant he was working on a fine misting. "Your librarian turned you down flat, didn't she?"

Clay folded his arms and frowned at Joe. "You mean *your* librarian, don't you? I seem to recall you're the one who suggested Ms. Andrews."

"After looking at the list of women you'd put together," Joe said dryly, "it was obvious your brain had followed your good sense right out the back door.

Minnie Wellmer, for God's sake. The women sets off car alarms when she laughs.''

"She was raised on a ranch and she likes kids," Clay defended.

Joe rolled his eyes. "And Marsha Carter? She's a sweet girl and nice to look at, but she's got the brain of an emu."

"So maybe I didn't think everything through," Clay agreed irritably. "And maybe you're right and this is a bad idea, but dammit, Joe, I need a wife and I need one now. I've got no choice but to go back to my list."

While Joe tended his plants, Clay paced. He had to admit, if only to himself, that after meeting Paige, he really hadn't the heart, or the stomach, to approach any of the other women on his list.

Joe had been right—Paige Andrews, in spite of the fact that she was a bit mousy and more than a little frumpy, was the best choice all around as a mother for his daughter. Clay knew she was educated and that she ran the reading program for children at the library where she worked. He also knew she'd been seeing Pratt at the bank for quite a while, but according to the gossip lines, Bernie had been dragging his feet, and the relationship didn't appear to be serious.

Paige wasn't a beauty queen, Clay thought, but she wasn't hard to look at, either. She had big, smoky-green eyes, skin that looked soft as rose petals and a mouth—when it wasn't pressed into a thin, firm line—that he'd found more than a little interesting. He remembered how those pretty lips of hers had parted into a small *o* when he'd told her that their marriage would be a real one. She'd blushed bright as a fire engine over that little bit of news.

As strange, and annoying, as it seemed, that strait-laced, Miss Prim manner of Paige's—and the fact that she'd turned his proposal down—had seemed to make him want her all the more.

Shaking his head in frustration, Clay turned his thoughts to the other candidates on his list. He needed a wife to help raise his daughter, and like it or not, tomorrow he was going to have to ask one of those women to marry him.

Paige had a routine. Monday through Thursday, she arrived home from work at precisely six-fifteen, boiled water for tea while she looked over her mail, set her teabag to steep while she changed her clothes, fed Eudora, then made herself dinner. After she ate, she read for one hour, quilted for one hour, then took a long, hot bath before she went to bed and read until ten o'clock. Fridays were different because she went to Bernie's. On the weekends she mostly gardened and cleaned her house, but for the most part, her days, and her nights, were pretty much the same.

Until today.

Since Clay had asked her to marry him, Paige had felt…disconnected. As if someone had pulled the plug on her brain. She'd finished off her shift at work, had gone through all the motions, but she really hadn't *been* there. She knew she'd walked home from work and picked up her mail, then she'd set her tea to boil and steep while she changed into tan slacks and a white sleeveless blouse. But now, as she sat at her cozy kitchen table and stared at the leftovers she'd reheated from the night before and the steaming mint tea she'd poured, she realized she had no precise recollection of doing any of those things.

It wasn't real, she told herself. It *couldn't* be. Men like Clay Bodine simply didn't ask women like herself to marry them.

But he *had* asked, she knew. She hadn't dreamed it, and she hadn't imagined it. Clay Bodine, the most eligible, the most desirable man in Wolf River had proposed to her.

And she'd turned him down.

Well, of course you turned him down, silly.

A woman shouldn't marry a man because he was handsome or sexy, or because he suddenly needed a wife. And there should definitely be love, Paige told herself, though Clay had made it clear that love was not a consideration for him. He wanted a dependable caretaker for his daughter, a wife to raise the child he'd never known.

Someone "dependable and stable," so he'd told her.

Paige straightened her back, then stabbed a green bean and popped it into her mouth. Had it been necessary to throw those qualities in her face, even if she did fit the bill? Now if he'd only added *boring* to his criteria, she'd have been perfect.

Considering all the women who would fight for the chance to be Mrs. Clay Bodine, Paige supposed she should be flattered that she had been his first choice. But his reasons for selecting her, though well-intentioned, were not exactly ego-boosting. What he really wanted was a nanny, she thought. One he could take to his bed at night.

That he'd actually wanted their marriage to be a "real one" as he'd put it, had shocked her more than the proposal itself. Paige knew she was no femme fatale. Men didn't turn their heads when she walked by, and other than her Friday nights with Bernie, she hadn't been asked out on a date in two years, though Rebecca had made numerous attempts to fix her up. The idea of marrying Clay, then sleeping with him, quite literally stole her breath away.

And sent a tingle of excitement rippling up her spine.

Even though she'd turned him down, she couldn't help but wonder what it would be like to be Clay's wife. What it would feel like to be in bed with him. For him to kiss her, to touch her, to slip her nightgown off and put his mouth on her breast—

Her fork slipped from her fingers and clattered to her plate, shaking Paige out of her fantasy. Heavens! Just thinking about the man made her pulse quicken and her skin hot. And, to her embarrassment, made her throb with a need she'd never experienced before. She pressed her thighs firmly together to ward the feeling off, but the dull ache between her legs persisted.

Needing a distraction, she picked up her plate and headed for the sink, turned on the faucet, then squirted dish soap under the spray. She was elbow deep in lemon-scented bubbles, doing her best to think about anything or anyone but Clay Bodine when she heard the knock at her front door.

Frowning, she reached for a dish towel. No one ever knocked on her door this late, except Rebecca, who wouldn't have knocked, anyway. She would have just walked in the back door. But Rebecca was on a buying trip in Austin for her antique store, Paige thought, so it couldn't be her, anyway.

Paige had nearly reached the door when she froze.

What if it was Clay?

Don't be ridiculous, she told herself. Of course it wasn't Clay. Unless he wanted to tell her that he realized he'd made a mistake and he wanted to apologize.

Still, she held her breath as she lifted her eye to the peephole. Her breath rushed out again when she saw who it was.

Bernie.

How absurd for her to be disappointed, she told herself and waited a moment for her nerves to steady. Of course it wasn't Clay.

When she opened the door, she smiled widely. He was still dressed in his dark-brown business suit and yellow-striped tie. "Bernie. What a nice surprise."

"Paige." He nodded stiffly. "May I come in?"

"Of course."

She stepped back, surprised not only by his visit, but by the fact that he was alone. Bernie rarely came to her house without his mother. Like Paige's grandmother, Mrs. Pratt didn't approve of them being completely alone together. Never mind her son was thirty years old, Bernie's mother ruled with an iron fist.

"Would you like some tea?" Paige offered.

"No, thank you. If you have a minute—" he slicked a hand over his short, blond hair, then shifted awkwardly "—I'd like to talk with you."

"Of course." Confused by his odd behavior, Paige finished wiping her hands dry, then led him to the sofa, where they both sat. While he adjusted his tie and suit jacket, she folded her hands and waited patiently for him to speak.

"Paige, I—" His voice broke. He cleared his throat, then turned on the sofa so their knees almost touched. "We've been dating for quite some time now, you know."

Paige had never seen Bernie so nervous before, except maybe the first time he'd kissed her. *He's going to dump me,* she thought.

"So, ah, you know that I have feelings for you," he went on. "Strong feelings."

Great, Paige thought. Here comes the, "but I think we should see other people for a while," part. She did her best to sit very still and let him finish, when she really wanted to just smack him with the wet towel in her hands.

She'd had a very long day, after all.

He cleared his throat again, then took her hand in both of his. "Paige, I think we should get married."

She stared at him for a long moment, letting his words sink in. *I think we should get married?*

This wasn't possible. *Two* proposals in *one* day? Had she suddenly slipped into some kind of alternate universe where every man she encountered asked her to marry him?

"Bernie, I—I don't know what to say."

"I have an excellent health plan at the bank," he said. "And since we'd have live-in child-care, you could keep working, which would help increase our retirement portfolio."

"Live-in child-care?" She stared down at his smooth, cool, manicured hands. "What are you talking about?"

"My mother," he said, gaining confidence. "You have three bedrooms here, more than we need. Now that she's getting on in years, I couldn't just leave her alone. She'll be wonderful company for you, another female in the house to talk to about girl things."

Of all the women in the world that Paige would talk "girl things" to, Bernie's mother was definitely not one of them.

"Let me get this straight," Paige said very carefully. "You want to get married, live in my house, with your mother, and I can keep working after we have children to 'increase our retirement portfolio.'"

He squeezed her hand and smiled. "If we're careful, we should be able to retire in thirty to thirty-five years."

Retire?

Live-in baby-sitter?

I have strong feelings for you?

Golly, Paige thought, a fantasy proposal come true.

What girl wouldn't swoon at such a romantic, tempestuous proposal? And to think it was her second one today, too! How lucky could one girl get? Any more luck and she'd throw herself off the roof.

She resisted the urge to yank her hand from Bernie's damp palm. "This is all so sudden."

"We've been seeing each other for almost two years, Paige," he reminded her. "And if we set the date before the end of the year, our tax liability will decrease, as well."

Well, now, *that* was certainly a reason to accept his wildly passionless offer of marriage, Paige thought. They'd save money on their taxes. Whooppee.

"I—I don't know what to say." Get out, was her first thought, but she simply stood. "There's so much to consider, and my head is simply reeling at the moment. Perhaps we can have lunch together tomorrow and discuss this more then."

"Oh, well—" Clearly confused that Paige hadn't immediately said yes, Bernie stood and smoothed a hand down the front of his tie. "Lunch would be fine."

Emotions held carefully in check, she walked Bernie to the door, offered a cheek when he bent to kiss her. "Good night."

Paige closed the door behind him, then walked numbly back to the kitchen and sipped on the cup of mint tea she'd made before dinner. To say that she was having one heck of a strange day was the understatement of the century. Eudora, who'd been curled up on a kitchen chair cushion, glanced up with a bored expression and gave a halfhearted meow.

''My feelings exactly,'' Paige said through gritted teeth as she plopped her hands back into the still-warm, sudsy sink water.

How many times had Paige envisioned the man she loved, and who loved her back, professing his love and asking her to be his wife? There'd been red roses and a sparkling diamond ring in her dream. Candle-light. Soft music. Flames dancing in a fireplace.

Not in one of those fantasies had the issue of re-tirement or tax benefits been mentioned. Not once had her true love suggested that his mother come live with them.

Tears burned her eyes as she stared at the snow-white mounds of soap bubbles. Fantasies were simply that, she thought. Fantasies. They held as much sub-stance as the bubbles in her sink.

She scooped up a handful of bubbles and blew on them, watched them scatter and float on the air. Maybe it was time for her to be more realistic about her future. She wanted children desperately. Bernie had offered that.

But then, so had Clay Bodine.

She picked up a glass tumbler and plunged a sponge inside. Not that it mattered what the rancher had offered, she told herself. Surely by now he'd found himself a wife and forgotten all about the col-orless, insipid Paige Andrews. Clay and his new fi-ancée were probably out celebrating right now, hav-ing dinner, sharing a bottle of champagne.

Practicing for the wedding night.

Knowing that she could have been that woman if she'd accepted Clay's offer made her skin tighten and her breath catch in her throat. Right at this very moment, he might have been holding her in his arms, kissing her, sliding his hand up her stomach to cup her—

At the sound of her front doorbell, Paige jerked her hand to the side. The glass cracked against the sink, then broke into several large pieces and fell back into the water. Groaning her annoyance out loud, she grabbed her dish towel again and headed back to the door.

Paige had never known Bernie to be persistent about anything, but she liked the idea that he'd returned. Maybe he'd realized his proposal had been a little too...limp, so to speak, and he'd come back to give it another go.

Only it wasn't Bernie, Paige realized as she opened the door.

It was Clay Bodine.

Chapter 3

For the second time that day, Clay made Paige's heart stumble, then race. Still dressed in the jeans and blue shirt he'd worn earlier in the day, he stood on her front porch, his expression somber as he leveled those incredible blue eyes on her.

"Paige." He nodded tightly. "May I come in?"

What was he doing here? she wondered, unless it was to tell her he'd found someone to marry him, and she needn't concern herself about his situation. Or that he'd come to his senses and realized how completely incompatible they would be together, then apologize for bothering her with his problem.

A strange disappointment flooded her at any of those prospects. How pathetic I am, Paige thought. That she would have preferred to let herself think that

Clay hadn't regretted asking her to marry him, even if he had found someone else.

"Of course. Please come in." Still gripping the dish towel tightly in her hands, she stood to the side of the door, then closed it behind him when he moved past her.

He said nothing for a long moment, just looked around her living room. She lived simply, Paige knew, but she'd made the house she'd inherited from her grandmother more than comfortable. Hand-quilted pillows on a burgundy floral sofa, lace curtains on the windows, an antique cherry-wood hutch that held crystal glassware passed down from her great-grandmother. The patchwork quilt she'd been working on lay across the overstuffed arm of a side chair.

And in the middle of the distinctly feminine room stood Clay, looking all the more rugged because of it.

When he turned to face her, her pulse skipped. Around the tight set of his strong jaw, he bore the faint shadow of a beard. His eyes held a razor-sharp edge to them she hadn't noticed this afternoon. He had a dangerous, wild look about him tonight, she thought, and licked her lips nervously. When his gaze dropped to her mouth and held there, Paige felt a little dizzy.

She forced herself to focus, let the years of etiquette her grandmother had imposed upon her to take over. "May I offer you some tea?"

Though she was certain she saw him wince at the

offer, he looked back into her eyes and nodded. "Thanks."

Grateful to have something to keep her hands busy, Paige took a step back toward the kitchen. "I'll just be a minute."

"Wait."

Clay moved across the room toward her, a frown darkening his face. Her breath caught when he took hold of her hand.

"You're bleeding."

She glanced down, saw the bright red circle of blood on the dish towel. She'd been so distracted since she'd opened the door, she hadn't realized she'd cut herself.

"I broke a glass in the kitchen sink." She tried to pull her hand back, but he held tight. "It's nothing."

"Relax." He turned her palm up and looked at the small gash just under the base of her thumb. "Let me have a look at it."

"Really, I'm fine."

But she wasn't fine. With Clay standing so close, holding her hand, she was anything *but* fine. He was just so…overwhelming. He was a powerfully built man, at least a foot taller than her, and she had to tilt her head to look up at him. His hands were large and callused, yet his touch was surprisingly gentle. When he lightly rubbed the center of her palm with his thumb, a shiver ran up her arm.

"It stopped bleeding." But he was still stroking her hand. "Shouldn't need any stitches."

"Clay." Paige had to pull herself back before she swayed into him. "What are you doing here?"

Clay realized he'd been so caught up in the smooth, silky feel of Paige's skin, at the sight of her shiny, sandy-blond hair brushing the tops of her slender shoulders, that he'd forgotten, for just a moment, the purpose of his visit.

What was it about Paige that set him on edge? he wondered. She wasn't what most men would consider beautiful, but she was certainly pretty, he realized. Especially now, with her hair loosened from that tight bun she usually wore, and the blouse and slacks she had on definitely displayed the fact that she did indeed have a woman's curves. And why hadn't he noticed the light splattering of freckles across her straight little nose, or the upward tilt in the corners of her full lips?

Realizing that he'd been sidetracked, he forced his attention back to the reason he was here and released her hand. "I want to apologize for this afternoon."

"That's not necessary." Her tone turned crisp as an autumn night. "Your need to get married was an impulsive decision based on the fear of losing your daughter."

He furrowed his brow. "My decision wasn't impulsive."

"Not your proposal, perhaps. But now that you've had time to reconsider, I completely understand."

He was glad she understood, because he sure as hell didn't. "I didn't come here to tell you I had reconsidered. I came here to ask *you* to reconsider."

That seemed to get her attention.

"You...what?"

"I know I scared you this afternoon," he said evenly. "I shouldn't have cornered you like I did. It wasn't fair to you."

"Are you telling me you still haven't found a wife?" She stared at him in disbelief. "That the other women on your list turned you down, too?"

Clay damned himself for ever mentioning he'd had a list. Lord, it was hard enough he'd done this once today. "Can we sit down?"

"I—I suppose we could sit in the kitchen while I make tea."

"Never mind the tea." He'd rather drink radiator fluid. He took her by the arm, then led her to the sofa and sat next to her. "I didn't ask anyone else to marry me. I want to marry you."

Her eyes widened, then she shook her head. "I don't understand."

"Look," he said on a heavy breath, "I know this is hardly conventional, but if you're worrying about the stigma of being married to the son of a convicted felon I can under—"

"I most certainly would not worry about such a thing!" she said indignantly. "And I resent your implication that I would have such a small mind to associate your father's crime with you."

Clay lifted a brow. It appeared that the little mouse could indeed roar when she was offended. He lifted one corner of his mouth and took her hand in his. "Paige, I'll treat you well. Give you a home, children.

Respect. All I ask is that you be a good mother to Julia and a wife to me. Once we're married, I won't look to other women, but I do have physical needs. You said you didn't find me repulsive.''

"Of course I don't,'' she muttered.

"We can build on that,'' he told her. "You can set the pace for intimacy between us.''

"What if I won't be able to—'' her gaze dropped and another blush brightened her cheeks ''—satisfy your needs? Maybe you won't even *like* me in that way.''

He was silent for a moment, then cupped her chin in his hand and lifted her face to his. "Easy way to settle that question.''

He felt her body stiffen, saw the fear flash in her eyes as he lowered his mouth to hers. She'd pressed her lips into a firm line, as if she was determined not to respond, to prove to him she would be the wrong choice for a wife.

Clay had always enjoyed a challenge.

Lightly he brushed his lips over hers, then moved to the corner of her mouth to nibble. When he caught her lower lip between his teeth, he felt the tremor move through her body.

A good sign, he thought, moving his mouth over hers with whisper-soft kisses. When her breath shuddered out, he slipped inside. She tasted like mint and smelled like lemon, he realized dimly. Her mouth softened under his; her tongue touched his tentatively, a sweet, shy movement that made his blood heat up.

Sliding a hand over her shoulder, he cupped the back of her head and brought her closer.

She made a sound, a soft murmur of surprise. She leaned into her, lifted a hand to his chest, then slid her fingers up to rest on his shoulder. He deepened the kiss, slid his other hand around her waist and up her back, bringing her upper body flush with his. Her breasts, soft and full, pressed against his chest, threatening to snap the control he carefully held in check.

Oh yeah, he thought. No doubt in his mind that he and Paige would be quite physically compatible in bed. He reined in the growing need inside him, concentrated on pleasing her, on seducing her into saying yes, if that's what it took. He wanted Paige more than ever now, and he was determined to have her.

From the moment Clay's lips had touched hers, Paige had lost the ability to think clearly. In her entire life, no man had ever kissed her this way. With such...intensity. With such tenderness, yet passion at the same time. Her blood warmed and a longing stirred inside her, made her heart beat wildly against her ribs.

Relentless, his mouth moved over hers, the taste of coffee and man arousing her more than she would have thought possible. She felt the heat of his muscular chest pressed so close to hers, felt her skin tighten and her nipples harden. Wave after wave of shining, silver-tipped pleasure coursed through her body.

The sound of her soft moan shocked her, but at the moment, she was too overwhelmed to even be embarrassed. And if his kiss wasn't a powerful enough assault on her senses, she wanted, *craved,* more. Her body ached to be touched, as well.

And to touch, she realized.

She curled her fingers into the soft cotton of his shirt, felt the ripple of muscle underneath her hands. She felt small against him, vulnerable, yet the idea of his large, strong body moving over her own did not frighten her, it excited. The pleasure she felt became a frustration she'd never experienced before. She moved against him, her breathing ragged, and pressed her aching breasts closer. The pressure between her legs became an unbearable, pounding throb.

And then he took her arms in his hands and pulled away. It was all she could do not to drag him back. Confused, disappointed, Paige slowly opened her eyes.

His hands tightened on her arms and for one, wonderful moment she thought he might kiss her again. His blue eyes glinted with desire, his jaw tightened and flexed. But he didn't kiss her. Instead, he dropped his hands and leaned away from her.

"Well, I'd say that answers any questions about our sexual compatibility," he said hoarsely.

She hadn't the voice to answer, but she had regained enough control to be embarrassed by her unbridled response to Clay's kiss. Good grief, she thought, she'd all but ripped his clothes off.

"We could get a license first thing in the morning," he said tightly. "Say yes, Paige."

First thing in the morning? Her head began to spin. "I—I have to work tomorrow."

"On your lunch hour, then. And that's the other thing I need from you." He reached for her again, took hold of her shoulders and met her gaze with his. "I need you to at least take the summer off to be home with Julia. She'll start school in the fall, so if you still want to work, you can go back then."

"But I can't just take the summer off. I have a responsibility. Schedules to make, orders to place, shipments to catalogue, a computer system that—"

Without warning, he kissed her again, cut off her protests with his mouth and made every other thought fly out of her head.

The sneaky bastard.

By the time he raised his head again, she would have agreed to anything. Anything and everything.

"We can be married on Friday."

"So soon?" Her voice sounded small and far away.

"Judge Winters can marry us in his chambers."

Judge Winters marry them in his chambers? The last of Paige's marriage fantasy—a church wedding—shattered into tiny pieces. Of course Clay wouldn't want a church wedding, she realized. He was in too much of a hurry for that. And like he'd said, this was hardly a conventional marriage.

She thought about Bernie, weighed his proposal against Clay's, and realized there wasn't much difference in the hearts and flowers department. Neither man had offered romance or love. Clay brought a child to their marriage, Bernie brought his retirement plan and mother. Paige shuddered at the thought.

But Bernie had never kissed her like that. Bernie had never made her heart slam in her chest or her toes curl. She'd never once considered ripping Bernie's clothes off.

Should she refuse both men and hold out for love? she wondered. Or should she face reality that a plain, dull librarian might never find her knight in shining armor?

She looked into Clay's somber gaze, believed that he would be a good husband and father. The lengths he was willing to go for his daughter were certainly admirable. She also believed that he would treat her well. If he didn't love her, Paige knew that he would at least respect her. All those things meant a great deal to her.

And maybe, just maybe, she thought, he might learn to love her, and she him. She knew the odds were against her, but as the saying went, all things were possible in love and war.

"Paige."

She looked at him, knew that he was waiting. The mantel clock over her fireplace loudly ticked off the seconds. "My house..."

"You can keep it or sell it, whatever you want," he said. "Just say yes."

"I—I suppose I could rent it. Rebecca's been looking for a place. I—" Her throat tightened and suddenly she couldn't speak.

She drew in a breath and nodded.

His hands loosened on her arms, then he let go of her and stood. "I'll meet you at the courthouse at noon tomorrow, by the county records desk."

"What—what will we tell people?" she asked through the haze surrounding her brain.

"It's easy enough to let it slip to a few people that we've been secretly dating for a few months," he said with a shrug. "I don't much give a damn what anyone thinks, but I realize a story like that might be easier for you."

She appreciated that he was considering her reputation in Wolf River and the kind of scrutiny and criticism she might be under for marrying him so unexpectedly. "Thank you."

She walked him to the door, then leaned back against it after he left, afraid her knees might buckle if she tried to walk back to her sofa.

"I'm getting married," she whispered in wonderment and touched her fingertips to her mouth. Her lips still tingled from his kiss. After several long minutes, she sighed, then pushed away from the door, making a mental note to call Bernie in the morning and cancel their lunch date.

A warm rain fell Friday morning. By Texas standards, barely a drizzle. But it was enough to wet the streets and raise puddles on the concrete steps of the courthouse. Enough to keep most people from walking idly along the sidewalks of town. More than likely, the weather would clear as quickly as it had come on, then the humidity would settle in like a hot, Turkish bath.

Inside the courthouse, in the corridor outside Judge Martin Winters's private chambers, Clay paced. He'd arrived with Joe twenty minutes ago and been informed by Helen Talbot, Judge Winters's matronly secretary, that she would call him inside when Paige was ready.

For the tenth time in as many minutes, Clay glanced at his wristwatch, then muttered a curse and looked at his foreman. Arms folded casually while he leaned against the opposite wall, Joe wore a gray tweed blazer, white dress shirt and black string tie. He shifted a toothpick lazily from one side of his mouth to the other, a habit he'd picked up since he'd quit smoking five years ago.

Clay glanced at the closed office door, had to shove his hands into his suit pockets to keep from reaching for the doorknob. "What the hell is taking so long?"

"Afraid your bride will change her mind?" Joe's deep brown eyes crinkled with amusement.

Your bride. Clay felt his throat close up at the term, then wiped at the fine sheen of sweat on his brow.

The truth was—Clay started to pace again—he *was* afraid that Paige might change her mind. Though they'd spoken on the phone every day since they'd filed for the license and taken their blood tests, he hadn't actually seen her. She'd hinted that her best friend, Rebecca Montgomery, had been less than thrilled at the news, but assured Clay she would proceed with the ceremony as planned.

And it wasn't as if he hadn't had second or third or even fourth thoughts about getting married himself. Hell, even a man who *wanted* to get married felt his feet getting a little cold before the big day. But every time he considered backing out, he thought about his daughter, thought about all the years he'd lost out on already. After two visitations with Julia, both in the Barringtons' house, Clay wasn't about to let one more day go by that he wouldn't be a part of her life. She was *his* child, and he intended to raise her. And if getting married would help him gain full custody of his daughter, then so be it.

And after kissing Paige the other night, he thought, getting married certainly wouldn't be all bad. He'd lain awake every night since then, thinking about the way her body had fit against his, how soft her lips had been, how sweet she'd tasted. Over and over in his head, he'd heard that little sound she'd made, half moan, half whimper, and he'd become aroused all over again.

He was more than anxious to take her to his bed and relieve the frustration she'd provoked in him.

On an oath, he glanced at his watch again. He'd give her five more minutes, he told himself. Then, ready or not, he was coming in.

"So let him wait," Rebecca said irritably behind the oak-paneled door of the judge's antechamber. "It'll do him good to sweat a little. Besides, I'm not finished with your hair. Now sit still and stop fidgeting."

"Easy for you to say," Paige mumbled. "You're not the one getting married."

Paige lifted a fingernail to chew on, but promptly had her hand slapped away.

"You'll mess up your manicure and your lipstick," Rebecca reprimanded. "And no, I'm not the one getting married. I'm not the one who's completely taken leave of my senses and agreed to marry a complete stranger, either."

As if Rebecca would have to, Paige thought. If Rebecca wanted a man, all she'd have to do was wiggle a finger at him. With her auburn hair, emerald-green eyes and stunning looks, she was the type of woman that had men tripping over their feet and tongues. But marriage was not in Rebecca's immediate plans right now. She was more interested in running her antique store and for the moment, seemed to be happy with her life just as it was.

"We've been through this already." Paige sat on her hands to resist temptation. "Clay wasn't a complete stranger to me. I told you. We met when he bought my grandmother's car."

"Oh, yeah, that's right, you'd met." Sarcasm dripped off Rebecca's voice. "First he shows up and wants Grandma's '57 Chevy, then he shows up and wants you."

"I know I'm not supermodel material," Paige said stiffly, "but I'd appreciate it if you didn't compare me to the purchase of an antique car."

"Oh, honey, I'm sorry. I didn't mean it that way." Rebecca knelt and took Paige's hands in her own.

"You're the most beautiful person I know, inside and out. Clay Bodine's the luckiest man in the world. Just wait until he gets a look at you. His eyes are gonna pop out. You're beautiful."

Paige doubted that Clay's eyes would pop out. She also doubted he'd think she looked beautiful. But after spending yesterday morning in a beauty salon, letting the hairdresser, a makeup artist and a hovering Rebecca have their way with her, Paige had to admit she at least *felt* pretty. Other than lipstick, she'd never worn cosmetics before, and was amazed at the difference a light application of mascara and blush made. Between the makeup and her new haircut of wispy bangs and layered sides, Paige barely recognized herself in the mirror. Her eyes looked bigger, her face softer, her lips fuller.

Next had come the manicure and pedicure, then an afternoon shopping trip to find an appropriate dress and shoes to wear for the ceremony. After two hours of disagreeing on everything they looked at, Paige finally agreed with Rebecca that a white silk suit dress and two inch white satin heels was perfect.

Rebecca hadn't let it end there. She'd insisted that the bride's trousseau include lingerie, too. Bras and panties in lace and silk, all definitely more sexy and more colorful than the boring, everyday cotton underwear Paige normally wore. Just thinking about wearing the thigh-skimming, white satin negligee with lace edging that Rebecca had bought her as a wedding present made Paige blush. The idea of putting on such a provocative, revealing negligee for

Clay, and the realization that he'd be taking it off, made her insides turn inside out.

He was waiting for her, she knew. Outside in the corridor.

The room started to spin.

"Whoa, Paige, you all right?" Rebecca's eyes narrowed. "My God, you're pale as a ghost and your hands are like ice."

"I—I'm all right." Paige closed her eyes and drew in a slow breath. "I'm just a little dizzy."

"Honey, you don't have to do this." Rebecca squeezed Paige's hands. "I'll go out there right now and tell Clay you've changed your mind. I'll take you home and we'll eat chocolate and watch old Doris Day movies."

Paige laughed, then shook her head. "I haven't changed my mind, I'm just scared to death."

"Every bride is scared to death, even under the best circumstances," Rebecca said gently. "But if you want to get really scared, just think about Bernie's mother living with you. That alone should eliminate any doubts you're marrying the right man."

Paige could still see Bernie's face when she'd gone to the bank three days ago and turned down his proposal, then told him she was marrying Clay Bodine. His face had turned chalk-white, then beet-red.

"Are you telling me that you'd marry a man you've barely met?" he had gasped. "A man whose father is a criminal, rather than marry me?"

"Clay's father paid his debt to society." Paige lifted her chin defensively. "And Clay worked hard and made a success out of his ranch so he could pay back every penny.''

Bernie's face had gone from red to deep purple. ''So you're marrying him because he's rich.''

''I most certainly am not marrying him because he's rich!'' Paige said loud enough to turn heads in the bank.

''Why else would you marry him?'' Bernie whispered harshly.

''Because—'' She had barely caught herself before telling Bernie about Clay's daughter. No one in town knew yet, and the bank was hardly the place to announce it. ''I don't have to explain myself to you, Bernie Pratt.''

''There's something going on here, Paige. Men like Clay Bodine don't marry women—'' he stopped, smoothed a hand down his tie ''—ah, women they don't know.''

Paige stiffened. ''You were going to say women like me, weren't you?''

He shifted awkwardly. ''No, of course not.''

Bernie was a terrible liar. Paige watched his gaze dart away as he nervously fiddled with a stack of papers on his desk.

''Yes, you were going to say that.'' She'd suddenly felt a deep sense of sadness. ''And you're right, Bernie. Women like me marry men like you. Which doesn't say much for either one of us, does it?''

''Paige—''

''I'm sorry, Bernie,'' she said quietly. ''I hope you'll find someone who deserves you.''

She rose from her chair and offered her hand. Bernie just stared at her as if she'd gone mad. Maybe she had, she thought. Because marrying Clay Bodine had to be insane.

But she hadn't changed her mind. If anything, she was determined. Determined to be more than she'd ever been before. Not necessarily better. Just more.

She'd left the bank then and hadn't looked back.

"Paige." Helen Talbot came into the room, looking a bit flustered. "Your groom is about to break down the door if I don't let him in soon. Are you ready, dear?"

Was she? Paige felt the low, deep drum of her heart.

"One word," Rebecca said soberly. "Just give me one word and we're gone."

Everything was in place. Rebecca was watching Eudora for the weekend, Paige had a leave of absence from the library for the summer, Clay was waiting outside...

But she could still stop this, Paige knew. She could say that one word and walk away.

Drawing in a long breath to steady her nerves, Paige stood and nodded.

"I'm ready."

"It's about damn time," Clay grumbled under his breath, then followed Helen Talbot into the inner office of Judge Winters's chambers. The office was spacious, with floor-to-ceiling oak bookshelves and a polished hardwood floor. Two brown leather armchairs faced a massive mahogany desk, where a bottle of champagne chilled in a silver bucket of ice.

Judge Winters, a white-haired, bushy-browed man with silver-rimmed glasses, entered through a side door.

"Clay."

"Judge."

Fifteen years ago, before he'd become a judge, Martin Winters had been the defense lawyer who'd represented Clay's father at the embezzlement trial. Even knowing that the Bodine family had no money to pay him, and that the case would hardly make him a popular man in Wolf River, Martin had nevertheless worked tirelessly to reduce Wesley Bodine's jail sentence. In the end, he'd managed to trim a five year sentence down to four, and even after the trial, after Clay's father had been sent away to prison, Martin had called and visited the Rocking B regularly to make sure that Clay was all right and offer any assistance he or his grandfather might need.

Other than Joe, Judge Winters was the only person in Wolf River who had seemed to give a damn. The only other man who Clay considered a friend. The judge was the first person Clay had called when he'd found out about Julia, the only person he'd asked for advice.

"You sure about this?" the judge asked him quietly.

Clay nodded. "I'm sure."

The judge sighed, then nodded at Mrs. Talbot when she stuck her head in from the anteroom.

Finally, Clay thought, adjusting the tie that felt much too tight around his neck. All he wanted to do was say what had to be said, sign what had to be signed, then get the hell out of here.

Rebecca walked into the room first, then Paige.

And Clay's mind went blank.

Paige?

Good Lord. He stared at the woman dressed in a white silk suit, could hardly believe this was the same woman he'd asked to marry him. When her smoky green gaze met his, his throat suddenly felt dry, and he could hear his pulse pounding in his brain.

He had to remind himself to breathe.

"Clay?"

"Yes?" He dragged his eyes off Paige and stared blankly at the judge. "What?"

Judge Winters smiled. "You stand here. Joe, you stand to Clay's right. Paige, you look lovely."

"Thank you, Your Honor."

Carrying a small bouquet of white rosebuds and baby's breath, Paige took her place beside Clay. She held her back straight as a post, kept her eyes locked on Judge Winters as he performed the ceremony. When Clay took her ice-cold hand and slipped a diamond solitaire and band on her finger, she looked up at him in surprise. They repeated the marriage vows, then Judge Winters proclaimed them man and wife.

It took less than five minutes.

"You may now kiss the bride."

Clay took Paige by the arms, felt her tremble as he

bent to kiss her. It was a light kiss, a mere brush of lips, then he straightened and shook the judge's hand. While Mrs. Talbot sniffled and hugged Paige, Joe opened the champagne and poured, then handed everyone a glass.

"To the groom and his beautiful bride."

Paige sipped her champagne. Clay downed his in one gulp.

He managed to endure the polite small talk for all of ten minutes. "Are you ready?" he finally asked Paige.

He saw the flash of fear in her eyes, the intake of breath. She nodded stiffly, then hugged Rebecca.

Clay wasn't certain whether to be amused or annoyed when Rebecca glared at him.

They said their goodbyes, then he took Paige by the arm. Outside, the rain had turned to a warm drizzle. When Paige hesitated in front of a large puddle, Clay scooped her up in his arms. Her eyes were wide, her body stiff as he carried her to the parking lot.

"My car and suitcase are back at my house," she said awkwardly.

"I've already asked Joe to get your suitcase, and you won't need your car today. If you need to drive into town before we pick it up, you can use your grandmother's car." He dumped her into the front cab of his truck, then came around and started the engine. "We aren't going directly to the ranch."

Paige narrowed her eyes in confusion. "Where are we going?"

"To The Four Winds Hotel."

Chapter 4

He was taking her to The Four Winds?

Paige had no idea what to say. Clay had never mentioned they'd be going to Wolf River's biggest, and most luxurious hotel. She had assumed they'd immediately go to the ranch after the ceremony, especially after he'd declined Rebecca's offer to prepare a luncheon for the wedding party.

The man continually surprised her. Not just because he'd asked her to marry him, but also the bridal bouquet he'd had delivered this morning to her house, the champagne he'd sent to Judge Winters's chambers, the stunning diamond ring he'd slipped on her finger. And now The Four Winds.

She realized he'd done everything for appearances, but still, she was grateful that he'd taken the time and consideration to make this day special for her. As if she mattered to him.

Foolish thinking, of course. But it *was* her wedding day, whether it was the real thing or not. And she *had* finished her glass of champagne, so she felt a little warm and tingly inside. Had he reserved the bridal suite for them? she wondered as he pulled into valet parking. Her heart beat faster at the idea that Clay might be anxious to start the wedding night now, even though it wasn't noon yet.

She cast a sideways glance at him, couldn't help but think how handsome he looked. The tailored black suit he wore accentuated his broad shoulders, and the silk teal tie around his neck made his eyes appear a deeper blue. She'd stood shoulder to shoulder with this man in front of Judge Winters and repeated her vows, as Clay had repeated his, but she barely remembered the words.

Married, she thought. Clay Bodine was truly her husband, and she was truly his wife. She still couldn't believe any of this was happening.

She slid out of the truck when the valet opened her door, waited until Clay came around and joined her. Casually, he placed a hand on her back as they walked inside the hotel. Her pulse jumped at the contact.

In the center of the marble-floored lobby, a huge bouquet of sweet-smelling flowers greeted the guests. Lush green plants spilled from fire-glazed pots of varying sizes. Classical music drifted softly from unseen speakers.

Paige had been here once before. Three months ago, she had treated Rebecca to a birthday dinner at Adagios, the five-star restaurant inside the hotel. The food and service had been memorable.

And now she was here with Clay.

As they approached the reservation desk, her hands trembled and excitement shivered up her spine. Anticipation of making love with Clay—in the middle of the day, no less—made her knees go weak.

"Welcome to The Four Winds." A pretty brunette desk clerk smiled at Clay. "May I help you, sir?"

"Would you please ring Mr. and Mrs. Barrington's room and tell them Clay Bodine is here to see them?"

Paige stiffened at Clay's words, and it felt as if all the air had been suddenly sucked from her lungs.

Clay wasn't bringing her here to be with him, Paige realized. He'd come to see the Barringtons. He hadn't even said Mr. and Mrs. Clay Bodine were here to see the Barringtons. He'd simply said Clay Bodine.

How ridiculous she'd been to think he'd wanted to be alone with her, intimately, in such a romantic setting as The Four Winds. Quickly she blinked back the moisture burning her eyes. She'd be careful not to make that mistake again, she told herself resolutely. If she was going to survive being Clay's wife, she needed to be strong. Any expectations that this marriage might be more than Clay had told her it would be was foolish.

And stupid.

"You can go up now, Mr. Bodine," the clerk said brightly. "Suite 1215."

They rode up the elevator in silence. Tension radiated from Clay as he knocked on the door. When it opened, a man, probably in his sixties, wearing black slacks and a white polo shirt stood on the other side. His neat, brown hair was gray at the sides and he wore silver-framed glasses over eyes the color of steel.

Clay nodded stiffly. "Barrington."

"Bodine."

Clay placed a hand on Paige's back, but kept his gaze on the elder man. "This is Paige, my wife. Paige, this is Robert Barrington."

She held her breath when the man's gaze moved to her. Had Clay told his ex-in-laws that he was getting married? she wondered. And had he mentioned that he'd be bringing his new bride here today, or was she a complete surprise?

Robert Barrington nodded politely, his gaze neither dismissive or inviting, then he opened the door wider and stepped to the side. "Come in."

Paige released the breath she'd been holding.

Inside the parlor of the well-appointed suite, sitting on a white sofa across the room, was a tall, slender woman, also around sixty, wearing a blue linen dress. Her thick, blond hair was swept into a French roll and knots of gold glittered on her earlobes. A dark-haired little girl wearing a pale pink jumper sat beside the woman. The child's features were delicate, her skin like porcelain, her deep blue eyes wide with worry.

"Go say hello to your father, Julia," the woman coaxed.

Julia glanced nervously from her grandmother to Clay, then slowly stood and walked across the room. Smiling, Clay knelt and held out a hand. "Julia, this is Paige, the lady I told you about. Remember?"

The little girl nodded, then held her hand out to Paige. "How do you do."

Well, she'd certainly been taught manners, Paige thought as she took the child's small hand. "I've looked forward to meeting you, Julia," Paige said with a smile.

"I'm Linda Barrington," the woman introduced herself. "I believe congratulations are in order."

"I—" Paige glanced at Clay, not certain what to say.

"Thank you," Clay replied as he straightened.

"Perhaps we could have lunch together, Clay," Linda Barrington suggested. "It would make the transition easier for Julia."

"It's just for the weekend, Linda," Clay said quietly. "I'm sure Julia will be fine." He smiled down at his daughter. "I have a little colt at my ranch that was born two weeks ago. Would you like to see him?"

Julia's face lit. "Can I pet him?"

"Sure can. Soon as we get back to the ranch and change our clothes, we'll go out to the barn." Clay's smile faded as he looked at Robert. "I'll have her back Sunday evening."

While Clay picked up Julia's suitcase, Paige stepped back and watched his daughter hug and kiss her grandparents goodbye. It was apparent that the

Barringtons adored their granddaughter and though they were smiling and pretending to be happy for Julia's sake, it was also clear they dreaded this first separation.

Ten minutes later, with Julia buckled in the front seat of the truck between Paige and Clay, busily chatting about the colt, they drove out of town.

In the side mirror, Paige watched the town, and her life as she'd known it, slowly disappear from view.

The Rocking B Ranch was ten thousand acres of prime land as far as the eye could see and beyond. Sleepy-eyed cattle grazed in meadows still green from a wet spring, then drank from wide streams and narrow creeks that bubbled through the lower valley. A grove of Spanish oak shaded a small pond behind the house. Wildflowers bloomed in nature's palette of blues, reds and yellows.

Clay's grandfather, and his great-grandfather, had worked this land for over a hundred years. Every post had been set, every road had been cleared, every well had been dug with Bodine hands. The hard, slow work had been a labor of love, for both the men and the women they'd married, as well. Their lives had been simple, but they'd been happy. Clay had hoped that he and Nancy might have that same happiness here.

What a fool he'd been.

Clay knew now that Nancy had married him not for love, but for adventure. For the fantasy of an exciting life on a Texas ranch. She'd been visiting a friend in Dallas whose father had just purchased a two-year-old from the Rocking B and Clay had personally delivered the horse. He and Nancy had been introduced at dinner that night and sparks had flown between them. Their courtship had been tempestuous, their elopement impulsive. On their week long, West Coast honeymoon, they'd actually been happy.

And then he'd brought her home.

Nancy had hated the simplicity of the town of Wolf River, the isolation on the ranch, the extremes and unpredictability of the weather. She'd hated the dust and the smell of the animals and the absence of Saks Fifth Avenue.

And it wasn't long before she'd hated him, too.

He obviously hadn't been thinking when he'd made Nancy his wife and brought her home to the Rocking B. Not with his head, anyway.

This time his marriage would not be based on lust or love, he thought as he pulled off the highway and turned onto a gravel road leading to the ranch. This time both he and Paige understood that this was a practical, logical marriage for both of them. Based on the kiss they'd shared the other night, a marriage that they would both find pleasurable, as well.

He thought of his big bed, knew that Paige would be sleeping there tonight, and he felt instantly aroused. It had been a long time since he'd been with a woman. He was anxious to consummate their marriage and relieve the frustration that had been building steadily this past week.

He still couldn't get over how different Paige

looked today. As a man, he fully appreciated her new style, but as her husband, he wasn't quite certain he was comfortable with the change. It made him… uneasy.

He scoffed at the idea, then glanced over at his new wife. She'd spent the thirty minute ride from town asking Julia questions about herself. If she liked to read books and play games, if she had a favorite television show or a movie. Because he hadn't a clue what to say to his own daughter, Clay was grateful that Paige had made his first time with his daughter— without the Barringtons standing guard—much easier for him.

"There's a horse!" Julia cried with delight when she caught sight of a roan gelding munching grass in the pasture beside the road. She pointed through the windshield. "And there's another one!"

"We can go see them after we take your suitcase inside," Clay told his daughter.

Eyes wide, Julia looked at Paige. "Will you come, too?"

"Of course, I will." Paige squeezed Julia's small hand. "But we all need to change our clothes first, okay?"

"I can do that real fast," Julia said with all sincerity.

Paige smiled at the little girl, felt her own trepidation grow at the new life that was suddenly facing them all. How strange it seemed that they were an instant family, yet they all knew so little about each other. Paige realized she'd taken a risk marrying Clay, just as he'd taken a risk marrying her. Other than the four- and five-year-olds she read to at the library for story-time days, Paige had never been around children. And now she was suddenly faced with raising one. What if she failed? Paige worried. Being a good parent couldn't be learned from a book. She was bound to make mistakes.

The enormity of the responsibility made Paige's stomach knot. She looked at the beautiful, dark-haired child sitting beside her, then at Clay. Love had not brought them together, she knew, but she was nonetheless determined to be the best mother to Julia, and the best wife to Clay, that she possibly could.

While Julia pointed out other horses in the pasture, Clay drove his truck through two red brick pillars and an open, wrought iron gate that delineated where the gravel road ended and a brick-lined concrete driveway began. A freshly-mowed lawn the size of a football field sparkled from the early morning rain, and the surrounding rose gardens bloomed in a riot of pinks and yellows. Though the skies had cleared, raindrops still clung to all the plants and dampened the ground.

Paige felt her breath catch when she saw the two-story red brick house at the end of the driveway. She had no idea what she'd been expecting, but certainly nothing this grand.

"It's beautiful," she heard herself whisper.

"My grandparents built it after they were married," Clay said as he turned off the engine. "They'd planned on having a large family, but my grandmother died two years after my father was born and my grandfather never remarried.''

"It looks brand-new.'' Paige noted the panels of leaded glass beside the oak, double-entry doors, the fresh, white paint on the eaves and shutters, the shiny brass lamp on top of a black wrought iron pole beside the porch steps.

"I've done a little refurbishing the past few months,'' Clay said with a shrug, then got out of the truck.

Paige waited while Clay came around to the passenger door and opened it. She took the hand he offered and slid out of the truck, then lifted her gaze to his. When their eyes met and held, she felt a tingle run up her spine. When his gaze dropped to her mouth, her heart skipped.

Something passed between them. It was sexual, to be sure. But there was more, Paige thought when Clay's hand tightened around hers. A momentary flicker of...oneness. And for that one instant, Paige felt as if she truly was a bride, that Clay truly was her husband.

The moment dissipated as quickly as it had risen, and once again, she was simply the woman Clay Bodine had married, chosen from a carefully predetermined list of prospective wives. If he hadn't married her, Paige knew, then another woman would be standing here at this very moment. Another woman would be mother to Julia.

Another woman would be sharing his bed tonight. Deciding this was hardly the time to be thinking about that, Paige stepped away as Clay helped his daughter out of the truck.

"The house is open," he said, nodding at the front doors. "Go ahead inside while I get the suitcases."

Paige took the little girl's hand and together they walked into the house. The tiled entry opened directly into a spacious, open-beam living room. To the right, Paige noticed her suitcase sitting beside an oak staircase that curved upward to the second story. To the left, a sparkling crystal chandelier hung from the ceiling of the formal dining room. The smell of fresh paint and wood stain hung heavy in the air.

Paige stared in wonder at the beauty of the large house, but was confused by one rather conspicuous detail.

There was no furniture.

Not one chair. Not one sofa. Not even a painting or a lamp.

Nothing.

She silently asked the question when Clay stepped into the entry carrying Julia's suitcase.

He shrugged. "Nancy took everything with her when she left, and I haven't needed much."

Obviously, Paige thought and stared at the barren house.

"We can pick up whatever you might want to bring here from your house." Clay picked up Paige's suitcase in his free hand. "And I've got the name of a decorator from Dallas you can work with. She told me she can put a rush order for anything you want."

Anything I want? Paige looked at the blank walls and empty rooms and felt overwhelmed.

"There are beds and linens upstairs," he said. "Plus the kitchen is stocked with everything you'll need for now, including a dinette set. There's food in the refrigerator that should hold us for at least a couple of days. I've also placed an ad for a housekeeper. I've narrowed a list of applicants down to two women you can interview whenever you're ready."

"You—you want *me* to hire a housekeeper?" Paige shook her head in disbelief. "And decorate your house?"

"The house is your domain now," he said flatly.

"But I don't know what style you like or don't like," she protested.

"You can paint the walls purple and green if it makes you happy. All I care about is the ranch and the livestock."

His words stung, but what did she expect? She knew he'd married her only to prove to the courts his daughter would be well cared for. In Clay's eyes, Paige thought, she was on the same par as the rest of the domestic help he intended to hire.

"Can I change my clothes and see the horses now?" Julia tugged on Paige's hand.

"Of course, you can, sweetheart." Paige smiled. "Maybe if you ask your daddy, we can find a carrot or apple to feed them, too."

"Can we?" Julia looked at Clay. "Can we, Daddy?"

"I think I can arrange that," Clay said with a nod,

then started up the stairs. "Let's go see where your room is first so you can change your clothes, okay?"

Bouncing with delight at the prospect of feeding the horses, Julia let go of Paige's hand and clambered up the stairs behind her father.

Paige waited a moment, then drew in a deep breath, and followed behind.

He couldn't concentrate. Clay had totaled the column of expenses in his ledger three different times and come up with three different numbers. Twice he'd mislabeled an account, and he couldn't count the times he'd transposed figures.

He'd bought new bookkeeping software for his computer, but he hadn't had time to install it, let alone learn how to run it, so he was still scribbling away in the ledger system he'd always used. He considered that Paige might be familiar with computers since she worked at the library, but he quickly discounted the idea of asking for her help. He'd managed to get along quite well up to now by himself, so he figured the new program could wait a few more weeks.

Tossing the pencil in his hand down on his cluttered desktop, he rubbed his hands over his face, then sat back in his chair. He'd been in his office for the past hour, working to balance his books while Paige helped Julia bathe and get ready for bed. He'd gotten nowhere fast. He'd never had this much trouble keeping his mind on his paperwork before, had certainly never used more eraser than lead.

But he'd never had a child in his home before,

either. *His* child, he thought, listening to the sound of laughter coming from Julia's bedroom down the hall. From the bits and pieces of conversation he'd managed to pick up, Clay knew that Paige had been acting out a bedtime story for his daughter. Something about a princess and a dragon and a forest filled with elves.

More than once, he'd been tempted to go stand in the hallway and listen himself. The sound of Paige's enthusiastic role-playing intrigued him, tugged at his curiosity. When she assumed her deepest dragon voice and warned all who approached to run away, he couldn't help but smile.

Paige had been terrific with Julia today, Clay mused. She'd helped his daughter feed carrots to the horses, even though Paige herself was obviously a little nervous around the large animals. Julia had been insistent on meeting every horse in the barn and learning their names, and she'd also picked up a friendship with Scooter, a stray border collie mix that Joe had brought home last year. Though Scooter had never given Clay the time of day, the dog had taken an instant fancy to Julia and had followed her around the entire afternoon.

The day had gone by quickly, then he and Julia had set the table while Paige made a salad to go with a tray of lasagna supplied by one of the ranch hands' wives. Julia, with her endless questions about the ranch and the horses, had kept their first dinner together from being awkward. Clay was used to eating by himself, but he was determined to be a good father to Julia, and that meant sharing meals. Once Paige hired a housekeeper, they could arrange a scheduled time for breakfast and dinner so that they would all eat together.

He could hear Paige now as she raised her voice and announced herself as Emlyn the Elf, king of all the woodland elves. The sound of Julia's laughter made his throat tighten. He'd lost out on almost five years of his daughter's life. He couldn't make up for that, but he'd be damned if he'd share her with the Barringtons, either. He would not settle for joint custody, and he sure as hell wouldn't settle for visitations.

Julia was *his* flesh and blood. *His* child. She belonged with him, dammit.

Without thinking, he pushed away from his desk and wandered down the hall, stopping just outside Julia's bedroom to listen as Paige finished her story.

"The elves gathered around the fallen knight," Paige said quite solemnly. "Afraid that their rescuer had succumbed to the dragon's fiery tongue, they wept over his still body. The dragon, with his green scales glistening in the morning light, lifted his great head and roared, 'I am the mightiest creature in the forest!'"

"But what happened to the princess?" Julia asked, her voice heavy with concern.

"The princess," Paige went on, "distraught over the loss of her knight, snatched the sword from his still hand, then lifted the weapon high and faced the fierce creature."

Amused, Clay stuck his head around the corner.

Dressed in pink-and-white striped pajamas, Julia sat transfixed on the edge of her bed, watching Paige as she lifted a hairbrush high to act out the scene of her story.

"What did she do?" Julia narrowed her eyes. "Did she kill the dragon?"

"Oh, no." Paige shook her head dramatically. "This dragon could not be killed by mortal man. The princess, with her wisdom and intelligence, knew there was only one way to conquer the mighty beast. A secret known only to a true princess."

"What is it?" Julia asked breathlessly. "What's the secret?"

"I can tell you." Paige glanced over her shoulder, then looked back at Julia and lowered her voice. "But you must never tell a dragon."

With her fingertip, Julia made the sign of an *X* over her heart, then pretended to zipper her lips closed.

Clay leaned forward, watched as Paige leaned close and whispered in Julia's ear. Julia's eyes went wide.

"Really?"

Paige nodded. "Really."

Damn, Clay frowned. He hadn't heard what Paige had said.

"And now it's time for you to go to sleep," Paige announced. "I'll go get your daddy to come tuck you in, okay?"

Not wanting to be caught eavesdropping, Clay strode back to his office, then sat at his desk and scribbled meaningless numbers in his ledger he knew he'd have to erase.

That was how Paige found him a moment later. Elbows on his desk, bent over his paperwork with a pencil in his hand. The light of a single desk lamp shone on the ledger in front of him. She knocked lightly on the open office door. "May I come in?"

"Sure." He did not look up, but kept his attention on his work. "Just give me a second."

Paige glanced around the room as she entered. Like the rest of the upstairs, Clay's office was wall-to-wall plush, beige carpeting. He had a computer on his cluttered desk, but it wasn't turned on. The room looked as if he were just moving in, or just moving out. Stacks of books leaned against one wall. Cardboard boxes served as file holders. A fax machine and telephone sat on the floor beside his desk.

Why did he live like this? she wondered. His house, his office. It certainly wasn't because he didn't have the money to buy things he needed. Everyone knew that the Rocking B ranch was extremely successful, and that Clay had invested wisely over the years, as well. No one knew exactly what Clay Bodine was worth, but Bernie had told her once that he'd heard Clay's portfolio with stocks alone was in the millions.

He didn't live this way because he was cheap, either. When he'd bought her grandmother's car, Paige remembered, he'd written a check for top dollar without any negotiations whatsoever. And then today, he'd also given her carte blanche to decorate the house and hire a housekeeper, too.

No, Clay Bodine was not cheap. Paige was absolutely certain of that. He lived this sparsely because none of those things had mattered to him before, because he'd had no use for them. Until he'd found out he was a father. That had changed his life, his thinking.

Good Lord, that was an understatement, Paige thought as she glanced down at the diamond ring on her finger. He suddenly had a child, and now a wife.

And she had a husband.

And tonight was her wedding night.

Her pulse jumped, but she forced the thought out of her mind and moved closer to the man who was now her husband. "I thought you might like to come say good-night to Julia. She's had a long day and she's ready for bed."

Rolling his shoulders, Clay leaned back in his chair and turned his deep blue gaze on Paige. He stared silently at her for a long moment, then said, "It's been quite a long day for you, too, I imagine. Go ahead and get ready for bed and I'll join you shortly."

"Clay—" she cleared her throat "—I think that I should, that we should talk about—"

"Let's save it until after I've said good-night to Julia, shall we?" he suggested. "Go ahead and get ready for bed and I'll be there in a few minutes."

Paige stared at Clay's back as he left the room. He'd told her straight out to get ready for bed and he'd join her. No innuendos there.

She swallowed hard.

I can do this, she told herself, then squared her shoulders and headed for the bedroom Clay had shown her to earlier. *Their* bedroom. She was a grown woman for heaven's sake. Even though she'd never actually *done it,* she knew perfectly well what happened between a man and woman. The act itself had always seemed as if it would be…awkward, but considering the amount of attention paid to sex, and all the hoopla about it, it must be something pretty good. Or at least tolerable.

Opening her suitcase, she pulled out the pretty white silk gown that Rebecca had bought for her. She and Clay were married. He'd been polite with her, had certainly never threatened her in any way. She had no reason to be afraid of him.

But the fact was, she was terrified.

She tossed the sexy gown back into her suitcase. She wasn't ready for it, she decided. Tonight she needed something she would feel more comfortable wearing. Like a pup tent.

Since a tent obviously wasn't an option, she pulled out one of her everyday, soft cotton gowns. The neckline was high, with scalloped edging in eyelet trim and a lacing of white satin ribbon. The sleeves were long and the hem skimmed her ankles. She realized she would look like a Victorian spinster, but at this moment, with her knees starting to shake and her palms turning damp, she didn't much care. He hadn't married her to be sexy or gorgeous, anyway.

She hurried into the large master bathroom, then took the quickest shower on record. She pulled the gown over her head, brushed her teeth, then ran a comb through her hair. Because she thought she'd be too embarrassed to take her underwear off in front of Clay, or for him to take them off her, Paige decided not to wear any.

She then sat on the edge of the bed, hands folded in her lap, and waited.

Chapter 5

"Was the baby cow scared?" Julia, clutching a worn teddy bear tightly to her chest, stared wide-eyed at her father. "Did she cry?"

"She cried a little bit," Clay said. "But not for very long. She was happy to get out of the mud."

"Did she find her mommy?" Worry furrowed Julia's small brow.

"Yes, she did."

"And her daddy?"

Not certain how to explain about the bulls and the cows, Clay decided to deviate from the truth a bit. "Ah, yeah. She found her mommy and her daddy, too."

When Julia relaxed and smiled brightly, Clay decided he'd made the right choice. Hell, what did he know about telling bedtime stories? When his daughter had asked for one, he'd simply related the rescue of a calf stuck in a mudhole, a fairly common occurrence for cows on a ranch.

"Time for bed now." Clay held the blanket up. "In you go."

Julia climbed under the covers and laid her head on her pillow. "Can I see the horses again tomorrow?"

"Sure."

"And feed them carrots?"

"All right."

Clay felt a hitch in his chest as he looked at Julia. My daughter, he thought in amazement. He'd taken a paternity test for the courts and it had been positive, but from the first moment he'd seen her, there'd never been a question in his mind she was his. He could see his ex-wife's traits in the little girl, especially in the shape of her face and her slender build, but Julia's eyes and hair color were his. She even had the same widow's peak in her hairline as he did.

"Good night, Daddy."

"Good night."

"Paige kissed me good-night," Julia said, her voice already sounding sleepy. "Aren't you going to?"

"Oh. Sure."

Leaning down, he pressed a kiss to her brow, felt the warmth of her skin, smelled the fresh scent of soap from her bath. Julia smiled, then closed her eyes and turned on her side as she snuggled into the bed.

He had to swallow the thickness in his throat as he flipped off the overhead light and stepped into the hallway.

Other than a few of his ranch hands' kids who'd shown up from time to time, Clay had never been around children. What kind of a father would he make? he wondered. He sure as hell didn't have much to fall back on. His father had worked long hours when Clay was growing up, and his mother had worked at spending all the money his father earned.

And all the money his father had stolen, as well.

Clay hadn't seen his mother since the day she'd left Wolf River. She'd called once several months later and tried to explain. Had told Clay that she'd been too humiliated to face the people of Wolf River, that she hadn't been able to handle the pressure. That was right before she'd dropped the bomb she'd divorced his father and was already remarried.

His mother hadn't called again after that day. Clay knew he was a reminder of a life she'd prefer to put behind her. She'd moved on, and so had he. His father obviously had, too, because after he'd been released from prison, he'd dropped out of sight. Clay rarely thought about his parents anymore, but now that he was a parent himself, he had to wonder, and worry, if he'd be able to make the cut.

He stared at the closed bedroom door where his daughter was sleeping. He would do everything in his power to make Julia happy. To provide for her, to protect her, to take care of her.

That's why he'd married Paige. He'd known instinctively she would be the best mother for Julia. After today, after seeing how terrific Paige had been with his daughter, Clay was certain he'd made the right decision.

With a sigh, he moved toward the closed master bedroom door at the end of the hall, then knocked lightly. At the sound of Paige's quiet response to enter, he turned the knob.

By most standards, the long, white gown she wore was much too conservative and covered too much skin to be considered sexy. Yet the sight of her sitting on the foot of the bed, her back straight as a fence post, her long, delicate hands intertwined in her lap, made his throat turn to dust. Her face was scrubbed clean; her shiny sandy-brown hair tumbled past her shoulders to her back.

When her gray-green gaze lifted to his, her cheeks flushed a deep pink.

"She's asleep," he said, closing the door behind him.

Paige nodded stiffly. "I'm not surprised. She had a lot of excitement today."

"I'd say we all have." Clay watched Paige's eyes widen, saw the intake of her breath when he moved across the room and sat beside her on the bed. "Wouldn't you?"

Her hands tightened in her lap. "I suppose we have."

"You were good with Julia today," he said, tugging one boot off, then the other.

"She's a wonderful child."

"I know it has to be a little scary for her, coming to a strange place, being separated from the Barringtons." He dropped his boots beside the bed. "You made a difficult situation easier for her. Thank you."

"You don't have to thank me," Paige said quietly. "She's a pleasure to be with, plus she's very well mannered and incredibly bright. Based on the books she brought with her, it appears she's already reading at a first-grade level."

When Clay tugged his shirt from his jeans, Paige quickly looked away.

"Her grandparents were going to send her to a fancy private school in Beverly Hills." Just thinking about his child going to one of those stuffy, pompous schools made Clay's eye twitch. "The same school that three generations of Barringtons had attended."

"I'm sure they only want what's best for Julia."

"I'm her father," he said irritably. "Being with me is what's best for Julia."

"I agree with you." She glanced back at him. "All I'm saying is that the Barringtons love her very much. I could see it in their eyes today. This has to be very hard for them."

"Finding out I was intentionally denied my own child for five years is a hell of a lot harder."

"It was a terrible thing she was kept from you," Paige said with nod. "And I absolutely believe you should raise her. But surely you must realize this is a big change in her life."

When Clay said nothing, just stared at her and

slowly began unbuttoning his shirt, Paige felt her heart jump into her throat.

Terrific, she thought dismally. Her first night here, their *wedding* night, and already she'd made Clay angry.

For someone who was supposed to be smart, Paige thought, she was showing very little common sense. This was hardly the time to be expressing an opinion that opposed Clay's, especially considering the fact that they would be sleeping in the same bed, and that he would be making love to her. The thought made her pulse skip and her palms damp.

Nevertheless, what she said was true. The Barringtons would always be a part of Julia's life, and whether he liked it or not, Clay was going to have to face that fact.

Just maybe not tonight.

He rose from the bed and stared down at her, tugging his open shirt from his jeans. Her breath caught at the sight of his bare, muscular chest. Dark hair swirled on his broad, upper torso, then narrowed over his flat, hard stomach to a vee pointing downward. Before she could think, her eyes followed that arrow and dropped to the bulge underneath the zipper of his jeans.

She barely knew this man, had been married to him only this morning. Other than the understanding that they would have sex, they'd never actually discussed the subject. She had no idea what he expected from her in bed. And she certainly had no idea what to expect from him.

Realizing that she was blatantly staring at his crotch, Paige snapped her head up to meet his gaze. The anger she'd seen in his deep blue eyes only a moment before was gone. Now his look glinted with sexual hunger. No man had ever looked at her that way before, with such raw, open need. It frightened and excited her at the same time.

"I—I haven't thanked you for the bouquet and the champagne," she said, feeling like an idiot that she was babbling, but too nervous to stop it. "And the ring is beautiful, too. I never expected anything so extravagant."

She practically jumped when he reached down and took her hand in his. He stared at the ring. "Joe made the arrangements."

"Oh." When would she learn not to assume anything when it came to Clay? she chastised herself. Soon, she hoped. "Well, just the same, thank you."

His thumb brushed over her knuckles. "How's your hand?"

"My hand?" she said, her voice breathless.

"You cut yourself the other night." He turned her hand over, then ran a fingertip over the faint red scar on her palm. "It looks much better."

"It was barely a scratch." The touch of his rough fingertip on the sensitive skin of her palm sent arrows of electricity up her arm. Her hand felt so small in his, Paige thought, and it fully occurred to her how large a man Clay was. He could do whatever he chose to do with her, whether she agreed or not, and there would be no way she could stop him.

But he wasn't doing *anything*, she realized, except holding her hand. And just that simple act had her nerves tied in knots of anticipation.

He released her hand.

"Paige," he said softly. "Stand up."

Though she wasn't certain her knees would hold her, she stood slowly, careful to keep her eyes straight ahead. She felt the heat of his gaze as it swept over her. Her heart hammered against her ribs.

"Clay," she whispered, careful to keep her eyes just below his chin. "I think we should probably...talk about a few things."

"What things?"

"I—" It was so embarrassing to say out loud. "I haven't, I'm..."

When she started to look away, he took her chin in his hand and brought her gaze back to his. "Paige, are you trying to tell me you've never had sex before?"

Her cheeks burned. "No."

"No, you haven't had sex before?" he murmured. "Or no, you aren't trying to tell me that?"

"I—" She furrowed her brow. Darn it! He was confusing her more than she already was. "I've never made—had sex before."

He didn't look the least bit surprised. As silly as it was, Paige felt slightly hurt by his casual acceptance of her admission. Why should he be surprised? she thought. The frumpy, plain librarian. The only thing that would make the stereotype more perfect would be if her name was Jane.

"Are you afraid of me?"

His question startled her out of her indignation. Was she afraid of him? Good Lord, *yes!*

"I'm just a little…nervous about…well—" She closed her eyes. "This is my first time and all."

His thumb lightly brushed her cheek. "But are you afraid of *me?*" he asked her again.

She drew in a slow breath and opened her eyes. "Maybe a little."

He lifted her chin until their eyes met. "I've never hurt a woman in my life, Paige. The first time we make love, I promise to make it as easy for you as I can."

He pressed his lips gently to hers, unleashing a cage of butterflies in her stomach. When he lightly swept his tongue over the seam of her lips, she felt the heat sweep through her body.

Then he dropped his hand from her chin and stepped away. "I'll just get my clothes and let you get some sleep now," he said, his voice rough and deep.

Paige's eyes fluttered open. "What?"

"I think it's best if I sleep in the bedroom at the other end of the hall."

Paige stared at Clay in confusion as he disappeared into the large master bedroom closet, then came back out carrying some clothes. "You—you aren't going to…"

He shook his head. "Not tonight."

Stunned, Paige watched Clay pick up his boots. He turned back to her, slowly slid his gaze from her feet back up to her face. She was certain she saw desire in his eyes, was certain she heard the hesitation in his voice. So why was he leaving her?

Julia, of course, Paige realized. It was Clay's daughter's first night in his house, his first night to have his child with him. Paige understood Clay's reluctance.

But they *were* married, she thought and barely managed to bite back the protest threatening to erupt. How pathetic was she that she would have to *ask* her husband to make love to her on their wedding night? Clearly, even with a new haircut and clothes, she was still resistible. He was more than willing to wait until the time suited him.

She lifted her chin. "What time shall I have breakfast ready?"

"Don't worry about me for breakfast," he said, shaking his head. "Joe and I have to get out early to the east pasture to repair a water valve. I should be back by noon and we can have lunch together."

She nodded, but when he turned to leave, she called to stop him. When he glanced back at her, Paige was amazed at how calm she suddenly was.

"About the housekeeper and decorator."

"What about them?"

"You said I could do whatever I wanted with the house, that your main concern was the livestock and ranch. Do you mean that?"

He narrowed a look at her. "What are you getting at?"

"I'd like to take care of the house and decorate it myself."

One dark brow lifted. "This is a big house, Paige. Julia needs to be your first concern."

"Of course she will be," Paige insisted. "But I'm not used to other people cleaning up after me. If I'm not able to adequately meet your standards of house-keeping, then I'll hire someone."

A muscle jumped in his jaw. "Fine."

"And Rebecca can help me with the decorating," Paige went on. "She not only owns an antique store, she also has a degree in interior design. If you don't mind me using your computer, I can also save money by buying most everything on the Internet."

"I'm not worried about saving money," he said tightly. "Buy whatever you want. Just don't expect me to look at fabric or paint or ask me which wall to hang a picture on."

"All right," she said with nod.

He stared at her for several long seconds, and she almost thought he was going to step toward her again. Her breath held, waiting, but then the moment passed.

"Good night, Paige."

"Good night, Clay."

When the door closed behind him, Paige sank back down on the bed with a sigh.

She wasn't sure if she was relieved or disappointed the evening had ended this way. Probably both. But one thing was for certain, Paige thought. Being married to Clay Bodine was not going to be a walk in the park.

* * *

Between the repair on the water valve and discovering a section of downed fencing, Clay didn't make it back for lunch. He'd called Paige from his cell phone to let her know, then told her he'd be there for dinner. It frustrated him that he'd missed a meal with his daughter and Paige, especially considering they only had the weekend together, but he'd long ago accepted the fact that the Rocking B was a seven-day-a-week, round-the-clock responsibility.

He loved the ranch. Loved the freedom of being outdoors and working with the animals. Hard work had never bothered him. He'd enjoyed putting his back into a job, using his hands. He found great satisfaction in knowing the land where his cattle and horses grazed was his own. He'd taken risks and been lucky, but he'd managed to turn the Rocking B from an average, mediocre business into an extremely lucrative enterprise. Between the ranch and his investments, Clay had more money than he could have ever dreamed.

In the beginning, his ambition to succeed had simply been to repay his father's debt to the bank. Clay had always been good at the hands-on aspect of ranching, but he'd discovered that he was good at the business end, as well. Then he'd ventured into stocks and bonds, and gotten lucky there, too.

Still, it was the challenge of making money and being successful that appealed to him, not the money or success itself. Before he'd found out about Julia, he could have lost every penny he'd ever made and he wouldn't have blinked an eye.

Now that he had Julia, though, his perception of life and money was different. He'd already set up a trust fund for her, and had recently rolled his high-risk stocks into more stable, secure investments. If anything ever happened to him, she would be well-cared for with *his* money, not the Barrington's.

And Paige, of course.

He thought about his new wife as he parked his truck in front of the barn. But then, he'd been thinking about her most of the day.

And certainly all last night.

It had taken a will of iron not to take her to bed last night. Lord knew, he'd desperately wanted to. He hadn't been able to get her out of his mind, had tossed most of the night, struggling with himself not to simply walk that short distance down the hall, slip between the sheets, then slide into her slender body and pleasure them both.

After he'd kissed her that first time in her house, he'd suspected she was a virgin. He'd tasted the sweetness of her innocence, but it hadn't diminished his desire for her in the least.

His daughter sleeping across the hall had not been the only reason he hadn't made love to Paige last night. She was his wife, after all, even though they'd only been married that morning. He'd always had a healthy appetite for sex, and he'd looked forward to having a woman in his bed every night. But even as much as he'd needed a wife, he wouldn't have gone through with a wedding if he hadn't thought that he and Paige would be compatible in bed.

But when he'd walked in the bedroom last night, when she'd looked at him with such shy, nervous anticipation, he'd nearly lost it right there. He'd taken that look to bed with him last night, had carried it with him all day.

He needed more time. Time to contain this unexpected *need* he felt for Paige. When they made love, he needed to be in control, for her sake, as much as his own. She'd admitted she was afraid of him, if only a little. He didn't want her to feel as if making love was her duty as his wife. He wanted her willing and eager. He wanted her to open to him, to rise up eagerly and take him inside her. To wrap her naked arms and legs around him and move her body in rhythm with his.

Scooter's bark from inside the barn snapped Clay out of his thoughts. *Good God.* He thumbed his Stetson back from his face and wiped at the sweat on his brow. He had to stop thinking about Paige like that, or he'd never make it through the weekend. Or when they did make love, he thought, it would be over much too quickly.

Stepping from the truck, he walked slowly toward the back door of the house, giving himself a few extra needed moments to let his blood cool. The air was warm and humid, a typical Texas summer evening. He hadn't even reached the back door before the scent of something wonderful drifted to him. When he stepped inside, the sound of Julia and Paige singing stopped him. He listened to the tune for a moment, smiled when he recognized it as the "spoonful of sugar" song from *Mary Poppins*.

They didn't see him when he entered the kitchen through the laundry area. Paige stood at the stove with her back to him, and Julia was placing forks beside the plates already on the table. A roast surrounded by quartered potatoes and carrots sat on a platter beside the stove, and it appeared that Paige was making gravy.

He'd assumed she'd hire a housekeeper to take care of the cooking and other mundane household chores. He could still see the proud upward tilt of her chin last night when she'd told him she would prefer to take care of the house herself. It didn't matter to him, but he had to admit, there was something very satisfying about walking into his house and seeing his family gathered in the kitchen, preparing a meal.

His family.

The thought caught him like a fist in the chest. It was going to take some getting used to, having a child and wife in the house. He'd been alone too long, and even with Nancy, this house had always been cold. And Nancy, who'd been a vegetarian and only ate salad and tofu, had never cooked him an edible meal once.

He hung his hat on a hook beside the back door and moved into the kitchen. "Smells good."

Paige turned at the movement and instantly stopped singing. When their eyes met, she blushed.

"Daddy!" Julia ran to him and threw her arms

around his waist. "We made you dinner and baked you a cake, too!"

"A cake, too?" He bent to hug his daughter, felt that familiar tightening in his chest at her enthusiastic greeting. "This must be my lucky day."

"It is," Julia said, her face beaming. "We wanted to s'prise you."

"You did."

"Dinner's ready." Paige turned back to the stove. "Why don't you wash up while we put everything on the table?"

"All right." He moved to the sink and rolled up his sleeves, then turned the water on and glanced over at Paige. She was dressed in a calf-length navy skirt and pale blue sleeveless blouse, and the sight of her bare, slender arms and lower legs sent a rush of heat through him.

"Paige and me used your computer and bought me a new bedroom set today," Julia said. "She let me pick it out myself and Betty Ballerina sheets, too!"

"Really?" Clay had never heard of Betty Ballerina, but he figured he had a lot to learn when it came to little girls. While he soaped up his hands, he looked at his daughter and smiled. "I'll bet you'll have the prettiest bedroom in Texas."

"I will," she said with a serious nod. "And California, too!"

"The pictures we printed out are on your daddy's desk," Paige said. "Why don't you run up and get them?"

Julia ran out of the room and Clay heard her singing the Mary Poppins song again as she skipped up the stairs.

Reaching for a towel, Clay turned back to Paige. "Sounds like you've kept busy."

"You haven't heard the half of it." Paige smiled. "We spent the morning saying hello to all the horses again and feeding them carrots. I'm sure you'll hear all about it over dinner."

Leaning back against the counter while he dried his hands, Clay watched Paige pour gravy from the saucepan into a bowl. Her hands fascinated him, and he couldn't take his eyes off her long, slender fingers, couldn't help but wonder what they'd feel like on his skin.

He sighed mentally, heard the sound of his daughter skipping back down the stairs, and he knew that it was going to be another long night ahead of him.

Chapter 6

Clay offered to help with the dishes after dinner, but Paige shooed both him and Julia out of the kitchen while she cleaned up. She knew that Julia would have to return to California with her grandparents the next afternoon, and she wanted him to be able to spend as much time with his daughter this weekend as possible.

Paige had also wanted a few minutes alone to absorb everything that had happened since she'd exchanged wedding vows with Clay. She was a married woman now. A wife. A mother.

While she loaded the dishwasher, Paige listened to the sound of Julia's laughter from the other room. Considering the circumstances, it amazed her how happy and well-adjusted the little girl was. From what

Clay had told her, Paige knew that the Barringtons, not Nancy, had raised Julia. The idea was unimaginable to Paige.

Without thinking, she touched her own stomach, wondered what it would feel like to carry a child, to give birth, then hold the tiny infant in her arms. Just the thought of it made her insides feel soft and warm.

At least she knew that Clay wanted more children. He'd made that clear to her when he'd told her that he intended her to be a wife to him in every manner. She was fairly certain they wouldn't consummate their marriage tonight, but what about tomorrow evening, after they'd taken Julia back to her grandparents? Her pulse quickened at the thought.

Heavens, she was wound tight as a clockmaker's spring. The waiting, and not knowing when they'd make love, was making her crazy. And frustrated, she realized. All last night, she'd lain in that big bed, *his* bed, and wondered what it would be like to have Clay beside her. Wondered what those big, rough hands would feel like on her skin. He'd kissed her before, on the mouth, but would he kiss her other places, too? Her breasts tightened at the thought and her nipples hardened. Would he kiss her there?

Oh, Lord, she hoped so.

"Paige!" Julia burst through the kitchen door, waving a sheet of paper. "Look what Daddy drew— a cow with three heads!"

Thankful for the interruption of her wayward thoughts, Paige smiled at the little girl. So that's what they'd been doing in the other room, she realized as

Clay strolled in behind his daughter. Wonders never ceased, she thought.

"See here?" Julia held the drawing up for Paige. "Right next to my picture of a horse. See?"

Paige looked at the drawing. "You're absolutely right. Do cows have three heads?"

"Of *course* not," Julia said with exasperation, then rolled her eyes. "He's just being funny. Don't you think he's funny?"

"I do think he's funny." Paige glanced up at Clay, though she couldn't imagine she'd have ever used that word to describe him. "Very funny."

"Hey, I like my cow." He had a twinkle of humor in his eyes, though his expression was quite serious. "Or should I say cows?"

Julia giggled at that, then looked back at Paige. "Can I put our picture on the refrigerator? My grandma always does. I have lots of pictures on my refrigerator at home."

Paige watched the humor disappear from Clay's eyes when Julia mentioned her grandmother. Clearly he didn't want to be reminded that, at least for the time being, he had to share his daughter, and that she didn't yet consider the ranch her home.

"Of course we can put your picture on the refrigerator." Paige dried her hands on a dish towel. "But first you have to sign your name in the corner. All artists sign their work."

"Okay." Julia handed the picture to her father. "We both have to sign it, 'cause it's both our pictures."

"Should I sign it three times?" he asked.

"No, silly." Julia giggled again. "I'm gonna go get my other pictures and sign them, too."

Paige watched Julia run out of the kitchen, then turned her attention back to Clay. "I'll take her upstairs now. We need to get her bath started and pack her suitcase."

"There's no rush." He dug through a drawer by the kitchen phone and pulled out a magnet advertising Peterson's Hay and Feed, then put the picture on the refrigerator. "You'll have plenty of time to pack her things in the morning."

"Not if we're going to make the ten o'clock service."

He glanced at her over his shoulder. "What are you talking about?"

"I'm talking about church service at ten o'clock. We'll need to leave the ranch no later than nine-thirty to make it in time."

Shaking his head, he turned to face her. "I don't go to church."

"Julia told me she goes every week with her grandparents." Paige folded the towel and laid it on the counter. "I go quite often myself, though I admit, not every week."

"So you and Julia go, then. I'll drive you."

Paige had known that Clay wasn't going to like the idea, but from the look on his face, she'd have thought she'd asked him to douse himself with fish oil and run naked through town.

"Clay, you were willing to marry me, a woman

you barely knew, in order to prove to the courts that you could provide the best home for your daughter. In comparison, spending an hour in church once in a while can't be that difficult."

He pressed his lips firmly together. "They're completely different issues."

"Are they?" she asked. "Or are they both about creating the illusion of being a family?"

"It's not an illusion." He narrowed his eyes. "We *are* a family now."

"Legally, yes," she agreed. "But maybe the courts will want to see a little more than that."

He stared at her for the longest ten seconds of her life, then said through gritted teeth, "Fine."

He turned and stomped out of the kitchen.

Stunned that she'd actually convinced him, Paige released the breath she'd been holding and leaned back against the counter.

Clearly, being married to Clay Bodine would be difficult, Paige thought, but it most certainly would not be boring.

Wolf River Grace Community Church hadn't changed much in twenty-two years. The clapboard exterior and tall steeple were still white, the steps leading through the wide double doors were still brick. Nothing had changed much inside, either, Clay thought as he stared at the cathedral ceiling and tall, stained glass windows behind the pulpit, though the church didn't appear quite as large as he'd thought it was when he was ten years old.

Especially the pews, Clay noted, shifting his legs so his knees wouldn't keep bumping the seat in front of him. On those few Sundays when he'd come to church with his grandmother, Clay had fit much easier into the long wooden bench.

Beside him, Julia and Paige joined in on the song that would finally end the crowded service. Paige might have managed to induce him into putting on a dress shirt and tie and coming here, but there was no way in hell he was going to sing. Arms folded, he skimmed his gaze over the congregation. Most of the faces were familiar to him, though there were several new ones, as well. He knew that Wolf River was growing by leaps and bounds, especially since The Four Winds Hotel had opened, bringing in more jobs along with tourists and businessmen. The last cattlemen's convention held at the hotel's newly built convention center had been filled to capacity.

Nothing stayed the same, he knew. Change was as certain as taxes and death. Lord knew *his* life had certainly changed just as dramatically, in a much shorter span of time.

He glanced at Julia, watched her fingers fiddle with the pink ribbon tie on the neck of her white dress. Though he hadn't spent as much time with his daughter as he would have liked this weekend, he knew that she'd be back in two weeks and they'd have two entire weeks together before the court hearing. After that, Clay thought, he was confident that Julia would be coming home with him to stay.

But the changes in his life had only begun with his

daughter, he thought and lifted his gaze to Paige. The yellow skirt she wore was long and flowing, her simple blouse with eyelet collar a crisp white. She'd pulled her soft, golden brown hair back into a bun, but the style didn't look as severe as it had before she'd changed her hairstyle. If anything, it made her neck look longer and her face softer.

Before he started to fantasize about his own wife while he sat in church, Clay looked away and focused his gaze two aisles over on the bald spot in the back of Hugh Foderman's head.

When he'd walked into church with Paige and Julia by his side this morning, Clay hadn't missed the slack jaws and open stares. He figured that by now, most everyone in Wolf River knew he and Paige had been married. There'd already been plenty of talk about them, Clay knew, and the fact that he'd had a child from his previous marriage. He also knew that there would be plenty more talk for some time to come, at least until something bigger and better came along to gossip about. He'd never paid any mind to loose tongues before, and he had no intention to start now.

But along with the curious stares, Clay had also noticed several disapproving glances directed at Paige. He'd considered that Paige might be the object of some criticism, but the snide, judgmental looks that had come from Judith Parcher and Maude Fetalmeyer had set Clay's teeth on edge.

But Paige hadn't appeared to notice the cool stares from the women, Clay thought, any more than she'd noticed the stares of interest from the men. More than one man had made Clay's eyes narrow in warning, and if Brett Rivers hadn't looked away when he had, Clay might have had to have a talk with the neighboring rancher about his lack of manners.

It's about time, Clay thought when the song ended, and was ready to get up and walk out when Pastor Sherman stepped up to the pulpit again.

"Before we leave today—" the young pastor smiled at his congregation "—I'd like to personally congratulate Clay Bodine and Paige Andrews on their very recent marriage."

Clay froze, then looked at Paige, who stared at the pastor in stunned disbelief. Terrific, Clay thought with a silent groan. It wasn't enough he'd shown up here, he and Paige and Julia were now suddenly under a microscope. Silence echoed as every head turned and stared. Then the church broke out in applause, with a few whistles and cheers.

"We'd also like everyone to join us in a celebration," the pastor continued when the room quieted down. "Sandwiches, drinks and cake, compliments of Rebecca Montgomery and the staff at Wolf River Library, will be served in the church garden."

Dammit to hell.

Based on the horrified look on Paige's face, she hadn't known about this, Clay realized. As the people filed out, Clay was met with a few slaps on the back and several well wishes.

Paige leaned across Julia and said quietly, "I—I didn't know. Rebecca asked me if we were coming to church and I told her yes, but I swear, I had no idea she was up to something.''

''Can I have some cake at the party, too?'' Julia asked hopefully.

Clay forced a smile as he looked at his daughter. ''Sure you can.''

With nowhere else to escape, Clay set his teeth, then followed Paige and Julia out of the church.

''I could tell something was up the minute he walked into the drugstore and looked at you.'' Sheila Gordon elbowed Paige and winked. ''You sure had everyone in this town fooled. To think you and Clay had something going on all this time, right under all our noses.''

Stuck between Sheila and Daphne Pringle on the crowded garden patio, Paige managed a stiff smile. She'd been cornered by the two women a few minutes ago and they'd been pumping her for details about Clay and their courtship. She'd managed to avoid or be vague with every answer so far, but Paige had the feeling Sheila and Daphne weren't going to leave her alone until she gave them something good to chew on.

The word had been spread by the women she'd worked with at the library that there would be a celebration in the church garden this morning, Paige realized, which would certainly explain why there'd been such a large turnout for today's service. She should have known something was up when she'd spotted Sheila and Daphne sitting two pews ahead of

her. Paige couldn't remember seeing the two women
at Sunday service since they were all little girls.

Paige looked around for Rebecca, who'd been serving punch a few minutes ago, but there was no sign
of her friend. *Friend.* Ha. That was certainly a loose
name for a traitor, Paige thought.

Holding her smile carefully in place while Sheila
rattled on about how surprised everyone in town was,
Paige glanced over Daphne's shoulder and spotted
Clay standing by the garden's three-tiered fountain.
He was talking with Lucas and Julianna Blackhawk.
The couple owned a ranch several miles west of town.
Julianna was currently holding the newest addition to
the Blackhawk family, four-month-old R.J., while the
twins, three-year-old Nathan and Nicole played with
Julia on the lawn.

Paige knew that Clay was unhappy about this unexpected reception, but there was nothing she could
do about it now. He would simply have to grin and
bear it, she thought, just the same as she would. Given
her druthers, though, Paige would take the Black-
hawks over Sheila and Daphne any day.

"And here we thought you and Bernie would be
tying the knot one day," Daphne said while she
sipped on a glass of punch. "I was in the bank on
Friday after you and Clay got married. Poor Bernie
was dragging round like a coon dog's jaw. Judith
Parcher told me you two got into a knock-down, drag-
out fight right there at the bank when you told him
you were marrying Clay. Is that true?"

Knock-down, drag-out? Oh, for heaven's sake,

Paige thought in exasperation. She'd barely raised her voice. Paige opened her mouth to answer Daphne, but Sheila beat her to the punch.

"Why do you listen to anything that old bat says?" Sheila curled her lip. "Judith lives for gossip and repeats everything she hears, whether it's true or not. Do you know she told MaryAnne Johnson and Stephanie Roberts that I was dating a married man?"

"You *were* dating a married man," Daphne said.

"But I didn't *know* he was married." Sheila folded her arms indignantly. "There's a difference."

When the two women began to argue, Paige decided it was time to leave. She started to back away and bumped into someone, who took hold of her arms to steady her.

"I'm so sorry," she said, turning around. "Please—" She stopped when she saw who it was.

Oh, dear.

"Hello, Paige," Bernie said without smiling.

"Hello, Bernie."

The conversation between Sheila and Daphne immediately went dead. Several other people standing around quieted, as well.

"So you went through with it," he said stiffly.

Terrific, Paige thought with a sigh. The last thing she wanted to do at this moment was discuss her marriage with Bernie.

"I didn't really think you'd do it." His frown deepened. "When I went to pick up my mother's prescription at the drugstore and Sheila told me about you and Clay, that he'd asked you to marry him, I thought it was a joke.''

What? Paige swiveled a look at Sheila. "You were listening?"

Sheila at least had the decency to look embarrassed. "Well, I wasn't really *listening,*" she said quickly. "I just caught a word or two from the vent by the cash register. Just enough to sort of catch the drift. It was just so romantic, the way he couldn't wait to propose to you."

Obviously Sheila hadn't caught enough of "the drift" to realize that Clay's proposal wasn't based on romance at all. If Sheila *had* heard everything, she'd have known the real reason Clay had married her. And if Sheila had known that little detail, then the entire town would have known, also.

But it was a little late to worry what the good people of Wolf River thought about her marriage to Clay Bodine. It was the price of living in a small town— Paige glanced at Sheila—with certain people who had small brains.

That's why Bernie had suddenly asked her to marry him, Paige realized. Because he'd heard from Sheila that Clay had proposed, and Bernie had been afraid he'd lose his "retirement portfolio," which had included Paige's income at the library.

At the beginning throb of a headache, Paige pressed her fingers to her temple. For a day that was supposed to be a celebration, she wasn't exactly having a stellar time.

Paige nearly jumped when Clay stepped behind her

and slid his arms around her waist, then pulled her back against his chest.

"You all right, sweetheart?" he asked.

Sweetheart? Her insides stampeded at Clay's endearment, but she did her best to look relaxed and comfortable in his arms. "I—yes. I'm fine."

"Good. I'm worried you haven't had enough sleep," he said, his tone suggestive.

Paige watched Daphne and Sheila's eyes widen and their jaws go slack.

"Congratulations," the two women said in unison.

"Thanks, ladies." Clay pulled Paige closer, then glanced at Bernie. "Hey, Pratt."

"Bodine." Bernie sounded, and looked, like he'd just drank starch. "Congratulations."

"Thanks."

When Clay bent his head and nibbled on her ear, Paige felt the heat of her blush work its way up her neck. Bernie turned bright red, while Sheila and Daphne watched with longing.

"Rebecca wants us to come over for a toast." Clay glanced up and smiled. "If you all don't mind that I pull my wife away, that is."

"Of course not," Sheila squeaked and Daphne nodded enthusiastically.

Clay looked at Bernie, who shrugged. "Sure."

"By the way, Pratt," Clay said. "I'll give you a call next week. I have some bonds maturing at my brokerage that I thought I'd transfer to your bank. Think you can handle the account?"

The prospect of personally managing even a piece

of Clay's sizeable funds visibly brightened Bernie. He straightened his shoulders and puffed up his chest. "I'd be happy to help wherever I can, Clay."

"Thanks."

Without warning, right in front of Sheila, Daphne, Bernie and everyone gathered around, Clay turned Paige in his arms and kissed her soundly on the mouth. Startled, she simply stood there. She knew the kiss was for show, but that didn't seem to stop her from slowly melting against him. Or stop her body from reacting. Vaguely, through the haze of pleasure radiating through her blood, Paige heard several "oohs" and "ahhs" and "isn't that sweet?"

When he finally pulled away and looked down into her eyes, Paige saw that same glint of desire she'd witnessed after the first time he'd kissed her. She shivered from the promise he held in his gaze, and knew that tonight they would truly be man and wife, at least physically.

It was going to be a long day, Paige thought as Clay took her hand and led her toward Rebecca.

And perhaps an even longer night.

Chapter 7

The ride back to the Rocking B that evening was tense. Clay drove silently, his gaze focused intently on the road, his large hands set firmly on the steering wheel. Paige glanced at him occasionally from the corner of her eye, but the tight set of his jaw and his obvious lack of desire to speak, kept Paige from even attempting to start a conversation.

She understood his dark mood, had felt a sense of loss herself when they'd had to return Julia to her grandparents after the wedding reception at the church. Clay had smiled at his daughter, then hugged her goodbye and told her that he'd see her in two weeks. His manner had been lighthearted and relaxed in front of the Barringtons, but Paige had seen the strain in his eyes when he'd watched his daughter drive off with her grandparents. Knew that his frustration and anger were simmering just beneath the surface, threatening to boil over at any moment.

He'd waited out in the truck when Paige had gone to pick up Eudora from Rebecca, and she was glad that her cat was now in its carrier, between them on the front seat of the cab. It helped somehow to keep a sort of barrier between them, something to create not only a physical space, but a mental one, as well. A distraction, of sorts, not only of what they'd left behind them in town, but what lay ahead at the ranch.

Not just in the days and weeks ahead of them, Paige thought, though that was certainly something to think about. But specifically, what lay ahead *tonight*.

It was the first time they'd be alone in the house, and though Paige was doing her best to relax, her insides were jumping like corn in a hot pan. Clay hadn't said anything to her, or made any innuendos about tonight, but she'd *felt* it. Knew instinctively that the tension between them wasn't just about Julia going back to California. It was about sharing a bed, and what would happen in that bed.

Though it had felt as if the ride to the ranch was taking a lifetime, when Clay finally pulled up in front of the house and stopped the engine, the journey suddenly felt too short. Without waiting for him, she quickly opened her door and slid out, then reached for the cat carrier and held it close. When Clay came around and offered to take the animal from her, she shook her head and told him she'd rather do it herself.

Thankfully, he didn't argue, just went ahead of her and opened the front door.

"Eudora's never been anywhere else," Paige said when they were inside. "She might be a little nervous for a while."

Clay looked at the cat carrier, then lifted his gaze to Paige. "The cat's not sleeping with us, Paige."

Us. Her heart slammed against her ribs. "No, of course not. She has a bed of her own she's used to. I've already set it up in one of the extra bathrooms for tonight."

He nodded. "I've got to go out to the barn. You do whatever you need to do. I'll be back in shortly."

She hurried upstairs to the bathroom and opened the door of the carrier, but Eudora simply glared at her and refused to come out. Paige sighed, then moved the cat's bed beside the carrier and left the bathroom, closing the door behind her, though she did leave a night-light on for the animal.

Eudora would be fine, Paige knew. Though it might take the animal a little time to adjust to her new surroundings, the cat had always been extremely independent. Right now, Paige had other, more pressing concerns on her mind.

She'd barely made it out of the shower and into her nightgown when she heard Clay come into the bedroom. She quickly pulled a brush through her hair, then stepped out of the bathroom. Her breath caught when she noticed the sheets had already been turned down. She glanced nervously at Clay, who stood in front of the large closet with his back to her. It surprised her that he'd apparently already showered, probably in the downstairs bathroom. Though he'd pulled his slacks back on, he was shirtless, a towel draped over one shoulder.

Her heart leaped at the sight of him. He'd slicked his hair back, and water still dripped from the dark ends, then beaded on his broad, bare back. Muscles rippled as he reached to hang up the shirt he'd worn that day.

She made a small noise, and he turned.

Heavens. She knew it wasn't polite to stare, but she couldn't take her eyes off him. The muscles in his shoulders and arms were well defined and appeared rock-hard. From what she could see, there wasn't an ounce of fat on the man.

Without taking his eyes off her, Clay snagged the towel from his shoulder and dragged it over his head and shoulders, then tossed it on top of a hamper inside the closet.

When he moved toward her, she held her breath. He stopped in front of her, then reached up to brush her hair off her shoulder; her breath shuddered out.

"You—you'll have to tell me—" she felt her cheeks burn as she dropped her gaze "—I mean, if there's something I should, or that you want me to—"

"What I want, Paige," he said softly, "is for you to relax. And to look at me."

She was at least able to do one of those things. Lifting her gaze, she saw a tenderness and patience in his eyes that startled her. And though only slightly, she did relax.

"We've got two weeks alone to find out what each of us likes and wants," he said. "Let's just let it happen, all right?"

She nodded slowly, was amazed at the soothing timbre of his voice, the gentle touch of his hand on her shoulder. He slid his fingers up to cup the back of her neck and eased her closer, then covered her mouth with his.

The kiss was a mere whisper, the slightest brush of his mouth over hers, but it was enough to quicken her pulse and warm her blood. Instinctively she placed her hands on his bare chest, felt the coarse sprinkling of hair under her fingertips and the steady, solid beat of his heart. His skin was warm, and he smelled of soap and man and sex. Dizzy from the sensations swirling through her mind and her body, she swayed into him on a sigh.

His lips were firm, unrelenting, yet—to Paige's delight, as well as her distress—clearly in no hurry. He took his time tasting, nipping the corner of her mouth, teasing the seam of her lips with the tip of his tongue, then retreating. Waves of heat rippled through her; her skin tingled, her breasts felt heavy and swollen. Her nipples grew hard and achy.

His hands slid down her back, then around her waist to pull her more intimately against him. Paige felt his arousal press against the vee of her thighs, and when she softly gasped, he slipped his tongue inside her mouth. He tasted like peppermint, she thought through the haze of sensual pleasure engulfing her. And when he deepened the kiss, she could barely think at all.

She met the easy slide of his tongue with her own, heard the sound of her own labored breathing. His hands tightened on her waist, then inched upward toward her rib cage. She felt as if she were on fire, and when his thumbs lightly brushed the undersides of her breasts, she trembled.

Lost in his kisses, Paige hadn't realized until now that he'd slowly inched her backwards toward the bed. For the past two nights, she'd lain in Clay's bed alone, wondering what it would be like when he finally made love to her. The moment was here, she knew.

She shivered in anticipation.

Clay slid his hands down her arms, then lifted his head. Slowly she opened her eyes and saw the raw need that burned in his gaze.

"I'm going to take this off you now," he said quietly, and began to bunch the fabric of her gown in his fingers.

She swallowed hard, felt her stomach lurch as he inched the gown higher and higher.

When he raised the hem of her gown up to her waist and hesitated, she held her breath, knowing that he'd just realized she had no underwear on. He muttered something, but her heart was slamming so hard against her ribs, she couldn't hear what he'd said. She raised her arms as he gently tugged the gown over her head and tossed it on the bed.

In spite of her fear and embarrassment, Paige lifted her chin and met Clay's narrowed gaze.

The fierce, primitive expression of pure lust in his eyes made her breath catch. Before they were even married, she had made a decision to be an active participant in making love with Clay. Even though her insides were shaking, even though her knees threatened to collapse, she was determined to stand firm.

His gaze slid slowly down her body, then lifted again. He said nothing, just stepped toward her, reached out and gently cupped her breasts in his large hands. She quivered at his touch, and when his callused thumbs rubbed back and forth over her hardened nipples, sharp arrows of pleasure shot to the juncture of her thighs.

Closing her eyes, Paige leaned into Clay's touch. She'd never experienced anything like this before, hadn't known she was capable of such intense feelings. She'd always thought there was something wrong with her, that she might even be frigid when it came to men. But she was quickly learning that she was far from frigid, and at the moment, she was actually burning up inside.

When Clay lowered his head to her breast and took her in his mouth, her eyes flew open again and she gasped in shock. She clutched at his head, arching back as he sucked lightly. The fire inside her spread; the ache became unbearable.

"Clay," she said between ragged breaths. "Please."

It seemed as though he hadn't heard her. He simply

moved to her other breast, swirled his hot tongue over the bud of her nipple, then once again pulled her into his mouth. If he hadn't slipped one of his arms around her back, Paige was certain she would have crumbled to the floor.

And just when she thought she might have to beg, he lifted his head, then slowly lowered her to the bed. The mattress was soft against her back, the sheets cool. Keeping his eyes on hers, he reached for the zipper of his slacks and pulled it down. Transfixed, Paige watched as he shed his trousers—the only article of clothing he'd bothered to put on after his shower.

Though Paige certainly knew what a man looked like without any clothes, she'd never actually *seen* one, not a living, breathing one, at least. And she'd absolutely never seen a naked, extremely aroused male before. She felt a mixture of fascination, fear and excitement as she looked at Clay.

How was this, this *joining,* possible? she wondered. Her confidence, and the burning desire she'd felt only a moment before, dipped slightly.

Clay sensed the hesitation in Paige and struggled to hold onto the last threads of his control. He'd nearly lost it when he'd taken off her nightgown and looked down at her naked body. She had a slender build, a narrow waist and long, curvy legs. Her breasts fit his hands perfectly, and her taste intoxicated him.

His need to be inside her consumed him, but this was her first time, and the last thing he wanted to do was spook her. If they were to share a bed, and a life together, he wanted her to trust him completely.

Strangely, her innocence did not take away from the pleasure, but aroused him all the more. It didn't seem to matter that this was the modern world, where relationships casually came and went. At a primitive level, Clay was pleased that his wife had belonged to no other man before him.

He stepped out of his slacks, then lay on the bed beside her, gently gathered her in his arms and kissed her, lingering over her sweet lips, then moving to the smooth column of her neck. Her skin was like silk, warm and soft and shimmering. When he slid his hand down her side and over her hip to caress her buttock, she made a small sound and pressed against him.

Clay wasn't certain how much more he could take himself, but he was determined to bring Paige every step of the way with him. Though his own body screamed for release, he concentrated on pleasuring the woman in his arms. He brought his mouth back to hers at the same time he slid his hand around to the triangle of soft curls between her legs. She jumped when he touched her there, then gasped against his lips when he slowly, intimately, slipped one finger inside her.

"Clay, I—"

"Shh." He gentled her with another kiss, slowly moved his finger over the most sensitive nub between her legs. She was moist, swollen. Tight. He slipped deeper inside her body, stroking her. Her hands clutched frantically at his shoulders. On a moan, she moved against his hand, wanting, needing more.

"*Please,*" she whimpered, wrapping her arms around his neck and pulling him closer. "Please... *now...*"

"Yes," he murmured, his own breath ragged and hoarse. "Now."

He moved over her, spread her legs with his knee, then eased inside her. She opened to him, dug her fingernails into his back and muffled her cry against his shoulder. With an effort that brought sweat to his brow, he stilled, waited for her to adjust to him. His muscles shook from the struggle between mind and body, but he waited, poised over her.

When she'd finally taken him fully into her body, she said on a rush of breath, "Don't stop. Please don't stop."

He hesitated, but then she began to move her hips and his mind went blank. Nothing else existed but the need for completion, the need to satisfy the intense, throbbing ache in his loins.

He thrust himself deeper inside the tight, velvet glove of her body. She met him, lifting her hips to take him deeper still, writhing under him in her own swirling world of emotions.

Clay felt the shudder move through her body, saw the surprise in her glazed eyes as she cried out. As she peaked, he thrust again and again, faster. On a groan, he shuddered violently into her, his body convulsing with his climax.

His lungs burning, his chest heaving, Clay rolled to his side, wrapping his arms around Paige as he brought her with him.

Paige was certain she would never move again. She felt as if she were drifting through soft, warm clouds. Dimly she heard the sound of her own slowed breathing and the slight rustle of sheets. If I'm dreaming, she thought, I don't ever want to wake.

But she wasn't dreaming, of course. She felt the long, hard length of Clay's body pressed against her own, heard the steady beat of his heart against her ear, and knew that this was real.

Turning her head, she pressed her lips against his chest and tasted the salty dampness of his skin. His arms tightened around her and pulled her closer.

Oh, yes, she thought with a sigh. This is definitely real.

"Are you all right?" he asked, breaking the silence between them.

She nodded, then lifted her gaze to his. The glint of desire still shone in his eyes and a thrill skipped through her. "That was…"

She hesitated, struggling to find the right word. There simply wasn't one to describe what she was feeling.

"What?" he murmured, pressing his lips to her forehead.

"Wonderful," she breathed, though it was so much more than that. "And amazing."

Smiling, he rolled to his back, bringing her on top

of him. She gasped at the sudden movement, laid her palms flat on his chest to steady herself.

"I'd definitely say that settles any question about how 'compatible' we might be," he said, then skimmed his hands down her back and cupped her buttocks.

Heavens, Paige thought. That was certainly an understatement. The rough feel of his palms on her bottom stirred the heat in her blood. The idea that she would feel the need again so quickly and—based on the hard press of his arousal between her legs—that he felt it, as well, stunned her.

One week ago, if anyone had told her that she'd be lying naked in Clay Bodine's bed, as his *wife*, she'd have told them they were insane.

It sobered her to think that if she'd refused Clay's offer, another woman would be lying here right now. Strangely, the idea bothered her more than a little. He might not have married her for love, she told herself, but the fact still remained that he had chosen her. She knew better than to expect more from him, but fool that she was, she couldn't stop the flicker of hope inside her that one day, in time, he might come to love her.

Because somewhere between the time they'd exchanged vows and this moment, she'd fallen in love with him.

Paige knew better than to tell him. Knew that it would spoil the moment, that he might even turn away from her if she did. She couldn't bear that. Not after what they'd just shared.

She wanted to cherish this night and the magic of the feelings he'd roused in her. Feelings that were building again as he caressed and stroked her backside.

And along with these feelings came a sense of power, she realized. A boldness she'd never experienced before.

Experimenting with this sudden bravado, she moved her hands over the hard planes and angles of Clay's chest. His muscles flexed underneath her fingertips and when she moved her hips ever so slightly against him, she heard his sharp intake of breath. She met his heated gaze, then lowered her mouth to his.

She kissed him as he'd kissed her before. A gentle tease, a soft nip, then finally tasting the firmness of his lips with her tongue. He moaned deeply, then cupped the back of her head and dragged her closer.

When she moved her hips against his, matching the rhythm of her tongue, she felt him harden again, felt the wild beating of his heart against her own.

She rose over him, then slowly lowered herself, taking him inside her.

And then she began to move.

His hands clutched frantically at her hips. When she arched upward, he lifted his head, then closed his mouth over her breast and ran his hot, moist tongue over the hardened nipple.

The pleasure was more than Paige could stand. The climax slammed into her, shattering her into tiny, shimmering pieces. When Clay groaned hoarsely, then shuddered inside her, she collapsed on top of him.

Pressing her lips against his neck, she closed her eyes.

And smiled.

Chapter 8

The week passed quickly. While Paige concentrated on decorating and furnishing the large house, Clay was busy at the west end of the ranch doctoring the freshly branded and marked cows. As the weather turned hot, screwworms were an ongoing problem for the cattle, and it was critical to find the affected cattle and treat them as soon as possible.

"Hold 'er tight, son." Joe jumped down from his horse and approached the cow Clay had just roped and tied down. "She's a bossy one and mad as a bottled bumblebee."

If he hadn't been so busy struggling to contain the angry animal, Clay might have responded to his foreman's uncanny knack to state the obvious.

Joe administered the medicine, then slapped the animal's rump and stepped back. Clay released the rope holding the cow's hind legs and jumped out of harm's way, too. Indignant, the cow rolled to its feet, glared at her tormentors, then turned and hurried back to the herd.

"Ingrate," Joe muttered, then climbed back on his horse.

Grinning, Clay coiled the rope in his hand, then tipped his Stetson back and wiped at the sweat on his brow with the handkerchief around his neck. It had been a long, hot day, but a productive one, and even though it was only midafternoon, Clay was itching to head back to the ranch.

In the past, Clay wouldn't have considered quitting work until it was dusk. There was always something to do, if not out on the range with the cattle, then back at the corral with the horses. Besides, there'd been no reason for him to hurry back home to an empty house and a frozen dinner.

But now that he'd married Paige, Clay found himself looking forward to the end of the day. Looking forward not only to the meal waiting for him, but the woman who'd prepared the meal, as well.

Not a day had gone by that she hadn't surprised him in one way or another. The downstairs bathroom she'd insisted on wallpapering herself. The arrangement of wildflowers she'd picked and placed on the kitchen table. Getting up at 5:00 a.m. every day to make coffee and breakfast for him.

And the nights. *Lord.* He wiped at the sweat on his

forehead again. Just thinking about the nights made his blood heat.

Damn, but he was one hell of a lucky guy.

From the first time he'd kissed her, Clay had suspected that there was a sensuality simmering underneath Paige's prim, straitlaced facade. He couldn't help but feel both pleasure and pride that he'd been the one to bring that sensuality to fruition. It seemed that with every passing day she grew slightly more bold, more curious, and last night she had come out of the bathroom wearing a sexy, white silk negligee.

At the sight of her long, curvy legs and the soft rise of her breasts under the plunging neckline, he'd been hard instantly. She'd walked slowly toward him, her gaze hesitant, her smile shy, and it had been all he could do not to drag her down on the mattress with him and slip into the sweetness of her body. Through a will of iron, he'd waited for her to walk to him, waited for her to slip beside him on the bed, waited for her to touch him.

He'd let her make all the moves, let her set the pace, and they'd made love slowly, drawing the passion out, making it all the more powerful between them.

He was already thinking about tonight, wondering what other surprises his new wife might still have for him.

"You gonna kiss that rope or maybe just sing to it?"

Startled out of his thoughts, Clay glanced up at Joe. A grin tweaked one corner of his foreman's mouth.

"Keep it up," Clay said, pulling at the slip knot on the rope, "and it'll be around your neck."

Amusement wrinkled the corners of the older man's eyes. Leather creaked as he leaned back casually in his saddle. "The way you been roping today, I'd probably die an old man before you managed to get hold of me. Even then I'd have to stand still and grab hold."

Clay glared at Joe, but he knew what the man said was true. He'd been so distracted today with thoughts about Paige, anyone looking on would have thought him a greenhorn for sure. It was downright embarrassing.

"You already are an old man," Clay said tightly.

"Not so old I can't see you got the bug."

"What bug is that?" Clay asked, though he really didn't care to hear the answer. Dropping the rope over his saddlehorn, he swung up onto his horse.

"The love bug, son." Joe tipped his hat back. "It's bit you square on the butt."

The absurdity of Joe's comment actually made Clay laugh and relieved some of the tension in his shoulders. "For God's sake, we've been married a week."

"The right woman is the right woman," Joe said flatly. "I knew the second I laid eyes on my Dory she was the one."

Clay couldn't imagine what it was like to love that deeply. He'd thought he'd loved Nancy, and that had ended in disaster. If he wanted his marriage with

Paige to work, then he needed to keep his head on straight and his emotions in check.

"Joe," Clay said quietly. "You, of all people, know how it is with Paige and me."

Joe nodded. "I know exactly how it is, boy. Trouble is, I don't think you do."

As if to agree, Clay's horse threw its head up with a snort. "Nothing's changed," Clay said firmly. "We respect each other and we get along just fine. That's all I want. I made that clear to Paige when I asked her to marry me. Love has nothing to do with our relationship."

Joe's grin widened. "So we'll see you at poker tonight?"

Poker. Damn. Clay hadn't gone last week because of Julia, and he'd completely forgotten about tonight. There'd been an ongoing game every Saturday night for years at Joe's place. Clay rarely missed, but if he cancelled tonight, he knew he'd be the brunt of "the little woman" jokes for weeks. Not only from Joe, but from the guys, as well.

"Of course I'll be there." His hands tightened on the reins. "Why wouldn't I?"

Joe shrugged. "No reason."

"Damn straight there's no reason," Clay snapped. "Now if this quilting circle is over, why don't we get back to work? We've got ten more head to check out before we ride back."

Clay didn't wait for Joe's response, just swung his horse around. He'd stay out all night and play poker if he damn well pleased, he told himself. He didn't have to spend every night at home.

The love bug, my ass, he thought, shaking his head. He and Paige barely knew each other, for crying out loud. Too much sun had obviously fried his foreman's brain.

He had a ranch to run, and at the moment, cattle to take care of. The last thing he needed, the last thing he *wanted,* was a woman on his mind.

The bed was mahogany—1880s plantation, four-poster, with a carved, massive headboard. The deep, rich wood was decidedly masculine, yet just soft enough around the edges to appeal to a woman, as well. The frame, with its new mattress, sat high off the bedroom floor.

It was a bed that a man could put his boots under, Paige thought while she tucked pillows into shams.

When Rebecca had shown her pictures of the bed, nightstands and matching armoire, Paige had negotiated the purchase from a dealer in Austin herself, and had it delivered immediately. She'd found the bedding—a deep chocolate and forest green print, with a green striped dust ruffle—on the Internet, then had the linens shipped special delivery so she'd be able to set everything up the same day.

Fluffing the pillow in her hands, she laid it beside its mate, then drew in the scent of freshly laundered cotton.

She'd ordered several other pieces of furniture and items for the house, some from the Internet, some from pictures Rebecca had shown her, but the bed for the master suite had been the first to arrive. Somehow, that seemed appropriate, Paige thought, since it was here, in this bedroom, where her marriage had truly began.

She couldn't believe that a week had passed since she and Clay had stood before Judge Winters and said their vows. Eight days, to be exact. It felt as if she'd been here forever, as if her entire life before had been a dream, and now, living here, was reality. Seeing her toothbrush beside Clay's, hanging her clothes in the same closet, using the same shower.

She smiled at that thought. Last night, when she'd gone in to shower before bed, Clay had shocked her when he'd stepped in and joined her. She'd been embarrassed at first, but when he'd pulled her into his arms and kissed her, she'd quickly forgotten her modesty. She'd spent most of today remembering the feel of his slick, muscular body against hers, the touch of his hands soaping her back, then her breasts, then moving down lower still.

With a sigh, Paige kicked off her flats and sat on the edge of the bed. She sank into the thick down comforter, then bounced to test the mattress underneath. It was firm and solid.

She couldn't wait to break it in.

Did all new brides feel this way? Paige wondered as she ran her fingertips over the soft cotton fabric. Tingly and excited and nervous, all at the same time? Every day was a beautiful day. Every task, no matter how menial or difficult, was a joy.

She especially enjoyed cooking, and tonight, to celebrate their new bed, she'd dragged out the cookbooks she'd brought with her and tried some new recipes. Wine-roasted chicken, garlic potatoes, fresh peas and a lemon-strawberry Bavarian cake for dessert. She knew that Clay worked a long, hard day, and he seemed to enjoy eating the food she set on the table each night as much as she enjoyed preparing the meal. Lord knew, he could certainly pack it away, but the physical labor of working on a ranch kept his muscular body rock hard.

She thought about that body, what it felt like on top of her own, how it felt when he slipped inside her, and she couldn't help but blush. She laid back on the bed, closed her eyes and ran her hand over the pillow, wishing it were Clay.

Would he make love to her slowly tonight, drawing out each exquisite moment with precalculated precision? Or would he take her fast, with wild, reckless abandon?

Or maybe both. Smiling, she burrowed her face into the soft mattress.

She certainly hoped so.

He found her like that several minutes later. Though he'd certainly noticed the four-poster bed, it was the woman lying on top of it that truly caught his attention. Her slender body was stretched out on the big bed, her soft brown hair spilling over her face while her fingers moved idly back and forth over the pillow beside her.

Clay's throat went dry at the sight of her lying there, her feet bare, the skirt of her lavender dress flowing over her long legs. His gaze feasted on the curve of her hip, the soft rise of her breasts above the scooped neckline of her dress, the smooth column of exposed neck. He knew the spot just below her earlobe that made her sigh, knew if he lingered there, she would moan. There were other places that made her moan, too. A soft bite on her shoulder, a brush of his lips on the inside of her elbow, a sweep of his tongue over the heart-shaped freckle beside her hip.

He loved that freckle.

There were other places, too. Intimate places where no man had been before him. Places that Paige hadn't known existed. He'd found great pleasure in exploring her body, committing to memory every sweet curve, every soft valley. She'd been an enthusiastic learner, as well. On more than one occasion, she'd pleasantly surprised him with her eagerness to explore new avenues—to enter into virgin territory, he thought with a wry smile.

He watched her now, felt himself harden when her hand slid to the vacant spot on the bed beside her. His blood raced, then pounded in his temples.

No woman had ever aroused him more. No woman had ever made him ache.

He swore at the need that overwhelmed him, then drew back into the hallway to rein in his emotions.

He could control this, he told himself firmly. Maybe he had gotten a little carried away with the domestic scene this past week, but it would pass. He was certain that the intense need would level off to simple lust. They could enjoy each other, as husband and wife, as man and woman, without further complicating an already complicated situation.

He just needed to hold off letting himself get too wrapped up in Paige. Stop wondering what she was doing while he was out working. Stop thinking about what she smelled like, how soft her skin was. That little sound she made deep in her throat when he touched the right spot.

A few more days and Julia would be back in the house with them. Having his daughter here would surely cool the heat between Paige and himself. In a few weeks, they would all naturally ease into a relaxed family routine.

But he had to get a handle on the situation, on his feelings, now. Had to contain the emotions threatening to disrupt his carefully structured life.

Careful not to disturb Paige, he quietly went back downstairs, faltered at the incredible smell of the dinner she'd prepared, then shook it off. Dammit, but he was getting soft when he couldn't make a decision and be firm about it.

He called out to her as if he'd just come in, then made his way slowly back up the stairs.

"I'm in the bedroom," she called back.

She was standing by the bed when he walked into the bedroom, her pretty face lit with a smile. Once again, his determination stumbled. Once again he recovered.

He glanced at the bed as if he were seeing it for the first time. "New bed," he said simply.

"Do you like it?"

He focused on the bed instead of the seductive way she was nibbling on her bottom lip. "It's fine."

"Just fine?" Her smile dimmed.

"It's a bed." He turned and headed for the closet. "By the way, I'm going to Joe's place."

"Tonight?"

"We have a standing poker game every Saturday night. I didn't think to mention it before."

"Oh."

The single word was filled with disappointment. Clay's hand tightened on the pair of jeans he'd pulled from a shelf in the closet. He didn't turn around to look at her.

"Will you eat before you go?" she asked hopefully. "It's ready, if you're hungry."

Dragging a clean shirt from a hanger, he shook his head. "You go ahead without me. I'll have pizza later with the guys."

If he stayed, even to eat dinner, there was no doubt in Clay's mind that he'd never leave this house tonight. He couldn't give that kind of control to Paige. To *anyone*.

"All right," she said evenly. "I'll leave a plate for you in case you're hungry when you come in."

She was certainly taking this well, Clay thought, then glanced over his shoulder at her. She stood beside the bed, her hands clasped primly in front of her.

She smiled at him when their eyes met. She not only didn't seem angry, she was being pleasant, to boot.

Dammit, anyway.

Maybe he'd been wrong about their situation, he thought. Maybe Paige hadn't got as caught up in their relationship as he had. Clearly she had control of her emotions, and seemed completely unfazed that he was going out to a poker game this evening.

Good, he told himself. That was what he'd wanted, hadn't he? What he and Paige had agreed on. A marriage without entanglements. He should be relieved, if not downright happy, that she wasn't upset.

"I'm going to take a shower," he said through clenched teeth, then turned and headed for the bathroom.

He stripped off his dirty clothes and stepped into the hot shower, determined not to think about Paige. But when the image of her lying on the big bed crept into his mind, he felt the need rise again.

Dammit, *dammit*.

Swearing under his breath, he stuck his head under the spray of water and turned the faucet to cold.

"It must seem strange to you." Rebecca sliced two pieces of cake and set them on gold-edged china plates. "Coming to your house and seeing someone else living here."

"For heaven's sake, Rebecca." Paige rolled her eyes. "You aren't exactly someone else, you're my best friend. I'm glad you're living here."

After Clay had left the house earlier, Paige couldn't

face the empty house—or the empty bed upstairs—
by herself. She'd called Rebecca to see if she was
home, made up a plate of food for Clay like she'd
promised, then packed up the rest in her grandmother's old Chevy and driven into town.

How she'd managed to hide her disappointment
and hurt from Clay when he'd so coolly told her he
was going out, Paige still didn't know. She'd let herself want, let herself hope, for too much in the short
time they'd been together. Today was a wake-up call
to get her head out of the clouds. Obviously, she was
going to have to be much more careful in the future.

"I'm glad I'm living here, too." Rebecca slid a
plate across the kitchen table, then sat across from
Paige. "My apartment over the store was getting
much too cramped, and with the shop doing so well,
I'm considering expanding upstairs. Since I already
have a kitchen up there, I even thought about opening
a tea room for lunch and small, private parties."

"What a wonderful idea." Paige could already picture the small, Victorian-style antique store serving
tea in pretty china cups, finger sandwiches and scones
with cream. "If you have it open by Christmas, I'm
sure the library would book you for their holiday luncheon."

Rebecca cut off a bite of cake with her fork. "What
makes you so sure?"

"Because I'm in charge of finding a restaurant,"
Paige said with a grin.

Rebecca grinned back, closed her eyes on a moan

when she took a bite of the Bavarian cake. "Ohmigod, I think I just died and went to heaven."

At least *someone* was enjoying the dessert, Paige thought.

"If I do open a tea room, I *have* to put this on my menu." Rebecca took another bite, sighed with pleasure, then leaned back in her chair and leveled a gaze at Paige. "Now you want to tell me why you're here, sharing this amazing meal with me, instead of your new husband?"

Paige knew she'd have to tell Rebecca sooner or later, had actually been surprised that her friend hadn't pushed her for information when she'd shown up on her doorstep with all this food.

Paige casually took a bite of her own cake, though she barely tasted it. "He had a poker game."

"Oh." Rebecca pursed her lips. "And I take it you didn't know."

"He forgot to mention it."

"I see." Rebecca lifted a brow. "So you had your first fight."

Paige glanced up sharply. "Of course not. It certainly wasn't important enough to argue about. I wouldn't have even minded at all if—"

She stopped, felt embarrassed to even say it.

"If what?"

"If our bed hadn't arrived today," she mumbled, then looked away. "I know it's silly, but I'd sort of thought that we'd…well, celebrate."

"And then he goes off to play poker." Rebecca shook her head. "Men. God, they can be such idiots."

"I shouldn't have assumed," Paige said firmly. "It's just that he's been home every other night, and he's been very, I mean, well, based on the past week, I thought that we would...that he might want to—"

"Have sex?"

Paige nearly choked.

"For heaven's sake, Paige." Rebecca rolled her eyes. "You're a married woman. Married women have sex, and sometimes lucky single ones, too. Which I haven't been one of lately," she said with a sigh. "But enough about me. So is it hot?"

"Rebecca!"

Laughing, Rebecca leaned forward. "Details, sister. I want details."

Paige felt her cheeks burn. "I can't talk about that."

"Okay, you don't have to talk about it. Just tell me—is it hot?"

Paige pressed her lips together, determined not to respond. But as Rebecca leaned closer, her brow lifted in anticipation, Paige couldn't help the slow smile that curved her lips.

"I knew it!" Rebecca grinned widely. "When you walked out of the anteroom in Judge Winters's chambers and Clay looked at you, I was ready to call the fire department. A person could weld steel with that look."

Paige knew the look only too well. That hungry, intense need she'd seen in his gaze this past week. Just thinking about it now made her pulse quicken.

"Clay is very..." Paige searched for the right word

"physical. Whoever he'd married, he would have looked at them the same way."

"That's horse puckey." Rebecca shook her head. "He wanted *you*, sweetheart."

"Only because I was dependable and stable." So dependable and stable, she thought, that he didn't have to mention when he wouldn't be home for dinner.

"More horse puckey." Rebecca shook her head. "He might have had that silly thought in the beginning, but I don't believe for a second he would have married you if he wasn't attracted to you physically. And if he hadn't gotten your juices flowing, you wouldn't have married him, either, my dear. You would have married Bernie Pratt," Rebecca said with a shudder, then leaned closer and leveled her I-know-you-better-than-you-know-yourself look at Paige. "Come on, Paige. Admit it."

What was the point in denying it? Paige knew that Rebecca would see right through her if she tried to lie. Rather than look her friend in the eye, Paige picked up her fork and played with the cake on the plate in front of her.

"So maybe I was physically attracted to Clay before I married him," Paige said quietly. "Name me one woman in this town—including yourself—who's under eighty that wouldn't look at the man and feel her insides go soft? One woman who didn't wonder, at least once, what it would be like to be with Clay Bodine?"

When Rebecca didn't answer, Paige glanced up and saw her friend staring wide-eyed at her.

"Well, for heaven's sake," Paige said irritably. "You tell me you want the truth, and when I give it to you, you stare at me as if I'd just told you I was a double-agent for the CIA. Why are you *looking* at me that way?"

"You're in love with him."

Paige went still, then her heart gave a sickening lurch. Was she so transparent? And if Rebecca could see it, then would Clay be able to see it, too? Maybe he had, she thought. Maybe that was why he'd gone out tonight without telling her. To keep an emotional distance between them.

"You *are* in love with him," Rebecca said breathlessly.

"I'd be a fool to fall in love with a man who married me simply to be a mother to his child." So Rebecca wouldn't see her hand shake, Paige slowly laid her fork down on the plate. "A man who made it perfectly clear not only that he doesn't love me, but he doesn't *believe* in love."

"Honey," Rebecca said, shaking her head, "those are the ones who fall the hardest."

Not Clay, Paige sighed as she pushed her plate away. Tonight she'd made a mistake and let him slip through her defenses. From now on, she thought, she was determined to be much more careful.

Chapter 9

When Paige woke on Sunday morning, the bed beside her was already empty. She'd heard Clay come into the bedroom last night just before 1:00 a.m., though she'd pretended to be asleep when he'd quietly called her name, not once, but twice.

Paige had recognized the husky tone in Clay's voice, and she knew if she'd turned to him that they would have made love. Unwillingly, her own body had responded to his soft whisper. She'd felt her skin tingle and her pulse quicken. Her breasts had ached to be touched.

Even when the mattress dipped beside her, Paige had kept her back to him, squeezed her eyes tightly closed and forced her breathing to be steady and relaxed. When he slid under the covers, then pressed his broad chest to her back, she'd had proof of his desire to make love. She'd wanted desperately to lose herself in that pleasure, had nearly given in to the need pulsing through her.

But she hadn't. The hurt from Clay's behavior the night before was still too fresh. The sting was too sharp. There were no emotions involved for Clay when he wanted sex, Paige knew. But for herself, the physical and the emotional were intertwined. When they made love, she gave herself to him completely. And she couldn't have done that last night, not while she was still upset with him.

She'd set herself up for it, of course. She'd let her guard down, let him get into her heart. But this was still all so new to her. Having a husband, being a wife, running a household. And soon she'd be taking care of a child full-time, too. It was more than a little overwhelming.

Maybe she was just being too sensitive right now, she told herself. Maybe in a few days, or a few weeks even, she'd get used to her life with Clay and little things like new beds and uneaten meals wouldn't bother her so much.

The possibility didn't make her feel any better.

On a sigh, she rose from the bed and showered, then dressed for church. Though Clay had attended the service last week because of Julia, he obviously did not feel the same compunction when it came to his wife. She could live with that, she told herself. It was not her intention, and certainly not in her nature, to force Clay to do anything he didn't want to do.

As if she—or anyone—could, she thought, buttoning the front of the red floral dress she'd bought before she'd married Clay. She'd never worn red before, but Rebecca had insisted the color was perfect for her. Now that she had it on, Paige stared at her reflection in the mirror. With the new hairstyle and dress, she barely recognized herself.

All her life, Paige had been a dowdy, colorless bookworm. She'd read stories of mystery and intrigue, with courageous heroines and dashing heroes. She realized now that she'd lived life through the characters in all those wonderful books. And for the first time in her life, she had an opportunity to *experience* life, not just read about it.

When it came to Clay, Paige prayed she could be just half as brave as those characters.

She quickly made the bed, slipped on a pair of white strappy sandals and as a last minute thought, went back into the bathroom where she ran a tube of rose-colored lip gloss over her lips and a touch of mascara on her lashes. She still wasn't used to applying cosmetics, but she did like the subtle way the makeup brightened her face.

She was disappointed that Clay wouldn't be joining her, but she was determined to enjoy the day in spite of everything. Leaving a note on the kitchen table to tell him where she'd gone, Paige gathered up her purse and the car keys to the Chevy, then drove into town.

* * *

Clay stomped the dust off his boots, brushed off his jeans, then limped through the back door. His thigh hurt like a sonofabitch, and though he couldn't be angry with the horse who'd kicked him, he was definitely angry at himself. He'd known better than to come up behind that two-year-old filly like he had. She was a pretty little roan, but high-spirited and a little nervous.

It certainly wasn't the horse's fault, Clay thought, that he'd had his mind on another high-spirited, nervous female. But he was infinitely glad that the blow hadn't been six inches to the left. If it had, he'd be singing soprano and very worried about his ability to ever father any future children.

Of course, after the way he'd left the house last night, Clay figured his chances of fathering any more children were greatly diminished, anyway. Though Paige hadn't seemed to mind that he'd gone off to play poker, she certainly hadn't received him warmly when he'd wanted to make love with her last night, either. She'd pretended to be asleep, but he'd felt her stiffen when he'd touched her, and he realized that maybe she hadn't been as unaffected by his leaving last night as he'd first thought.

But what had really surprised—and annoyed—him, was the fact that he'd felt like a heel all night. He hadn't been able to concentrate on one single hand, had made three bets out of order, and forgotten what game they were playing twice. He'd been forced to listen to constant ribbing about separation anxiety from his wife and then laugh it off, when what he really felt like doing was reaching down someone—anyone's—throat and ripping out that person's liver.

So much for a friendly game of cards.

He wasn't used to feeling guilty, didn't like it one little bit. He'd make it up to her, he told himself as he closed the back door behind him and walked through the laundry area into the kitchen.

He could take her into town for dinner tonight, or maybe even offer to look at some of the paint chips or drapery samples she had laid out on the living room floor. He shuddered at the thought, but he knew women liked men to do that kind of stuff.

He realized how quiet the house was as he walked through the kitchen. Paige usually had classical music playing on the intercom system, but today, the house was absolutely still. He called out to her, but she didn't answer.

For one heart-stopping moment he thought she'd left him. That she'd packed up her cat and clothes and driven back to town. He hadn't thought she was upset enough to do anything like that, but who the hell could figure out what was going on in a female's head? Lord knew he'd never been good at it.

His eyes narrowed with anger. If she thought she could walk away that easy, she had another thing coming. Dammit, if he had to go to town and have it out with her in front of everyone, then that's what he'd do and if she—

Then he saw the cat. Eudora sat in the kitchen doorway, looking at him like he was an idiot. Clay released the breath he'd been holding. Paige wouldn't have left without taking her cat, he was sure of that.

He spotted the note on the table and snatched it up, then groaned.

Church. He'd forgotten all about that. He hadn't even thought about it being Sunday. Shaking his head, he raked a hand through his hair, then looked at Eudora.

"So I jumped the gun a little," Clay said irritably. "What was I supposed to think when she wasn't here?"

The cat meowed.

"She should have reminded me about church last night," Clay said in his defense. "It's my Sunday to tend to the horses."

Eudora flicked her own tail at that little bit of information.

"Yeah, well, what do you suggest?" Clay scowled at the animal.

The tabby got up and walked away.

"Thanks for the help," Clay called after the retreating cat.

He glanced at the clock on the kitchen stove. If Paige had come home after the service, she would have been home an hour already. Obviously, she'd gone somewhere else and hadn't bothered to call him.

He knew she'd gone out last night, too, because the Chevy had been parked in a different spot. He'd assumed she'd gone to Rebecca's, but what if she hadn't? What if she'd gone to see Bernie to cry on her old boyfriend's shoulder? His eyes narrowed at the thought, then he shook his head.

No. Paige might not be predictable, but she was honest. As much as he could trust anyone, he trusted Paige.

Shaking his head, he limped upstairs to take a shower. When he stepped into the bedroom, he stared at the new furniture and decided he liked it. Especially the antique four-poster bed. It was large enough to easily accommodate his tall frame, the mattress was firm, but extremely comfortable.

His ex-wife's taste had been the complete opposite of Paige's. When Nancy had moved into the house, she'd carted away every piece of furniture Clay had owned, then retained a designer from Beverly Hills to fly out and furnish the house. Everything she'd bought had been ultracontemporary. Sharp lines, bold colors, lots of white, glossy woods with steel trim. When she'd left him, she'd hired a moving company to pack up every last piece of furniture. Every lamp, every chair, every god-awful eye-straining painting that she'd considered "art."

And even though he'd paid exorbitant prices for everything, Clay had still appreciated the fact that Nancy had emptied the house. It had saved him the trouble of dragging everything off to the nearest charity organization.

For the past five years, he'd been comfortable with just a dining table, bed and office furniture. He hadn't needed anything else. He worked most of the time, and even when he had dated, he never brought women here, anyway.

His gaze traveled from the mahogany armoire to the nightstands, then finally back to the bed. He'd always liked the idea of a four-poster bed. It stimulated certain fantasies that would no doubt make his wife blush, but hey, he thought as he headed for the shower, a guy could only hope, couldn't he?

He had no idea what mood Paige would be in when she got back from town. Nancy had always given him the silent treatment when she was mad at him—right after she'd yelled at him.

But Clay was already well aware of the fact that Paige was nothing like Nancy. Paige was not selfish or condescending, and she certainly wasn't lazy.

She also wasn't predictable, Clay thought as he quickly soaped up. And that, strangely enough, was the one thing that worried him the most.

Arms loaded with groceries, Paige shoved her way in through the back door, dumped the paper bags and her purse on the kitchen table, then began to unload the items that needed refrigeration first. She'd stopped at Bud and Joe's Market to pick up fresh produce and meats for the week, along with several spices that had been missing in the kitchen pantry, especially some of the more uncommon ones.

After last night, Paige had seriously considered serving Clay frozen dinners from now on. Or maybe slap some lunch meat and cheese between some bread and toss that down on the table for his dinner. She'd

even seen meals from the shelf that could be micro-
waved and ready in under ten minutes. The hours
she'd save could certainly be put to use painting Julia's bedroom that lovely pale shade of yellow she'd
picked out from the samples.

But the fact was, she *liked* to cook. Because of her
grandmother's sensitive stomach, Paige had mostly
made bland soups and boiled chicken for the past few
years. Trying new and interesting recipes had been
fun, and watching Clay enjoy her cooking had been
extremely satisfying.

There was no point in staying upset with him, Paige
told herself as she dropped a head of romaine lettuce
inside the vegetable crisper. They'd both lose.

But at the same time, she thought as she pulled a
bag of apples from a shopping bag, she had no intention of being a doormat, either. Clay might not love
her, but if their marriage was going to succeed, he
needed to respect her. Not only as his wife, but as a
person. He'd caught her in a vulnerable moment last
night. If it happened again, she'd be ready to stand
up to him and speak her mind.

Why wait for there to be a next time? she asked
herself boldly. She'd speak to him now. Tell him how
she felt. While she stared at the bag of fruit in her
hands, she ran through various scenarios.

I would appreciate prior notice…

No, that sounded too prudish.

Clay, maybe next time…

Absolutely not. Much too timid.

Unless you'd like to make your own meals, Clay Bodine, I suggest...

She shook her head. Too combative.

I'm your wife, Clay. My time is valuable, too, and I feel that I deserve respect and consideration in this marriage.

That was pretty good, she decided.

"So how do like *them* apples?" she said with a nod.

"They look pretty good."

Startled, Paige squeaked at the unexpected sound of Clay's voice behind her. She whirled around to see him leaning against the kitchen doorjamb, watching her.

"Clay," she gasped. "You scared me."

"Sorry."

The black T-shirt he wore fit snugly over his muscled chest and arms. His jeans were clean, as were his black boots, which meant he'd just showered and changed. She watched as he pushed away from the doorjamb and walked toward her, stopped a foot away and dropped his gaze to her mouth. Her heart started to beat like a drum. When he bent to lightly brush his lips over hers, the scent of man and apples assailed her senses.

"New dress?" he asked softly.

Between his closeness and his lips on hers, Paige could barely remember what she had on. Oh, right. The red one. "Yes."

"Pretty," he murmured and traced the seam of her lips with his tongue.

"Thank you." She held back the threatening moan, had to remind herself to breathe.

"Can I help with anything?" he murmured softly.

Yes! You certainly can, her body screamed. Her knees went weak as she thought about all the ways he could "help" her.

But as tempting as it was, she wasn't ready to fall into Clay's arms just yet. There were things they needed to discuss first, and she was determined to stay focused on those issues, not the feel of his lips on her own.

"There is something," she whispered against his lips.

"What?" he asked huskily.

She pulled her head back, then shoved the apples at him. "You can put these in the refrigerator."

She turned away from him and began to empty the contents of another shopping bag. She said nothing about church and he didn't ask. They worked side by side in awkward silence, the tension between them tightening with each passing minute. Paige knew it wouldn't be any easier later to discuss what had happened last night. Which meant there was no time like the present. She slid a box of raisins in the cupboard, drew in a breath to steady herself, then turned toward him.

A bottle of apple juice in his hand, he walked toward the refrigerator. That's when she noticed the limp.

"What's wrong with your leg?"

He opened the refrigerator door and put the juice on the top shelf. "Horse kicked me."

"A horse kicked you?" she repeated in alarm.

"Nothing's broke." He snagged one of the apples he'd put in the fridge a moment ago and rubbed it on his chest.

The impulse to touch him, to soothe and fuss, overwhelmed her. Concern narrowed her eyes as she stepped closer to him. "But you're limping."

"All in a day's work," he said with a shrug, then bit into the apple.

"Where did it kick you?"

"In the barn."

She rolled her eyes. "Don't be smart."

He rubbed his hand over the top of his thigh. "Here."

Paige sucked in a sharp breath as she noted the proximity of the kick to Clay's groin. Eyes wide, she quickly looked back up. "Are you all right?"

"I'm sure everything still works." He chewed slowly. "We could test it out, if you're worried."

The light tease in his words was heavy with sexual innuendo. Paige felt her body respond to the deep, low timbre of his voice, and the hungry, fierce look in his eyes. Her pulse skipped, and the heat of his stare warmed her insides.

She was torn between her mind and her body, but determined not to let him use sex to clear the air between them. She swallowed hard, then met his steady gaze. "Clay, I think we should talk about—"

"I was an ass."

Surprised at his interruption, she simply stared, her mouth still open. He set his apple on the counter, then stepped closer to her, cupped her chin in his hand and looked down at her.

"I can't promise I won't be an ass again," he said evenly, "but I will promise that I'll be more considerate."

It wasn't exactly an apology, but it was close enough that Paige was too stunned to reply. Had he really called himself an *ass?* When she just continued to stare at him, he frowned, then dropped his hand and stepped back.

"Look, this isn't easy for me," he said flatly. "I've always come and gone as I pleased. I never had to think about anyone else. Now suddenly I have a wife and a kid. I'm bound to make some mistakes. For God's sake, you could at least *say* something."

First he'd thrown her off with his almost-apology, now he was getting irritable because she hadn't replied to his outburst. Heavens. Living with Clay was obviously going to be like riding a roller coaster. But even as she opened her mouth to speak, he started up again.

"Dammit, Paige." Hands on his hips, he paced to the other side of the kitchen, then back again. "What do you want from me?"

If he was trying to make her mad in a ridiculous attempt to ease his own guilty conscience, he was doing an excellent job, she thought. Folding her arms, Paige pointed her chin at him. "I don't believe I've asked you for anything."

That stopped him. He looked down at her, and the anger slowly drained from his eyes. "No, you haven't," he said quietly. "Maybe you should."

"There's nothing I want." *Except for you to love me,* she thought, but she might as well wish for the moon.

On a sigh, he reached for her hand and ran his thumb over the diamond on her ring, then suddenly he was pulling her toward the back door.

"Clay!" she gasped. "What are you doing?"

"I want to show you something behind the barn." He dragged her down the back steps.

"I've heard that one before," she said, but he just chuckled and kept pulling her along.

She could barely keep up with his long strides. Scooter came out of the barn, barking with pleasure as he joined the game. The sun beat down hard, and the smell of hay and horses filled the hot mid-afternoon air.

Other than a trip to the barn with Julia the weekend she'd visited, Paige hadn't spent much time outside since she'd come to the Rocking B. She'd been too busy inside the house to truly explore the ranch yet, and wasn't sure if Clay would object to her wandering around where his men were working. For the past week she'd heard the low growl of tractors, the whistles and shouts as the ranch hands worked the horses in the corrals, the occasional snorts and whinnies from the horses or the deep moo of a cow. Life on the Rocking B was very different from her house and job in town, but she'd come to love the ranch and already felt at home.

Because it was Sunday and midafternoon, the corrals were thankfully empty of horses and men. Paige would have been embarrassed if any of the ranch hands could see the way Clay was dragging her across the yard, despite her protests.

When they rounded the side of the barn, Clay stopped abruptly and turned, causing Paige to collide with the hard wall of his chest. He steadied her with his arms, then looked down at her. "Close your eyes."

"Clay, for heaven's sake, what are you—"

"Just do it," he insisted.

She sighed heavily, then closed her eyes, felt the anticipation and thrill of waiting for him to kiss her.

But he didn't. Instead, he stepped away and took both of her hands in his, then kept walking. "Don't open your eyes until I tell you."

She did as he asked, felt the dirt path under her shoes as he guided her. He continued to warn her to keep her eyes closed while he pulled her along several feet, then turned her to the left and kept walking.

When he finally stopped, she heard the sound of a door opening, then felt the warm, moist rush of sweetly scented air.

"Eyes closed," he reminded her and pulled her forward.

Paige furrowed her brow, resisted the temptation to open her eyes. The smell of damp earth filled her nostrils. She felt and heard the crunch of gravel under her feet. The quiet strains of Mozart played overhead.

Clay let go of her, and she heard the door close again, felt a fine mist fall on her cheeks and arms.

Where in the world had he brought her?

"Okay," he said from behind her. "Open your eyes."

She did, then gasped.

Orchids.

Hundreds of them. She was too stunned to speak, just turned in a slow circle, taking in the kaleidoscope of colors and shapes. From the palest lavender to the deepest purple, from creamy yellow to startling gold. Pinks and whites and reds. The shapes on the flowers were as individual and as varied as the designs. She felt as if she were in a rainforest somewhere. All she needed was the sound of rushing waterfalls and screeching, colorful macaws to complete the picture.

"It's so beautiful," she breathed.

"They're Joe's," Clay said. "It's a hobby, of sorts."

Joe's? It was hard to imagine Clay's foreman cultivating orchids. Cactus, maybe, Paige thought, but *orchids?*

"What do you mean, 'of sorts'?"

"It was actually his wife's hobby." Clay looked around the greenhouse. "Joe took over when she got too sick to care for them. After she died, he just kept them going. That was ten years ago."

"Ten years?" Paige examined the delicate stalk of

a tiny yellow flower that looked like a lion's head. "That's a long time."

"There were only twenty plants or so back then. Somehow it just kept growing. We've expanded the greenhouse twice."

She stepped toward and lightly touched the thick, waxy leaf of a large, white orchid with purple stripes in the center of the bloom. "How long were they married?"

"Twenty-six years." Clay shoved his hands into his front pockets. "She was a nice lady."

Paige bent to smell the tropical scent of a creamy white flower. "Did they have children?"

"Two sons and a daughter," he replied. "All of them scattered across the country now. We all kind of grew up together, though they're all younger than me. Joe sees them mostly around the holidays, but they stay in touch."

"He obviously loved her very much," Paige said wistfully.

Clay didn't answer, but he didn't need to. Love shimmered in every plant, every bloom, every leaf. The kind of love that endured beyond the bounds of life. Paige *felt* it, in the air, in her heart. Not just Joe's love for his wife, Paige knew, but her own love for Clay.

Why had he brought her here today? she wondered. Was this his way of saying he was sorry, without actually saying the words?

She wasn't sure, but she did know that him bringing her here, sharing this place with her, was something special. Something to cherish.

She walked to him, placed her palms on his chest and smiled up at him. "Thank you," she said softly, then rose on her tiptoes and pressed her lips to his.

His arms came around her, and he deepened the kiss. Her breath quickened as his tongue met hers, her heart beat heavy. He tasted like apple and dark, sweet desire. His hands slid down to her waist, pulling her tightly against him. He wanted her, she felt his arousal press against the junction of her thighs. And she wanted him. In every way, but for now, she would take whatever he offered.

He pulled away from her, his breathing ragged, and stared down at her. "Why don't we go try out our new bed?" he said huskily. "See how it holds up."

Our new bed, he'd said, and that simple word sent joy shivering up her spine. She smiled at him. "I'm sure it will hold up just fine."

Grinning, he took her hand and they hurried back across the yard toward the house.

Chapter 10

The following Friday morning, Clay and Paige drove into town to pick Julia up from the Barringtons. The morning was pleasant and they rode along the highway with the truck windows rolled down and a Tim McGraw-Faith Hill duet on the radio. Knowing that Clay was tense over meeting with the Barringtons again, Paige did not try to make conversation, she simply sat back and enjoyed the passing countryside and the wind lifting the ends of her hair.

This past week had flown by for Paige. The furniture for the living room, guest room and Julia's bedroom had arrived and already been situated, plus she'd had shelves delivered for Clay's office. If there was one thing Paige felt completely comfortable with, it was arranging the piles of books he'd had stacked on the floor. She'd also ordered a bigger desk, chair and file cabinet that would be delivered in a few days.

The house was slowly evolving into a home, especially since Paige had found a large steamer trunk in the attic that had belonged to Clay's great-grandmother. It was like finding a treasure chest. She'd been giddy with delight as she'd pulled the items out. An entire set of china, two crystal vases, a patchwork quilt and a needlepoint that read HOME SWEET HOME. Old photographs, including several of Clay, that she couldn't wait to frame and put up on the walls. Small toys, some antique, some from Clay's childhood. Baby clothes.

Paige had felt a longing rise in her as she'd brushed her fingers over a hand-knitted baby blanket. She was anxious to give Clay another child, and Julia a sister or brother. Anxious to feel life inside her, to hold a baby in her arms and place it to her breast. She and Clay hadn't discussed when they would try for a baby, but she considered bringing the subject up in a day or two.

Instinctively, Paige laid a hand on her stomach, then glanced over at Clay. Soon, she hoped.

While he was absorbed in his own thoughts, she studied the profile of the man she loved. She'd thought him handsome before, but now, just looking at him made her insides take flight. His rugged looks and size didn't intimidate her any longer and she'd become accustomed to the strong lines of his face and jaw. The sharp cut of his chin, the straight angle of his cheekbones, the slight bend in his nose. When he

smiled, the blue of his eyes softened to the color of
worn denim, but when he looked at her with desire,
his eyes darkened to the color of an ocean at sunset.

She remembered making love after he'd shown her
the orchid greenhouse last week, and the memory
shivered through her like an electrical current. Something special had happened between them that day,
something that hadn't happened before or since.
Though only for a little while, Clay had let his guard
down. His lovemaking had been more tender, more
gentle, than it ever had before. There'd been no rush,
no sense of desperation or urgency, just long, slow
kisses that built ever-so-slightly, until the pleasure
spiraled to what felt like torture and she'd begged him
to hurry.

She'd felt something from him that day, something
he hadn't given her before. Paige was too cautious,
too afraid to give it a name, but it was more than sex
and more than pleasure.

When Clay pulled into town, the sound of a
friendly honk from a passing pickup brought Paige
out of her reverie. From the sidewalks, several people
smiled and waved as she and Clay drove down Main
Street toward The Four Winds. For the past fifteen
years, Clay had kept to himself on the Rocking B.
But it wasn't going to be so easy for him now, Paige
realized. With a wife and a child, he wouldn't be able
to keep that same cool distance. It was obvious he
wasn't comfortable with the outward display of attention from the townspeople, but he'd get used to it,
Paige told herself. When he wanted to, she knew first-

hand how quickly her husband could turn on the charm.

When Linda Barrington opened the hotel room door, however, Clay's charm was definitely in the Off mode. He nodded stiffly at the woman.

"Linda."

"Clay, Paige, please, come in." Linda Barrington offered a weak smile as she stepped aside to allow them entrance to the suite.

The simple emerald-green suit dress Linda wore hung loosely on her slender frame and Paige thought that the woman looked thinner than the last time she'd seen her, her face more gaunt. It was apparent that the custody battle, and knowing that Clay would most likely win, was taking its toll on her.

Paige felt for the woman, could only imagine how difficult this situation must be for her. She wanted to comfort her, assure her that she wouldn't be cut out of her granddaughter's life, but based on the hard press of Clay's mouth, this wasn't the time.

"I've just ordered some coffee and pastries." Linda gestured toward a room service cart. "May I offer you something?"

"I'd love a cup of coffee," Paige said before Clay could answer. It was obvious that Julia's grandmother had something to say, and Paige understood it would be easier for the woman if she were able to keep her hands busy. "Cream, no sugar, please."

"Please have a seat," Linda said, gesturing to the sofa.

Clay watched Paige move to the sofa and he shot

his wife a disapproving glance. What the hell was the matter with her? he thought irritably. She knew perfectly well that he wanted to get Julia and get out as quickly as possible, yet here she sat primly on the sofa, her hands folded in her lap, watching while Linda poured coffee from a silver pot into a cup on a saucer.

Reluctantly, Clay slipped his hat off his head and held it in his lap as he sat on a chair beside the sofa, only half listening while Paige politely asked Linda about their flight. All he wanted to do was gather up his daughter and take her home, not listen to a bunch of female chitchat.

So where was Julia?

He looked at both of the closed bedroom doors and realized how quiet it was. A knot formed in his stomach. He didn't think the Barringtons would try to oppose the court-ordered visit, but then, he really didn't know them very well. Nancy had told him that her parents had objected to her marrying him, but he'd only actually met Linda and Bob once before he and Nancy had eloped and then once after.

"Where's Julia?" he asked Linda.

"With her grandfather, at the park on the edge of town," Linda said while she added cream to Paige's coffee. "She saw the swings there yesterday and asked if she could go. I said it would be all right."

The knot loosened in Clay's gut. "We could have taken her."

"You'll have plenty of times to take her," Linda

said, her voice strained. "I wanted a few moments to speak privately with you."

"Is everything all right with Julia?" He hated not knowing what was going on in his own daughter's life, that he had to be kept updated by Linda and Bob. But no longer, he told himself. Julia would come back to the ranch with him today, and in two weeks, after the court hearing, he was completely confident she would be coming home with him to stay.

"Yes, of course she's all right," Linda reassured Clay. "She's wonderful. You know how much we adore her."

This was exactly why he hadn't wanted to stay here, Clay thought. He'd known Linda would try to talk him into compromising on his decision for full custody. "Linda—"

"We're only asking for a few weeks a year, that's all. Maybe a holiday or two."

"We've been over this a hundred times," Clay said firmly. "I've told you and Bob that as long as you call me first and make arrangements, you can come and visit Julia as often as you want."

"Why is it so difficult for you to let her come and stay with us on an arranged schedule?" Moisture filled her eyes. "We've done a good job raising her, haven't we?"

"Dammit, Linda," Clay said under his breath. "Don't do this."

"Clay—" The woman drew in a slow breath to compose herself. "We know that Nancy wasn't a good wife or mother, but don't punish us for that. Julia's all we have. If you would just agree to—''

''You kept my daughter from me for almost five years.'' He felt the heat of his temper rising and struggled to contain it. ''Why should I trust you now? Why should I ever trust you?''

''We wanted to tell you about Julia. We told Nancy you had a right to know. That Julia had a right to know.'' Linda's hands were visibly shaking. ''But she threatened to take Julia to Europe with her and that musician and never return if we told you. She would have done it, Clay. You know she would. How could we have taken that chance?''

''If you'd have come to me before, we would've worked something out.'' Clay stood, his hands tightly gripping his hat. ''I will not sign papers that give you legal decisions of any kind over Julia.''

''We aren't asking for that,'' Linda said, her voice desperate. ''We just want to know that we'll be able to spend time with her in California.'' Linda glanced at Paige, then touched her knee. ''Paige, you're a woman, surely you can—''

''This discussion is over.'' Clay jammed his hat back on his head. ''Paige.''

Paige looked up at him, and when he saw the indecision in her eyes, he thought for a moment that he was going to have to argue with her, too. But thankfully, she simply set her coffee cup down and stood.

''Thank you for the coffee, Mrs. Barrington,'' Paige said softly, and the sympathy in her voice set Clay's teeth on edge.

"Linda, please." Forcing a smile as she rose from the sofa, Linda looked at Paige. "We bought her a new pair of shoes for casual wear, but we thought you'd know best what to buy her for wearing around the ranch. She might need a pair of jeans, too. She's growing so fast, we can barely keep up with her."

"We'll take care of it," Paige answered, her tone gentle. "You don't need to worry."

"I know." Linda swallowed hard and hugged her arms close. "I'll go get her suitcase."

Paige was quiet in the hallway after they left Linda, but when they stepped into the elevator, she looked up at him, her gray-green eyes somber. "Clay, there must be some kind of a compromise, something that you can work out."

"I don't want to talk about this." He punched the elevator button to the lobby. "I'd at least expect my own wife to be on my side."

"This isn't about sides, Clay," she insisted. "This is about Julia."

"*I* know what's best for my daughter," he said more sharply than he intended. "And that's the end of it."

Paige pressed her lips into a thin line and lifted her chin. She didn't say another word, not in the elevator or the lobby, or on the drive over to the park.

When Julia saw them pull into the parking lot at the park, she jumped off the swings.

"Daddy!"

His heart tripped at the sight of her running toward him. He stepped out of the truck and Julia jumped into the arms he held out to her. She laughed when he swung her around, and when he put her down again, she ran to Paige and hugged her, too.

Bob hugged and kissed his granddaughter goodbye, then looked at Clay and nodded stiffly. There'd been no arrogance in the man's demeanor today. If anything, Clay thought, Barrington had appeared humbled as he'd cast one last look at his granddaughter before he walked away.

He wouldn't feel guilty, dammit. He *wouldn't.* Shaking the feeling off, Clay turned his attention back to his daughter.

"Will you push me on the swings?" Julia asked Paige.

"Your daddy will." Paige smiled brightly at Julia. "I have some errands to run. Your daddy is going to take you to lunch and shopping for some new shoes and pants. I'll see you both back at the ranch later, okay?"

"Okay." Julia kissed Paige's cheek, then ran back to the swings and called out, "Come push me, Daddy."

"Be right there." Clay kept his gaze on Paige. "*I'm* taking her shopping? I don't know anything about girl stuff."

"All the more reason for you to learn," she said evenly. "I'm sure you'll do fine."

He frowned at her, knew she was doing this because he'd snapped at her in the elevator. Women were just too damn sensitive, he thought irritably, but he certainly wasn't going to argue with her in front of Julia. "Where shall I pick you up when we're done?"

"I still have my own car at my house," she reminded him. "I'm going to go look at some curtain samples at Rebecca's shop now, then I'll drive myself back to the ranch."

A muscle jumped in his cheek. "You could have lunch with us."

The smile she gave him didn't reach her eyes. "I'm not really hungry. Maybe I'll have something in a little while with Rebecca."

"I'll drive you," he said, knew that it sounded like a command, not a request.

She shook her head. "Rebecca's shop is half a block from here, Clay. It's a nice day and I could use the exercise. Enjoy the time alone with your daughter."

She turned from him and waved at Julia, who sat on a nearby swing, waiting to be pushed.

"Come on, Daddy," Julia called.

Clay watched Paige walk away, her back stiff and shoulders squared. He wanted to go after her, wanted to explain to her why he couldn't compromise when it came to Julia. But he wasn't sure he could explain, wasn't sure he understood himself why he felt so strongly against any kind of written agreement with the Barringtons. Julia's visits with her grandparents would be on *his* terms, not the courts.

"Daddy."

With a sigh, Clay turned and walked toward the

swings, felt his mood lighten slightly when Julia smiled at him.

He could pick out a pair of shoes and jeans for his daughter, he told himself. She was just a little girl, for crying out loud. How difficult could it be?

Paige was in the kitchen chopping carrots when she heard the slam of the truck door from the backyard, then Julia's excited shriek. It was nearly five o'clock, and though Paige would never admit it to Clay, she'd been slightly worried.

She'd had mixed feelings this morning when she'd left Clay and Julia at the park. Part of her was upset at Clay for refusing to even listen to what she had to say regarding Julia's grandparents, part of her was hurt that he continually referred to Julia as *his* daughter and *he* knew what was best for her. Paige understood Clay's bitter feelings toward his ex-wife, keeping Julia from him was a despicable thing to do. But she didn't understand why that bitterness extended so strongly to the Barringtons.

If he wasn't so pigheaded, Paige thought as she dumped the cut-up carrots into a pan, he wouldn't think that she was taking sides because she wanted him to try and understand how Julia's grandparents felt. How terrified they were of losing their only grandchild.

For Julia's sake, Paige hoped that Clay would be able to set his own feelings aside long enough to realize that there was room in his daughter's life for *all* the people who loved her.

The back door flew open at that moment and Julia came running into the kitchen. "Paige! Wait till you see what Daddy bought me!"

Wiping her hands on a towel, Paige turned. Good heavens! Julia was certainly not the same, neat little girl Paige had seen only that morning. Her ponytail was askew and her hair and face were covered with sparkling, iridescent glitter. Chocolate dotted both corners of her mouth and stained the front of her white tank top and green print shorts.

And on her feet, she wore a pair of brand-new, shiny black cowboy boots.

"Aren't they great?" Excitement danced in Julia's blue eyes. "I couldn't decide if I like the brown or the black, so Daddy bought me both!"

Based on the number of packages in Clay's arms as he came into the kitchen, he'd bought Julia a great deal more than two pairs of boots.

"They're beautiful, sweetheart." Paige smiled at Julia. "They look just like your daddy's."

"I got a new dress and some pretty shoes for church, too," Julia said brightly. "And a Betty Ballerina instant-bake oven, and a Patsy Poodle stuffed animal, and a really cool jewelry-making kit with five hundred thousand beads."

"My goodness, you've had a busy day shopping, haven't you?"

"I even got my own big person's hot fudge sundae," Julia said with a nod. "With extra whipped cream and sprinkles on top. Isn't he the best daddy in the whole world?"

Paige watched Clay dump the day's purchases on the table and lifted a brow. "The absolute best."

"I want to go make a bracelet." Julia rifled through the bags, then pulled out a bright pink box with dozens of pictures of bracelets and rings on the front. "I can't wait to tell my grandma all the stuff I got."

Tucking the box under her arm, Julia stomped out of the kitchen in her new cowboy boots, then stomped up the stairs toward her bedroom.

Paige turned her attention to Clay and met his sheepish gaze.

"I guess I got a little carried away," he said with a shrug.

"A *little?*"

"Yeah, well, I know we were just going for shoes and jeans, but—" He stopped, then swore. "Jeans."

Paige looked at him in disbelief, then glanced at all the bags. "You didn't get the jeans."

"I guess I forgot." He slipped his hat off his head and scratched the back of his neck. "I could take her—"

Shaking her head, Paige put up her hand. "I'll take her. You'll need a semi if you go shopping with her again."

He grinned, then reached into one of the bags and pulled out a small, black velvet box. "I bought you something, too."

Her heart tripped when he handed the box to her. She opened it, then gasped at the heart-shaped diamond necklace inside.

"You can take it back if you don't like it." He

jammed his hat back on his head, then shoved his hands into the back pocket of his jeans. "Get something else, if you prefer."

"It's beautiful." Bernie had given her a subscription to *Time* magazine, a Dustbuster and a desk calendar, but no man have ever given her a present this nice before. In awe, Paige stared at the sparkling diamonds.

"Try it on," he said, inclining his head.

Lifting the delicate gold chain from the box, Paige tried to open the clasp, but her shaking fingers refused to work. Clay stepped behind her, then took the chain out of her hands and settled it around her neck. He hooked the clasp, then gently ran his fingertip down the necklace to the diamond heart.

"Thank you," she whispered, shivering at his touch. "But you didn't have to buy me anything."

"Of course I didn't have to." He wrapped his arms around her, pulled her close against his chest and lowered his head. "I wanted to."

I wanted to. She felt herself melt against him, felt as if her bones had softened at his tender words. She thought she could stand like this forever, with his arms holding her close, his lips brushing her ear.

"I want to give you things, Paige." He nipped at the shell of her ear. "Anything you want, just name it."

She blinked back the moisture burning her eyes. "There's nothing I want, Clay," she said quietly, though it was a lie.

There was one thing she wanted, Paige thought. Only one thing. Something that didn't come in a box, and no amount of money could buy.

Chapter 11

''The water is too cold,' Mindy Marmot said to Rosie Raccoon. 'I'll wait here on the shore for you and Sydney.'

'''But Mindy,' Rosie said. 'You're going to miss all the fun. We want you to come swimming with us.'''

Paige held the book up high so all the four- and five-year-olds gathered around her could see the illustrations in *Picnic by the Pond*. The popular children's book was one in a series of adventure stories about three friends, Mindy Marmot, Rosie Raccoon and Sydney Squirrel.

Today, Mindy, the fraidy-cat of the three, refused to go swimming in the pond.

'''There might be octopuses out there,' Mindy said.

"'Octopuses don't live in ponds, silly,' Rosie said. 'They live in the ocean.' Rosie and Sydney both laughed, which made Mindy very mad and she made a face at her friends.''

Paige held the book up again for the children to see the funny face that Mindy had made and the youngsters all laughed.

Paige had brought Julia to the library today for Thursday morning story time, and Elissa, the scheduled storyteller, had asked Paige if she would mind reading instead. Since reading to the children had always been one of Paige's favorite tasks when she'd been working at the library, she'd been happy to take over for the head librarian.

Paige still hadn't made a decision whether she would be returning to work part-time after Julia started kindergarten in late summer. Lord knew that between caring for an energetic five-year-old and a big house, there was plenty to keep her busy. Since Julia had returned to the ranch nearly two weeks ago, the time had flown by.

The court hearing was scheduled for tomorrow morning at ten, and even though Clay's lawyer had reassured him that he would be awarded full custody, Clay had grown more tense as the day had approached. In fact, he'd been downright cranky, Paige thought as she held up a picture of Sydney and Rosie diving into the pond and splashing Mindy Marmot.

Paige knew that Clay was anxious something might go wrong tomorrow, but she was certain he would relax after the hearing. Once he knew he had full custody of his daughter, he would have no need to worry.

He'll have no need for you, either, a little voice whispered. *You'll have served your purpose.*

The thought had been niggling at her all week. She'd known from the beginning, of course, that was the only reason he'd asked her to be his wife, but she couldn't seem to get her heart to cooperate with her mind. She would simply have to accept that Clay had married her as a means to an end and that was all. That fact that she'd fallen in love with him was her problem, not Clay's.

Shaking her thoughts off, Paige turned her attention back to the storybook, which ended with Mindy Marmot overcoming her fear of the water and coming out to swim and play with her friends.

The children all clapped when Paige finished reading, then jumped up and ran to the table where one of the moms was serving punch and cookies. Paige watched Julia giggling with one of the other little girls while two little boys made funny faces at them. Paige was happy to see how well Julia fit in with the other children that she would soon be going to school with. After the custody hearing was settled, Paige intended to enroll her at Wolf River Elementary.

"Paige?"

Paige turned at the sound of a woman quietly calling her name and was surprised to see Linda Barrington standing by the row of childrens' history books.

"Mrs. Barrington?" Paige returned the book in her

hand to the shelf behind her, then walked over to the woman. "I thought you and Mr. Barrington were flying in tomorrow morning."

"Please," Mrs. Barrington said with a tired smile. "Call me Linda."

"Of course." Paige returned the smile. "Linda."

"We changed our flight and flew in late last night instead," Linda said. "I was hoping I might have a few words with you privately before the hearing tomorrow."

"But how did you know we'd be in town today?"

"Julia told me on the phone yesterday that you were bringing her to the library this morning for story time." Linda's smile brightened as she glanced over at her granddaughter, who was busy playing with the other children. "She was very excited."

The sadness in Linda's eyes as she watched her granddaughter was evident. Once again, Paige wanted to comfort the woman, but wasn't sure what to do or say. She could only imagine the anguish Linda Barrington was going through.

"She looks happy." Linda clutched the small white purse in her hands to her stomach, then brought her gaze back to Paige's. "Have you any idea what it feels like to lose a child?"

"I can't imagine anything worse," Paige said quietly. Just the thought of it made her heart ache.

"There isn't anything worse." Linda blinked at the gathering moisture in her eyes. "I know our daughter wasn't perfect, but we miss our Nancy so."

Paige put her hand on the woman's arm. "I'm sorry for your loss."

Linda nodded sadly. "We know we don't stand a chance winning custody of Julia. The only reason we tried, was because we were hoping that Clay would compromise and let Julia come visit with us on a regular basis."

"You can come here and see her as often as you want." Paige covered Linda's icy hands with her own. "Clay told you that."

Linda shook her head. "It's not the same as having her come stay with us. Now that Bob is retired, we have lots of time to spend with her. Places we'd like to take her. Clay won't allow that. He hates us for keeping Julia from him."

"I'm sure he doesn't hate you," Paige reassured the woman.

"If we were in his shoes, I'd be angry, too." Linda closed her eyes on a sigh. "We're just so afraid that Julia will forget us. If we could just have some kind of reassurance that he won't try to keep her from us."

"He won't do that," Paige insisted. "I know he can be stubborn, but maybe if we just asked him—"

"Maybe if you just asked me what?"

Paige felt her breath catch at the sound of Clay's voice behind her. She and Linda had both been so intent on their conversation, neither one of them had seen Clay walk into the library.

And based on the tight set of his face, he wasn't at all happy about finding her speaking with Julia's grandmother.

"Clay." Paige dropped her hand from Linda's. "What are you doing here?"

"I was picking up an order at Peterson's." His voice was flat. He looked at Linda. "Linda."

"Clay, please don't be mad at Paige for talking to me." Linda's face had turned pale. "She didn't know I was coming here. I just thought that, as a woman, Paige might be able to—"

"Influence me?"

Linda shook her head. "Talk to you."

"Paige understands that I'm the one who makes the decisions when it comes to my daughter. There's nothing to talk about."

Paige felt her insides twist at the cold tone of his voice. When he turned his ice-blue gaze to her, a chill shivered up her spine.

"Grandma!" Julia suddenly spotted her grandmother and ran across the library. "Grandma, you're here!"

Linda knelt and Julia flew into her open arms. "How's my baby?"

"Where's Grandpa?" Julia hugged Linda.

"Back at the hotel." Linda smoothed a hand over Julia's head. "He told me to tell you he misses you."

"Can I come and see him?" Julia asked. "I want to tell him Paige got me a library card."

"You'll have to ask your daddy, sweetheart." Linda looked at Clay, her eyes pleading. "Just for a little while?"

"I want to sleep at the hotel with you, too," Julia

said insistently. "Just tonight. Can I, Daddy, please? I can sleep in one of Grandpa's T-shirts."

Paige couldn't bear the thought of separating Julia from her grandmother, especially considering the court hearing was tomorrow. She knew she would be stepping onto thin ice if she interfered, but it was impossible to stand back and say nothing.

"We could pick her up in the morning and bring her fresh clothes," Paige told Clay, refused to allow herself to flinch when he shot her a look.

"Please, Daddy," Julia begged. "Pleeaasee."

A muscle worked in Clay's jaw, then he nodded stiffly. "We'll pick her up at ten."

Julia flung herself at Clay's legs. "I love you, Daddy," she said brightly, then jumped into Paige's arms and hugged her, as well.

"I love you, too, Paige."

Holding her grandma's hand, Julia skipped out of the library. Clay watched them go, then turned back to Paige, his mouth set in a hard line. "I want to talk to you. Outside. Now."

Paige lifted her chin and met his steely gaze. "Fine."

She followed him to the back parking lot, managing to smile and wave goodbye to Elissa and several other people she knew as she left the library. He stood beside his truck, a grim expression on his face as he held the passenger door open for her. She didn't bother to thank him when she slid into the cab and folded her hands in her lap.

He slammed the door, then stormed around and

climbed into the truck beside her. Hands gripping the steering wheel, he stared straight ahead. Determined to wait him out, Paige kept her attention on a crew of workmen repairing a pothole on the street behind the library.

"Why would you do this?" he said after several long, tense moments.

"Why would I do what?" she asked calmly, though her stomach had more knots than a fishing net.

His fingers tightened around the steering wheel. "Go behind my back and meet with Linda like that."

Paige swiveled her head to meet his dark gaze. "I did *not* go behind your back, Clay Bodine. Linda knew that Julia and I would be at the library today and she wanted to speak with me."

"Convince you to change my mind about the joint custody, you mean."

Paige prayed for patience. "Not about joint custody. She told me that she and Bob never expected joint custody. They were just hoping to work out an arrangement of scheduled visits in California."

"Dammit, Paige, we've been over this," he said, raising his voice. "How can they expect me to trust them? If I drop this custody battle and give them what they want, what am I left with legally? We'll constantly be arguing over who has Julia when and for how long."

"Clay, that's not true." Lowering her voice, she leaned toward him and laid a hand on his arm. "They just want some kind of assurance that you won't keep Julia from them."

"How can you come into this and after a few weeks think you know what the Barringtons will or won't do?" He jerked his arm away. "I was married to their daughter, remember? More than once, they tried to stop the marriage, and afterwards, when Nancy came to Texas, the phone calls begging her to leave me were almost daily."

"Did you hear the phone calls?" Paige asked. "Or did Nancy *tell* you about them?"

His eyes narrowed at Paige's question. Clearly, he hadn't considered the possibility that Nancy might have lied. "Linda and Bob had made it clear before the wedding that they didn't think I was good enough for their precious daughter," he said tightly. "Why should I think their opinion of me now is any different?"

"Even if they did have their doubts about you marrying Nancy," Paige said, determined to get through to him, "that was nearly six years ago. They aren't the same people. They have Julia now, and they lost their only daughter. Things like that change a person."

"You're naive to think that people like the Barrington's can change. They will say and do anything to keep control of Julia's life."

"Isn't that what you've done, too?" she asked carefully.

His face turned to stone, then he snapped his gaze away and white-knuckled the steering wheel. "I won't do it and that's that."

Paige straightened her back. "So I have no say in this."

"I make the decisions when it comes to my daughter."

"I see."

He swore under his breath, then drew in a deep, impatient breath. "We had an understanding about Julia."

"Which understanding was that?" she asked calmly. "The one that I'm a glorified nanny to *your* daughter, or the one where I keep *your* house, and conveniently share *your* bed?"

His gaze shot back to her, dark and cold and angry. A muscle jumped in his jaw. "This is about Julia. Not about you and me."

"Maybe you can separate the two," she said quietly. "But I can't. Not anymore."

"What the hell is that supposed to mean?"

She knew what she had to do, knew that it was the right thing for everyone, but knowing that didn't make it any easier. A numbing cold settled over her as she looked into Clay's eyes.

"You're right, Clay." A knot of ice formed in her stomach. "We did have 'an understanding' as you put it. But things have changed since then, at least, for me, they have. It wouldn't be fair to Julia for me to stay and pretend to be a mother to her. She deserves honesty, not lies."

For a split second, fear replaced the anger in Clay's eyes, but then it was back again, as cold and dark as before. "You're leaving Julia and me now, the day before the court hearing?"

She realized how desperately she'd wanted him to say something, *anything* that might have given her a reason to stay. Her heart felt as if it were ripping apart.

"Don't worry, I'll be at the hearing tomorrow," she managed to say through the thickness in her throat. "I'll clear out my things this afternoon, and I'll call one of the housekeepers from the list you interviewed. I'm sure we can work out the details over the next few days. I realize you probably won't want me to see Julia, but I'm asking anyway. I can come to the ranch, or when you come to town, maybe she can spend some time with me."

"Dammit, Paige." Frustration rumbled in his voice. "You can't just walk away like this. Not now."

"When's a good time, Clay? Next week? The week after that? Like you said, people don't change. And for the record—" she opened the door and slid out of the cab, felt the warmth of the sun on her skin, even though she was chilled to the bone "—I'm not leaving Julia. I'm leaving you."

How she managed to stand when her knees felt like soggy noodles, Paige didn't know. But somehow she held her head up, her shoulders straight, then put one foot in front of the other and walked away.

Clay couldn't remember the last time he'd gotten stewed to the gills drunk. Though he drank a beer or two on poker nights, he'd never been one to consume hard liquor in vast quantities. Too much alcohol numbed the senses and dulled the brain, made a person act stupid and lose control.

Which was exactly why he was currently nursing his third whiskey. If he'd ever needed a reason to numb his senses and dull his brain, it was definitely tonight.

He sat at Joe's kitchen table, frustrated that the whiskey had not yet quieted the roar in his head or the ache in his chest. When he'd showed up at his foreman's back door an hour ago, Joe had taken one look at him, then turned around and broke open a new bottle of Jack Daniel's. Joe hadn't said one word, just poured the shots into two glasses, handed one to Clay, then sat down at the kitchen table with a book about orchids and started to read.

Clay had tossed back the first two shots, but he truly didn't want to get completely smashed. He had a court hearing in the morning, and the last thing he wanted to do was to walk into the courtroom looking as miserable as he felt.

Dammit to hell, anyway.

"She left me," he said, finally breaking the silence.

Joe looked up from his book.

"Just like that." He swept a hand up to emphasize his sense of futility. "Packed up her suitcases, took her cat and went back to town."

That's why he'd come here, Clay knew. Because he couldn't stand the empty house. Couldn't stand being there, knowing that Paige was gone, that she wasn't coming back. Even after their argument, he hadn't really thought she'd follow through on her threat to leave.

When he'd driven back to the ranch this afternoon and she was gone, he felt as if he'd been sucker punched. He'd known she was angry, he'd been angry, too. That's why he'd waited to cool off before he'd gone back home.

But in his heart, he truly hadn't believed that she would go. He'd been so certain she'd calm down and realize that Julia needed her.

That *he* needed her.

The thought rocked him to the core, had him tightening his hand around his glass. He'd never needed anyone before. Didn't *want* to need anyone.

Joe took his glasses off, then closed his book and reached for the bottle of whiskey. "Is that so?"

Clay frowned. "That's what I just said, didn't I?"

"Can't imagine why she'd leave, considering your congenial nature," Joe said and topped off Clay's glass.

"I warned her I wouldn't be easy to live with," Clay defended himself. "She knew how it was between us, why we got married."

"So I guess you should have married Minnie Wellman." Joe sipped on his own glass of whiskey. "She wouldn't have given you two licks of trouble. Bet you could boss her around all day without a peep of backtalk."

"Damn straight." Clay nodded in agreement, then winced and dropped his head in his hand. "Good

God, no. It makes my brain hurt to even think about it.''

And his heart, he realized. His heart hurt, too, dammit.

He didn't know how to handle these emotions. Even when Nancy had left, he hadn't felt this... empty. He had no idea what to do, which way to turn. After the way he'd treated her, the things he'd said, why would Paige come back to him now?

She wouldn't. Not without a good reason.

So he'd give her a reason, then. A very good one.

But first, he knew he'd have to get her attention.

The alarm startled Paige awake at seven the next morning. Though she wanted nothing more than to simply burrow back into the haven of her soft bed, she slipped out from under the covers, sighing heavily as she turned off the persistent beep coming from the bedside clock radio. Too tired to stand just yet, she sat on the edge of the bed, waiting for her mind to come into focus with her surroundings, was once again hit with the reality that she was back in her own house, in her bed.

Yesterday afternoon, not knowing where else to go after she'd left the ranch, Paige had shown up on Rebecca's doorstep.

''You're staying with me,'' Rebecca had said emphatically and Paige hadn't argued. After her showdown with Clay, she hadn't the strength to argue with anyone. She could barely remember packing her things and driving back to town. After calmly explaining her situation to Rebecca, who'd listened and offered solace, Paige had retreated to the quiet of her old bedroom and let the tears come. It had been like opening a floodgate, but even when she'd finally been too exhausted and spent to cry any longer, she'd still tossed and turned all night.

Closing her eyes against the oppressive darkness that filled her, Paige drew in a long, deep breath. Her body felt limp, her limbs heavy, her brain like cotton. She considered slipping back into bed, only for a few minutes, but knew that a few minutes or a few hours wouldn't make a difference. The pain wrapped around her heart was too tight to let her rest. She knew she needed every ounce of strength she had in her to face this day. To face Clay, to look into Julia's eyes and tell her that she wouldn't be living with her and her daddy anymore.

She'd spent the entire night worrying about the little girl, several times had nearly driven back to the ranch. And though her heart told her to go, her gut told her no. She loved Clay. She would always love him. But she knew her love alone would not sustain their marriage. Respect and trust between two people were vital to any relationship. What kind of home could they provide for Julia, if they didn't have those elements?

Paige loved Julia, too. But she couldn't lie to the child, couldn't pretend to be someone, or something, that she wasn't. Julia deserved better.

Combing her hands through her hair, Paige sighed, then rose from the bed and tugged on her robe. After barely three hours sleep, she could only imagine what she was going to look like in the courtroom today. Her eyes would still be red from crying, and there were certain to be dark circles under her eyes. She could only hope that all those cosmetics she'd bought worked as well as they promised in the ads. Today she was definitely going to need all the help she could get.

When Paige opened her bedroom door, Rebecca was waiting outside with a cup of steaming coffee.

"I heard the alarm." Rebecca pressed the warm mug into Paige's hand and guided her toward the bathroom. "You have a warm bath waiting for you. Have a nice long soak. I'll go find you some clothes and bring them in."

Paige opened her mouth to protest being waited on, but Rebecca shook her head and shoved her gently into the bathroom. "Not one word, Paige Andrews Bodine. In the tub."

Rebecca's use of Paige's married name tightened the pain around her heart, but she simply hadn't the energy to resist. After Rebecca closed the door, Paige combed her hair and clipped it on top of her head, brushed her teeth, then pulled off her robe and gown and stepped through a mound of lavender-scented bubbles. Tugging the white lace shower curtain closed, Paige eased her body into the tub, sighed as she sank neck-deep into the popping bubbles.

"Bless you, Rebecca," she murmured. A bath was just what she needed to revitalize and confront what was going to be the most difficult day of her life.

Slowly, the kinks in her neck and shoulders loosened and her brain began to clear. She reached around the closed shower curtain for the coffee she'd set beside the tub, took a long sip, then set the mug back down and closed her eyes.

Mentally she began to prepare herself for the day. She had more than enough time to kill before she had to be at the courthouse. Too much time, she thought. The waiting was going to be as difficult as actually sitting in the courtroom beside Clay, pretending that they were a happily married couple.

I can do this, she told herself firmly. For Clay and for Julia, she would pretend one last time.

She hadn't thought about divorce yet. Though she suspected that was inevitable, she supposed there wasn't any rush for at least a few months.

Her eyes popped open.

Unless Clay wanted to remarry.

Her breath caught at the possibility. She didn't think she could bear it if he married someone else. Couldn't imagine knowing another woman was in Clay's house.

In Clay's bed.

In *her* house, in *her* bed.

Just the thought was like a knife in Paige's heart.

Who was she kidding? she thought on a small whimper. Of course he would remarry.

Hoping to drown the painful idea, she closed her eyes tightly and sank deeper into the bubbles. She couldn't think about that now. She'd never get through this day if she did.

Through the bubbles popping in her ears, Paige heard the bathroom door open, then the sound of Rebecca bringing her clothes in. Paige wasn't ready to get out and get dressed yet, though she wasn't certain that she'd ever truly be ready.

"Thank you, Rebecca," she said through the bubbles rising over her chin.

"It's not Rebecca."

At the sound of Clay's deep voice, Paige opened her eyes on a small gasp. She sat abruptly, then realized the mistake and quickly slid back down in the water.

"Clay!" She was at least thankful that she had the shower curtain between them. "Get out of here!"

"We *are* married, sweetheart."

How dare he come in here like this and call her sweetheart! And how could her best friend—her *ex*-best friend—let him in? Paige was definitely going to have words with Rebecca over this.

"If you're coming to check up on me," she said, keeping herself discreetly covered with bubbles, "I told you I'd be at the courthouse and I will. Now please leave."

"I'm not coming to check up on you. I'm here to give something to you."

When he reached to open the shower curtain, Paige grabbed hold to keep it closed. "I don't want anything from you, Clay Bodine," she lied. "I just want you to leave me alone."

"I can't, sweetheart," he said with a sigh. "Now

let go, or I'll come in there with you and we'll talk about it some more.''

He meant it. Paige could hear the determination in his voice. Fuming, she made sure the critical parts of her naked body were covered with bubbles, then let go of the shower curtain.

When he opened it, her breath caught in her throat. *Orchids.*

The bathroom was filled with them. On the floor, the toilet lid, the counter. All wrapped in silver foil and tied with pretty red bows. He'd managed to bring in at least eight pots, all blooming, in purples and pinks and yellows.

''How did you…?'' She leaned close to the side of the tub, placed her hands on the rim as she stared at the beautiful plants. Confused, she lifted her gaze to his. ''I don't understand.''

''Rebecca gave me a little assistance.'' He knelt beside the tub, then reached out and touched her cheek with his fingertip. ''Though I admit, when I showed up on your doorstep at six-thirty, it took me a while to convince her to let me in.''

''You've been here since six-thirty?'' She hadn't heard the door, but then, she'd been in such a deep sleep, a tornado could have come through and she wouldn't have known. ''But the hearing isn't until ten.''

''I cancelled the hearing.''

''You cancelled it?'' She furrowed her brow. ''Why?''

''I went to see the Barringtons last night,'' he said

quietly. "After Julia was asleep. We sat and talked, really talked. We've never done that before."

Not certain what to say, Paige simply waited for Clay to continue. He looked as tired as she felt, and he hadn't shaved this morning, either. And yet he looked wonderful, she thought, doing her best to concentrate on anything other than the gentle touch of his finger on her cheek.

"I asked them if they had tried to convince Nancy to leave me. They admitted they had, but only because Nancy had told them I neglected her, and that I'd had an affair." He shook his head on a sigh. "I should have known, should have considered that we'd all been lied to."

He slid his fingertip under Paige's chin and pulled away a dollop of bubbles. "They're coming to the ranch later and I've asked them to stay for as long as they like."

"The Barringtons are staying at the ranch?" she asked incredulously. "For as long as they like?"

"Well, for at least two weeks."

Two weeks! Clay and the Barringtons under one roof? Her mind was reeling in disbelief.

Despite the fact that her heart had began to pump faster, she shivered from the cooling water. Clay reached for her robe, held it up for her. "Now will you come out of there?"

When she hesitated, he rolled his eyes, then closed them. She stood, quickly grabbed her robe and tugged it on, then stepped out of the tub.

Clay opened his eyes and it took a will of iron for

him not to drag Paige into his arms and kiss her sense-less. There were blue-gray circles under her eyes and though her cheeks were flushed, her skin looked pale. He thought she'd never looked more beautiful.

"Come home, Paige," he said quietly. "Please."

He saw the startled look in her eyes, but she only pulled her robe tighter.

"I can't, Clay."

"You're my wife," he said softly.

"You've worked out your problems with the Bar-ringtons." She looked away, then whispered, "You don't need a wife now."

"That's true. I don't need a wife." He stepped closer, cupped her chin in his hand and lifted her face. "But I need you."

Her eyes widened, but then she pulled away from him and shook her head. "I know you're worried about Julia, but she'll be fine with a housekeeper. She's amazingly strong, and she knows you love her, plus she can come see me—"

He swooped down on her mouth, cutting off her words with a kiss. He felt her stiffen and thought for a moment she might pull away, but then she leaned into him, her lips softening against his as she kissed him back.

Blood pumped hot through his veins, his heart slammed against his chest. He wrapped his arms around her and breathed in the sweet lavender scent of her skin, knew that he could never be without this woman. *His* woman, he thought. His wife.

When he lifted his head, her eyes slowly fluttered

open. "*I* need you," he repeated firmly. "I'm asking, no, *begging* you to come back not for Julia, but for me."

She blinked in confusion. "For you?"

Lightly he brushed her lips again with his own. "I love you, Paige."

"You love me?" she said, her voice breathless.

"I love you," he whispered against her lips. "I want you to be my wife. Not a 'glorified house-keeper,' as you put it. But a real wife."

"But yesterday—"

"Yesterday I was a jerk. Like I told you before, I can't promise I won't be one again. I also can't promise that I won't beat my chest and growl when I want my way, either." He kissed the tip of her nose. "But I will promise that we'll be equal partners in marriage and parenting, for *all* our children."

Longing filled her eyes as she met his gaze. "All our children?"

"As many as you say, sweetheart, though personally, I'd like to fill every bedroom." Sliding his hand up her back, he pulled her closer. "When I came home to that empty house last night, I knew I had to get you back. Tell me you love me, Paige. Tell me you'll come home with me."

"I love you," she said softly, laying her palm on his cheek. "I think I loved you the first time you showed up at my door to buy my grandmother's car. My knees nearly gave out when you smiled at me. Lord, my knees are weak now, too."

"I was so afraid I'd lost you." Relief poured

through his body. "I didn't know if I would be able to tell you what I'm feeling," he said, kissing her lightly. "I thought the orchids might show you how I feel. That I'll always love you, no matter what happens."

Tears glistened in her eyes. "And I'll love you," she whispered. "Always."

He knew there would be many years ahead of them, years of happiness, of pleasure, and certainly some heartaches. He could handle whatever life threw at him, just as long as Paige was by his side.

He'd tell her later that he was taking her on the honeymoon he'd never given her, that after church on Sunday morning, they'd be on a plane for a two week stay in Paris.

For now, he was content to hold her close, to thank his lucky stars, and God, for giving him the woman in his arms.

*   *   *   *   *

Be sure to catch
Barbara McCauley's next release,
the lead book in the new
DYNASTIES: THE DANFORTHS *series,*
available January 2004
from Silhouette Desire.